Where You Belong

STACY WILLIAMS

ISBN: 979-8-9890449-3-1 (ebook)
979-8-9890449-4-8 (paperback)

To the lost.

Those looking for a place to call home. A place to belong.

Keep searching. Don't give up.

Who knows? Home just might find you.

Chapter 1

ANDIE

"No. No. No, no, no, no, no, noooooo." My forehead presses against the smooth, cool wall. "This can't be happening," I whisper as the emergency lights flick on.

I stay perfectly still, hoping if I don't move, the elevator will. Of course, this would happen to me today. I don't even want to be here and now this. It's a sign. When these steel doors open, I'm going to find Miranda, whoever she is, and kindly explain that I can't do this.

I hear shuffling behind me and spin, remembering the man who slid into the elevator just as the doors were closing.

"Great. Are you going to freak out?" He quickly pulls his phone out of his pocket, clearly annoyed.

I stare at him long enough to see one eyebrow raise a quarter of an inch.

"No. I'm ok," I say quietly, feeling just a bit confined in our dim little box.

He hits a button on his phone and, in the next second, is talking to someone about getting us out of here. I study him, knowing for the next however long we're in here, we'll be comrades, partners in suspended confinement.

His deep voice rapidly explains in detail which elevator we're in, and I realize he's familiar with the stadium. He sounds a little breathy and completely irritated, like whoever is on the other end of the phone is responsible for this.

He's wearing a hoodie, joggers, and a backward cap over close-cut light blond hair. The bagginess of his clothes hides his massive build and likely defined muscles because I'm pretty sure this guy is one of the players for the Tennessee Tigers.

I have no idea who he is or even that he's a player, but I want to smile because I know Josh would be out of his ever-loving mind at this. Of anyone who could've gotten stuck in an elevator with some high-profile professional football player, it's me.

The only thing I know about football is that they play on a field outlined with 100 yards, and there's a weird, oval-shaped ball they fight over. Ok. I know a little more than that, but not enough to care who this guy is.

"Yes. It's just me and one other person," he says into the phone. "You need to hurry up. I don't have time for this. Plus, my partner here isn't looking so comfortable in our tight quarters." His eyes flick to mine, clearly outlined with displeasure and maybe a hint of alarm. "Yeah. Put a rush on it."

He hangs up, and his fingers immediately take over the screen, flying around at the speed of a hummingbird's wings. His light blue eyes, almost translucent in the horrible lighting, sneak a peek at me, but only for a second before returning to his phone.

"It's going to be a little bit, but they're getting someone on it," he informs me casually, but his attention stays on his screen, shifting his weight from one foot to another.

Well, ok then.

I remove my backpack, deciding I might as well make myself comfortable, and take a seat on the floor. I'm tired, thanks to the four hours of sleep I got last night, and now I'm really mad at myself for letting my nerves keep me from eating breakfast on my drive here. At least I was smart and arrived early, giving me time for this little glitch. Although, dangling in thin air isn't going to do my quivering stomach any favors.

The man sits on the floor against the adjacent wall and stretches out his legs as he rolls his neck, irritation roaring from his every move.

"Do you work here?" I know it's likely a stupid question, but I go with it anyway.

A flash of ice blue darts to me out of the corner of his eye like he's surprised I can speak, then moves right back to his phone. "Something like that."

Clearly, he doesn't want to make small talk. *Whatever.* I guess I'm just going to sit here for the next however many minutes or hours, or for the rest of my life, and keep my mouth shut.

"Do *you* work here?" His low, raspy voice comes out of nowhere.

I look up. His head is still down, focused on his screen.

"No. I'm supposed to meet Miranda or her assistant, I think. I guess it's a good thing I'm early."

"Miranda from PR?" His question is quipped.

I wonder why he's even talking to me when he clearly has better things to do.

"Yeah. I guess so. I wasn't supposed to be here until noon, but…" I decide to keep the part about my nerves to myself. "Are you a…player?"

I should feel really dumb because anyone setting foot in this stadium would likely know the answer to this question, but something about him makes me not want to give a crap about what he thinks.

I watch him inhale slowly, waiting for a response. Then what I think is just a glimmer of an arrogant smirk appears like I should be embarrassed.

"You could say that."

"Are you going to be late for warm-up or whatever you do on game days?" I might as well just be out with my ignorance. If we're going to be stuck here, there's no reason we can't be open and honest. Although, something tells me this openness will be totally one-sided.

"I'll be fine. I just hope they don't take too long. You going to be in trouble if you don't find Miranda on time?"

I shrug. "Not much I can do about it if I am."

His crystal blue eyes finally rise from his phone and meet mine, expressionless. "So, if it's not about a job, and you aren't here as a fan, what are you doing here?"

Wow. This guy's a real charmer.

I look down at my freshly painted light pink fingernails because that's the question of the hour. What in the world am I doing here? Every part of me wants to be released from this box on a string and hightail it back where I belong. To the safety of my home, surrounded by the things that are comforting and familiar, and to the one person who still dwells there but doesn't exist anymore.

A lump rises in my throat, and I quickly swallow it down. The last thing I need is a full-on breakdown that's been threatening for the last few days. My best friend, Nora, keeps telling me I have to do this. She all but belted me in my car and tied the accelerator down. She says it's not goodbye, just a place to start. A fork in the road where I have a choice to remain living in the past or see what might lie on the other side.

When I don't answer right away, I feel the burn of his gaze.

"Actually, I'm here to sing the national anthem." I try to sound confident, though I feel anything but.

A noise comes from his throat. "Really?"

Did he just scoff that reply?

His eyes run over me like he's trying to figure out if he should know who I am, and I don't miss his unimpressed conclusion.

I hold back my ass-eating grin. My ripped jeans and wide-neck graphic t-shirt definitely don't scream superstar, but he could be a little less obvious. *Jerk.*

"Yeah, really."

"Are you an artist?" His brows tip inward like he doesn't understand as he tugs at the neck of his hoodie.

"I guess that's debatable. My…someone entered me into a contest. I didn't even know about it until I got an email."

"Huh." He flips his phone over and over in his hands. Flip. Rest. Flip. Rest. Flip. Rest.

It's not that I expected someone of his esteemed caliber to know about the contest, but does he have to be so skeptical? I freaking won.

"So…can you even sing?" His words come out slow and hoarse.

I want to reach out and smack him. Is he socially inept or just a dick?

"I guess we'll find out now, won't we?"

Flip. Rest. Flip. He's focusing on his phone like it's his most prized possession. "So, you don't normally sing…for crowds?"

I smile at his condescending tone. "No. I don't. Although, karaoke on Tuesdays at the bowling alley is usually a packed house."

Flip. Stop. So, so slowly, his eyes pull away from his phone and drag up to study my face, maybe trying to interpret if I'm serious. But then, apparently, I'm not interesting enough for any follow-up questions.

Feeling my snarky side switch to on, I toss a softball back at him. "So, how long have you played for the Tigers, or do you just warm the bench?"

"A couple of seasons," he says, dryly ignoring my sarcasm.

Well, Chatty Cathy is going to have to do better than that. "How's the South treating you? I can see the southern charm has taken full effect." I wait to see what kind of reaction I get from Mr. Social.

"Fine. The weather is nice." His phone rests on his leg, and he pushes his arm out to stretch like we've been sitting here for hours.

Because I can't help myself, I add, "You really should tone down the excitement. We don't want you running out of steam before the big game."

His unamused look makes me want to kick it up a notch higher, but I stop.

This guy seriously has a football stuck up his butt. I hope they find it before game time. *Sheesh.*

I look around the elevator, more than ready to get out of here. "Does this get stuck often?"

He's moved on to some other kind of stretch that involves moving his feet. "If it did, I wouldn't have gotten on."

Good grief, this guy. I should cut him slack. All that arrogance would be a heavy load to carry.

My stomach growls in the quiet, and my jail mate raises his eyebrows, hunger gaining another strike against me.

He reaches for his bag and digs around before tossing an energy bar at me. "You should eat."

"Do I need to worry it's laced with something?" I just can't help myself.

He goes back to his silent…whatever he's doing, and I know I need to eat if I'm going to make it. I pull the wrapper open and take a bite of the peanut butter bar just as my phone starts ringing. I slip it out of the side pocket of my backpack. It's my mom. *Just great.*

I don't want to answer it, not only because talking to her in front of another person, let alone this guy, will be uncomfortable at best, but also if she knew what I was doing today, I'd never hear the end of it. What I know, though, is that if I don't answer it, she'll just keep calling, and I don't need anything else hanging over my head today.

I swallow my bite of the bar, shove my chin to my chest, and swipe to answer. "Hey."

"Andrea, is that any way to greet a caller? The informality is impolite."

"Hello. How's that?" I peek from underneath my eyelashes as my partner in captivity is back to being engrossed in his phone, but I know there's no way to avoid listening to this exchange.

"Andrea, I don't have time for your dramatics. I'm calling you about the benefit. I've yet to receive your response in the mail, and even though you must come, I want to be sure that you aren't trying to slip your way out of this one. You know how important this is. I already have a piece picked out for you."

Only my mother would send a formal invitation in the mail to her only daughter, which is bad enough, but then also expect a proper reply.

"I told you I'd think about it." It's best to keep it short and sweet, but this response will be unacceptable.

"Andrea, you've used one excuse after another for far too long. You can't keep going on like this. It's time to come home and finally get your life together. I'll put you down for the chicken and expect you an hour early."

I close my eyes, inhaling through my nose. I accepted long ago that my parents would never change. Someday, maybe they'll understand that I won't be returning to the only lifestyle or the facade acceptable to them.

"We both know that extra seat won't put you out if I can't make it." I attempt to stay as calm and quiet as possible.

"Andrea, you've been avoiding your place long enough. It's time to put these silly, rebellious antics behind you. Besides, your father and I have decided to make you the focus of this year's event. Please don't embarrass us by not showing. There's no way to find someone to replace you this close to the date."

I clench my jaw. She just had to wiggle the knife in a little further. She seriously should be the one who holds a scalpel for a living. She'll never understand that my silly little choices brought me the greatest joys of my life.

Screw it. I rest back against the wall. "Sorry, I couldn't hear you. Either the connection is bad, or your nose has finally reached a height where the blood isn't flowing properly to your brain. Either way, I'll let you know when I'm good and ready. Until then, I have to go."

I hang up and toss my phone back into my bag, forgetting about the man sitting next to me. My eyes snap to him, and he's looking at me like…something.

"Sounded like a lovely conversation."

"Yeah. This morning has been full of delightful exchanges," I huff. "If you ever want to talk to the devil herself, let me know. I'll give you her number."

He laughs. He actually laughs, his head falling back against his wall. It's low and soft, and I expect the elevator to start free-falling at any moment. One dimple pops in his cheek. Who would've ever guessed there was a dimple hidden in there? I bet no one's ever seen it before. This could be a monumental discovery, and I almost reach for my phone to capture it. *Sports Illustrated* would probably pay millions for the rare glimpse. I resist, feeling sorry for the little concave patch of skin. That cute little dimple never gets show time with all that stiffness.

I smile, and somehow, it loosens the tightness around my chest that could only be caused by my mother.

I survey our space, not wanting to talk anymore about what he just overheard. "I feel like we should be taking stock of our supplies and figuring out what we can use to unscrew the ceiling panel."

As if he's turned into a sloth, his head drags sooooo slowly in my direction like he's back to being bored, and I feel like I should take offense to that, but whatever. Our little moment born of my misery and embarrassment is over.

All I know is they better get us out of here before I have to go to the bathroom. This guy already thinks very little of me. Going number anything in front of him will put us on a whole new level that I'm not at all comfortable with.

"So, do you have family coming later to see your big performance?" my partner asks out of the blue in his same bored, monotonous tone.

I shake my head. "Nope, it's just me today."

His light eyebrows scrunch together, forming a crease between them, and he lets out a long, disapproving breath. "You won a competition to sing the national anthem in a stadium filled with thousands, and no one will be here to see it?"

Why does he have to say it like that? I don't like his patronizing tone or know how to answer this.

I don't want to, but given that we are stuck together, I decide to just put it out there, trying not to sound defensive. "This was a surprise. I didn't know I was entered into the competition, and honestly, I wasn't even going to come, but my best friend replied and said I'd do it. She thinks…" I stop but realize I'll likely never see this man again after we leave this little box on a cable, so I continue. "She thinks it will help me move past some things and be the start of something new."

I shake my head and find him listening intently. "That probably doesn't make any sense to someone like you. The truth is I'm only here singing for one person, so no matter the reason and whether it's just me or thousands are listening, the one that matters will be."

He returns to his normal state of phone-focused silence while his fingers tap on his thigh. One. At. A. Time. Repeat. I'm beginning to think he wasn't really listening, but after a minute, he surprises me.

"You're the only one who gets to decide when it's enough. You know, when it's time to move on and find out what else might be out there waiting."

I'm shocked by this lug's insight and how much it seems like he might understand. "Huh. I'm impressed. It sounds like you might have a soul in there somewhere."

His chest rises with a long inhale and then falls. "Don't read too far into it."

Ok. There we go. I was worried for a second we might become friends through our time stuck together.

"Don't worry. I won't. There's also the little thing of not wanting to embarrass anyone." That earns me a heavy dose of side-eye.

Interestingly, this joker seems to have given me the permission I was looking for. Today can be about whatever I want it to be. Maybe that's why we're stuck here together because it sure wasn't for the good company. I needed to hear that, even if it had to come from a giant egotistical jerk.

This doesn't have to be the end, or it can be the start of something new. Either way, I get to decide.

The sounds of Mariah Carey's "Make It Happen" fill my earbuds, and my pump-up song is working. Every part of me wants to jump up and dance, letting it all out. But one, this temperamental turd doesn't deserve the greatness of what is the best just-do-it songs of all time. And two, and more importantly, the thought of shifting the elevator even the slightest bit freaks me the hell out. Just the idea almost takes me to level seven on the anxiety scale.

I check my watch. We've been in our little dangling cocoon for just over an hour, and the air is starting to feel stale. My trapped companion has been busying himself with a nap or meditation for the past few minutes while I've been enjoying the sounds of the queen herself.

I stretch my feet out towards the middle, and they come close to reaching his legs, which are seriously the size of tree trunks, but I don't care that we're almost touching. I may be on the shorter side, but I shouldn't have to stay tucked into a ball because he's a space hog, even if he can't help it. I've sat curled up for an hour and can't do it any longer.

Moving slightly with the beat, I open my eyes again to find him staring at me.

"Do you have to have that so loud? It's bad for your hearing."

I pull one earbud out, and even though I heard him, I can't help myself. "Eh?"

He rolls those pale blue eyes, full of irritation, and repeats himself.

I tip my head to the side. "Is it bothering you? I'm trying to get pumped, you know, for my performance. Isn't that what you big-time football players do to get in the zone?"

Is there an award for looking most bored with life and emotionally unavailable? Because folks, we have a winner.

"I like quiet." He rests his head back against the wall, staring at the lights like he's hoping to catch some rays from the horrible twin fluorescent lights that shine dimly down on us.

"You also look like you could stand to let loose a little. Maybe if you found a pump-up song, you'd look a little less…constipated." He sighs, long and slow, the toe-tapping thing starting again. "I know! Since we have time, we should find you the perfect song."

I start scrolling my phone, thinking, not being able to help pushing his buttons. "I know! I know! How about a little jazz? Soft and smooth with the spice of the sax."

He peels his eyes away from the ceiling to look at me but doesn't move his head. "Jazz," he repeats matter-of-factly.

"No? Ok, let's see. Something calm and quiet. Ocean sounds. No, you don't need anything more snoozy. You have enough of that going on."

He makes some kind of throaty noise.

"You need something with a little more pizazz. 'Poker Face?' Can't read minds, can't read minds," I sing off-key while he listens unaffected. "It's fitting with all the deadpan you've got going on, but it might just be a little too…pop-y."

I scroll in silence for a minute and then gasp. "I've got it, grumpy pants! Your new jam. Are you ready? It's smooth and soulful and just completely perfect. From now on, this in your ears before each game will have you playing like never before. So long solitary gloom, hello potency and sunshine!"

I look at him wide-eyed with anticipation, knowing I'm getting under his skin, but I Just. Can't. Stop. It's like a bug bite that itches so bad you have to scratch it raw. This guy needs to get off his high horse and settle down here on earth with the rest of us.

I wiggle my eyebrows at him, waiting for him to ask me. His cool stare doesn't weaken my excitement.

"Ok, sunshine. I can tell happiness is your truth. Are you ready to clap along? Your new pregame jam." I let the song play, and Pharrell's "Happy" fills our tiny space. I start moving, and he continues to ignore me.

I turn it down and look at him, lip-singing the lyrics.

I bop my shoulders up and down for effect. "Can't bring me down, baby. It's perfect."

I let the song play for a bit and then turn it off just as the ceiling lights flicker. We both look around, waiting. Nothing.

His cool exterior suddenly doesn't look so calm. He's pale, knees to chest, and gripping the railing like at any moment we're going to be in for a ride.

"You alright, big stuff?" I sit forward a little, trying to get a better look at his face.

Like he forgot I was here, his head snaps in my direction, and I watch him morph back to calm and collected like a plastic shield melting into place. *Huh?* He stretches his legs out again, reaches into his bag, and pulls out a water bottle.

I rest back while he takes a long drink. "Careful, there won't be any tinkling in here." He eyes me, twisting the cap back on. "I don't care if you own this stadium. I draw the line in your entitlement there."

"Shouldn't you be saving your voice for the big performance?" His voice is filled with agitation.

His previous disinterest is suddenly full of tender care. *Not.* "I don't need to save my voice. It's my sanity I'm concerned about at the moment."

"So, you're seriously here to sing the anthem, then what?" He picks up his phone again and starts tapping away.

What in the hell is his problem? I shrug, pulling my knees to my chest. "Oh, you know, dance a little jig, strip down to nothing, and hit on as many players as I can in hopes that one will see the real me and bring life full circle. The usual."

He rolls his neck like he's trying to loosen up. "Does the bitterness ever get tiring?"

I let out a laugh filled with sarcasm. "Ugh, we've been here so long we're starting to think alike. Scary. I was just thinking how the helmet and pads are probably a good buffer for all that narcissistic arrogance."

He groans. "This is ridiculous," he says, resting his head against the wall, one leg bent and bouncing. In the next second, he pulls his hoodie over his head and tosses it on top of his bag. The t-shirt he's left in confirms my previous assumptions about his muscular physique.

His phone vibrates. He looks at it and tosses it down, creating a soft thud in our tiny space. He tips his head back again and closes his eyes. I hear him breathe in and push it out, likely getting antsy about game time.

I'm just as ready to spring this pendulous joint so I can get on with what I came here to do and go back home where it's safe and sound. Where I can hide and ignore the fact that life is going on around me—where nothing has to change.

Even though this likely famous football star has been a little prickly and a whole lot self-absorbed, he did provide one insightful nugget of input. Maybe I can be grateful for that tiny portion of our captive time together.

My eyes square in on him again while he sits stiffly, jaw clenched, brow beaded with sweat, and looking like he's about to come unglued. I know I should just keep my mouth shut, but it's never been very good at listening.

"What you said earlier about it being my choice to move forward and see what's out there. That's actually pretty good advice. I wasn't sure you had that kind of depth."

His head turns in my direction, his eyes full of tension and something else I can't identify. Surprise maybe. But after a moment, I see him relax just slightly, his eyes softening.

I bite my lip as his intense stare causes the air around me to suddenly feel thick. When he continues to say nothing, my mouth takes over. "I'm so glad you were able to come down to my level for that brief moment. I was certain we'd leave this experience, never really knowing each other."

There's a sudden jolt as the lights pop on, and the elevator starts to move. We both stand, and there's a ding that has the doors opening.

As I reach down for my backpack, my cordial bestie flees our holding space and disappears. No goodbye or nice meeting you, although we bypassed introductions. No, have a nice life. Nothing. *What-ever.*

I step out onto solid ground and into a group of waiting people, thankful this little mishap is over. A couple of custodians stand waiting.

"Welcome out in the fresh air." One of them smiles, holding out his arms.

"Thanks for getting us out of there." I throw my backpack over my shoulder.

I take in my surroundings and then pull out my pass and phone to look at my instructions for where I'm supposed to meet Miranda. I follow the directions that will hopefully take me to wherever the lower-level conference rooms are. I wind through the painted cinder block hallways and what feels like down into the bowels of the stadium.

I have to be headed in the right direction when I start seeing more people, including cameras and reporters. I spot a couple of people in business suits and ask if they know where I can find my contact. They kindly point out a woman in a navy blue power suit with perfectly styled short blond hair, makeup, and poise. She appears to be in her early forties and has a welcoming smile as I approach.

"Ms. Parks." She takes a step towards me, extending her hand.

Knowing I'm this much closer to singing, my stomach flips. I push the nerves aside and extend my hand in return, trying to muster up a believing smile. "Yes. I assume you are Miranda. It's nice to meet you."

She smiles warmly. "I understand you've already had quite the adventure this morning. I'm so sorry. At least you were stuck with someone as collected as Sean. He's a great guy and so cool under pressure."

I nod and smile but wonder if the Sean she is talking about is the same guy I was stuck with. Maybe she heard wrong.

"Ok." She jumps in. "Let's get you to your dressing room, and then we'll talk specifics." She starts walking, and I follow. "We'll end up back out here where you'll be taken out onto the field, but for now, we'll get you all set up with whatever you need."

"Great." I suck in a deep breath wanting to believe I can do this.

After a short walk, Miranda opens the door to a bright room with a large lit mirror, a loveseat, and a table with a basket of snacks and bottles of water. I set my backpack down on the counter, turning to Miranda.

She must sense my nerves because she asks, "Are you doing ok? I know this is all a lot if you're not used to it."

"Yeah, I just need to get out of my head. I'll get there." I try to smile, but it'll take a miracle for me to make it through this emotionally intact.

"Ok. Sound check is in thirty, and then you'll have time to dress and get ready. We're really hoping you can stay after the game. We invite some families into a conference room to meet some of the players. They sign autographs and talk with the fans for a bit. If we have guests like yourself, we invite you to stay and do the same."

I laugh. "I don't think anyone will want my autograph in a room full of football stars."

Miranda smiles. "You'd be surprised. You're very talented and have a touching story. The crowd is going to eat you up." She pats my arm. "Anyway, we have a piano all set for you, so I hope you'll join us."

I nod. "Sure."

"Ok. Well then, I'm going to leave you to get settled. My assistant will come to get you in a bit, and we'll get that sound check out of the way."

"Ok. Thanks."

In a blink, Miranda is gone, and I'm left in another tiny space, only this time, I'm alone with my overly active thoughts, emotions, and fears.

I open my backpack and pull out my neatly folded short black dress and fitted leather jacket. I hang them on the rack, then set my shoes underneath. My favorite glittery silver heels.

I set out my makeup, deciding if I'm going to do this, I better get to it. I put in my earbuds, find my song, and this time, since I'm all alone, I dance and sing like nobody's watching.

Chapter 2

SEAN

Twenty minutes. I have twenty minutes to get my ass out on the field if I'm going to have any amount of pregame warm-up. I use my shirt sleeve to wipe the sweat from my brow as I wind through the hallway toward the locker room.

I round a corner, almost plowing over one of my teammates.

"Hey, they finally got you out. Remind me never to take that elevator. I would've been scaling the inside of the shaft. Man!"

He shakes his head, and I bump his fist as he passes, knowing if I had sat in the tiny, locked box one second longer, I'm pretty sure I would have completely lost my shit. I inhale another long, deep breath, feeling my lungs expand with freedom.

I'm out. I made it out, and everything is ok.

Now, I have to get my mind and body back under control and ready for the game.

I push into the locker room, trying to get my head in game mode. My calm and quiet pregame ritual got blown to pieces the minute I set foot in that elevator. That needed peace was replaced with two torturous hours of suffocation and incessant sass.

A part of me knew the second I squeezed through those closing doors I'd made a mistake, but it was too little too late. Elevators are a hell no for me, but today, when I was already running late and filled with my newly discovered discontent, I convinced myself it'd be fine. I was a damn fool.

I spent two hours being poked and prodded when I needed to be focused and controlled. I needed calm and serenity. The closed quarters were enough, but that woman got under my skin. She seemed to know exactly where to stick the needle and pry. Under different circumstances, I might have been annoyed as hell.

I'm not used to people seeing anything beyond the pro-athlete persona I glue on, but she made me feel transparent and vulnerable. My skin literally feels like it's been scraped off, leaving me raw and defenseless, and I cannot step out onto the field in this condition.

The locker room is empty. I change quickly and get on the field to do what I can with the minimal time left, hoping it will help my frame of mind. I've been preparing for today for months, just as I have every season before. I need my mind and body aligned so I can do my job.

Instead, my head is still spinning, and my body is fatigued with everything that happened in the last two hours. Ironically, it might be fitting, given my attempt to rediscover my priorities and rearrange my life to reflect something more meaningful–more real.

I wake up each day with everything a man could dream of: the dream job, the massive house, the supermodel girlfriend, the car, the fame. I have it all, and what I don't have, I can buy. But there's a fear surfacing even with it all, I have nothing I actually need–nothing that really matters.

So, it's fitting, after these past weeks spent recovering from an injury and examining my life, that when I'm supposed to step back out on the field good as new and ready to kick ass, I get stuck in an elevator of all places…with someone. A woman, I'm certain, could give any man a run for his money.

On the field, I'm unable to get my mental state to cooperate and ready itself for the battle ahead. I knew I should've just sat there and not engaged. I know better than to open my big mouth to a stranger who will probably blow up the internet with some nonsense about me, which may or may not be true.

It's not like I confessed anything, but people will take liberty in pulling anything out of context. Being trapped in an elevator with the wrong person could be a full-blown catastrophe. If portions of our time alone together make it to the internet, my agent will have a mountain of damage control to undertake.

It was evident by her incessant witty banter that she assumed I'm some cocky, chauvinistic baller who thinks the world revolves around me. I can be cocky, and I'm good at what I do. But I know with one hundred percent certainty that the world would go on just fine without me. In fact, what I'm struggling with, which no one seems to understand, is what happens when you have the whole world but feel like you're losing your soul.

Trying to center myself, I slowly take a deep breath, hold it for three seconds, then let it out. Then, I do it again while my teammates move around me, pumped and ready.

With each deep breath, I try to let it all go. Only time will tell the level of danger I encountered with the woman and her smart mouth, but at least it provided a really nice distraction.

I thought if I stayed quiet, she'd follow my lead, but that was not the case. The only thing I have going for me is that she seemed sincere in having no idea who I am, and it was clear she didn't care.

I stretch for another minute before a trainer throws me a ball, and I sprint a few yards, trying my best to get my body warmed up while my mind has other plans.

Time runs out, and I'm back in the locker room listening to Coach's pregame pep talk. Without my routine, I'm feeling off and uncomfortable. My body is stiff and tense, and I try to concentrate, but that freaking *Happy* song has infiltrated my brain.

When Coach finishes, I stand and attempt to shake myself loose. My buddy, Tyrell, bumps my shoulder.

"I heard you got trapped with some chick. Was it like in the movies? Did she freak out and get all starry-eyed when she realized she was locked in with the one and only Sean Greyson?"

I huff. "Quite the opposite. She didn't have any idea who I was."

He snickers. "Just wait until she tells all her friends. Then she'll be selling elaborate and steamy stories to the highest bidder."

I frown, thinking back through our time in the elevator again. "I don't think she's like that. I'm pretty sure she didn't like me all that well." I could tell him that she said I looked constipated, but I decide to keep that little jab to myself.

"Right." He slaps me on the back, walking away.

My hands fist at his disbelieving tone, and I'm feeling a little more ready to get out on the field.

Padded up and jersey on, I make my way down the corralled hallway to wait in the tunnel with the rest of my team. My body finally shifts into game mode. I feel a little more amped up and ready to go, but my mind wanders to the woman about to sing.

I realize I don't know her name. I wonder what her voice will sound like and whether or not she'll be nervous up there alone in front of all these people. She said she was here because she won a competition, but what if her voice isn't good? What if she's terrible? I cringe at memories of people trying to hit that high note and not quite making it.

The guys in front of me jump around, getting hyped up, when I hear some shuffling behind us. Then I see her. She's being led off to the side, listening to instructions. She looks different, but not in an unrecognizable way.

Instead of jeans and a t-shirt, she has on a short dress partially covered by a black leather jacket and silver shoes. Something about them makes me smile. It's fitting–the spice under all that misleading innocence. She's carrying an insulated cup and catches me staring.

Like we didn't spend two hours locked in an elevator earlier, she stares back blankly. Her spirited green eyes are even brighter now with dark eye makeup, but not the kind that makes a woman look like a raccoon. It's subtle. Her dark curls frame her face, and her soft pink lips turn up into a slight smile as she stops on the other side of the metal fencing in front of me. She's still strikingly beautiful in a natural way, and I have a strong suspicion there's nothing fake about her.

We're caught in some sort of staring contest as she stands, the metal barrier between us. She's petite, and even in heels, I lower my chin to match her gaze. She doesn't move as Miranda lingers beside her, tapping away on a tablet.

"Hey, roomie. Glad to see you made it." One sparkly eye squints just slightly in amusement.

"You ready for your big break?"

She shrugs and steps away like it's a joke. She takes a sip of her drink, almost backing into the team owner. I'm surprised to see him down here. He's a nice man with a generous heart, but he takes the game seriously, and we don't usually find him down here before games.

"Ms. Parks," he says, and she spins toward him. "Ed McNeil." He holds out his hand. "I'm glad I made it down to welcome you. I understand you were trapped a bit earlier. My apologies."

She smiles. "Yes, sir. It all worked out fine."

Ed turns to me. "Well, you could've had worse company. Sean's a good guy. Good luck today." He slaps my shoulder with a grin.

"Thanks," I say as his attention returns to...Ms. Parks.

"You were my vote for the competition, and after what your husband said on the tape, I'm even more honored to meet your acquaintance."

Husband? I didn't notice a ring, but that doesn't mean anything. My gaze unconsciously turns to her hand.

"I'm so very sorry for your loss," Ed continues. "Your husband's dedication and service will be honored and remembered here tonight."

A smile touches her lips, but not the same one as when she gave me endless doses of shit.

"Thank you, sir," she says quietly. "He would have loved every second of this. He was a huge fan."

Her comment about singing for only one person suddenly makes sense, and I feel like a giant ass.

"Please join us in the owner's box when you finish up here. My wife would love to meet you, and I understand afterward you're treating some kids and their families to a performance while these tough guys sign autographs."

Her eyes grow wide, but she recovers. "Yes. It'll be a pleasure."

"Ok, then," Ed says. "Go knock our socks off, and I'll see you in a bit."

"Yes, sir," she says, turning away and taking a deep breath. She takes another sip of her drink and walks towards the opening.

I play football in front of thousands of people week after week, but I can't imagine getting up on a stage and singing for these people, knowing the whole time that my husband, who organized this, isn't here because…

The cheering starts, and we're on the move, jogging out of the tunnel. I look back as I pass her, but her attention is elsewhere. We line up on the sideline as the fans scream and yell, but I'm having a hard time hearing them over the noise in my head.

I often feel misunderstood, especially lately, and here I judged this woman based on her casual look and unrelenting sass. However, I'm not sure she was teasing when she was calling me out.

I step in line with my team as she's escorted to the small platform. I can't help but think that if she can do this and move forward in life after losing her husband, then there's no reason I shouldn't be able to figure out why I feel so removed from mine.

Chapter 3

ANDIE

I grip the mic tightly as I step up on the platform and turn to face center. The lights are blinding. I suck in air, knowing I need to drown out the noise and get in my head.

I can do this.

I've sung the national anthem a thousand times before, and maybe it was only to myself, but I made it. I can do it again because that's what I'm doing here. I'm singing for myself.

At first, when I agreed to this after Nora's sneaky butt replied to the email, I was doing this for Josh. But now, maybe she's right. Maybe this is me singing for the start of something new–the beginning of life without Josh.

It's not goodbye. I'll never be able to say goodbye to him. The time we had together, even when we were apart, I'll cherish forever. He'll always have a piece of my heart, but if I don't start attending to what's left, I'm worried it's going to shrivel up and die from keeping it closed off and on hold for something that will never be again.

Sean, AKA football's smuggest ass, said something about the possibility of so much more waiting for me, and it's stuck with me all afternoon. I can't miss out on living life because I'm waiting for someone who's never coming back. Josh wouldn't want that.

So, I guess I am doing this for me, mostly. The other part is for Josh because his shenanigans got me into this in the first place.

I look out at the crowd, trying to see, but all I can make out is the fifty feet in front of me where the home team is lined up.

"Ladies and gentlemen, please rise and remove your hats for the singing of our national anthem. Tonight, we're honored to have a very special guest, singer and songwriter Andie Parks. She's the winner of our Show Us What You've Got competition where her husband secretly submitted a recording on her behalf."

The jumbo screen flicks to Josh's face. My mouth goes dry, and a raw burn climbs up my throat. He's wearing his BDUs and a smile, and he's as handsome as ever. The sound of his voice makes my stomach squeeze. I've missed it so much.

"My wife would kill me if she knew I was submitting this, but you've seen for yourself that she has the voice of an angel. One that the rest of the world needs to hear." His mouth turns into that mischievous grin. "I'm the luckiest man to get to be the one who stands in the hallway and listens to the songs of her heart. So even if it's only this one time and in a stadium filled with people, all of you will get to see what I've always known. She has a gift that needs to be shared because it will make the world better."

I can't help but let out a little laugh as tears fill my eyes.

"So baby, if you get to see this," he grins, and then it fades a little. "I know you may hate me for doing this, but I love you. Show these people exactly what you're made to do and make them feel what you've made me feel since the moment your voice reached my ears."

The screen flicks to a giant me staring back at myself, trying to hold back tears, and I want him to come back. I want to see his smiling face one more time. I have no idea how I'm supposed to sing after that.

The stadium is silent, and I turn my attention back, front and center. My lungs are paralyzed. It's like trying to breathe through a straw, only able to suck in a little air at a time as I try to remember the words that need to come out of my mouth in the next few seconds.

I look up, blinking the blurriness away and willing myself to hold it together. The loud voice comes back over the speakers.

"Tonight, we honor the memory of Staff Sergeant Joshua Parks, remembering him for his sacrifice and duty. Please place your hand over your heart for the singing of our national anthem."

One, two, three…I count. It's all I can do as the military drums roll and the flag is marched forward. In my moment of panic, I search the line of players for Sean and his massive ego, waiting for me to fail. It might be the thing that gets me through this.

I find him–number twenty-four. With his helmet off, I see those clear blue eyes on me, and as if he somehow knows, one side of his mouth tips up into a jerky, smug smirk. His chin dips just an inch, maybe in a nod. That does it.

The first notes hit the speakers. This is it. I close my eyes. *This is for you, Josh, and…for me.*

Chapter 4

ANDIE

I did it. I did it! I. Did. It. I sang the national anthem in a stadium filled with 50,000 fans and nailed it. I freaking nailed it.

When I finish, I'm whisked off the platform and given just a moment to myself in my dressing room to collect my things before I join Ed McNeil, owner of the Tennessee Tigers, his wife, and whoever else in their box.

I had no idea how I'd make it through after seeing Josh and hearing his voice again, but I made it with only a single tear as I hit the word 'brave.' I did it, and now all I want to do is go home, but I'll stay because they had me at the word 'kids.' So, I'll stay and play for them and their families.

I dig my phone out of my bag to find five texts from Nora, all in some form of yelling and cheering. I hit her number.

"Oh my gosh! You did it, and girl, you nailed it! I had chills from my head to my toes. I cried the whole time." She's talking so loudly that I have to turn down the volume.

"They played a clip from Josh's submission right beforehand. I had no idea how I was going to make it through."

"Oh honey, but you did. You did it. Andie, this was huge. I've never heard it sung so beautifully. Well, maybe except Whitney Houston, but it was seriously the best I've ever heard."

"Thank you." I close my eyes, letting out another breath of relief.

"So, get your tail back here, and we're going to celebrate with…I don't know, ice cream and cupcakes."

I laugh, and there's a knock at the door. "Actually, I have to stay until after the game. I hope that's ok. They invite kids and their families to stay to meet the players and want me to play a bit. You know I can't say no when it comes to kids."

"Yeah. Ok, well, things are fine here, so take your time. You deserve every moment of this."

"Yeah?"

"Yeah."

"Ok."

"Hey, Andie." Nora stops me from hanging up. "How do you feel?"

I'm not sure how I feel. Like I'm on a high: excited, relieved, sad. My eyes burn, just trying to figure out how to describe it.

"A little bit of everything." I pause. "You know how when you do something you never thought you would or could, and then when you do, and it's over, you feel like something changed inside you?"

"Yeah. It's like when I dye my hair a new color and feel like I can take on the world."

I laugh. "Something like that. Anyway, I've had a few moments today where I've felt something start to shift inside me like maybe I might really be able to climb out of the dark because I can see the light filtering through."

"Good. That's so good. I'm so proud of you. Now, go play your heart out for those kids."

We hang up, and I throw my backpack over my shoulders, stopping to look at myself in the mirror. Yes, something's shifting. It started in the elevator, then again out on the field, and maybe even a little when one big, annoying football-playing fool dared me to actually do what I came to do.

Mingling is not my thing, especially in a room full of people who remind me of the life I left behind when I chose Josh. Joining the owners in their box to watch the game is like stepping into a reality show for the rich and famous.

Ed quickly greets me and then his wife, Elaine, who spends a few minutes asking me about Josh and songwriting. Both are warm and welcoming and introduce me to their family and friends. After introductions, I score a plate of food and back myself into a corner.

Unsurprisingly, it's delicious. I mean, these people wouldn't eat crap. I have no idea how long I'm expected to stay after the game, and if I'm going to do anything other than fall into a chair, I need the energy. Starving, I take my time savoring each bite.

After a bit, I decide I can't hide in the corner any longer, and move out into the open-air seating in front of the box, taking a seat in the back. To my left is a group of women who look like a cast of supermodels dressed in team colors and different players' names and numbers. They stand posing and snapping pictures of each other while my eyes don't miss that one is wearing number twenty-four.

She's tall, long-legged, with dark, almost black hair, and looks like she just stepped off a runway. I smile. Of course, the pretty boy superstar football player I spent two hours with, having no idea who he was, has a wife or girlfriend who looks like she belongs on the cover of Vogue. She's beautiful. Flawless.

I settle into my designated ordinary girls' section, party of one, and try to watch the game. I'm here, and this really is a once-in-a-lifetime experience. I check the score, and the Tigers are up by seven. I watch the tiny players move the ball from one end of the field to the other, only briefly thinking about what I'm supposed to do when the game is over.

"Girl! You gave me chills!" I turn my head, and the model who belongs to number ninety-eight is looking at me. "The whole thing brought tears to my eyes."

I watch as the group of women all nod in agreement. It's a little creepy how much they all look alike.

"Thank you," I say awkwardly, not really knowing what else to say.

"Seriously. It was so beautiful, and that clip beforehand. I don't even know how you were able to do that after–" She stops.

"I'm so sorry for your loss," Number forty-five says, tipping her head in sincerity. "What a great guy."

Again, I have no idea what to say. "Thanks. He was."

Number twenty-four stands. "You should come sit over here with us."

I sit, trying to figure out how to get out of it. After all the stress and emotions, I really just want to be by myself, but knowing I shouldn't be rude, I stand and scoot down.

Number ninety-eight looks at me. "You really have the most beautiful voice. They said you're a songwriter? We tried to look you up. Have you released any albums?"

This I can talk about. It's business. "Actually, I write and sell to other artists."

"Really?" Number forty-five's perfect eyebrows almost hit her hairline. "You should definitely be singing your own stuff. I wish I had your voice. I'd be touring the world."

The group agrees, and their quest to spur me to stardom becomes their top priority. I've heard this all before, and it's a big 'no thanks' for me. I let them go on and dream about the life they think I should have. Eventually, they move on to other topics, and I keep to myself.

"So, what's up with Sean?" Number ninety-eight asks number twenty-four, who has Greyson across her back in an oversized jersey and maybe nothing else. I can't help it that my ears perk up at this. "Tyrell said that he's been different since being released. Are his ribs still bothering him?"

Number twenty-four straightens. "No, he's feeling good. He's glad to be back out there. It was hard for him to sit out. Too much downtime."

"Well, I love Sean. You're so lucky. He's the sweetest guy." Number ninety-eight squeezes her arm.

"I know." Number twenty-four squeals and scrunches her nose like a giddy schoolgirl. "And he's all mine."

Yes, honey, that giant tool is all yours.

In the next breath, the primped and primed decide it's time for more selfies, and seeing there are only a few minutes left in the game, I'm ready to excuse myself.

Back in the box, I thank the McNeils and search for Miranda so she can help me find the room with the waiting piano. Having time to warm up and a moment to myself will help put me at ease after such a surreal day.

She's easy to find amidst the sea of people outside the box and escorts me to the large conference room, where the kids and families will be ushered after the game.

After a quick jaunt, I find myself back down in the same area I was before the game, but in an open room with a few tables up against the wall covered with Tigers memorabilia. The upright piano sits off to the side, and suddenly, I'm unsure of myself. Not in my ability but in what exactly I'm supposed to do or play.

I turn to Miranda. "I thought I'd warm up a bit, but what would you like me to play?"

Not taking her attention off her tablet, she says, "Whatever you want. I'm sure the families will love to hear about the contest and some of the songs you've written, but it's really up to you." She pauses. "I have to go check on a couple of things, but make yourself at home. It'll probably be half an hour or so before someone brings the families in."

I nod, slightly frustrated by the lack of direction, but step into the room and toward the piano. I set my backpack on the floor next to it and sit on the bench, running my fingers over the slick keys. The smooth, cool ivory under my fingertips instantly makes me feel at home.

After today, there's a song begging to take shape, but that'll have to wait. For now, I play what's on my heart, and given that I have this time alone, I raise my voice to sing the way I like best…when no one is listening.

Chapter 5

SEAN

Another hand slaps my back as the room erupts with celebratory praises for clinching the victory. I dress quickly, ready to get the post-game interviews out of the way so I can hit up the meet and greet and go home.

I'm happy with the win, but I'm not the type to go overboard when we still have a whole season ahead. I like to take it one game at a time, focusing on keeping myself in shape and off the bench.

Above all the racket, I hear my name. "Greyson, you're up next."

I finish dressing and grab my duffle on the way out of the locker room, setting it aside before stepping up to the mic. I don't mind the interviews as long as they stay on topic and off my personal life. Today, I know I'll get asked about how my ribs felt during the game, and luckily, they're feeling good.

Weeks back, during preseason, a helmet collided with my ribs, and I was benched until the medical team released me, which is always torture. Not only is it hard to watch the game go on without me, but I never know when the sub will outperform and end up being my replacement. It's the name of the game. One minute, you're on fire, and everyone is chanting your name. The next, you're ancient history with the new guy tearing up the field.

It ended up being the wake-up call I needed. While sitting around waiting for my bruised ribs to heal, I realized that outside of football, I was completely detached. It was like I'd been flying high for so long that once back on the ground, the world surrounding me was unrecognizable. It was a revelation I couldn't ignore.

I sat at home for days, wondering how I'd gotten so far from where I started. I grew up with nothing. No family, no home, no consistency or security. I spent my childhood in the foster system and eventually moved into a group home. Until a few years ago, I didn't have a clue as to where I even began.

But the years since playing college ball and being drafted into the NFL have been like a whirlwind. It's been a dream come true, but sitting on my couch resting my body, something hit differently this time. The question I couldn't get out of my head was what happens when the dream is over.

These past years playing at the highest level have moved fast, and my life outside of football has turned into something I don't recognize or even like. I've started to question everything. Who are my friends, my real friends? The people who actually know me and care about me beyond my name or that I play football. From what I could come up with, that list was very, very small.

All my pondering and self-examination left me with the sad reality that I have it all, but very little of it really matters. At the end of the day, the house, the car, the grand vacations...what's it all worth?

I even woke up one day wondering why I was dating my girlfriend. She's beautiful, smart, and strong, and I care about her, but I don't love her, which was shameful. I enjoyed the companionship and having someone there, but that isn't what a relationship should be. At least not for me or the man I want to be, the man I used to be.

But here I stand, again, answering questions like everything is fine, with a group of people who think they know me and believe that football is the only thing that matters. For years that was true. I can't say that anymore, so I'm trying to get back to those things that mean something, the things that, at the end of the day, I can't live without. The terrifying thing is I'm having trouble finding them.

I answer about ten easy questions, then let the next guy take my place while I head down the hall to the meet and greet, where I'll shake hands and sign autographs for kids whose dream is to be me one day.

As I approach the doors to the conference room, I hear piano music, which is not typical of these sessions. Reaching the doorway, I see her and stop, flashing back to her standing on the podium, looking tiny, and then hearing the most unexpectedly soulful voice come pouring out.

I feel like a real asshole. I misjudged her and not only her but her ability. She plays the piano almost as beautifully as she sings. Whatever it is, it's soft and soothing. Her husband was right; her voice, her music–it's a sound the world should hear.

"Sean, come on in. We have kids waiting to see you." Miranda pushes me forward into the room, but I find it hard to concentrate on anything but the woman at the piano. Her head is down, eyes focused on the keys, almost like she's somewhere else.

I drop my bag on the floor, sidle up next to my teammates to shake hands, and sign footballs and jerseys. After a bit, I notice Andie, Ms. Parks, is standing next to the table getting a bottle of water, and I excuse myself.

She notices my approach, and I see her stiffen as if she's readying herself for battle. I don't like that I make that happen. I'm not the guy I might have led her to believe I am.

"I guess you knew what you were doing out there." I nod, gesturing toward the field.

She shrugs. "Who knew?"

I survey the room, hoping no one is paying attention to our closeness. "I guess it might really be your big break after all."

She crosses her arms over her chest as she peers up at me. "Look, if you're so uncomfortable standing here talking to me, why did you come over? I'm certain it's not to talk about my future prospects."

I want to groan, but I keep it in. "I wanted to say I'm sorry. I didn't mean to be insensitive earlier today. I had no idea…about your situation."

Her head falls to the side an inch. "My situation?"

I sigh. "Yes. I didn't know about your husband. I'm…sorry."

"So, if you'd known my husband was dead, you wouldn't have acted like a prick?" She says it quietly to ensure the kids around us don't hear.

This is not at all how I envisioned this going, and now I wish I'd just kept my distance.

"No. I mean, yes." I'm stumbling all over myself. *What is it about this woman?* "I just mean, I think I gave you the wrong impression." I glance around again, relieved to see everyone is still going about their business.

"Your husband was right. You're clearly very talented. You should definitely do something with it."

She glares. *Why is she glaring at me?*

"Because *clearly,* I can't possibly already be doing anything of value?"

I set my hands on my hips while my eyes find the floor, trying to understand why this is so difficult and why everything that seems to come out of my mouth isn't even remotely close to the apology I was hoping for. Something about this woman jumbles my thoughts and twists my tongue. Everything I want to say remains unsaid, while everything I do say gets misinterpreted.

She leans in a little closer, and that same calming, distinctive scent that filled the elevator wafts to my nostrils. It's contradictory. I've never smelled anything like it, and although this is not the time to notice, I like it. It's unique and completely…her.

It's her turn to survey our surroundings before her eyes return to me.

"It might come as a surprise to you, but not everyone needs a spotlight or have their face on the front of a cereal box to feel like they've made it in life. Some people are very happy living a mundane, ordinary, everyday life. People who work hard and try to do good with what they have." She takes a breath, her bright green eyes boring into mine. "Maybe if you climb off your high horse for just a second, you'd see that your whole world is just shallow enough for your presumptuous pompous ass."

I'm left speechless as I feel an arm snake around my waist.

"Hey, babe." Morgan snuggles in next to me.

I try to make sense of how all of this went so wrong while figuring out why in the hell Morgan is here. We broke up. Weeks ago.

"Wasn't she amazing earlier?" Morgan beams up at me. "I was telling her that she should be headlining a tour."

My eyes turn back to the green ones across from me, and the fire in them still burns. "Yes. She was, but I don't think headlining a tour is her calling."

I search her eyes to see if I can find what I'm missing. I know I wasn't the most courteous or charming version of myself during our time together. I have a feeling there's more to this than my lack of being personable, and for some reason, I want to know what it is.

"Excuse me." A tiny voice comes from down low.

We all turn to see a little girl standing, shyly peering up at Andie.

Andie immediately crouches down next to the girl. "Hi."

The little girl looks around at all the people before leaning closer to Andie. "Don't tell all these big guys, but I want to be just like you when I grow up."

Andie smiles, and it's genuine and striking. "Well, you are way too cute to want to be like these tough guys, but you know what I think?" She grabs the little girl's hand and places it between hers. "I think you shouldn't want to be anyone other than yourself. God made you very special and needs you to be exactly who you are. Nobody else. Ok?"

The little girl smiles and nods. "I like your shoes."

Andie looks down at her feet. "Thank you. They're kind of my favorite. Someone I love very much gave them to me. Do you want to help me play a song?"

"Yeah!" she says with a toothless grin.

"Ok. Let's go show them what we've got." Andie stands, still holding the girl's hand, and turns back to Morgan and me. "If you'll excuse us. It was nice meeting you." Her eyes meet mine. "Good luck with things."

We watch as she sits at the piano, and the little girl scoots beside her.

"What was that all about?" Morgan asks.

"Nothing. What are you doing here?" I don't even try to hide my irritation.

Morgan pulls away from me. She's wearing my oversized jersey that barely covers her. It's falling off one shoulder and has nothing else on except thigh-high black boots. There was a time when this wouldn't have bothered me, but in a room full of kids, I can't help but feel it's entirely inappropriate.

"I wanted to see you. Are you ready to get out of here? I made reservations."

"Morgan, kids are waiting, and then I'm going home," I whisper. "We've already talked about this, and I can't get into it again right now." I cross the room and sneak back in line as Morgan joins some of the other girlfriends and wives chatting.

I sign more footballs and take more pictures, wondering when I can leave. I don't want to have this conversation with Morgan again, especially tonight. I'm tired and want to go home where it's calm and quiet.

My eyes jet back to Andie, along with the rest of the room, when the piano erupts with the theme song from *Star Wars.* I see Andie whisper to the little girl, who laughs. She keeps playing, and then it morphs into something else. Something I recognize. She's playing *Happy,* and the room starts moving and clapping along to the song. Next to me, Tyrell starts singing.

She focuses on the keys in front of her, but after a second, her eyes flick up to mine, and she tips her head to the side, glaring ever so slightly with just a hint of a smirk. I will the corners of my mouth to stay put.

Tyrell bumps my shoulder. "Don't think I didn't notice you snuck over there to talk with her. Something happen in the elevator I should know about?"

"Nope. I didn't know about her husband. I told her I was sorry." I pause. "I wasn't real pleasant while we were trapped together."

Tyrell turns to grab his water and takes a drink. "She's beautiful, talented, and seems pretty smart, too. And that voice–"

"Alright." I cut him off.

He holds up his hands. "I'm just saying I would've been on my best behavior. Even pulled out the Simmons charm." He grins and winks.

"Not interested. For some reason, she can't stand me. Besides, I've got plenty on my plate right now."

"Yeah. For real. Speaking of which…" He leans close. "What's Morgan even doing here? I thought you broke up."

"We did."

"Huh." He rubs his chin. "Good luck with that. I'm finding my wife and going home. See you Tuesday." He slaps me on the back.

"See ya," I say, thinking it must be nice to be that settled. I hope to someday have a wife and kids waiting for me at the end of this room, but right now, that idea seems so far off it almost feels impossible.

The room quickly starts to empty, and I see Miranda talking with Andie, who's wearing her backpack and looks ready to go. I grab my bag and think about making one last attempt at apologizing, but then decide against it.

Something about her combative nature gets under my skin and pushes all my non-easygoing buttons. It's time to go our separate ways and let our time in the elevator and all other interactions today be history.

I throw my bag over my shoulder, and like she's been ready to pounce, Morgan joins me.

"Are you ready?" She takes hold of my arm.

"Yeah."

Andie's eyes meet mine one more time, and I think about what she said earlier, that today was about moving forward for her. I hope she was able to do that. What I know is I'm ready. I'm tired of feeling like I'm missing out on reality because I've gotten wrapped up in all the wrong things. Superficial things. All of which have left me with not much, if anything, real and lasting.

We may have misunderstood each other today, but one thing is certain. Andie was right. I've been living in the shallow. If I want more, I'm going to have to wade out and dive deep until I find what I'm looking for.

Chapter 6

ANDIE

I tiptoe into the dark room and peek over the crib's railing. He lays there, arms stretched over his head, and his chubby cheeks and kissy lips so innocent and relaxed on his sweet face. Every time I look at him, my heart squeezes at the realization that he's actually mine.

I turn the soft music off, head down the short hallway, and out to the living room, where Nora is sprawled out on the couch, Sniper on the floor beside her.

I bought this little cottage, perfectly tucked in the outskirts of Nashville. It's a small three-bedroom home with an open floor concept, but it's spacious enough for Axel and me. Besides time in the studio, this is where I spend my time caring for my little guy.

I brush by my grand piano, which takes up a large portion of my living room, but when you don't really have visitors, who cares? I spend more time sitting at that piano than talking to people, so I can have it wherever I want. Part of me wants to get right to work on the song that's eating away at me, but I also feel the need to let it simmer, giving it the space it needs to really come alive.

I grab my tea from the counter and curl up in a chair beside the couch facing Nora. Sniper, Josh's German Shepherd mix, who's now my constant companion, crawls to lie at my feet. The retired service dog is smarter than I am, and given all of his training and the bond we've formed in Josh's absence, he's likely sensing my emotional overload from today.

"Sooooo…tell me everything," Nora says through a yawn.

I hired Nora five years ago when my workload became more than I could handle on my own, and in those five years, she's become my best friend and confidant. She's the best when it comes to assistants. She's wild, energetic, my complete opposite, and I love her.

I look over at my friend. Her blue hair is piled on top of her head, dark-framed glasses crooked on her face, and one pierced eyebrow arches upward in wait.

"I didn't want to do it, but you know, all in all, it was pretty amazing." I sit, knowing I'll get a reaction out of her.

"I knew it!" Nora pushes to sit up and throws her arms in the air like she won the competition. "What was the best part?"

I tug on the tag attached to my tea, and the scent of peppermint and vanilla rises with the steam. "The whole thing was just…surreal. Getting stuck in the elevator, seeing Josh on the big screen, singing the final word, and knowing I did it." I pause, remembering it all. "Leaving there, I felt…lighter. Like I could breathe again or at least like I was alive again. I don't know if it was seeing Josh's face, hearing him say he loves me…"

I try to think of how to put my feelings into words. "I walked in there this morning wanting to turn around and come back home. I thought I was just doing it for him, wanting to get it over with. But really, in the end, I think I did it for me. I feel like I took a step in a different direction, and I'm not sure where I'm going yet, but somewhere, and it feels really good."

I hear Nora sniff. The girl seriously tears up if someone has a hangnail.

"I'm so happy for you. You were amazing. I don't know why you don't put yourself out there more. The web is blowing up with reposts of you singing. Labels and producers will be coming out of the woodwork tomorrow."

I roll my head. "You know why. I don't want that life, especially now with Axel."

"I know, I know. You're just so talented. I wish I had an ounce of what you have." She adjusts her crooked glasses. "Anyway, tell me what you did after you were done singing. Did they treat you like the queen you are?"

I laugh. "No. I joined the owners in their box to watch the game. They were gracious and so kind. Then I sat in the outdoor area, trying to collect myself a little and let my emotions settle when some of the players' wives or girlfriends asked me to sit with them."

Nora snorts. "Look at you making friends with the Tiger elite. They didn't have you strip down and pose with kissy faces that I'm going to have to somehow get removed before your mother sees them, am I?"

I laugh. "Haha. Yeah, right. Although, now that you mention it, that would've been a fun way to torture her. Speaking of Countess Dracula, she called me while I was stuck in the elevator, and I had to have that fantastic conversation in front of Sean."

"Oh, we're calling him *Sean* now." She sets her arms in her lap with a smug look on her face.

I roll my eyes. "Anyway, I have to decide about the benefit."

"We both know you're going, so stop pretending."

I groan. "I know. Why can't I just say no?"

"Because you've got a heart so big it'll just slap your mother right out of the way while you do so much good." I rub my temples, feeling the stress of it seep into me. "You could take me as your date, which will really set her off."

"You know I would, but I need you to watch Axel."

Nora grins. "Yep. I'm totally the winner in this deal. Plus, my tattoos and piercings might shock those stiffs into a tizzy."

"You'd give them all something to talk about and love every minute of it." I'm already dreading it since staying home with Axel is my favorite thing in the entire world.

Nora clears her throat. "You think they'll want to meet Axel at some point?"

I close my eyes and rub my face, feeling drained from the emotional day. "I don't know. They haven't mentioned it, and I'm fine with that. I know the minute they see him, they'll have his whole life planned out for him, and he'll carry around all that pressure his whole life. Or worse, they'll treat him like they treated Josh. I just want to protect him from all of that."

Nora sits up straighter. "No, that won't be how it is. He has you. You get to dictate who and how much they're involved in his life. I just want to see the look on your mother's face when momma bear lays down the law. Your dad might have to resuscitate her."

I sink down in my chair a little, knowing it's likely inevitable at some point, but I'm just not ready yet. I'm perfectly happy keeping Axel far from their ridiculous standards he will never meet.

"They don't even ask about him. They only care about how this looks to their small, superficial world. They still haven't forgiven me for marrying Josh when they had Brice lined up. I'm just waiting for the talk about how improper it is for me to be a single mom. Then she'll arrange a moving truck filled with Brice's stuff to arrive at whatever house she's picked out for us so she can tell all of her friends I'm finally coming back into the fold."

Brice. The egotistical slimeball I stupidly dated when I was nineteen for about five minutes until I realized he's a dirtbag of the worst kind. Of course, my mother will see and hear none of it. He remains her answer to the kind of life she wants to demand I live.

Nora shivers, wrinkling her nose. "Yuck, Brice. He's like the scum that lives on top of algae at the bottom of a swamp."

She's not even wrong. "They're just so...pretentious and condescending. Without Josh, I have no doubt this benefit is a ploy to drag me back into their world. At least my mom was mostly honest about that. She didn't even try to hide it. They'll look at Axel as collateral damage they can explain away with bogus grief and military honors. It makes me sick, and if it weren't for the kids I know will benefit, there's no way in hell I'd be going."

"I'm so sorry, Andie." Nora's soft sympathy tugs at my heart. "I guess it's just one night, and you can blow the sticks out of all those uptight asses. And well, Brice, I'll let you borrow my mace. I'd like to see how well he functions without those creepy wandering eyeballs."

I smile. "She said she has a piece chosen for me."

Nora scoffs. "I'm sure she does, but you can work your magic on that sheet music and bring down the house. You're the one that will raise funds so she can stick that piece where the sun doesn't shine and let you do your thing." Her finger taps her lips. "I bet Jonesy and the girls would be on board to help you out, taking one for the team to attend your hoity-toity ball. They'll be amazing, as always, putting on a real show. The money will roll in."

She's right, and I just need to accept that I'll have to tolerate my overbearing, ridiculously shallow, and uptight mother for one evening.

"Annnnndddd," Nora raises her eyebrows, "Gem will be there, so you can bet your cute little behind she's going to set your mother's overly sprayed hair on fire before she even gets to you."

I smile, knowing Gem will have my back. "Let's ask Jonesy and get something set up."

"Sure thing," she nods. "Now, I want the whole scoop on Sean Greyson. You can't tell me that you didn't swoon just a little. I don't care how much you try to deny it. He's so freaking hot. Did he smell good? I bet he smells amazing."

I roll my eyes while she sniffs the air like she imagines it. "He's completely full of himself."

"I don't care. I'd get stuck with him anywhere, anytime." She lets her head fall back like she's dreaming about the possibility.

I pull a pillow out from behind me and throw it at her. "He's not even your type. He was so…irritating. Half the time, he was a stuck-up jerk. The other half, he was zoned out on his phone. He looked at me like I was so far beneath him, and when he realized I could actually sing, I think he tried to apologize."

"Wait." Nora pops up. "You talked to him after the elevator?"

I shrug. "Yeah. I ran into him heading to the field and then again at the meet and greet. I think he thought he was apologizing for judging me and felt bad once he learned about Josh, but he stood there like he didn't want anyone seeing him talking to me like I was some leper."

"Really?" Nora says like this can't possibly be true.

"Yeah. Really. He said I should do something with my talent."

"Oh, man." Nora knows where that comment got him.

I grin. "I let him have it, and then his supermodel girlfriend showed up to save him."

"I'm guessing there were no sparks." Nora huffs, looking totally bummed.

I laugh. "No, sorry my little lovebird. Two hours alone in an elevator is all it will ever be."

Chapter 7

SEAN

"I'm not sure what you want me to do," Craig says. I hold the phone with my shoulder as I grab a bottle of water from the fridge. "You hired me to represent you. If you're just going to decline or worse, not show up, that makes us both look bad."

I don't know how to respond. We keep having the same conversation, and it's complete bullshit. If he doesn't know where I stand by now, we have a real problem.

A week ago, after being stuck in that damn elevator, I called my agent and told him I was done. I'm done spending time at pointless media stunts to get my picture taken, only to have it blasted everywhere, like I'm some great guy making an impact in the world of beverages, athletic gear, celebrity parties, and other high-profile events. I've done it for too long, and I'm not doing it anymore.

I'm done spending my time building a life that's no longer mine. I want to give back. I want to be part of something bigger than myself that goes beyond the game I play for a living. I'm through with playing the part that's written for me, the one I let myself buy into. The guy living the high life with all his other high lifers, ignoring the reality around us.

I got lost in it all, but I'm beginning to see clearly now. Getting lost was easy, going from a world of having nothing and no one into a world fabricated to my preferences. People will do anything, morph into anyone to be a part of this life.

I wanted to fit in. I liked the feeling of being valued, but it's clear to me now that those people have no idea who I really am, and they don't care to know that person. They want the pro football player who has fame and money. They don't want the man who grew up being tossed from one home to another or the one who'd give up the fame and money and still play the game for the love of it.

What mattered so much to me at one time doesn't mean a thing to me anymore. I'm getting back to me, the kid I used to be and the man I liked and respected. The one who understands there's a world full of people who are hurting and in need, and I'm fortunate enough to have made it to a place where I can help.

I step out on the field each day as part of a team. A team that works hard to be the best we can be for each other, our organization, and our fans. When the game is over, I find the kids in the stands, hand over a glove or ball, sign their shirts, and talk to families at the meet and greets.

I'm no longer attending events or premieres or anything else just so it can be posted to some social site or someone can use my name for their gain. I'm doing things that benefit tangibly from me and my donations, whether time or money.

I hear Craig's huff of building annoyance on the other end of the phone, but I'll make myself clear one more time. "I told you, I'm done with bogus events. When you have something for me that's bringing good to the world, let me know."

"I'm guessing a spread for *Sports Elite* is out." He says it teasingly, but I know underneath it all, he thinks I'm a fool for not doing it.

"I have to go. Morgan will be here any minute to finally get the three items she's been nagging me about."

"You sure you want to do this? She's good for you. Not many women can handle your lifestyle, and she's stuck by you. When news breaks, this could be a mess to clean up."

I let my head fall back toward the ceiling but withhold my groan. Craig needs to get on board with what I'm doing here. I'm tired of feeling like I'm talking to myself.

When I'm done with this repeated conversation, I have no doubt Morgan and I will be having the same talk, for the sixth time, about why I can no longer be in a relationship with her. It's funny, really. When you've told someone your feelings for them aren't what they should be, and they're perfectly fine to continue in the relationship anyway, it's a giant red flag if I've ever seen one. I want to punch myself in the face for not seeing it sooner.

I like Morgan. She's genuinely a nice person, but I also think she became more attached to my name than me. I need this to be over today. No more lingering.

"Craig, Morgan and I are over. You need to understand this and everything else we've discussed. I'm done with it all. I'm not interested in feeding social media with anything other than what happens on the field. My private life is going back to being just that, private. I'm no longer lining the pockets of anyone or anything unless I believe in the cause and know where my money is being used."

I hear Craig's frustrated sigh. "Got it. I'll review some charities and community events and get back to you."

"Thanks." I click the end button, hoping we're finally on the same page. If not, I'll have to find a new agent. I'm making changes, and Craig will either keep up or not.

I stretch out on my couch, enjoying the quiet breeze filtering through the open doors leading to my large screened-in porch. I spent days sitting on this couch, letting my bruised ribs and spirit heal, realizing I had everything I wanted and nothing I needed.

My house is massive and beautiful, filled with the finest of everything, yet it's completely empty. I look around, thinking again about moving into something smaller, closer to the city and the training facility. I wonder if it would be another change that could get me back to a simpler life. A life where I wouldn't be surrounded by all of the noise of the pretension and duplicity I let myself get caught up in.

It's not who I am, but I might have given the world the wrong impression, or maybe I'm just afraid I have. No more. Off the field, I want to be someone who lives by authenticity. I'm hoping, bit by bit, I'll find myself there again.

There's a light knock on my front door, and after my chat with Craig, the thought of breaking up with Morgan again has my level of frustration inching higher. We've been broken up for a month now, and she still doesn't seem to get it or won't accept it.

I unlock and open the door.

"Hey!" She bounces right past me with that chipper voice that never changes, no matter her circumstances. There was a time when I found that attractive. Morgan is never in a bad mood, but recently, I realized that's unnatural. Who is *always* in a good mood?

Like right now, here to collect her remaining things, I'd really like to see her good and pissed, but nope, she's peppy as usual.

"Hey." I quickly close the door and step into her path to stop her from taking over my space. This needs to be quick and to the point. She needs to collect her things and figure out how to move on…on her own. "I gathered your things." I gesture to the box on the long table in my entryway.

I see her pull back like she wasn't expecting this.

"I didn't realize you'd be in such a hurry." She peers into the box, her long, dark ponytail hanging over her shoulder.

She uses her hand to poke around inside the shoebox that contains only a few of her personal items as if something might be missing. I know it's all there. She only spent a few nights here every now and then.

Between my training schedule and her constant travel for photoshoots and modeling gigs, our time together was limited. In the off-season, I train out of state or spend time with my brothers. It should have been a sign that I didn't miss her or wasn't disappointed to come home and for her not to be here. The thought has me tugging at my shirt collar, which suddenly feels tight as I find I dislike who I let myself become even more.

She leans against the table, planting herself, then crossing her arms over her chest. *Here we go. Round seven.*

"So, this is it, then?" Her puppy dog eyes appear, and I find I'm unaffected.

"Yes."

She pulls in a breath and bites her bottom lip. "I don't understand. I thought…I thought you cared about me. We're great together. You said a million times how grateful you were that I could put up with your life. That I understood, and it made us a good fit."

I hang my head. It's all true. The fact I didn't recognize all that was wrong is my fault. It wasn't that I lied. I do care about her, but not the way a man should care about the woman in his life. The person who is supposed to be my best friend and the one who, when everything falls apart, I want and need to hold me up.

We don't even know each other well enough to be any of those things. I didn't spend the time getting to know her in those ways, and I have a feeling she didn't care to.

These past months, I've spent a lot of time evaluating every part of my life. I've watched my brother fall in love, and I now see what a relationship should be, what I want it to be, and what Morgan and I are not.

I take a deep breath through my nose and let it out, readying myself to try to explain it again.

"Morgan, you and I were great together. We had some amazing times, but we weren't what we should be. I'm not ok with that. You like my life, but I'm not sure that you really like me or at least the me I'm trying to be. We've been together for almost two years, and I'm not blaming you because I got sucked up in my own superficial existence. But I can't live like that anymore, and I'm pretty sure the parts of me you like are gone."

She tips her head to the side. "And now, suddenly, you just don't want me to be a part of this new life you're making for yourself?"

It might be the first time I hear just a hint of spite. "I don't know what my life will end up looking like, but you have to ask yourself, if I wasn't a football player, if I wasn't Sean Greyson and playing for the Tigers, would you even be here right now?"

Her eyes roam over me while she ponders what I just asked her. "But that is who you are?"

"I won't be that forever."

She scoffs like it's a ridiculous statement, but it's true. The more I evaluate things, the more I see that door closing at some point, maybe sooner than I've ever imagined.

"Morgan, if you really think about it, we don't even know each other that well."

She laughs, and it's filled with sarcasm. "And whose fault is that?"

I rub the back of my neck, my frustration igniting my temper, and I need to hold it together. "I'm not pointing fingers. I'm just saying that what we've been doing isn't really being in a relationship, at least not what I consider a relationship should be."

She looks down at her crossed ankles and sniffs, but not in a sniffly way. It's more the kind that's full of irritation. "If I leave here, that's it.

When your temporary breakdown is over, and you realize this was a mistake, I won't be there."

Her thinking all of this is temporary and a part of some midlife crisis only confirms again how far apart and wrong for each other we are.

"I don't expect you to be." I'm ready for her to leave.

She stares at me for a long few seconds like she's waiting to see if I'll change my mind. When I don't, she huffs and grabs her box.

"Good luck figuring out your life. When you find yourself or whatever, I hope you don't regret everything you're giving up."

I would say thank you, but I get the feeling she doesn't really mean it.

Taking her small box, she opens the door and closes it behind her. It's horrible. I know it's horrible, but the finality of this gets me one step closer to being a person I recognize again.

I never wanted to hurt her, but I wonder how much of what just happened is actually emotional hurt versus me scuffing up her pride. We were never going to be right together. I know that with certainty.

With that reminder, I walk onto my screened porch, the sounds of early nightfall and cool air calming my heated skin and temper. The crisp and rhythmic sounds of the cricket chirps and the locusts in the distance are peaceful and familiar. I stand listening, and for the first time in a very long time, I feel something like excitement stirring within me.

Morgan called it a breakdown. Craig has called it a midlife crisis. Whatever it is, it doesn't matter. All I know is I feel like I'm standing on the precipice of something real and tangible, and I haven't been anywhere like that in a really long time.

Chapter 8

ANDIE

I crumple another piece of paper into a ball and toss it to the ground, where it lands with the other twenty that are representative of my morning. Snipe bumps my elbow with his cold, wet nose, letting out a grunt like he, too, is disgusted. I let my head fall forward onto the piano, the deep tones matching my emotional state.

Sometimes, songs pour out of me like an escapee from an asylum, fast and manic. Other times, it's like pulling the truth from a toddler when the bowl of Halloween candy goes missing, and their mouth is smeared with chocolate. The truth is evident, but you might never get to it.

There's a melody and words that need to come forth. It's agonizing and painful when I can't get them to surface. I keep digging and searching, but…nothing.

I press my hands to the keys quick and fast in frustration, knowing my time for this morning is about to expire. My little man has been napping but will be up and ready to eat soon.

I stand and stretch my arms overhead, moving to my small kitchen to fill my kettle with water and place it on the stove. I lean against the counter and hear tires crunch against my gravel drive. There are only two people it could be. When I peer out the window and see the black town car, I know I'm in for it. *Bugger.*

I lie in wait for the click of heels on the front porch, the door to swish open, and the woman to appear like she's on a hunt and found her prey.

She steps in, removes her massive black sunglasses, and looks around until she spies me. She stands there, the epitome of the Nashville royalty she is, in her bright red pantsuit, black designer purse, shoes, and jewelry to match, along with professionally styled hair and makeup. If there's ever a woman who knows how to make an entrance, it's Gemma Taninbaugh, my grandmother.

Those squinting eyes land on me for a long second before calling over her shoulder. "She's here, Gerald. I'll be just a bit." Then she closes the door.

Without saying a word, she sets her purse on the couch and sits on the edge, poised and ready. "Rough morning?" Her eyes roam over me again.

I look down at my knee-high socks and oversized sweatshirt, which is so large you can't tell I have shorts on underneath. I can't see it, but I'm certain my curly hair is in knots on top of my head. Even though I have a headband to help keep the mess contained, it's likely not doing its job.

I shrug. "Rough life."

I see just a hint of a smirk. "Well, sweet cheeks, whoever told you this was easy should be taken out back and given a swift kick in their lying ass."

I look down at my turquoise socks, covered in sloths. They're ironically fitting today.

"Want to talk about it? You look like hell."

"Gee, thanks." I want to laugh because she's seen me in a worse state than this. "There's a song. I can't get it out. It's like it's stuck in there, and it's…suffocating. I have something to say. I just don't know what yet, I guess." I shake my head, trying to put it out of my mind for now. I need a break.

"Like me, you don't lack vocabulary, so I have no doubt it's coming. The question is, are you going to be ready for it?"

I bite my lip. "Not sure yet."

She nods like she understands, and really, I think she does.

"Maybe that's the problem." She points at me, changing the subject. "You keep looking like that, and your mother is going to call the authorities to haul you to a rehab facility."

"Well, then I'll spend my time in therapy talking about all of the years she tried to make me into some freaking beauty queen lookalike, readying me to be sold off to the highest bidder." I smile. "Looking like this is like giving her a giant middle finger."

That lights up my Gem's face, and I remember why I love this woman so much. She settles on the couch, crossing her legs.

Crap. Here we go.

"I heard something that might have a similar effect on her. If word gets to those gaudy pearled ears, we might just see a little cloud go poof in the distance that was her head." Her fingers mimic an explosion.

I try to hide my smile. "What exactly is this gossip that you speak of?"

"Is it gossip if I've seen evidence with my own eyes and heard the magnificence of it with my delicate but very working ears?"

"I guess that makes it factual."

She sniffs. "Want to tell me why you didn't mention it? Why *I* didn't get to sit in the stands and watch my only granddaughter sing the national anthem like she was born to do it? Baby girl, you made grown men weep."

I take a breath and hold it, wanting to get this right with the only woman who's ever had my back and always will.

I let the breath out. "I'm not sure if you'll understand this, but I just felt like it was something I had to do on my own. Josh sent in the video, and I had no idea. I didn't even want to do it, but Nora accepted on my behalf."

Gem cuts in. "Remind me to give that girl a swat and a hug and an allowance for a new hair color. I knew she'd be good for you."

"Anyway," I continue. "I went, hoping it would help me say goodbye one last time. Like doing this for Josh would somehow help me move forward or in any direction other than standing still."

Her head bobs slightly in understanding. "Did it work?"

I think over the past couple of weeks since. "Maybe. I left there feeling different, lighter. When I got there, I got stuck in the elevator with this big-time football player who was completely full of himself. All I wanted was to run right back here like it was some kind of sign. But after dealing with him and his condescension, I just kept pushing forward, wanting it for myself. Then I was in the middle of the field, and the drums started, and I did it. It felt so good." I smile, thinking back to hitting that final note.

I rub my temples. "Now, I'm just kind of angry. I want him back. I want to go back to the way it was, but it's been over a year, and everything has changed. I've changed, and it's becoming harder to remember, you know?"

I look up to see her watching, listening intently.

"I'm sorry I didn't tell you about it, but I just couldn't have you waltzing in there like the Queen of England, letting everyone know how it was going to go down. I needed to have it naturally unfold how it was supposed to. I just…needed to do it on my own. To try to say goodbye and find a way to let myself live again."

She smiles this time, and it's the real deal, not one filled with sass. "Andie, don't be sorry. Don't apologize. You took the bull by the balls and squeezed them." I laugh, her face relaxing into a more solemn look. "It's ok to let yourself be happy again. You know that, right? Josh was a good man. He'd want that for you and for Ax."

I nod, knowing it's true and finally feeling like I might be able to allow myself. If there's anyone who understands, it's my Gem. She married my grandfather right out of high school and buried him after thirty years together. There's never been a single man since, but I don't think it's that she didn't try. She's just never found someone who made her feel anything compared to the way she felt with him.

I hear a squeak from the baby monitor and move to grab it off the counter.

"Well, look at that." Gem claps her hands together. "Perfect timing. I get to see the most handsome man in the entire world. You go make yourself smell and look better, then we'll go to lunch."

"I need to feed him first, and then he's all yours while I think about putting actual clothes on."

She smacks my butt as I pass by. "Clothes or no clothes, Andie. Makes no difference to me."

"I have to be back by 1:30. Jonesy is coming over so I can try to convince him to help me at the benefit, and don't even think about staying and monopolizing his time, Gram."

"Oh, pfft." I hear her puff like I'm ridiculous, but I know her. "You call me Gram again, and I'll call Ed McNeil and see when we can do a duet."

That stops me in my tracks. I know this woman knows people, but freaking Ed McNiel, owner of the Tennessee Tigers. *Really?*

I spin. "You know him?"

I see her meticulously drawn eyebrows rise. "Sweet cheeks, I know everyone. He thought you were fabulous but was shocked to find out we were related. He was quite sorry to hear about Josh and felt terrible that you spent two hours in the elevator with what I now understand is a whole lot of man."

I groan. "You really should save Nora from her horrific apartment and have her move in with you. This whole town wouldn't know what to do with themselves if you two were ever in cahoots."

She studies her bright red fingernails, and then her rings. "We'd paint the whole town every color but gray…and that dreadful beige color that looks like shit."

I turn back around to go find my guy. This woman, it's no wonder she's my favorite.

"What exactly are you looking to do at this benefit?" Jonesy's hesitancy has me smiling.

I sit Axel on my lap. At six months, he's so close to sitting up on his own, but I prop him up against me so he can grab at the teethers on the table in front of us.

"I need you to work your magic. I have a classical piece my mother insists I play. I'll start with that and fade it into something more…me. Then, I want you, Natasha, and Cici to back me up."

Jonesy taps his pen on the table. "You want me to mix something up for a bunch of old people?"

I laugh at the young, remarkable man sitting across from me who, in my opinion, is the next Quincy Jones. I have no idea why he's still sitting here with me instead of in a high-rise in New York, but I'm grateful. Not only do I love working with him, he's my friend.

We've worked together for the past couple of years after being introduced by a label. When he learned I write songs, we paired up to produce demos, and he's been killing it ever since. I'm just waiting for the day when someone hears one of his tracks and he leaves me in the dust.

"Yes, that's exactly what I want. I say we start with my classical piece fast and stark but then bring it down into something…smooth and soulful. Then maybe we kick it back up with something fun to get the old people tapping their toes."

He sits back and crosses his arms, a smile tugging at his lips. "Sounds like a challenge."

Jonesy is not a large man. He can't be more than 5' 10." His uniform consists of skinny jeans and tight t-shirts, accented by the gold chains around his neck. But when it comes to music, he's a genius. And when it comes to a challenge, just watch him work.

I raise my eyebrows. "And it's the perfect job for you. Plus, it's for an amazing cause. All proceeds will go to the children's wing at the hospital."

If I haven't hooked him, I know that'll do it. I spend a lot of time in the children's wing at the hospital playing piano or guitar and singing with the kids. Since Jonesy learned about my standing dates, he's often joined me, and the kids can't get enough of him. His dancing and rapping are a complete hit.

He glares at me. "You just had to throw the kids in there."

I grin. "Gets'em every time. I'd definitely like to forego the benefit, but it will be so much better with you and the girls there. If I have to sing in front of these people, I want to bring down the house."

He chuckles. "Fine, Miss Andie. I'll do it." His bright smile shines against his dark skin.

"You're the best." I grin, so happy to have his help and know I don't have to do this alone. "Oh, and also, I've been working on something. I'm stuck, and I wondered if you'd listen to what I have so far. I don't know if I should keep going or toss it."

"Sounds good. If we're going to do this, let's get to it." He stands and heads to the piano. "Don't think you don't owe me for this." I roll my eyes, and he laughs, holding out his hands. "Give me that boy, and let me hear what you've got."

I hand over Ax, and we spend part of the next hour at the piano and the other part brainstorming for the benefit before his time is up. If I have to go to this benefit and face these people, including my mother, at least I can do it on my own terms. Her head might explode when she finds out, but my father can pick up the plastic pieces and cauterize them back together.

I settle on the floor and lean against the couch, putting Ax between my legs and pulling his toys closer. He grabs one and tries to shove it in his gummy mouth while drool trickles down his arm. I kiss the top of his soft head and breathe in his clean baby scent.

I watch as he pushes around a bumpy ball, trying to get it with both hands, then looks up at me with those big blue eyes like he wants to make sure I'm still here. I smile as he returns to the ball, running my hand over his light brown hair that's finally getting long enough I'm starting to see some curls. It's hard for me to believe this is my life.

I'd do anything for this kid, absolutely anything. I think back to my conversation with Gem earlier about what I gained from stepping out of my comfort zone and singing for thousands. What I know is I don't want Ax to see me like this, not living, standing still because I can't get myself to move forward. I want to live and experience life with him. I don't want him to see me afraid or holding back because I won't move on from what was and won't ever be again.

I want to live life for him. So, no matter how much I might have to push myself, I'm going to figure it out. Even if it's baby steps, I'm doing it for him. Gem's right. It's what Josh would want, too.

So, I'll go to this benefit. I'll appease my parents and let them carry on the facade of their fancy little life, but I'm doing it my way. I'll play, sing, and entertain, and when I'm done, I'll have taken another step toward seeing whatever this new chapter in my life might hold.

Chapter 9

SEAN

CRAIG: How do you feel about a benefit for the children's ward at Mercy Hospital?
CRAIG: All proceeds go to upgrades and the latest technology. Great cause and a perfect way to start getting involved.

ME: When?

CRAIG: Wednesday night. Shouldn't impact your schedule.
CRAIG: I can't promise there won't be cameras or press. Looks like a pretty big deal from what I've gathered, but it's not a stunt.

ME: Sign me up.

"You, GQ Man of Last Year. You're going to this thing alone?"

Mark's teasing astonishment comes through my phone, sitting on my dresser. I expect this from him. My brother from another mother doesn't do events alone.

Mark, Shane, and I found each other at a group home. Growing up in the system formed a bond between us that cannot be broken. They're my brothers in every sense that matters. But just like all siblings, we don't always see eye-to-eye.

"Yeah. Believe it or not, people can attend functions without a date."

Mark scoffs. "What's the fun in that?"

I ignore the question. "Anyway, you don't go to enough of these things. You're too busy hitting up the next party and hot young thing.

You should send a check. One hundred percent goes to the children's hospital."

"Why aren't you just sending a check? Then you could sit at home and rest. Don't you have a game?"

I do. I have a game in two days, so I should stay home and rest, but this is important. Even though my body is sore and I have a slight ankle sprain, I'm going. I've been looking for opportunities to give back, and this is only a few hours of my time and a click of a button to donate.

I've made enough excuses over the years and told myself enough lies that kept me from doing things that matter and spending a whole lot of time doing things that don't. So, I'm going. I want to see how this bit of time and money benefits these doctors, nurses, and kids. I'm hopeful it might lead to other ways of helping and providing.

I unbutton the top button on my shirt, deciding to go without a tie this evening. It's a formal event, but what will they do, kick me out? In the bathroom, I splash on some aftershave and then grab my suit coat.

"I still don't understand what the hell is going on with you," Mark grumbles. "Look, I think I understand breaking up with Morgan, but the rest of this, the no more parties, events, magazine spreads…I don't get it. It's just part of what we do."

I stop on my way to the garage and look out at my backyard. The sun is setting, and the dim light filters through the trees. It's peaceful. Serene. Growing up, peace wasn't something I understood or experienced, so when I see it or feel it now, it overwhelms me.

The beauty of the fading sun, the stillness and quiet, makes me pause. I realized I'd stopped noticing it. Rushing from one thing to the next or sitting in pain and discomfort, I've taken moments like this for granted. Something at one time I thought I'd never do.

As a boy fighting to survive in foster homes, I could only dream and hope for this–moments of calm and quiet, safety and security. I have it now, but I've been flying right past them, seeking the next offer of praise or approval. Now, I wouldn't mind just sitting here and watching the sun work its way below the horizon.

Hearing Mark cuss at something, I'm pulled back to the phone.

"Don't you ever just get tired of all the bullshit?" I keep my voice soft, not wanting to disturb the sight before me. "It's not real, Mark. The girls you hang out with, the parties you go to with all those people, the fans chanting your name who think they know you...it's only because of what you do on the field. It's not because of who you really are. Don't you just get sick of wondering if any of it is real?" I pause. "When all that is stripped away, those fans, those parties, those girls…what's left?"

"It's just part of what we do, man." He says it like it's no big deal. "Someday, no one will give a shit about who we are. We'll just be some has-beens, so for now, I'm living it up."

I think about that for a moment. I know someday, all of the fame and notoriety will be long gone, only a memory to go back and visit from time to time. Are there perks to this life? Absolutely. Is it amazing to walk out onto the field and hear the fans chanting my name or have a kid approach me, dreaming of being me one day? It's an honor, especially coming from my background.

What I know is, though, it will all fade sooner than we think or want it to, and when it does, I don't want to be standing in sinking sand because I didn't see the danger of it when I should have.

"That may work for you, but it's not for me. I've already taken a good look around, and besides you, Shane, Maggie, and the kids, I'm not sure what's real, and it scares me."

Last year, Shane married his wife, Maggie, and gained an entire family. I've watched him fall in love and start a new kind of life. One that, if I'm honest, I'm completely jealous of. What he has is beautiful, and I can't help but want that someday, but I'd never get there with how I was living.

I let a breath out, remembering what it was like to sit on the couch, resting and healing, wondering how I'd let myself get lost. It'd been a long time since I remembered being scared, not since I was a teenager, maybe before that. Once I'd left the system and the horrors I'd faced, I promised myself I'd never let myself feel that way again.

"You and I know what it's like to have absolutely nothing." I remind him. "Now, I have everything and sometimes recently…I've felt like I'm there again, just in a big house, with a ridiculously expensive truck, the best job… I have it all, and yet, I'm completely alone."

I'm met with silence, and I wonder if he's listening. "We've spent so much time alone, worse than alone. We didn't have a choice. We do now. I don't want to wake up one day and realize I've let the best things pass me by while I got caught up in being surrounded by people and things. Reality is these people, and these things are only surface deep. When my body gives out, or the rookie outshines me, it'll all fade and then disappear. None of it is real."

I hear Mark inhale and let it out. I know he's finally letting what I'm saying register.

"You're not alone, bro. I do understand feeling that way. I don't like it much either."

"That's just it. Now that I see it, I can't stand it. It's eating at me, and I'm tired of it. I don't want to feel that way anymore. I'm done wasting my time on things that don't matter, and I'm going to find what does. When we turned eighteen, we didn't take a single thing for granted. I'm getting back there."

I want to get back to the boy that I was. The one who sat praying that I'd make it, and if I did, I'd build a life that I was proud of and filled with happiness and joy. I've been happy, but somewhere along the way, I've lost it and replaced it with contentment, only moving from one game or event to the next.

"I'm proud of you. You always were the smart one." Mark's uncharacteristic sentimental tone hits me in the chest. "I really hope you find what you're looking for. Have a good time tonight."

"Thanks." I press the end call button and grab my keys.

In the garage, I climb into my truck, ready to find out what this feels like and disappointed in myself that it's taken me this long. It's a place to start, and I want to leave the benefit tonight feeling like I've actually made a difference somehow. Maybe if I'm lucky, it will lead to something more.

Chapter 10

ANDIE

My reflection stares back at me in the horribly lit bathroom. Am I hiding? Yes, I am. If I'm going to make it through this night, I need a minute before I face my mother's wrath. She'll be toting a list a mile long of all the things she finds fault with.

At the very top will be what I have planned for tonight. Next will be my dress since I'm not wearing the one she sent me. She'll have to add the 'hell no' I'm going to give her when she talks about me playing nice with that scumsucker Brice. If I'm going to suffer through her barrage of complaints, I'm damn well going to make sure it's in a ballroom filled with her people, not tucked back into some corner.

I grab my phone to see if Nora responded to my text, checking in on Ax. Once I leave the bathroom, I won't be able to check my phone for a bit. Seeing her thumbs up, I inhale another deep breath, hoping there's courage in the air.

In through my nose, out through my mouth.

I smooth my hand down the front of my black satin high-low dress. The sleeveless, fitted bodice hugs my torso and flares out with layers of tulle, which are shorter in the front and longer in the back. At the hem are two solid stripes of satin of different widths, giving it just an extra hint of rocker chic. It's the best I could find without going overboard. What I know is I love it, but it will trigger the start of my mother's complaints.

Oh well. We all can't be people pleasers.

I lean forward, checking my makeup for smudges. My light smokey eye and pink-tinted glossy lips are good enough. I don't usually wear much makeup, so a little sparkle and shine go a long way.

I grab my purse off the worn chair, hearing the click of my silver ankle wrap heels against the tile as I exit. Just the shoes I need if I'm going to remain standing tall despite the forceful hot air that's about to blow in.

I step out into the hallway that leads into the ballroom and find people are arriving. I know my parents are here somewhere. I need to get myself geared up to sing, so I risk running into them trying to get a hot tea from the bar. Thankfully, I make it back out to the safety of the atrium to wait for Jonesy and the girls.

I balance my tea while pulling my phone out for one last quick check. Nothing. When I glance toward the doors, hoping to see Jonesy, I squint, seeing a familiar broad, muscular figure pushing through the door. It's that same pretty boy face I see plastered everywhere now that I know who it belongs to.

He glances around like he's unsure where to go, and then his gaze snags on me. His forward motion slows, and I see the instant those almost translucent blue eyes find recognition.

Well, juussssstttt fan-freaking-tastic. If this isn't the icing on the big pretentious cake.

He nears with the slightest hint of a smirk creeping across that quiet mouth, and I want to wipe it off his way-too-handsome-for-his-arrogant-self-face. His big, nicely dressed body stops in front of me.

"What in the world are you doing here?" I ask, seriously wanting to know.

"Hi. It's nice seeing you again." His lips turn up just a little more into something resembling amusement like there's some universe where we can stand each other. "I was just about to ask you the same thing. Did you win another competition, or are you here for other purposes this time?"

I'm pretty sure I glare, readying my response, when I hear my name called from behind me. It's that tone that instantly makes steam shoot out of my ears, and part of me wonders if my eardrums have suffered trauma from years of enduring it.

I turn in that direction, praying the large masculine presence behind me won't stick around for the showdown that's about to take place.

I can only watch as the woman who is my mother approaches. Her blond hair is delicately swept up, her pearl necklace in place, and her soft blue ball gown crisp as usual.

My mother and I could not be more different regarding practically everything. From our looks to our personalities to how we think I should live my life.

"Andrea, what are you doing out here, and what in the world are you wearing? That is not the dress that I sent over for you. This..." She reaches out, gesturing with her hand. "This dress is–"

"Stunning." I hear a low voice come from just behind me.

The shock on my mother's face probably matches mine, and it might be the very first time we've ever encountered common ground. I have no doubt it'll only last a second. The thought makes me smile as I turn to peer over my shoulder at Sean, who I find standing just inches from me, his brow furrowed.

"You look incredible." His eyes meet mine before floating over my head to my mother.

"Andrea. Who is this man?" Her quick question has my head whipping around, but her panic continues. "You're...Brice is here. He's sitting at our table. It's full, so there's no room for your...friend."

"Mother," I cut in, intending to tell her that Sean is not my date, but then I hear my name again.

"Andie." Jonesy joins our growing little group. "You all set?"

I try to smile as he leans in to hug me, but the comfort is fleeting. "I will be now that you're here."

"Good. The ladies are just behind me." Ignoring my mom, Jonesy looks at Sean, one eyebrow arching up as he offers his hand. "Jonesy."

"Sean." He sticks his hand out in return.

Jonesy looks back at me with a questioning look, and I stand there like an idiot, letting whatever conclusion be drawn for now.

"Andrea," my mother snaps, but a little more quietly this time. "What exactly is going on here?"

"Jonesy and a couple of other friends are helping me out this evening." I really hope she'll let this be, buuuuutttt I know better.

"What kind of help? I picked out the piece you'll be playing. *That* is what you're performing tonight."

Jonsey lets out a tiny chuckle while I hold back my own smirk. "I'll find you in a few." He squeezes my forearm before leaving me.

I'd really like Sean not to witness this bit of humiliation, but for some reason, his large presence is anchored in place.

When I don't respond, she gets even more agitated, lowering her voice and stepping in just a little closer. "Andrea, there are very important people here tonight. Your father's colleagues, our friends, people of the community…They're expecting you to play–"

I cut her off. "I don't care if Santa Claus himself is here. I'm doing this my way or not at all. Your choice, Mother." I pin her with a look so she understands I mean what I say.

She pulls back, stiffening, but doesn't say anything. In her silence, a hot flash envelops my body, and sweat starts to collect under my arms. I wonder if it's possibly radiating from the big guy behind me. I peek to find he's stepped even closer, almost pressed against me.

What…is going on?

This guy was concerned about being seen with me before but clearly doesn't have an issue when it's my public dress-down.

"Darling, there you are." I close my eyes but hold in my groan as my head falls back. I stop it just before it meets Sean's chest. My dad rolls up to our little hallway party and puts an arm around my mother. "Andrea, I didn't see you come in." He leans in to kiss my cheek.

My father is a tall man with gray hair and has always been the absent, easier-going of the two. The problem is, my mother runs the show. I guess it makes sense, given his time was spent with a scalpel in his hand rather than at home or with me. I've understood it's part of the career and consumes his life.

He looks at Sean, who's still standing with me.

"Dr. Taninbaugh." My dad sticks out his hand, and Sean accepts it.

"Sean Greyson."

As if Sean standing here is really of no matter to him, he returns to my mother. "Donna, people are arriving. We need to get back in there. Also, what's this I hear about Andrea singing at a Tigers game?" My dad frowns as my mother's face takes on a whole new dimension of horror.

Why does he ask the questions like I'm not standing right here?

"Andrea, what is he talking about?" Her eyes are wide and wild like someone just told her I took up stripping.

I let out a breath, but just as I'm scrambling to come up with an appropriate way to answer without getting into this with her, my Gem comes sauntering over like she's just busted through saloon doors. I can almost hear the music from an old western playing in the background. The look in her eye tells me she knows exactly what's up and is ready to draw if necessary.

"Hello." Gem's innocent tone makes me smile. "Donna, you really should be inside welcoming your guests." Her attention moves to Sean, eyeing him, and then her beady, little, mischievous eyes find mine.

As my mother tries to gather herself, Jonesy walks by with my guitar case in hand, and he gives me a strange look, likely not understanding why I brought it based on what we discussed.

"Andrea, what is that?" My mother's voice rises an octave.

I'd hoped she didn't notice, but that's never my luck.

"A giant fiddle. I thought it would be perfect for this little hoedown."

I hear Sean clear his throat next to me like he's trying to stifle a laugh.

"And who are you?" Gem steps forward, not even trying to hide her blatant perusal. I know damn well she knows who he is.

"This is Sean." I cut in, needing to get this show on the road. I look up at him. "You probably want to go get seated or something, right?" I'm past ready for him to excuse himself from this little shitshow that is my family.

"Andrea," my mother hisses. "You will be sitting with us. Brice is waiting. Your…friend will be seated at a different table."

I scoff. "Yeah. Not happening. I wouldn't sit next to Brice if it was the last seat on the last bus out of hell. But hey, he's into ignoring the whole married thing, so feel free to keep him company."

"Andrea!" my mother spits as my Gem grins, and I roll my lips to prevent them from tugging upward and making this worse.

"Alright," my dad says, trying to smooth things. The problem is, the man is oblivious and always has been when it comes to the horrendous relationship between my mother and me. There's no smoothing things over here. It's just one giant load of horse crap after another that even years of therapy haven't helped me trudge all the way through. "Let's go welcome our guests, and we'll figure out seating in a bit." He tries to be diplomatic.

I should correct the idea that Sean and I are here together, but we've gone this far, and he hasn't said anything, so I keep my mouth shut for the sake of moving this along.

"I need to get ready." I try to break this up. "You can get back to all that pomp and circumstance. Just leave the entertainment to me."

"Andrea," my mother says in warning. "You better not make a spectacle of this and, for heaven's sake, try to do something with your hair." She reaches out like she's going to smooth down my curls.

I move out of the way, bumping into Sean, and his hands grip my hips for just a second to steady me, and then they're gone. The feel of his hands on me is momentarily alarming, but it doesn't prevent the roll of my eyes directed at my mother. I'm a grown woman, but my eyeballs do their own thing when it comes to that tone of voice.

"Look," I say, trying to ignore the foreign lingering feel of the two large hands encircling my pelvis area. "I'm here to raise money for the hospital and these kids. That's why I'm here. Whether you like it or not, *I* am the entertainment for this evening. So, I will put on a show. It's what I'm good for, right?" I don't expect an answer. "Don't worry, the money will roll in, and your precious reputation will not be tarnished in the process. You might find your so-called friends even like it." I just couldn't help myself.

Finally caught speechless, my mother huffs as my dad guides her away.

"Well, just like old times," Gem says, moving closer to loop an arm through mine as they disappear into the ballroom.

I let out a breath.

"Sean, is it?" she says, and I ignore her, seeing Jonesy talking to Natasha and Cici.

I call to him, interrupting Gem. "Jonsey." He looks at me from across the space. "That thing I was working on, we're putting that in."

"You sure?"

I nod.

He grins. "You got it."

I look back at Gem and then at Sean. "Well, this has been a blast, but I must get going."

Gem holds my arm. "You get that little issue sorted out?"

I know she's referring to our conversation last week about the song I was struggling with. She knows what this means to me. Even though she'll only hear it for the first time tonight, she knows this song is a piece of me going out into the world. It's me taking a big step forward, letting the pain, anger, and heartache go.

"Yeah, I think so."

She smiles and leans in to kiss my cheek, holding my chin with her thumb and forefinger for just a second. "I'm proud of you, my girl. You play what's in here." She taps my chest. "No matter what anyone else ever tells you. There's a load of knockoffs here, so show them something real."

I give her a quick nod, unable to let her words sink in too deeply. I can already feel my emotions coming to life, knowing I'm going to sing something so personal in just a little while.

I step away but stop, looking back at Sean. "Sorry for all of that. I guess you got two shows for the price of one."

"It's ok. I'm looking forward to the second." The corners of his eyes crinkle. "At least it wasn't my ass getting roasted this time."

"The night's still young, and it looks like I'll have the mic." I smile, and he laughs. I notice his face is different tonight. It's less stoic and more relaxed. I wonder again why he stood there through all that and why he's even here. He's the last person I'd expect to see at one of these, especially alone. Where's his entourage? His girlfriend?

I let it go, not having time to think about it. "Careful hanging out with this one." I step away, pointing to my grandmother. "She's taught me everything I know."

I leave Gem and Sean as I make my way to find Jonesy and the girls, ready to treat these people to something original. It's all I know how to do, even if my mother despises it.

Chapter 11

SEAN

I watch Andie Parks disappear down a hallway, and I have no idea what to think about what just happened over the past few minutes.

When I walked through the doors and saw her piercing green eyes, my shock instantly morphed into a pleasant surprise. I don't know why, exactly. Especially when it was clear I was the absolute last person she expected or wanted to see here. Although, after our previous encounter, I get it.

"So, Sean," the older woman next to me says. I feel her eyeing me as I drag my gaze away from the crowded room and to the woman whom I imagine looks the epitome of Mrs. Robinson–all youth under the wisdom and snark.

I meet her glare as she steps closer, but just as she's about to say something, someone grabs her attention.

"Gemma Taninbaugh, in the flesh." A woman approaches, and I take the opportunity to escape.

I step aside, but the spry older woman snatches my arm. "I'll be catching up with you later," she winks.

I give her a quick nod, heading straight into the ballroom and bypassing the cameras and reporters, looking for their morning story or latest social media post. It doesn't take long for a man to recognize me, and once again, I'm cornered. Trying to be polite, I answer a few questions about my season so far but search the large room for a place I might hide for the evening.

I don't mind socializing, but I'd rather learn more about how the funds raised tonight will be spent. I also might be just a bit curious about this little performance that will occur at some point.

When an opportunity presents itself, I step away, finding a quiet spot along the wall to pull out my phone. I Google the name Taninbaugh. Beyond being surprised to see Andie, I was even more caught off guard by the interaction between her and her parents.

At first, I was going to excuse myself, but once I heard how her mother spoke to her, my instinctual defenses flipped on, and I wasn't going anywhere. If there's one thing I cannot stand, it's hearing someone berate another. Being the recipient of a verbal pummel is something I'm entirely too familiar with and won't tolerate.

I couldn't believe her mother would talk to her like that, especially in front of others. First, it was about her dress, which was freaking stunning, exactly as I said. Andie was beautiful at the stadium, but tonight, she looks striking in a way that is all her own. Her petite figure, wrapped in black with skinny silver heels, gives her a devastatingly badass look. All her curly dark hair spilling around her, and her soft pink smart mouth that, for some reason, just makes me want to smile every time she opens it.

When her mom started in on her about playing tonight and only now getting wind of her singing at the stadium, some of what she said to me at the meet and greet might be starting to make sense.

In the elevator, I'm sure I gave Andie the impression that I'm too good for my own reflection and that I was judging her. Maybe I did, or maybe I just wanted to understand why she would be there alone. But given my state that day, I definitely wasn't the most gentle in my curiosity. I think I might be starting to understand her pushback, at least partially.

But her comment about performing tonight, and that being all she's good for, really bothers me. I wonder if she really feels that way. Based on that little altercation in the hallway, I wouldn't be surprised if she did. That might be something the two of us have in common–that feeling of only being wanted for your talent or what someone can get out of you and never interested in anything more.

After scrolling for a second, I find what I'm looking for. Gemma Taninbaugh, the woman I was just standing with, is Nashville's daughter. She descended from the line that founded Nashville. Scrolling a little further, I see Dr. Jeffrey Taninibaugh is now Chief of Staff of the children's hospital funds are being raised for tonight.

Damn. After two hours in an elevator and a few quick interactions, I realize how wrong I was about the woman who picked out my pre-game hype song. That day, I had no idea about her losing her husband. If tonight showed me anything, it's that her parents clearly don't respect her or her talent, and that's probably only half of it. Never in a million years would I have seen this coming, and now I'm curious to know more.

My thoughts are interrupted when a speaker takes the stage, asking us to find our seats. I wander to the seating chart, hoping I don't find myself at a table full of fans. I'd be happy to sit quietly with people who have no clue who I am.

I find my table in the middle of the room and see Andie's parents seated up front. I can't help but search the faces surrounding them, wondering which one is the guy Andie was talking about. That thought brings to mind the fact that these people thought I was here as her date, and she didn't correct them. I find that very interesting, given our minimal history and her inability to tolerate me.

The current speaker is replaced by another as I take a seat. Everyone's eyes are focused on the stage, and luckily, no one at my table seems to notice my late arrival. Dinner is served as I listen and learn about the research being conducted and how the funds raised tonight will help further their efforts. Afterward, a short video showcases the hospital and staff before Dr. Taninbaugh takes the stage.

The screen rises as he welcomes everyone, and behind it sits a shiny black grand piano, some microphones, and a lone guitar. My mind wanders to Andie as her dad speaks about his role at the hospital. Her standing on the small podium in the middle of the field flashes through my mind, and the look of grief and fear in her eyes just before she started to sing. Then, the glow of those green eyes when she challenged me afterward. The same ones that stared back at me tonight when I entered. But as she walked away, leaving me with her grandmother, her eyes were softer. Still full of sass, but a gentler version, maybe as if it's used as a shield.

"Well, without further ado, I'm happy to introduce you all to my daughter. Some of you may have seen her around the hospital, playing and singing for the kids. Tonight, she's here to help us raise funds to continue our progress in our mission of saving lives. I'm told she's performing a classical piece, and the more money you dish out, the longer she'll play. So, get those wallets out, and please welcome Andrea Taninbaugh."

The crowd claps as Andie steps out, walking directly to the piano. Her father didn't address her as Andie Parks, and it feels like another puzzle piece is falling into place.

She sits at the piano and gets comfortable before resting her hands on the keys. The room is silent, except for the subtle sound of forks scraping against plates. People are eating, but I sit back anxiously, waiting to see what she can do.

The room fills with the soft sounds of her fingers on the keys, which quickly ramps up into a fast-tempo classical piece. It's sharp and loud, and I'm amazed at her precision and expertise. The song must go on for minutes before she winds down, playing more softly again as it comes to an end. The room erupts with applause as Andie stands and turns to face us.

She walks to a microphone, adjusting it so she can speak. "Thank you. I'm sure you all saw those amazing kids in the video earlier, and you heard what my dad said. If you want more, you have to pay up." She smiles as laughter makes its way around the room.

"I've spent a lot of time with the kids over the years. It's one of my favorite places to visit, so I can tell you that not one penny will go unappreciated or unused for something amazing."

She pauses. "These kids need people like you to help them in the fight of their lives. So, pull out your wallets, purses, and phones and help my dad and all of the amazing doctors, nurses, and staff continue to give these kids the best, most innovative care possible." She clasps her hands together. "And hurry up because you'll get another song out of me, but that might be it."

She smiles and adjusts the mic stand as the man I met earlier, Jonsey, steps out with a stool and hands her a guitar. My eyes are glued to her as she gets comfortable with the guitar across her lap. She pulls a pick from between her teeth, pushes her curls out of her face, and tucks them behind her ear. She adjusts the mic, taking just a second to look around.

I see her take a deep breath before she speaks. "This is something new."

She starts strumming, and instantly, it's beautiful. The sound is soft and melodic. Then, her voice takes over, hitting a whole new dimension. The room is silent except for her, and you can't help but be drawn in.

I listen to the words, and understanding hits. Andie told me she was looking to move on…forward, and I remember the hesitancy in her tone when she said it. Her words speak of unbelievable loss, broken promises, and people warning her that it was bound to happen. Her anger fades into sadness as she sings about wanting them to be wrong but never believing it would turn out this way.

I'm frozen in awe. Not just by her ability and incredible talent but by her sheer rawness and the emotions pouring out with each word. To be so completely vulnerable and…honest, especially when only minutes ago she was warned not to be.

The final note rings in the air, and the room erupts again, much louder this time. Andie smiles with glossy eyes. Her head drops forward as if she's relieved, but it only lasts a second before Jonesy comes out to collect her guitar. He stops to hug her long and hard before stepping away again. After a second, she takes the mic again as two women join her off to the side, with Jonesy at the piano this time.

A new tune fills the space, and she laughs. "I see what you're doing, Jonesy." She looks back at the crowd as the music picks up the beat. "Apparently, I'm doing this one next. It's called *Make It Happen,* and it's one of my very favorites."

For the next half hour, Andie puts on a show. The room comes alive, and the people are into it. She's giving them what they want and more. For reasons I find I really want to understand, this woman doesn't want this. To be on stage, in the limelight, even though she's amazing in it. But for tonight and for the kids and the hospital, she's giving her talent away. That shows me the kind of person she is.

She wraps another song and tells the crowd goodnight, much to their displeasure. The waiter comes by and takes away my untouched plate. I didn't come for the food or the attention or anything besides seeing my money going to good use, but I've gained something from Andie about the kind of person I want to be. The kind that gives away, not just because they can, but because it matters and it's important–it's personal.

That's what I need more of in my life. That's what's missing at the end of the day, leaving a giant hole where the tangible, authentic, and absolute should reside and hold true, regardless of my name or profession and the fame that comes with it.

I leave the table and make my way to the bar, ordering a whiskey on the rocks and try to let it sink in. I watch from a distance as the dance floor fills with couples, moving to the music pumped through the speakers. A second later, Ms. Taninbaugh sidles up next to me, and I have no doubt it's not coincidental.

"Hey, handsome, another VO and water." She lifts her empty glass to the bartender, swirling the ice before setting it on the bar. She turns to peek up at me. "I understand you and my granddaughter spent a little quality time together recently."

I take a sip of my drink. "Just a bit." Without knowing what Andie said and the misunderstanding of me being her date, I don't offer more.

Her focus remains forward, and I'm curious to see where this is going.

"She's quite something, isn't she?" she asks, and I suspect she's talking about more than just her performance tonight.

"Yes, ma'am. Seems so."

Turning to look at me, she arches one dark penciled eyebrow. "You call me ma'am again, and you might lose a testicle."

I almost choke on my whiskey but catch it before it goes down the wrong pipe. The bartender sets her drink on the bar, and she lifts it, turning to face me straight on.

"You helped her earlier when you didn't have to. Something tells me you've got balls. It takes big ones to make it in this world." She squints her eyes, inspecting me, and it feels like she has the ability to see more than I want her to. "I might like you, Sean Greyson, and I don't like many people." She takes a slow sip of her drink and turns away, glancing back for just a second. "Now, if you're smart, you'll go save her from that handsy prick who's got her trapped on the dance floor."

I watch her walk away before my eyes search and zero in on Andie. She's being held tightly, and by the look on her face, not willingly. The man has one hand splayed close to her butt and the other white-knuckled on her hand. He's short, with dark hair, and seems to have an issue with no.

I drain my glass, willing myself to ignore what I might get into as I push away from the bar and stride toward her.

I stop just behind the bastard who's holding her hostage. He's inches shorter than I am, and I can make out Andie telling him to let her go.

"I'm cutting in." I make it clear that I'm not asking.

Their staggered motion stops immediately as the guy turns to look at me over his shoulder, but he doesn't let her go.

"Sorry, she's with me the rest of the night." He turns back to face Andie as if that's the end of the conversation.

"If you want to remain standing, let me go. Now." Andie tries to pull away again.

"Who is this, Andie?" he asks, in a territorial tone that I don't care for.

"Her date," I say before she responds, or I can stop myself. I don't like this guy's attitude, his roughness with Andie, or his face.

I see the shock on her face and then his, but she recovers quickly, taking advantage of catching him off guard to yank away and move to stand next to me.

He doesn't hide his displeasure. "Seriously, Andie. You're dating…" He takes a second to inspect me. "You're Sean Greyson." He states rather than asks. I don't respond.

His dark eyes move back to Andie. "You're finally ready to date, and you're dating a football player." He half scoffs, half laughs. "This figures. First, a soldier, and now this guy. What a joke!"

I see Andie physically pull herself up. *This guy is a chauvinistic dick.* I don't like how he speaks to her or the hurtful things he just said. I'm not sure where he gets his entitlement, but he's way too close to Andie. I slip my hand around her waist and pull her into me.

"Brice, the only joke here is you and maybe anyone who believes you are anything other than a pathetic excuse for a human being. Stay away from me. And if you ever talk about Josh or–"

Not letting her be in this asshole's presence one second longer, I pull her away from him, turning her into me instead. She comes along willingly as I lead her to the middle of the floor and far away from him.

We sway for a minute, my hand on her waist, the other locked with hers. She avoids looking at me, her anger having morphed into either embarrassment or shame, and it makes me want to haul that skinny dick's ass outside.

I break the silence and hopefully her negative thoughts. "You killed it up there tonight."

"Thanks." Her quiet response is uncharacteristic. "I'm glad it's over."

"The new song was…" I search for the right word. "Moving. It was beautiful."

She finally looks at me, her eyes flicking between mine for a moment. "Thanks for earlier and then now, with Brice. He's an entitled jerk and has never quite gotten the clue that Gem has no problem being my alibi if he disappears."

"He's worse than a jerk."

Her pink lips turn upward just slightly. "I'm sorry you were dragged into all of that. My parents and then him." Her eyes fall to my chest before bouncing back up. "What are you doing here, anyway? I would've never guessed this would be your scene."

"It's not…or at least it wasn't. I'm trying something new."

She nods like she's thinking about it as she surveys the couples around us. "We probably shouldn't be dancing or standing this close. People might think we're actually dating, which would not be good for your reputation or girlfriend."

"I don't have a girlfriend," I correct quickly. "And my reputation could use some tweaking."

Her head falls to the side, her eyebrows pinching inward. "I met her at the game, in the owner's box. I can't remember her name, but…"

"Morgan. Yeah, I'm not sure why she was there. We broke up weeks before that."

Her brows move upward this time. "Apparently, she didn't get the memo because she clearly thought she was."

"She didn't take it well. I should've broken it off a long time ago."

The song ends, and we stop moving. Andie's eyes dart around the room before meeting mine again. "I'm going to grab my guitar and get out of here. Thank you for–"

I cut her off. "Let's go get it, and I'll walk you out. I wouldn't feel right leaving you here if that guy is still loitering."

She ponders it and doesn't argue.

I follow her off the dancefloor and through a door that takes us backstage. After she gathers her things, we exit a side door and into the parking lot.

"Look, thanks for rescuing me back there and for sticking up for me when my mother was about to lose her cookies over a dress," she says as we approach what must be her SUV.

"She shouldn't talk to you like that," I say with more force than I mean to.

Andie smiles. "It only hurts if I let it. I've learned you can't wish a blind person into seeing."

That makes me smile. "So true. Doesn't make it right."

"Nope." She unlocks her car and puts her guitar in the back. "If you ever want to try something else new, the kids at the hospital would lose their minds if you visited."

"I'll consider it." I step away, leaving her.

"Hey, Sean," she calls, and I turn back to see her standing with her door open. "I still don't like you, but I might've pegged you wrong."

I laugh. "You weren't wrong, but fortunately, I'm not blind. I've just got to pay attention to where I'm going from now on."

She smiles. "Good luck."

I walk back to my car with a giant grin on my face. For the first time in a very long time, I feel something a little like…happiness.

Chapter 12

ANDIE

My phone is ringing. I reach out from under the covers, trying to find it so I can throw it against the wall and make it stop. Nora knows better than to call this early, and Gem isn't up yet, so when I can't find it, I ignore it. Two seconds after it stops ringing, it starts again.

I finally find it and rip it off my nightstand, squinting to see the name.

"Nora, there better be a–"

"Oh, my goodness, have you seen it?"

Is she whispering?

Ugh. It's too early for her dramatics.

"Have I seen what?" I whine.

"Andie." Her alarmed snap has my eyes popping back open.

"What? I'm tired, and Ax is still sleeping, so can this wait?"

"Annnndieeeee," she says more softly this time.

"Noorrrraaaa."

"Andie." The careful way she says my name this time has me paying attention. "You might want to check Instagram. Maybe search Sean. You know, your new buddy? Then call me back." She says the last part quickly and hangs up.

What? What is she talking about now? I don't need to see pictures of whatever Sean has going on. I just saw the man last night. I lie back down and pull the covers over my head. Then it hits me. *Last night.*

I pop up, open Instagram, and search for him. I don't even need to scroll before I see it. I tap on the little box. It's pictures of the two of us.

The first is of us dancing, then of us standing next to each other, and from the angle, it really does look like we were…together.

I hit back and tap on another post. It's only more pictures captioning me as Sean's new girl. Discussions carry on in comments speculating about what happened between him and his ex. Then, comments turn their attention to me, wondering who I am and how the female population is in mourning.

I rub my forehead, running through what this actually means. It's only a matter of time before people figure it out, and then…well. *Shit…Shit!*

I call Nora.

"Soooo…"

"Don't 'so' me. What does this mean?" I sit perfectly still, trying desperately not to panic. Panicking is not in my nature, but right now, I'm about to freak the hell out.

She doesn't answer right away, which only makes my nerves hike higher.

"Ummmm…maybe call him and see what he thinks about it? Maybe he has some ideas about how to handle this, or maybe it will blow over quickly, and people will mind their own business."

I laugh, sounding hysterical. "Right. Call him, like I have his number."

"Well, you're apparently dating him. You should have his number."

I can tell that Nora thinks this is funny, and I feel like a hair tie trying to hold my curls in place and about ready to snap. I look back at the posts and see hundreds of comments, growing by the minute.

Suddenly, on fire, I kick the covers off of me. "Ok. Maybe you're right. Maybe it won't go any further, and it will fade into the background or be taken over by pictures of him with someone else, someone he's actually dating."

I remember Sean said he broke up with his girlfriend, and if he was being truthful about his priorities shifting, it didn't sound like dating was on the top of that list. *Shoot. Crap. Shit!*

"You know, if my mother sees this and realizes who Sean really is–"

Nora yawns like I'm boring her now that she's spilled the beans. "Maybe you should just really date him and drive her crazy while enjoying Sean in the process."

"Have you lost your mind? I'm not dating Sean or enjoying him in any way."

"That's not what the pics look like."

"Nora Renee," I say, warning her.

She dials it back. "Didn't you say he was nice last night, that he rescued you from Brice, the bottom-feeder-scum-sucker?" She asks the rhetorical question like in some universe dating or internet dating, Sean makes logical sense.

"I think you and I may need to part ways. You can collect your last check, and I'll provide a good reference."

She laughs. "Andie, this is all going to be ok. I really think you should see if you can figure out how to contact him. He's probably not loving this, either, but might be used to this kind of thing and knows how to handle it."

I flop back on my bed just as grunts erupt from the baby monitor. "I can't deal with this. I'm ignoring it for now and praying that this just goes away."

"There you go." Her peppy voice makes me want to puke. "Denial solves everything."

"It's not a big deal, right? People wouldn't actually think Sean Greyson would be dating or hanging out with me."

"Why?" Now, Nora's instantly irritated. "You're smokin', smart, talented beyond belief, kind, and have a real way with words. He'd be a complete idiot not to date you."

"I'm not dating anyone!" Ax starts crying, and I pull myself up. "I have to go. Let me know when all of this goes away. Until then, I'll be hibernating, completely removed from the outside world."

"Want me to come over?" Nora asks, and I sense amusement.

I haul my butt out of bed. "Nah. I'm fine. Surely this can't get any worse, right?"

She laughs, and we disconnect.

I know if my mother finds out, this will definitely get worse, but at least I will be the only one affected by that lashing.

I drag myself across the hall to Axel's room and lean over the crib to snatch him up. "Hey, monster. Did you sleep well?"

I kiss his cheeks and neck as we make our way to the kitchen. I turn the burner on to heat my kettle and make him a bottle. On mornings like today, snuggling him on the couch while the rest of the world stays far away is my favorite kind of morning.

I scroll on my phone for a few minutes, flipping through pictures of Sean and me before tossing it down, not wanting to see anymore.

Don't people have anything better to do than look at completely innocent pictures of the two of us and then actually take the time to comment on them?

Thinking back to last night and seeing him walk in the doors, looking all…Sean. Tall, muscular, incredibly handsome, and then he had to go and be nice to me. He just jumped in there and shut my mother up, which in a different place and time, I'd find that pretty damn attractive.

Then, he saved me from Brice, who was one second away from getting a fist to the throat.

I look down at Ax and run my hand over his head, realizing that I'm here and have him, and that's all that really matters. People can think that I'm dating Sean if they want. They can say what they want or hate me because I've apparently taken him off the market.

Who cares?

When no more pictures surface, it will die, and then, another woman standing next to Sean will take over the feed.

It's fine. It's all going to be fine. I just need to give it time.

Chapter 13

SEAN

I scroll to a new song and grab a set of dumbbells. The weight room is quiet. It's just me and a couple of other guys getting a head start before a team meeting to discuss tomorrow's game and then practice.

After last night, I'm feeling good. I woke up ready to get to work and focus on the game. Then, I'm getting in touch with Craig to figure out where I can help next.

I make it through a couple of sets, and Tyrell struts in.

"You're here early."

I turn off my music. "Yeah. I'm ready for tomorrow."

"Yeah? I thought you'd be in later after your big night last night." He smirks like something is funny.

I start on another set. "What are you talking about? I went to a benefit last night for the children's hospital."

"Yeah, I saw. I didn't know you and *The Show Me What You Got* girl were getting up close and personal."

"What? Her name is Andie." I set the weights down.

"Oh, sorry. I didn't know you and *Andie* were hanging out." He grins, and I don't like the smugness behind it one bit.

"I don't know what makes you think we're hanging out, but–"

"You haven't seen it." He laughs, covering his mouth with his hand. "Man, you know better than anyone there's no sneaking around."

"I'm not sneaking around." I wipe my brow with my shirt, my muscles contracting with irritation.

"That's not what it looks like. You should see the pics. The two of you look pret-ty cozy."

"What pictures?" I grab my phone, scrolling, wanting to know exactly what he's talking about. It only takes a second, and I see them. "Shit!"

I run a hand over my face, my jaw clenching. "I just went to the benefit. I had no idea she'd be there. This guy was being a complete asshole, and I cut in so he'd leave her alone."

Tyrell puts his hands on his hips as his head falls to the side.

"We barely know each other, but I couldn't just let this guy put his hands on her and treat her like…" I inhale and let it out, wondering if Andie knows about these.

I sit down on the weight bench, looking through more photos and comments. People want to know who she is, and others answer with clips of her singing the anthem. They're discussing how she looks and comparing her to Morgan.

Tyrell's right. I know better, and I'm pissed that my life and who I am is impacting her. I know she has strong reasons for not wanting to be in the public eye, even if I don't know what they are. I should've known this could happen and been so much more careful.

"She doesn't need this." I rest my arms on my knees. "You're right. I know better, but I'm not trying to hide anything."

Tyrell laughs. "Don't worry, you just put her face in front of millions. She's probably sitting back and eating this up. You should be more worried about your female fans. They're angry. First, they didn't know you broke up with Morgan, and now they've missed their chance."

I shake my head. "Andie's not eating this up."

He pushes his lips to the side and raises an eyebrow in disbelief.

My temper awakens, and he must see it. He sits down beside me. "Just call her and give her a heads up. It's not a big deal. Give it a day or two, and people will move on."

"I don't have her number." I shoot back a little louder than I intended, and one of the other guys looks in our direction.

Tyrell leans back. "You don't have her number?" He says it like it's the most ridiculous thing in the world. "Man, she's hot, so why not?"

"I told you, I barely know her. We spent time in the elevator, and then I saw her last night. That's it." I keep the few personal things we exchanged and all I witnessed with her parents to myself.

"Sounds to me like you know her at least a little if you know this isn't her dream come true."

I hang my head, trying to figure out what I need to do if anything. Maybe Andie doesn't know about it and won't.

"Your agent is going to love this."

"Shit." I rub my hand over my face. "He's going to be blowing up my phone any minute. I don't want him or anyone else involved in this. There isn't anything to it."

"Well," he stands. "Maybe there should be. Maybe you should ask her out and then just let the story fly. It wouldn't be a bad thing."

"Dude, she lost her husband, and I'm not dating anyone. I have other things to focus on. I should be focusing on the game right now, not this."

He nods and slaps me on the back. "You're right. Good luck. I hope you get it figured out. See you in the meeting."

He leaves the weight room, and my mind is spinning. I have no idea what to do about this, and I don't have time to figure it out. Since dating Morgan, I haven't had issues like this. I didn't think about the potential of someone from last night posting pictures.

If I had Andie's number, I'd text her and apologize. I can only hope this fades before it reaches her.

I check my phone, knowing I need to get to the meeting, but of course, I have messages.

MARK: Pic attached: Andie and me dancing.
MARK: Who dis? Going alone, my ass.
CRAIG: The national anthem girl, really? What do you want me to do? Are you releasing a statement?
SHANE: Been a while since you brought the drama, bro.
MAGGIE: Seriously, why didn't I know about this? Who is she?

Not responding to any of them, I put my phone in my pocket so I can sit through a meeting and try to focus on tomorrow's game. I hope this all dies quickly and disappears into some other major news story.

I toss my jersey to the floor. I made it through practice, but not without the guys throwing jabs about me taking over social media. My good mood and positive outlook have tanked, and I just want to go home and sit in my hot tub. Why anybody cares about what I do with my personal life, I'll never understand.

The snickering around me continues, and I've had it.

"Seriously, what?" I growl as I shove my stuff in my bag, ready to ditch these fools who are clearly entertained by my misery.

Charles, one of our tight ends, walks over with his phone in his hand. "Man, I'm not sure you want to see this, but..."

I let out a breath, knowing I've had enough. He hands me his phone, and I see a picture of Morgan underneath a headline that claims I've been cheating on her.

I look at Charles and then back at the phone, wanting to throw it against the wall.

He holds up his hands. "Don't kill the messenger."

"Dude, this is messed up," someone says from behind me. "Didn't you break up with her, like forever ago?"

I don't respond.

Tyrell comes to stand next to me and shakes his head. "I didn't see this coming. What's her deal?" I close my eyes, trying not to let my anger swallow me whole. I feel his hand on my back and stop myself from jerking away. "Are you going to talk to Andie?" His voice is soft to prevent the room from hearing. "The comments are getting out of hand. Morgan's followers are coming for her."

I hang my head. I don't have to read the comments to know what they likely say. If Andie knows about this, I'm certain I'm the absolute last person she wants to hear from right now.

My head begins to pound, and the walls are closing in. "I have to get out of here."

Craig is relentless and waiting for me to respond. I guess I have to figure out if I should risk adding fuel to the fire or say nothing and wait for it to die.

Tyrell looks at me with sympathy. "Try to get some rest. We need you to be all in tomorrow."

I grab my bag and hightail it out of there. I have no doubt it's not just Craig who'd like to get a hold of me. The team's PR reps are probably hot after my ass right now too. If I can help it, I'm skipping out before they catch me. Then maybe I can stay under the radar until this whole thing sinks.

Not wanting to, I look at my phone. I have a hundred texts from Craig but ignore them, jumping to a group text.

MAGGIE: I'm going to kick her tight model ass. Tell me where to find her.
SHANE: Calm down, Firefly.
MARK: Maggie, I'm down. I don't discriminate.
SHANE: Sean, you ok, man?
MARK: Hell no, he's not ok. He's the nice one and would never step out.
MAGGIE: The kids and I are getting on a plane.
SHANE: Maggie, he doesn't have time to bail you out.
MARK: I'm her alibi.
SHANE: Sean? Seriously? If you don't answer, I'm sending Maggie.
MAGGIE: Sean? Time is ticking.
MARK: Sean? I'm willing to take one for the team and cause a ruckus to take the pressure off. I still want to know who she is, though. I hope she's worth it.

In my truck, I almost dial Craig but decide to call Shane first. He's sound and reasonable and will give me no grief about this.

"Hey, bro. How's life treating you?" Shane's no-nonsense tone is refreshing after the day I'm having.

"I have no freaking clue what to do about this." I tighten my grip on my steering wheel, needing it to help me hold it together.

"I bet Craig's loving this." Shane's calm voice makes me feel a little less panicked.

"I haven't talked to him yet. His texts are pinging as we speak, but I'm not sure I can handle hearing his advice right now. He'll want to make a statement or get Andie involved." I run a hand through my hair. "I have no idea why Morgan would do this. She isn't this person, or at least, I didn't think so."

Shane is silent for a moment. "Her name is Andie?" he asks cautiously, creating a pressure in my chest that's not normal.

"Yeah. She's the one I got stuck in the elevator with a few weeks back who was there to sing the anthem."

"The chick who thought you were a self-centered bastard." Shane chuckles, and the sound makes the band tightening around my ribs lessen just slightly.

"Yeah. I ran into her at the benefit last night, but that was it. Some jerkoff was getting handsy, and I put a stop to it. I walked her to her car, and she reminded me that she doesn't like me."

"I like her already," Shane says matter-of-factly.

I roll my eyes. "Actually, you probably would. She doesn't take anyone's shit. I've seen that first hand."

"Have you talked to her?"

"No! We aren't friends. I don't have her number." *Why does no one get this?* "I know from our time in the elevator that she has no interest in being in the public eye…and now this. I feel terrible. The organization will be all over me for this. This is the last thing I need after coming off the bench. I know to be careful, but I just didn't think…I had no idea someone at the benefit would post pics like that. Now Morgan…"

Shane lets out a breath, and I envision him running a hand over his face. "Maggie's losing her mind over this if it makes you feel any better. One minute she's ranting about kicking ass, and the next, she's booking a flight to hug you." A smile tugs at my lips. "What do you want to do?"

"I don't know, man. I can't believe Morgan would do this. I feel like such an idiot for not seeing something like this coming."

"Don't blame yourself, Sean. Not for one second. You didn't do anything wrong. We both know some women will do anything for attention. Let her say whatever she wants. Just don't let her get you by the balls. Keep your head up and facing the right direction. Whatever dumbass lie Morgan or anyone else wants to make up next can't withstand the truth. It may just take a little time."

I want to believe what Shane is saying, but the world thrives on drama and heartache, not happy endings.

"Craig wants me to release a statement, but you and I both know how lame that will sound, and nobody wants honesty anyway. They've already made up their mind." I think about my team and the game tomorrow. "PR is going to chew my ass out, and the GM is probably all fired up. This is another strike against me." I push out a breath.

"You've been there a long time. They know you. It might be worth seeing what they have to say. They're good at making things go away. It's their job."

I groan. "Yeah, maybe."

"Let it go for today. Get your head in the game and see what tomorrow brings." I know he knows it's going to be difficult as hell.

"Thanks. Hug Maggie and the kids for me."

"Will do. I wish we could be there tomorrow, but we'll be watching."

I hang up, pulling into my garage and closing the door. I rest my head on the steering wheel, my hands in fists, wanting to punch something. If it were any other night, but before a game, I'd take it out on my heavy bag.

Grabbing my phone, I see another text from Craig.

CRAIG: I've been taking calls all day. Meeting tomorrow 8:00 a.m. at the stadium. I'll send you the room number in the morning.

I climb out of my truck, slamming the door shut with force and wishing I'd just called him back. Dealing with Craig is one thing, but now Craig and PR and whoever else, before a game, will be a freaking nightmare. I already know it.

I head straight to my room to find my swim trunks before heading to my hot tub. I sink down, needing the rhythmic pounding in my head that started hours ago to ease. But as I try to relax and let go of all of the anger and frustration of the day, my mind drifts to Andie. I wonder, for the millionth time today, how she's handling this. Maybe she has no idea. It's not likely, but a man can hope.

I sit there until I can no longer stand it, then shower and crawl into bed. I just have to get through the meeting and then the game. Maybe a win tomorrow will push this to the background.

Shane told me to keep my head up and moving in the right direction. It's all I can do. And pray somehow, I can show them all the truth when faith in my word has already been destroyed.

Chapter 14

ANDIE

"Sweetheart, I never knew you were so scandalous," Gem says. "But then again, you are my granddaughter."

Another call beeps through, and I hit ignore. My phone has been blowing up since this morning, but it's taken on a whole new level since Morgan freaking Monroe took to the streets with cheating allegations. Other than sitting near her for fifteen minutes, I don't know this chick, but this tells me exactly who she is.

"Please tell me you aren't sulking about this phony's ridiculous little attempt to manufacture sympathy over getting kicked to the curb."

"I'm not sulking. I'm pissed."

"That's my girl."

"I don't, however, care for being labeled…pick any of the things you've read this morning."

It's impressive what some people come up with based on an allegiance to a fictitious person. I mean, these people don't know Morgan. They're loyal to the plastic person on their screen, who they want to believe is everything she sells them. Well, today, she's selling them that I'm a lowlife, cheating whore.

"Is it really so bad to be accused of cheating with such a fine specimen as Sean Greyson? I mean, Andie, the man is–"

I cut her off. "Uh, yes. It would be horrible under normal circumstances, but Gem, I have Ax. This has to end. I won't let this get near him. Not to mention, when you know who gets wind of this, it's just one more thing that will be added to the list of Andie's-most-horrifically-disappointing-decisions. It actually might replace number one, and I'll never hear the end of how embarrassed they are and what poor decisions I always make, and on and on and on."

I take a breath and curl up tighter on the couch. Snipe moves closer to me, knowing I need comfort.

"I can't take any more of her condescending, presumptuous comments. It's bad enough when it's just me, but then in front of Sean and Jonesy. It never stops. I can't have Ax around that. I won't. And now this. I can only imagine…"

"I know, baby girl," Gem says softly. "You shouldn't have to. I do believe she wants the best for you. She just thinks that the best can only be achieved her way."

I put a hand on my forehead. "I can't believe this." My skin is hot, my face is flushed, and I'm certain I've burnt a thousand calories just in anger management today. "I can't read any more comments. Comments about Sean. Comments about me. I feel like it's only a matter of time before someone starts beating on my door."

I've wondered all day what Sean thinks about this. *Why in the world isn't he doing anything?* The pictures are one thing. Fine. Whatever. We were photographed together. People are speculating. But the moment his ex started spouting lies, he should have Shut. It. Down.

Now, I'm being marked as a low-dollar slut in front of the entire world, including my business associates. Sean, on the other hand, is off playing football and making millions while being called a sorry lying cheat. BIG DIFFERENCE.

At first, I was ready to drive to the stadium and hunt him down. I wondered if he lied to me about breaking up with Morgan. But then I realized he had no reason to lie to me, nor did he have any reason to tell me that they'd broken up. He wasn't hitting on me or making any sort of move. So, I can't hate him for his ex's blatant attempts at getting attention or retaliating or whatever it is she's trying to do.

I can, however, think he totally sucks for this being a part of his life and, now, mine. I know he's probably used to this and not concerned about it, but I'm not good with people putting a tag on me that is the wrong label and price.

I get that this kind of messed up revenge happens when you live your life on stage, and someone's pride gets bruised, but I've avoided that kind of life. One very brief trip down that crooked lane was enough for me.

I hear Gem take a sip of something, likely her evening VO and water, the one I definitely should be drinking instead. "What are we going to do about it, sweet cheeks?"

"I don't know," I whine. "People I work with have been calling Nora all day. It's just so…uncomfortable. I'd be embarrassed, but I didn't do anything. I stood next to him and danced with him for one minute when he saved me from Brice's handsy ass."

"That narcissistic son of a…" Gem spats and can't help but smile. "If I see that skinny, sorry excuse of a man, I'll make sure he never procreates."

"You won't have to if I see him first."

"What can I do?" Gem asks, back to business.

"Nothing. Hope that tomorrow they've all moved on to something else."

"Honey, we can always do something. When the storms out, we play in the rain." I can feel her smirk through the phone. "You know, I could call Ed McNeil and get tickets for the next game, and we could parade in there and show this Morgan nobody exactly how we Taninbaughs handle lying twats."

"I bet Sean would just love that." I snort.

I hear her sniff. "I have a feeling Sean wouldn't mind."

"Yeah, right. He and I don't run on the same frequency."

"You're saying sparks fly when you two get just a little too close."

"Oh, good grief. Keep dreaming, Grandma."

"Andie," she warns. "I'll let that one go since you're having a crap day."

I smile but hear my phone beep again. "Do you hear that?"

"What?"

"The eerie silence and gentle breeze before a lashing." Gem snorts. "The Countess of Bigotry has gotten the word and is ready to throw down the gauntlet. I have to go. If you hear a boom, you know my head exploded." Snipe growls low and steady like he can tell it's her from twenty miles away.

"Be calm and try explaining how amazing the sex is."

I laugh, hanging up and readying myself for this battle. I pat Snipe, hoping he'll give me the courage I need as I slide from the couch to the floor. The hard surface is appropriate for this fun conversation.

"Hello, Mother. To what do I owe this pleasure?"

"Andrea, don't be smart with me. Tell me there is some sort of explanation. Your father and I have been hearing things all day and…"

I let her carry on for a second before cutting her off. "Look, you know people will say anything to make the headlines. I am not, nor will I ever be, in a relationship with someone who is *already* in a relationship with someone else."

"You're saying this Monroe woman is making this up. Andrea, you can't possibly think dating some…football player is acceptable. How did you not think that something like this would happen? What would Josh think of this?"

How dare she? I see red. "Don't talk about Josh and what he'd think. You have no idea. You'd barely even address him when he was alive. Don't think for a second you can use him now that he's gone. I know exactly what he'd want for me, and that's for me to be happy and loved and find the things and people that make those things true."

My chest heaves, and I try to catch my breath as my heart feels like it might pound right out of my chest. "Unless you have something worthwhile to say, this conversation is over. I'm sorry if this upsets you and your little world, but what I do with my life and who I date or spend time with is none of your business."

"Andrea…" She pauses like she doesn't know what to say, and I just need her to be quiet.

"Bye, Mother." I hang up, and Snipe rests his head on my thigh, puffing out a breath.

A lump aches in my throat for the first time today, and I need it to go away. I won't cry. Not about this and not because of what she said.

My phone buzzes, and I want to throw it across the room. All of this is too much. It's too much, and it wasn't even anything. I laugh at the absurdity of it all because if I don't, I'll cry, and I'm not doing that.

I pick up my phone and look at the screen.

NORA: I got a call. Miranda from the Tigers wants to meet in the morning. Don't hate me, but I said we'd be there. She wouldn't tell me what it was about. 8:00 a.m. I'll pick you up.
NORA: If you aren't speaking to me, it's ok. I'll wait. *Kissy face emoji*

I groan and pick myself up off the floor, although staying there would be entirely appropriate at the moment. I tiptoe down the hallway and peek in at Axel. His sweet, innocent face is just what I need to remind me that there is good in the world. I run the back of my finger over his cheek and leave him.

I grab my guitar and notebook from the back room and settle on my bed. There has to be a song in all of this. It's so completely messed up that I'm not sure where I'd even begin.

I start strumming, closing my eyes. I've been trying so hard to pick myself up, and the second I feel like I might actually be able to stand, it's like the world wants to tear me down. I want to run right back into hiding.

I jot down some notes but stop, tossing my pen down. I rest my head in my hands, my throat feeling tight. I know I can't hide anymore. I want to. I want to stay where it's safe, and I don't have to face reality.

Josh would have never wanted that, and that's all I've been doing, but I can't hide from this. It's everywhere. He'd tell me to get up and fight. Quit sitting around feeling sorry for myself and show them all what I can do and, in this case, who I am.

I'm not a cheater or a slut or some chick looking for her five minutes of fame hanging off some baller's arm. So, I'll go to this meeting in the morning to see what Miranda wants, and if it has anything to do with this, I'll do what I need to and tear the lies down.

Chapter 15

SEAN

"What's this about?" I step into the large conference room, leaving the door open as I take a seat next to Craig. His nose is in his phone, and Miranda is across from us.

It was a long night, and I'm more than ready to get this over with and down on the field.

"We're waiting for a couple more people to arrive." Miranda takes a sip of her coffee.

I look at Craig. "Who? Who else is coming? If this has to do with the lies my ex is spreading, then that only has to do with me." I try to keep my temper in check, but the last twenty-four hours have tried every ounce of my patience.

Miranda frowns, setting her coffee down. "Actually, that's not true."

Before I can ask her to clarify, there's a knock on the door jam. A woman with long bright blue hair and glasses walks in, followed by…Andie.

"Andie, it's so good to see you again." Miranda stands, moving to shake her hand. "And you must be Nora. It's nice to put the face with the name. Thank you so much for coming today. I know it's early."

I sit stunned by this turn of events but stand briefly when Craig gets up to shake hands and introduce himself.

I feel like I'm the only one in the dark, and the darkness is not my friend. I don't like it one bit. I meet Andie's eyes, and by the cool glare she sends me, she's not happy about it either. Or maybe it's just me she's unhappy with.

"Well, since we're all here, let's get started. I'll try to keep this short." Miranda jumps in as Andie and Nora sit. "Craig and I spoke yesterday after the press let loose on the two of you." She gestures between Andie and me. "It's safe to say damage control would do everyone some good."

"Wait." Nora stops her, pushing her glasses up her nose. "The only damage control that needs to happen is for Sean, here, to step out there and clear this whole thing up."

Craig stiffens beside me before speaking. "And who are you? Are you representing Ms. Parks?"

Nora looks like she's about to give him the middle finger but holds back.

"I'm her assistant. You must be the imbecile who doesn't know how to do his job."

"You think it's just that simple," Craig scoffs. "Anyone in this business knows it's not as easy as just saying these two aren't sleeping together." He points between Andie and me, and I want to smack his finger away.

"It sure was easy enough for an innocent picture to lead to–"

Andie puts a hand on Nora's arm to stop her. "Why don't you just tell us why we're here," she says softly, making sure her eyes never wander in my direction.

"Tigers management wants to get this under control quickly." Miranda looks at me. "Sean, you are a figurehead of our organization, and what's bad for you is bad for the Tigers. Doug couldn't join us this morning, but he's insistent we turn this around."

Great. Doug, my GM, is sending a warning, and I hear it loud and clear.

Miranda sips her coffee. "Craig and I think it would help if we teamed up to offer some kind of community outreach. The two of you working together to give back would be a good way to break down some of the…negative press."

"Hold on." I raise my hand. "We just started the season. I don't have time to organize some event to try to negate a bunch of lies."

"I'm not sure you have much of a choice. If this continues, you need to consider the repercussions," Craig says. I know he's talking about my affiliation with the team and sponsors. "I'm sure Ms. Parks is facing similar issues."

Andie's eyes finally land on mine when I glance her way. "What do you mean, like being called his dollar store arm candy or a coin purse slut or having all of my business associates questioning whether or not they want to work with someone like me?" She air-quotes the last part.

I drop my head, unable to look at her any longer. I've seen the comments, and they're despicable.

"Sean, you could always kiss and make up with Morgan, and then this whole thing will vanish," Craig offers.

I turn to face him. "There's not a chance in hell I'm doing that."

Miranda takes over again. "What we're suggesting is the two of you collaborating to bring an event to the stadium. We think the best thing is to let your fans and the community see the two of you working together. Turn the negative into a positive. You were at the benefit for the children's hospital when this all broke loose. Andie, I understand your father is the Chief of Staff, so maybe a day for the kids at the stadium? Or a benefit for veterans since your husband–"

"Stop." I put my hand up, not wanting to listen to another word. I stare at Andie, who looks like she's ready to rip my head off. "Can Andie and I have a minute, please?"

She doesn't move, but Nora leans over and says something to her. When no one moves, I stand. "Would you step outside with me? Please?" I ask her directly.

The room is silent for what seems like a solid minute before she pushes her chair back and stands, coming around the table toward the door. We step out, and I close it. She stands with her arms crossed, looking up at me expectantly.

"I'm sorry. I'm sorry about the pictures and what's being said. I had no idea they were going to–"

She cuts me off. "What do you want, Sean?"

I look down at her. Her green eyes look tired and miserable, which is an exact reflection of how I feel.

"Are you ok?" I ask, not wanting her to blow me off. I really want to know.

"No, not really, but it's a feeling I'm becoming entirely too comfortable with."

I close my eyes, reeling in the outburst building in my throat, not at Andie, but at the situation. "I know it doesn't make it any better, but I hope you know nothing my ex said is true. I have no idea why she's doing this."

Her head falls to the side. "Well, that's a relief."

I inhale and let it out, but Andie's frustration only adds to mine. I know she's angry and has every right to be, but I didn't do this.

"Look, they want us to do this, but if you don't want to do it, I'm fine with that. If you do, if it will help you through this, then I'll do what I can to help."

"That's awfully generous of you." Her sarcasm is clear. She, too, lets out a breath like she's trying to reel it in. "Listen, I don't know what the right thing is here, but I know that I need this to stop, and I can't have people following me or showing up at my house."

I frown. "Has that happened?"

"Sean, does it really matter?"

"Yes, it matters!" My last nerve waves at me as it flees like a rock in a slingshot. "I need to know you're safe." I rub my face. "This has gotten way out of hand."

"Do you think us working together on something will even help?" she asks softly, sounding defeated.

I lift my eyes to meet hers, not wanting to, given how horrible I feel. "I don't know. It would be a reason why we were together, and the more people see us working together professionally, the more they'll see we're just…friends."

"We aren't friends." She throws out quickly. "Don't you think us doing anything together could make this worse?"

"Possibly."

She looks down at her shoes. "Let's just go hear the rest of what they're suggesting, and then maybe we can talk about it before we decide."

I nod. "Ok." She moves to open the door, but I stop her. "Wait. Give me your number." She crosses her arms again. "Then we can figure out what we want to do. I don't want to talk in front of them. They have their own agendas, and I want to be sure you and I are on the same page."

She contemplates it for a second. "Fine." She pulls out her phone, and we exchange numbers.

"Andie," I say, waiting for her to look at me. "I am sorry…about all of this."

She nods, opening the door, and we step back into Nora and Craig, sparring while Miranda taps away on her phone. They stop when they notice us, and we take our seats.

"So, what do you have in mind?" I ask, willing my body to relax enough to listen.

Miranda sets her phone down. "You two combine efforts to give the kids at the hospital a day out at the stadium or something similar and a concert. Andie, we had rave reviews from your night here at the stadium. The video of you singing the national anthem is one of our top-viewed posts, and the families loved you, so I know it will be a hit. I've spoken with Ed, and he's more than on board. He loves the idea and is excited to hear what you come up with."

I look at Andie, but her focus is on Miranda.

"Can we have a day or two to think about it?" I ask.

"The sooner you guys get to work, and we can announce it, the better. It gives the world a reason to question Morgan's…claims." Craig says, and I'm surprised he's toned down his aggressiveness.

"I understand," I say, needing him to back off and willing Andie to look at me, but she doesn't.

"Ok. Well, let us know soon. We'll do whatever we can to help." Miranda starts gathering her stuff. "Sean, I know you have a game to get ready for, and Andie, I'm sure you have life to get back to. Unless there's anything else, I'll wait to hear from you. Please be quick. We need to start blasting all outlets, make arrangements, add it to the schedule, draft press releases, and get your names back in good standing."

I want to curse but hold it in. I'm sick of everyone acting like we did something wrong. Miranda stands, and the rest of us follow.

Nora glares at Craig as she passes. "You really should rethink the suit. It makes you look extra prickish."

Andie groans but also kind of smiles.

I stop Andie in the doorway. "Think about it. I'll text you later."

She nods and then moves to catch up with Nora. I run a hand over my head, realizing this quiet Andie makes me nervous. I've only been around her twice, but both times, she came out swinging. Seeing her turned down or muted makes me think this really rattled her. I hate it.

I know how this affects me, but I don't know how it's screwing up her life. The thought of people following her or showing up at her house rouses a wave of anger I haven't felt in a long time, and it feels dangerous. I wonder if Morgan has any idea what she's done.

"You need to do this," Craig says, breaking through my thoughts. "I realize this may die down in a week or two, but it's too long. People are already forming opinions, and we have to change their minds."

"I need to give her a minute to decide what she wants to do. She deserves that."

"Yeah, well, your other option is to play this up. Date her. Make the world fall in love with the two of you and shove Morgan into the background."

"Craig, have you not heard a single word that's come out of my mouth these past months? I'm not pretending to date Andie or anything else."

"Then you make sure she does this event. This is your future, and looking out for you is my job. With your injuries and now this…this organization is going to be taking a serious look at what you're bringing to the table. From their end, it's not looking good. Tell her she's doing it." He slaps my shoulder and walks away. "Good luck today, Sean." He says over his shoulder, but it feels like a smack in the face.

I run a hand over my face and then head to the locker room. I have plenty of time, but I need to think…about a lot of things. One of which is maybe finding a new agent.

My phone buzzes in my hand, and I look at it.

MARK: Heard you talked to Shane. Thanks for letting me know you weren't drowning in a pool of self-pity.

ME: Been busy sorting through a pile of bullshit.

MARK: Fair enough. I'll consider forgiving you.
MARK: Put your head down and get to work. Then, put an end to this.

I huff, putting my phone in my locker, hoping it'll get lost. My head is full and overwhelmed with too many things to process and sort through. Sitting in the chair in front of my locker with my head in my hands, I try to focus on one thing at a time.

First, I need to do my job. Then, I'll have to deal with the press. At some point, I'll check in with Andie and see what she wants to do. One thing at a time. It's all I can do.

But Mark is right. I'm done being a coward. Morgan can say whatever, and people will believe it or not. That doesn't mean I should lie down and take it. If Andie is willing to work with me, I'll make time, and we'll show these drama queens exactly what's up.

I change, getting ready for warm-ups as my teammates file in. Some give me a sympathetic nod or a slap on the back, while others eye me like they're still deciding whose side they're on. I'm already tired of that shit too. I've never needed someone's pity or consolation, and I don't want it now. If these guys want to believe the lies, fine. They can get in line with all my former fans.

I've been through hell and back growing up, seeing and facing things I could only pray to forget. This is just another bump in the road, and just like the others I've encountered in my life, I'll step over it and face whatever is on the other side.

Chapter 16

ANDIE

"For real? We're going to watch the Tigers, and you're going to pretend that I'm not here?"

She's sitting with her arms crossed over her chest, her glasses forever crooked on her face. Her blue strands are pulled back now, and the sunlight catches on the diamond stud in her nose, casting a rainbow droplet on the wall opposite me.

I've never watched football in my life. Even when Josh had it on, I spent that time doing anything but watching the game. Today, however, I can't help but want to see just what kind of reception Sean gets.

"Andie, if you keep this up, I'll no longer support your sulking and will call Gem to yank you out of it. You know what that means."

I roll my eyes. "I'm not sulking, you big nark. As if you haven't been reporting every tidbit of the last forty-eight hours to her like my life is some kind of daytime drama."

"Well, it kind of is. I mean, the only other thing needed in that meeting this morning with Sean and that imbecile agent of his was a door slam and a slap, and the Daytime Emmy would go to us."

I laugh. "Five more minutes with Craig, and you would've conquered the slap."

"I'm sure he gets paid way too much for adding absolutely no value," she says with disgust. "Now that you've finally cracked, what did you and Sean discuss in the hall? If it hadn't been for that pinhead in a suit, my ear would've been pressed to the door."

"Calm down. It's not that exciting." I think back to our conversation and my surprise at how concerned Sean seemed to be. This guy just messes with my dislike–to–hate scale like it's his job.

She scoffs. "Right. You and I both know if you decide to do this, the social media aspect on your end will be all me. So, I fall into the need-to-know category."

"He apologized for this whole thing and then asked what I wanted to do."

She stares at me. "He apologized?"

"Yes, he said he was sorry."

"That was nice of him, but why? It's not like any of this is his fault. His crazy ex is selling stories to get some kind of rise or pay out of it. Clearly, this isn't easy on him either."

"Since you're all team Sean, maybe I should give you his number, and you can convince him to fire Craig and hire you instead."

She weighs her head from side to side. "I wouldn't mind working for all that hot muscular manliness, but…I'd miss you too much. I'm just saying he seems like a genuine person. This wasn't his fault. He can't help what other people will do to get back at him. In fact, I imagine his friend pool is quite small."

I groan, not wanting to hear about how amazing Sean *probably* is, but she's right. He seemed genuinely apologetic and upset about something he didn't do, but I can't think about that. I have to figure out if I want to work with him to try to 'clear' our names. *Ugh. People just really suck.*

I'm really good at waiting for the storm to blow over and would like to sit on this couch until this all goes away, but I'd told myself I wasn't doing that anymore. I'm supposed to be living, no longer wallowing in grief and heartbreak. I'm *trying* to step back into the land of the living, one baby step at a time. This little setback isn't good for my progress.

A round of baby babbles comes through the monitor, and Nora and Snipe pop up like they just heard the word 'treat.'

"Can I get him?" Nora sits forward, ready to bounce. "I've missed that little booger so much."

I smile as she jumps up like she's won the lottery. "Yeah. Just keep all that Sean's-so-great rhetoric to yourself. Ax is on my team the whole way, forever."

Nora snorts from down the hallway, and I pat Snipe as he lays back down at my feet. "You've always got my back, you good boy." I scratch behind his ear and watch the Tigers take the field. The crowd cheers, but as the camera scans, they breeze by women holding posters calling out Sean as a cheater.

One says, 'Tigers cheat.' Another says, 'Tigers don't keep Cheatahs.' The signs are held high, and the boos go on as number twenty-four is announced and runs onto the field.

My stomach twists for him as I watch him take his place on the sideline with the rest of his team. Regardless of my wishy-washy feelings toward Sean and not understanding what he's all about, he doesn't deserve this. No one should have to just stand by and watch their dreams and hard work go down the drain because of one person's bald-faced lie.

I think about Gem asking what we were going to do about it. I know that woman, and she'd do anything but sit back and let someone work her over. My Gem would sit with her VO and water, getting the last laugh. She's never hunkered down and waited for the storm to pass. She'd be out there dancing in the rain. Maybe she was onto something when she said we should parade in there and show them how we Taninbaughs deal with liars.

Nora returns, holding my favorite guy in the entire world. He's just a baby, but I want to be the kind of mom who shows him strength and resilience.

"I'm going to do it," I blurt, stopping Nora in her tracks. "I'm going to work with Sean and give these jokers the big middle finger by doing something really great for some deserving people."

Nora grins. "Yeah?"

"Yeah." A smile creeps across my face in return.

"Can Gem and I literally flip them all off?"

I laugh. "You, no. You work for me, and we're going to be professional about it. Gem, well, she'll likely have her own ideas."

"Damn straight, she will. I want to be her when I grow up."

I smile. "Don't we all."

Chapter 17

SEAN

"You guys brought in a win today, thanks to your touchdown that tied up the game. Any thoughts on what happened in the first quarter and what was going wrong?"

I need this to be the last question as I try to escape from the podium before they address the crowd boos and all of the negative press that's aimed at me.

I quickly make up some generic response I'm not even sure I hear myself say, then lift my hand as in thanks as I step away to let them know I'm done.

A hand shoots up, and the reporter speaks before I can make my getaway. When I hear the start of the question, I freeze, my temper spiking as they continue to push forth this fabricated story.

"Sean, can you say if your recent break up with Morgan Monroe and her claims will have any impact on your relationship with the Tigers organization or your sponsors?"

I push out a breath, dragging myself back up to the podium. My hands grip the sides to prevent myself from letting loose on the room. All eyes are on me, expectant and waiting for any bone I will throw, giving them their next headline.

I steady myself, hoping they can catch this. "My contract does not specify relationship status or lack thereof as a condition of employment. As far as sponsors, they have been gracious in understanding that one person's claim does not equal truth."

I shake my head, so freaking sick of this. "As far as what's being said about me and my personal life, this is all I'm going to say. If you all want to spend your time listening to and reporting on far-fetched ideas, fine, but leave innocent people who have nothing to do with those things to their lives. You can come at me all you want. Surely, you have better, more important things to report than trying to hunt down false narratives to get another like or follow that will boost your career."

I step down and grab my bag, ready to go home to peace and quiet. I need to text Andie and see what she's thinking so we can get on with this or not.

Halfway home, my phone starts ringing. It's Mark.

"Now, that's what I'm talking about! About time you whoop some ass!" Mark yells through the phone. "Who's next, bro? I want asses and names!"

I laugh for the first time in days. "The next person that follows me or shows up at my house or calls my phone looking for a comment."

"Alright, now. There you go! That wallowing shit was getting really old. I saw the game. That touchdown had to feel good. You showed those fans what you got."

"Yeah, I wasn't sure how today was going to go. I had to meet with Craig and PR beforehand. Andie was there. They want us to battle the press with community outreach and positive press."

Mark groans. "So, Andie, huh?"

Of course, this is what he'd pick out of that. "Yes. Her name is Andie, and no, nothing is going on."

"Why not?"

If I weren't driving, I'd ram my head into the steering wheel. "Dude, after this whole thing, I'm likely never dating again. She's the one I was stuck in the elevator with."

"The one who hates your handsomely covered guts?"

"Yeah, this didn't help her see me in a better light. I told you she lost her husband, and this…they're after her, and it's not right."

"What are you going to do? What exactly do they want?"

"I'm leaving it up to Andie. They want to show us working together in a professional capacity. Put on an event for kids that are hospitalized or something. It'll be difficult during the season, but if she wants to, I'll do it. A local organization would benefit, so that's good."

"Sounds like fun," he grumbles. "Keep me posted."

"Yeah. Sure." I pull my truck into my garage, happy only two cars are sitting outside my gate tonight, hoping to catch something they can use.

"And you should definitely rethink this no-dating thing. If this Andie chick doesn't like you, something tells me she might just be exactly what you need."

The asswipe hangs up before I can respond. I climb out of my truck, ready to sit in the sauna and rest my sore body. I feel like I was hit by a freight train, and sometimes I wonder why I'm still doing this. But then I'm reminded of what it feels like to stand on the field with my team and carry the ball to the end zone. It's a rush like no other.

After I sit in the steam for a while, I shower and find my phone to text Andie. She's the last item on my list today, and something about that has a swirling feeling erupting in my gut as I sit to find her number.

Looking at my phone, I see she's beat me to it.

ANDIE: Thank you for what you said today.

I don't know if I'm more shocked that she said something nice or that she apparently watched the press conference and maybe the game. Because I'm ready to move forward from the doom and gloom, I can't help but mess with her. For some reason, a world where Andie is nice to me seems dangerous.

ME: Who is this???

ANDIE: Nevermind *eye roll emoji*

ME: Phew. I was worried someone might have broken in and stolen your phone. I think that's the nicest thing you've ever said to me.

ANDIE: Don't let it go to your head. I still don't like you.

ME: Ok. Good. I was worried we might become friends through this whole ordeal.

ANDIE: No chance of that. I have enough friends…people I actually like.

ME: What? Like two and your grandma?

ANDIE: Actually, three. People aren't my thing.

ANDIE: Careful. You better never let her hear you say that 'G' word, and her ears are sonar-rated.

ME: Since there's not much competition, I think it might be time you had one you don't like…all that much.

ANDIE: No thanks. I'm good. *Smiley face emoji*

ME: What do you want to do about the outreach?

ANDIE: Are we talking just outreach or outreach with a little ass-kicking?

ME: Definitely ass-kicking involved. Preferably the lying, cheating, propagating kind.

ANDIE: I'm in, then.

ME: You sure? We'll have to pretend to be civil.

ANDIE: No pretending involved. We're going to show these cowards what happens when you take something mean-spirited and turn it into good. And we'll show them what real looks like while we're doing it.
ANDIE: To be clear, that means we don't have to pretend to like each other.

ME: I never said I didn't like you.
ME: I'm in. When do you want to meet?

Chapter 18

ANDIE

The door to my favorite little coffee shop chimes, and I look up expecting to see Sean, but it's an older woman with a white fluffy dog peeking out of her purse. Annoyed he's fifteen minutes late, I go back to the word game on my phone.

I need a break from…everything. I just spent the last hour meeting with a label that's hunting down songs and demos for an up-and-coming artist. I've worked with them before, so they know my style and how I work, but of course, the first twenty minutes were focused on my 'relationship' with Sean Greyson. I left unsure if they were more interested in my music or trying to see if they could somehow capitalize on me and the man who is close to twenty minutes late and counting.

Ready to call it a day and go home to snuggle my little guy, the door chimes again, and Mr. Popular himself strolls in. He's wearing gym shorts, a long-sleeved Tigers t-shirt, and a backward ball cap. I'm pretty sure even if I were blind, I'd still know exactly how attractive he is. Physically, he's beautiful. He's got that pretty boy face but with a rugged edge. The kind of handsome that's swoon-worthy even to the most attached. Add to that he's taller than most women with the sort of defined muscles that tell you his body is a machine and that blond hair that's barely dark enough to make his light blue eyes pop. But it's his quiet confidence that's both alluring and mysterious, and it all annoys the crap out of me.

He stops at the table, setting his keys and phone down. "I'm sorry I'm late. Have you ordered?"

"Nope. I waited for you."

He surveys the few small tables around us. At first, I took offense to his constant audit of his surroundings, like I was somehow inferior, but I've learned my lesson about jumping to conclusions. Given our predicament, I understand his need to ensure our privacy.

I chose this place, knowing it's quiet in the afternoons. I used to spend time here working before Axel was born. It's out of the way, low-key, and has a consistent clientele.

A young woman, wearing headphones, is working on her laptop. A couple with a toddler occupies a corner, and the older woman now sits in the window reading a book while her dog naps next to her in the bag.

Sean's gaze returns to me. "If you tell me what you want, I'll order it, and then we can get to work."

I could protest, telling him I'll get my own, but given I've sat here waiting on his privileged muscled behind for twenty minutes, he can pay for my tea.

"A peppermint tea with honey. Please."

He nods and walks to the counter behind me to order. I pull a notebook and a pen from my bag, hoping we can hammer this out quickly. Nora is watching Axel but has to leave at a certain time, so we need to get to it.

I open my notebook to a blank sheet, but in my periphery, I see the couple from the corner approaching.

"Hi," the woman says cautiously. She smiles as she reaches down to pick up her son, and her husband joins her. She continues to smile at me nervously.

"Hi." I rack my brain, trying to figure out if I know her somehow, but I come up short.

"I'm sorry to bother you, but are you...is that…" She tips her head in Sean's direction, and the lightbulb goes on. I have no freaking clue how to handle this. This is one of the reasons we're here. We need to figure out what in the hell to do about all of the attention.

"Oh, um." I frantically search for words while my eyes dart over my shoulder to Sean, willing him to get back over here and help me.

"I'm sorry." She jumps in. "We watch every game. You sang the national anthem, and it was breathtaking. Your story…it just hit so close to home."

With his hands full, Sean returns to our table and sits, looking between me and the couple.

I peek at him quickly. "Thank you."

"I'm so sorry about your husband," she says with genuine sympathy, and I sense understanding in her voice. She gestures to her husband. "He's getting ready to deploy. It never gets easier."

I nod and try to smile, but there's a pinch of recognition in my gut as I remember every time Josh left, knowing that truth.

My eyes drift to the little boy who reaches for his father, and I hold my breath, willing my mind not to wonder what it would be like to see Josh holding Ax.

"Anyway, I'm sorry we interrupted, but we love 'you guys. You're absolutely the cutest, and our military family is rooting for you." She looks at me. "Your story is so inspirational. Would it be possible to get a picture?"

I look at Sean, and he stares back at me like he doesn't know how to answer either.

"Actually…we just work together." I stammer all over myself like I'm new to the world. "But…sure."

The woman's brow scrunches, her eyes flicking between the two of us like she doesn't believe a word of it. *Ugh. This isn't going to work.*

I stand as she pulls her phone out of her pocket, and Sean follows.

He shakes the husband's hand. "Thank you for your service, and stay safe."

My mind floods with memories, and sadness for what will never be creeps up my throat. The man nods and tells Sean what a big fan he is, and then we squish together to fit into the frame. After a few clicks, we separate, and they thank us again before leaving.

Once we're seated again, Sean studies me for a second. I want to crawl under the table with the way his eyes are lingering on my face.

"Are you alright?" His voice is soft and full of concern, and I can't help but wonder what he sees that makes him ask that question.

Can he see me swimming in the emotions of telling Josh goodbye the last time or the excruciating reminder that he'll never hold his son? The son he didn't get the chance to know he'd have. So many things are running through my mind, but I push it all down to get back to working together, worried it's a terrible idea.

"Yeah." I push my hair behind my ear, trying to shake it all off. "Thanks for the tea." I take a sip, readying myself to get down to business, but first, I want to revisit what we're doing. "Do you think this is a good idea?"

He looks around, his hand rotating his bottle of water. "For you and me, I don't know. The more we're together, the more people will think whatever they want. If that bothers you, then we shouldn't do this. If we want to join forces to do something good, I say to hell with whatever people think we are or aren't. I mean, what more can they really say? I'm kind of done giving a shit."

That makes me smile, and I don't even try to hide it.

One of his light eyebrows hitches up toward the clasp of his hat. "Why are you smiling?"

I lift a shoulder. "The guy in the elevator definitely gave a shit, Sean. This is a fast turnaround, and in my experience, it takes a while to get to the level of truly not giving a single crap."

"Are you telling me you don't care that people think we're sleeping together and may continue to spin stories as long as Morgan wants to feed them?"

I glare at him, knowing he's right. I do care, but only because it affects my business and, if this doesn't stop it, at some point, possibly my son.

When I don't respond, he pushes forward. "Andie, at this point, I'm just ready to try to turn this around, so unless you've changed your mind, tell me what you're thinking."

I lean back in my chair. "I'm thinking, if we can use the attention to help some people in need, then maybe all this nonsensical noise will be worth it."

"Ok. Let's do it." He downs about half of his water. "What ideas do you have?"

I fiddle with my pen. "I thought we could combine things we're passionate about. The couple just here gave me the idea of honoring military families and veterans. The stress and hardship of that life is real. It's a big sacrifice for servicemen and women and their families."

"What about the kids at the hospital?"

I weigh my head from side to side. "Most of them are currently in treatment or recovering. Not all days are good days, and it would be sad for some to miss out. Plus, getting them to the stadium could be a challenge. Really, just stopping in to see them would be amazing. That's where they need their spirits lifted."

He nods, thinking about what I said.

"How about you? Is there something you're passionate about you'd like to call attention to or honor?" I'm curious to see if there really is something deeper to this man.

He rolls the cap to his water bottle between his fingers as the self-assured guy looks just a little bit uneasy. "I was thinking we could do something with local foster families."

Well, that's not what I was expecting. "Foster families?"

"Yeah. I grew up in foster care and would have lost my mind if I'd been able to go to a game, let alone spend a morning with some players. It would've been a dream come true for a kid with nothing to look forward to. Adding you to the mix only makes the deal that much sweeter. Those kids…"

He doesn't finish his statement as I stare at him. I'm not sure, but my mouth might be hanging open. I'm speechless, and I'm never caught without words. When I pull my mind back from the brink of being blown to pieces, I have to ask, "You were a foster kid?"

He adjusts the cap on his head before resting his arms on the table. "Yeah, until I aged out. I moved into a group home as a teen but was shuffled between homes before that. Not many people know that, though."

I don't even know what to do with this information. I can tell he's ready to be done answering questions, but I can't stop. "So…you don't have any family?" I have a thousand questions running through my mind, but for some reason, this one floats to the top.

He rests back in his chair, crossing his arms over his chest like he's guarding himself from an interrogation. "No, but I have two brothers. Two guys I lived with in the group home. One is married with a son, and they're raising his wife's younger siblings. The other lives in New York City. They're my family, but that's it."

I have to sit for a minute, letting this sink in. This in no way makes sense…or maybe it does. Sean Greyson is a foster kid. I need to peel back the layers of that for a second.

"So…what do you think?" He breaks into my rapid-fire attempt to piece things together. "Craig isn't going to like it, but–"

I cut him off right there. "Does Craig dictate your whole life?

"Not everything." I see his honesty. "Does Nora run yours?"

"Nope. She helps keep me organized, but I make the decisions."

"Unfortunately, that's not how it works for me. My life is not my own sometimes, especially during the season. Team management, sponsors, fans...they're all a factor. Craig's job is to keep it all running smoothly."

That sounds oddly similar to my life with my parents, although I didn't have someone trying to run interference.

"Sounds fun," I say, feeling just a little sad he lets his life be run by other people. "Did Craig arrange your relationship with Morgan, too?"

Sean pulls back slightly at my question, his fingers running over his jaw like he has to think about it. Now, I want to know if that jerk pushed Morgan on him because of how good they look together.

"He did, didn't he?" I can't even hide my irritated shock. "He sure lowered his bar, allowing you to work with me. I definitely don't fit the mold. He's probably off, pacing somewhere, worried I'm ruining your image."

Sean's brows pinch together, a crease forming between his eyes. "I think my image could stand some improvement. I'm not sure if you noticed at the game, but all of the women look...similar?"

"Well, it must not have bothered you. They're all freakishly beautiful. Isn't that what Morgan is, an influencer-turned-model?" I'm not sure why I care about this, but I do. Maybe it's because I've been pulled into this by simply being near this man for longer than a second.

He leans forward, resting his muscled forearms on the table. "Andie, it's my fault you're involved in this, so I should be clear about something. Craig may have introduced Morgan to me, but I dated her for the past two years. And by dated, I mean I saw her maybe a handful of times a month at the most. When we were together, it was usually a quick dinner before I had to get to bed or attend an event where we went our separate ways to talk to different people. Rarely, she came over to watch a game or hang out with friends. That was it. All this stuff she's spreading around is false."

He pauses but doesn't take his eyes off me, an energy in them that tells me I hit a nerve.

"My life and schedule are not my own, which is an issue I'm working on. Morgan clearly thought we were dating, but not by my definition, and

I should have broken it off with her long before I did. That superficial, unattached life doesn't work for me anymore. Everything from women who look a certain way because they think they fit my life to people telling me what to do and who to be. I'm done with it, but change takes time, and I'm doing what I can."

He sits back in his seat like he's finally satisfied. "Andie, I'm pretty sure there isn't a mold you'd fit into, and that is a compliment in the highest regard."

There are just too many little revelations in that speech for me to fully process right now, but what I know is the look on Sean's face tells me he's seriously pissed about how things are. There's nothing like finally having had enough to shove you off the ledge. I wonder exactly what it was for Sean that did it, but that's a question for another day.

He and I are two very different people, but in the last few minutes, I've realized we have some things in common. If doing this event is part of him getting more of his life back, there's even more reason to do it.

I jot down a few notes so we can lay something out for Miranda, giving him a moment to chill out. He looks all riled up like I took a hot poker to a fresh wound. *Why does that make me want to smile?*

I set my pen down and find him staring at me. "I think foster families would be awesome." I roll my lips to keep them from betraying me.

Apparently, I'm unsuccessful.

His head falls back, and he groans at the ceiling. "Andie, you're infuriating. What in the hell is amusing about what I just told you?"

I'm not blind to the level of emotions rolling through Sean at the moment. I also know he's likely used to being surrounded by people who never notice the man who exists underneath. They only want surface-level Sean.

I understand what it's like to live feeling like no one ever actually sees you or cares enough to find out who you really are. So, in solidarity, I'll ease his tortured, vulnerable soul. I know he gave me just a little bit of himself today, and I don't take that lightly.

"Nothing…" I tap my lips with my pen, trying to contain the grin that's desperate to escape. "I'm just not sure what to make of that verbal vomit. I didn't know you had that in you. I'm impressed."

He hangs his head. "Alright. Are we done here?"

I laugh, and his bright blue eyes form slits as they drag up to mine. It takes everything in me not to reach across the table and pry them open with my fingers because glaring Sean doesn't feel authentic. I know there's a smug smirk in there somewhere instead.

"Yes, I think we should touch base with Miranda, and you can deal with your agent if you want, but I'm warning you. I don't give two diddly dos what he thinks or wants."

"Fine. I imagine Miranda will want to meet soon to begin planning on her end and report to Mr. McNeil."

I close my notebook and put it back in my purse. "Sure." Sean gathers his keys and phone, but I stop him just before he stands. "Hey. What we're doing is personal. We aren't doing this to polish your image, and let's be real. It won't make the lies about us disappear. What Craig or anyone else wants doesn't matter. This is you and me giving back. So, if he doesn't like it, that's just too damn bad."

His mouth curves upward, and I see recognition that his words didn't go wasted on me today.

Chapter 19

SEAN

"Hey, man." I slap Tyrell's hand as we cross paths in the hallway of the practice facility. I've been here since early this morning, and I'm ready to go home where I can be alone and away from the depressing mess that has become my life.

These past few days have been filled with me dodging the media as much as possible and trying not to take offense to some of my so-called friends and teammates treating me like the lying, cheating bastard Morgan has convinced everyone I am.

The attitude and disbelief of my teammates have been the hardest to comprehend. I know some of their wives and girlfriends are friends with Morgan, but I thought they knew me better. Apparently, I was wrong.

Tyrell has done his best to keep me focused and away from the cold shoulders in the locker room, but even his exuberant positivity and constant upbeat demeanor can only stretch so far. Some things just are what they are, and today, I feel like I want to crawl into a hole and stay there.

"Where are you headed? I figured you'd be out of here by now. You need to rest." He points to my elbow, wrapped with an ice pack around it. "That's not looking good."

He's right. I need to get home. I just left the physical therapist who's been working with me since I overextended my elbow last game. It's been bothering me all week, but it's worse today. Forget the ice pack. What I really need is an ice bath. My whole body aches, and I wouldn't mind feeling numb for a little bit.

If only it would work on my brain, too. My body took a beating last weekend against one of our rivals, but my mental state has been taking a nosedive for a while now.

"I have a meeting with Miranda about an event I'm working on with Andie. She and Craig thought it would help settle some of the negative press." The press release went out, but the rumors continue to fly. I need this meeting to be short and get things rolling so I can go home.

Tyrell nods. "Huh? So, this involves you spending time with Andie."

I roll my eyes. "It's not like that, man. It's pure business, and we hope something good comes from this mess."

"Well, let me know what's up. If I can make it, I'm in."

That makes me think about what Andie said about visiting the kids at the hospital. "What do you think about making some time for the kids at the children's hospital on our day off?"

"Yeah. I'm down. Those kids would rather see this face than your ugly mug, anyway." His white teeth shine against his dark skin. "Does this also have to do with Miss Andie?" I ignore him, and his punk-ass grin grows even wider like he knows something I don't. He slaps me on the back. "Well, good luck with the meeting. Rest up. We need you to be one hundred percent this weekend."

I salute, and he laughs as I turn to find the meeting room Miranda sent me. I haven't talked to Andie since the coffee shop, where I divulged more personal information than intended. I don't talk about my childhood with anyone except Shane and Mark, and even then, we don't talk about it often.

I also didn't mean to share details of my relationship with Morgan or really lack thereof, but her comment about not fitting the mold of my world sent my temper soaring.

The idea that anyone, but for some reason, specifically Andie, thinks they don't fit into my life because of how they look, their profession, or where they come from, set me off. I'm a guy whose very existence came from trauma and horror, and I'm beginning to think Andie is exactly the kind of person I should surround myself with. But I don't deserve that kind of honest friendship with how I've been living and acting.

I didn't intend to share any of that with Andie, but she sat and listened. She may have made light of it, but on some level, I felt like she understood. It was like she knew talking about the personal details of my life was not something I was comfortable with. She took my uneasiness, tossed it up in the air, and let it float back down gently, reminding me that I don't have to live like that anymore.

I turn the corner of a short hallway and find Andie leaning against the wall. She's holding her phone close to her face, frowning, with her lips pushed to the side. Her long, curly, dark brown hair is tied back loosely. She's wearing holey jeans and a black and red flannel shirt with the sleeves rolled up. In this facility, she sticks out like a sore thumb, and it's…refreshing.

"Hey. What's up?" I rest up against the wall beside her, wondering what she's so focused on. I really hope it's not more pics or comments about us. It just won't stop.

She side-eyes me and then returns to her phone. "I need a five-letter word that starts with 'F' and ends with an 'E' for a triple word score. I have an 'A,' a 'U,' 'R,' 'K,' and a 'C.' If I hit this, Gem will go bananas."

"What?" She tips her phone in my direction, and I see what looks like a Scrabble board.

"Gem says she needs to keep her mind sharp. She usually beats the pants off me. I'm determined to win this round if it takes me the next year to figure out a word." She gestures to the door next to her. "There's a meeting still going on in there. Where's your keeper?"

"He'll be here any minute, I'm sure." I study the letters on her phone. "Flake."

"I don't have an 'L,' dumb dumb."

A small smile tugs at my lips. "Dumb dumb?"

She rolls her eyes. "Force. Crap. I don't have an 'O.'"

"Farce."

Her green eyes snap up to mine and grow wide. Then she types it in, and there's a dinging sound. "Ha. Eat that, Grandma. I better text her and tell her to pull out the ole checkbook for that one."

She taps away on the screen and then drops her phone in her bag. She turns to face me, leaning her shoulder against the wall.

"You two wager on a word game?"

"You've met my Gem. Does she strike you as a woman who'd give a single brain cell away for free?"

"That woman frightens me."

Andie laughs, her green eyes like two rare shiny emeralds. "You're a smart man to be afraid."

"So, what's my cut?" Her dark eyebrows come together. "I gave you the winning word."

"Ha. You're not getting a dime from me. I've given that woman more money, and it's finally her turn to pay up. You'd have to beat me in Words all on your own, buddy."

Her phone dings. She retrieves it and turns the screen to show me.

GEMMA: Next round, you're going down, sweet cheeks.

Her face shines brighter than the sun. Andie is really beautiful, and something tells me she has no idea. If I were in a different place, I'd take advantage of this whole working together thing and spend every spare minute with her. Her spunk, sassiness, and authenticity are contagious, and I'm finding the more I'm around her, the more I want to be.

Andie has this way of setting me on edge and pushing all of my buttons no one else seems to know are there. At the same time, she makes me feel so completely normal in a way that I haven't experienced in a very long time, maybe ever. There's no pretense with this woman or anything artificial about her. She's a what-you-see-is-what-you-get kind of person, and it's invigorating.

"What happened to your elbow?" She pokes the ice pack with her finger.

"Overextension. It'll be fine."

"Does that prevent you from playing?"

I shake my head. "Not much keeps me from playing. It has to be pretty bad for us to sit out." I adjust the ice pack, and she watches me like she wants to ask something but doesn't.

The door next to us opens, and a couple of people step out as Miranda calls us in. The room is tiny, with a table and chairs crammed inside and no windows. I gesture for Andie to go in first, being polite but also allowing me to keep the door open. We sit opposite Miranda, and a second later, Craig scurries in, and I hear the door click behind me.

While I try to remind myself the door is easily pulled back open, he takes a seat at the end of the eight-person table, barely acknowledging us as he taps away on his phone.

"Sorry to keep you all waiting." Miranda starts. "Nora's provided me with a detailed outline of your plans so far, and it's better than I could have ever imagined." She clasps her hands together in front of her. "Let's talk logistics. I need to get my team working, and we need to set a date. From Nora's notes, it would be ideal if it matches up with a game day so that we can offer the families a box, and Mr. McNeil would like to welcome them as well. He's onboard with what I've shared."

She pauses, scrolling through the email Nora sent, which was extremely detailed and contained my desire to invite local foster kids and their families. I roll my neck, trying to stretch, reminding myself I can breathe.

"Andie, Nora provided me with a list of what your band will need for the event. I'll get someone to review it and ensure we've got everything covered. You're welcome to invite any additional family or guests, and they'll also receive passes to the game."

"Thank you," Andie says.

"Based on what Nora has here, you'll be reaching out to the local VA so they know how to register families."

Andie nods. "Yes, we'll do that as soon as we have approval so they have time to register."

"Perfect. Sean." Miranda says my name, pulling me out of the tiny hole I'm sinking into. "How do you want to handle getting in touch with foster families? Do you have a specific organization you want to work with or–"

"What?" Craig finally pulls his head out of his phone and stares down the table at us. "What's this talk about foster families?"

I pull in air, slowly and quietly, trying to calm my nervous system. I knew he'd have an issue with this, so I purposely didn't discuss it with him. Now, I wish I had so I don't have to argue with him in front of Andie and Miranda.

I run a hand over the back of my neck and clear my throat. "I'd like to invite foster families. These kids often don't have many positive things going for them, and this would be huge."

"Mr. McNeil and I think it's a wonderful idea," Miranda pops in.

"Sean, have you really thought about this?" he asks, pinning me with a look. He's one of the few people who knows about my past, and that's only because I've had to explain to him that I have no family. "We're trying to repair your image here, and this isn't the time to stir the pot even further."

I bristle at his comment but ignore it for time's sake. Plus, my current state can't handle his superiority complex. "I've thought about it. This matters."

I'm not sure if it's by accident, but I feel Andie's knee press against mine underneath the table, and it's calming. It's the distraction I need to bring my anxiety down a few notches.

Craig scoffs, setting his phone on the table like I'm putting him out. "Sean, your sponsors, fans, even this team and the organization depend on you. You're not one of these young guns anymore who can do whatever they want and think the world will forgive them."

Anger replaces the panic at my core, and the heat of it rises to the surface. *What in the hell is he talking about? What does my age have to do with this?*

"What are you talking about? We're putting together an event to give people with hard, difficult lives something to look forward to. An experience they'd never have otherwise."

He glances at the ceiling like he's willing his patience to stay intact and then leans forward as if getting closer will help me catch up.

"That's only part of this. The bigger part is showing people that you aren't the lying cheater they think you are. Whatever you want doesn't matter. Dragging up some sob story will only make them roll their eyes and further convince them this is all some big publicity stunt to get you back in their good graces."

"Hey. Craig, is it?" Andie says, shocking me still, which is the only thing that prevents me from grabbing him by his lapels and letting him know exactly what does matter.

Andie's tone is calm and collected, and I can only stare at her, wondering where this is going.

"I'm not sure you understand what's going on here." She rests her arms on the table. "No one was asking for your permission. Sean and I agreed to do this, and the only thing *we're* interested in is providing a little joy to people who otherwise often live in a dark world of despair. The kind of world I hope you never have to face."

She takes a breath, and I realize she's not finished.

"These two groups of people we're talking about wear shoes that your tiny, self-absorbed feet would never ever be able to stand in, let alone survive. So, I don't really care what you want or who you think needs to be impressed. We're not here to massage anyone's image or work this for some kind of publicity stunt to look better in anyone's eyes. It's called kindness, and you'd do well to try it on, although I'm not sure they make it in your size."

Andie concludes her verbal slap with a grin spreading across her face, pointed directly at Craig. I can't speak. I can't remember the last time someone besides my brothers stood in my corner or laid down the law on my behalf. Actually, I do remember. It was never.

I'm completely taken aback, and it's not until I feel Andie's hand rest on top of mine that I realize, at some point during her declaration on how this will be, that my hand moved to her thigh and is squeezing. I quickly remove it, knowing it's completely inappropriate, but it itches to jet right back and reclaim her leg when I see Craig's face turning a shade of red that I've not seen before.

His dark and furious eyes aim at me, and I'm certain if they were loaded, I'd be dead.

"Sean, what is this? Are the two of you sleeping together? You're going to let some widow who writes songs for other people use you to make a name for herself while your reputation and career die in the process?"

I hear Miranda gasp, reminding me she's in the room. If it weren't for the fact that these two women are sitting here, I'd rip his damn head off. Out of respect for them, I won't show him the severity of his mistake.

"Craig," I say with as much patience as I can muster while my blood boils under my skin. "What I do from this point forward, personally or professionally, is no longer any of your concern. You're fired. I suggest you move quickly before I help you find the way out."

He makes a sound of disgust. "We have a contract."

"Yes, one that dictates that I can terminate it at any time for a fee. I'll pay. Now, get out."

He swipes his phone off the table and stands. "I hope she's worth it." He gestures towards Andie. "At least the last one made you look a whole lot better."

I stand, but Andie's hands grip my forearm, pulling me back down. I let him go, but I better never see his face again.

He scurries out, slamming the door behind him, and it takes me a minute to meet Miranda's eyes, which are wide and full of alarm. I can't even look at Andie after what he said.

Bile rises in my throat, and I'm in serious need of a punching bag, but I can't even hit it because my fucking elbow feels like someone took a hammer to it. *How in the world did I let it come to this?*

Miranda's tentative voice breaks through the dead silence and my misery. "Well, I guess we should continue?" She pauses. "Sean, if it's ok with you, I'd be happy to have my assistant reach out to some of the foster care organizations and get registration all set up."

"Sure. That would be great. Thank you." It's all I can say. My mind spins out of control as my skin prickles with a cool sweat.

Miranda continues as a cinch tightens around my chest, making it hard to breathe. "So, we'll start posting about the upcoming event and work on getting the word out. Andie, if we can get a picture of you and your band, that would be great. Sean, we'll use some of the photos we already have of you with kids."

I hear Andie respond, but I can't make out what she said through the beating of my own heart. I try to take some slow, steady breaths.

Miranda pushes a piece of paper toward Andie and then stands. "You two look at the dates and pick one that works. Once we have the date, we'll be off and running full speed ahead."

"Thanks. We'll get back to you shortly with a date," Andie says softly.

Miranda gives me a long look. "If you need a number for a new agent, I can get you a list of some of the best."

"Thanks, but I've got someone in mind," I say, trying to get a handle on myself and whatever is happening.

She nods, tells Andie goodbye, and then leaves the room.

The silence is thick before Andie turns in her seat, and I can feel her eyes on me. "I'm sorry–"

"Don't." I can't stand to hear her apologize.

She puts the paper Miranda handed her in her bag and stands. "I'm sorry if I made things worse for you."

I push up from my chair, completely drained and exhausted. Her eyes stay trained on the floor, but I need her to look at me.

"Andie, besides my brothers, I've never had anyone stick up for me like that."

As if in slow motion, her head tips upward, her eyes searching mine. Without thinking about it, I pull her to me, hugging the shit out of her. Her body hits mine, and every one of my muscles instantly relaxes. The pressure across my chest begins to lift.

I'm not sure what my life will look like after all the dust settles, but hugging Andie, hearing what she said, and having her in my arms feels more powerful than anything I've ever experienced.

"Thank you," I whisper.

Her arms come around my waist, and her stiffness eases. I don't notice that she smells like peppermint or how soft her hair is against my cheek. I can't think about the feel of her body next to mine or how she fits perfectly inside my arms, wrapped up, safe, and warm. All of this would lead me to want things I'm not ready for and she's not interested in.

I loosen my arms, and Andie takes a step back, pushing her hair behind her ear.

"Are you going to be ok?" I hear the concern in her voice, which makes something deep in my chest squeeze.

"Yeah. I should've fired him after our last meeting. I'm sorry about what he said–"

She holds up her hand and lays it gently on the center of my chest. It's not an intimate gesture but supportive and caring. It doesn't prevent me from wanting to clasp it in mine and hold the warmth and comfort of it for a long while.

"Don't apologize for something someone else said. My Gem says words can only hurt when they come from someone who actually knows you." Her lips turn upward.

"How about I walk you out, and we'll see if we can find a date that works?" I need to get out of here and have a second to take everything in.

"Fine, but no elevators. I got stuck with this guy once, and let me tell you…" She smiles and steps out into the hall. "You know, I should've just let Nora take Craig out into the hall last time. She's small but freakishly scrappy. She could definitely have taken him and would've enjoyed every minute."

"Andie," I say, stopping her. "You're a really good person and friend."

Her head tips to the side, and then she starts walking again. She bumps my arm with her shoulder. "We aren't friends, Pretty Boy. In fact, I don't even like you."

It's been a shitty day. A. Really. Shitty. Day, but somehow, I leave the practice facility with a slight smile on my face.

ME: I need Rob's number.

SHANE: Finally, kick that dipshit to the curb?
MARK: Still kicking ass and taking names.
MARK: What happened?

ME: A story for another day. Send me Rob's contact. I have a bad feeling Craig wasn't being upfront about everything.

SHANE: You alright, bro?

Chapter 20

ANDIE

Ax's pudgy little hands strike another set of keys, letting the sound ring out while I watch the Tigers score. Nora is in the kitchen making some kind of snack she promises is amazing, but I'm skeptical.

The constant clicking of Sniper's nails on the floor fills the momentary interlude as he pounces around, waiting for Nora to drop something. By the sound of it, she's making a mess.

All I know is this chick is too sweet to be hanging out with my pissy pants today and should be out with her friends, who are way more lively and fun than I am. But she's here, and I'm grateful.

"So, are we watching all of Sean's games now?"

She might be teasing, but I don't want to talk about Sean anymore today or ever.

This morning after the meeting, I spent fifteen minutes too long on the phone with my mother, trying to explain that whatever was happening with Sean and me was none of her business. She lost the right to know anything about my life when she refused to acknowledge Josh because he didn't fit into 'our' world. I imagine my decline to comment on the status of my 'intimate' relationship with Sean was about to make her pull out her regularly dyed hair. I find that amusing, and if that makes me a masochist, so be it. I may even have gone as far as to tell her what an amazingly sweet and dedicated man he is.

The last part wasn't even a lie. After we met with Miranda, where Craig all but called me a leech who was only after Sean's fame, I saw a different side to Sean. He was vulnerable at the coffee shop, telling me he grew up in foster care and the uninteresting details of his relationship with Morgan. But in that meeting room, I thought he was going to combust.

I could feel him vibrating as his large hand grabbed my thigh and squeezed. I couldn't stand any more of Craig's degrading demands. His grip held strong like I was a grounding point. It shocked me at first, but weirdly, the contact felt like we were actually in this foxhole together. It wasn't sensual or arousing. It was simply a connecting point that seemed essential to him remaining intact.

Then, there was the hug that was both bold and urgent. I'm not really sure what to make of it. I would've never pictured Sean as a hugger, so that has me pondering just exactly what was going through his mind. He told me he'd never had someone stick up for him, and I believe him. But that hug, his arms so tight around me, holding me to his large, forceful frame, made me just a little uncomfortable. The effects are lingering, and I don't like it.

It was just a hug, but I'm not sure I've experienced one similar to it in my life. I felt warm and safe tucked against him, but it was more than that. It felt desperate and dire. It was as if he needed *me* in that moment.

I roll my shoulders and neck, trying to shake loose the memory.

"Seriously, I'm cooking for you, and you're just going to ignore me." Nora's annoyance comes through loud and clear.

"I'm not sure you can call what's going on over there cooking." I adjust Ax on my lap. "I'm only watching, so I understand the game better when all these fans show up for our event." And because I know Sean hurt his elbow, and I want to see how he's doing, but I will never admit that to Princess Sassy Sparkle Pants.

As the game goes into halftime, Snipe barks, and seconds later, the front door swings open. Gem saunters through as if she owns the place.

"Ladies, tell me you have alcohol. I spent thirty minutes on the phone with your mother, listening to her yowl like a cat in heat. If I had to listen to her go on one more minute about you punishing her with this football player and how Brice is hanging on patiently for you to come to your senses, my nicely manicured nails would've reached through that phone and wrung her skinny, wrinkled neck."

She plops down in a chair across from me. "Andie, give me that handsome fella, and Nora, anything on the rocks will do."

"It's nice to see you too, Gemma. How may I serve you, madam?" Nora croons from the kitchen and then laughs. "All we have on tap this evening is beer."

"Oh, good Lord. You uncivilized ladies these days, sitting around drinking toilet water."

"BYOB, Gem," I say, handing Axel over to her.

"Come here, young man." She kisses his cheek, marking him with her red lips.

I settle into a spot on the couch, and it only takes a second before her beady little dagger eyes focus on me.

"What? I haven't done anything. Not today anyway."

"We're watching football these days?" Gem's eyes remain on Ax, but I hear her too-sweet tone as Nora snickers echo from the kitchen. "How's the elbow?"

I know this woman. She thinks she's so smooth tossing out that little tidbit as bait, but I'm no amateur. I've learned from the best. I school my face to remain impassive and train my eyes on the screen like I have no idea what she's talking about. What I want to know is how she knows about Sean's elbow.

"Whose elbow?" I'm as cool as a cucumber.

I feel the heat of her glare inspecting me, looking for any piece of evidence that I might be trying to pull one over on her.

"Yeah, whose elbow?" Nora chimes in. "Andie's doing research so she can speak intelligently about the game at the event. We just happen to be watching Sean play at the same time." The snitch adds that last part with just a hint of flare, knowing Gem will jump all over it. I want to reach into the kitchen and pinch her. Gem doesn't need any more fuel for her fireball eyes.

"Hmmmm," she hums, bouncing Ax on her lap. "Well, see, Gerald helped me download this little app that gives me the latest updates on the Tigers. Apparently, Sean overextended his elbow last weekend and has been dealing with some pain. Thought you might know something about that since you two are in…cahoots these days. I'd imagine that discomfort makes things a little less enjoyable in the sack."

This woman cracks a joke with such cool ease it almost passes for truth. *Why didn't I get that genetic trait?*

"Oh, good grief, Grandma. You've seriously lost the last two screws still intact up there." I point to my head. Nora cackles in the kitchen while stirring her brew. "Don't you have anything better to do than keep tabs on Sean? Unless you have a little crush. Is that it? Should I warn Sean that you're his newest stalker and he should beware of lurking old ladies outside his windows at night?"

"Sweet cheeks, if I had a crush on that gorgeous man, I wouldn't need you to pass on that information. What I want to know is, why you aren't making some truth out of all these lies?"

"Yeah, Andie. Why aren't you making whoopie with that gorgeous, muscled football star? I bet he smells amazing." Nora stares off into space like she's imagining how good he smells again.

The innate female part of my brain betrays me and pulls forth the sensory memory of his clean, crisp scent from that meeting room hug. Even with a little sweat mixed in, he does smell pretty damn good, but no way am I letting that accidentally spill from my lips.

I let my head fall to the back of the couch. "Oh, for Pete's sake. Why does there need to be something going on between Sean and me? His life is full. My life is…Axel and music, and that's enough. He's good-looking and nice most of the time when he's not wearing his self-absorbed football persona. But I'm not looking to get attached to him or anyone else who could just decide at any moment that they're done with me, or worse, have them just disappear."

Well, bugger. I didn't mean to say all of that. Besides the sound of the commentators informing us that the second half is starting, there is dead silence all around. Even Snipe got bored and is now asleep at my feet.

I keep my face pointed to the ceiling, not wanting to face these ladies. Eventually, though, I make myself be brave and pull my head forward to see Gem patiently waiting for me. Axel sits in her lap with a teething ring shoved between his gums and drool running down his chin and arm. My beautiful boy. I force myself to meet Gem's eyes.

"Baby girl, I'm going to tell you something I wouldn't dare tell another soul." Her voice is uncharacteristically gentle, and I have to swallow hard to force the burning lump down. "There is a time and a place to be afraid, scared senseless, and then there is a time to let it go. When your granddaddy died, I thought I'd never feel a single thing again, and I haven't."

She pauses, pulling Ax to her chest and holding him tighter. "But Andie, it wasn't that I couldn't. I just never let myself. I closed myself off to the possibility, and because of that, I've spent the last almost thirty years alone."

She straightens herself, and I see what I believe just might be tears in her old wise eyes. "You listen to me." She holds my gaze, not wavering. "We are not meant to spend this life alone. We were not created for it. Don't do what I did and shut out the possibility because you're afraid. You are stronger and braver than I've ever been."

That golf ball-sized lump returns in my throat, constricting my airway and causing tears to blur my vision. It only worsens when I hear Nora sniffle and then, a second later, blow her nose.

Gem leans down and kisses Ax's head. "Now, I'm not saying you should give Sean a shot, although I like that young man. He has a soft, quiet confidence that comes from something much deeper than the football field. Andie, he may not even want a shot with you, but when a nice, beautiful man comes your way that drives you absolutely out of your mind, make sure you don't push him away for the wrong reasons."

I don't say anything, but I'll hold on to everything she just said, and she knows it. She's loved me better and longer than most, and I know what she's saying is true. I don't want to spend my life alone. I don't want thirty years to go by and wish I'd been brave enough to let someone in, but the thought of losing someone again terrifies me beyond belief.

Trying to blink back tears that are determined to fall, I glance up at the TV and see Sean. He's sitting on the sidelines, squirting water into his mouth while someone puts a bandage on his knee–that punk looking too good to be true in his pads and jersey.

A smile tugs at my lips. The idea of Sean and me is alarming and ridiculous. We're like fire and water. Both of us have things to work through and move on from, and for some reason, that's comforting.

Nora comes to sit on the couch with me, pulling her feet up to her chest, still sniffling. "Gemma, I know that wasn't for me, but that is the most honest and heart-wrenching thing I have ever heard. You make me want to be a better woman. You need to write a book or something." She dabs her nose with a Kleenex.

"Oh, good night, hot pants. We need a drink. There is too much estrogen in this house." Gem stands, bringing Ax to me. "I'll have Gerald run to the store and get us something to lighten things up. For two exceedingly attractive young women who should be out spinning heads, you sure are depressing."

We laugh and joke as we eat Nora's cashew dip with crackers and finish watching the game. After giving Axel a bath, Gem robbed us of everything we had in a game of rummy, and since it was late, Nora passed out in the spare bedroom. I can hear her snoring from my own bed two doors down.

Sitting on my bed, I mess around with my guitar, thoughts of all that Gem admitted running circles in my head. There's a song in all that vulnerability and truth just waiting to be born.

I'm still trying to process what she said. I'd always thought she'd never met someone who made her feel the way my granddad had. In a million years, I would've never thought fear held her back. She's the strongest, most kick-ass woman I know.

My phone dings next to me, and I pick it up. A Words game request appears from…Sean.

ME: What are we playing for?

SEAN: I need a friend who gives verbal beatdowns like it's her day job.

ME: Send the request to Gem.

SEAN: She frightens me, and I'm sure she'd kick my ass.

ME: What do I get if I win, loser?
ME: Be careful. I play the word wizard.

SEAN: What do you want?

ME: Oh, the list of possibilities is endless.

SEAN: Maybe we should just play for fun.

ME: Are you worried?

SEAN: Hell, yes, I'm worried.

ME: How's your elbow?

SEAN: Hurts like a mother.

ME: How's your knee?

SEAN: You watched?

ME: I can't be caught completely uneducated at our event. Gem wouldn't have it.

SEAN: What'd you think?

ME: I think 24 sucks. He kept getting the ball and then getting tackled. Who let him on the team?

SEAN: You clearly need someone to explain the game.

ME: Nah, I'm a quick study. It's pretty clear that guy is a slacker.

SEAN: Alright, wiseass, I played the first word. We'll just see who's the slacker.

ME: Oh my gosh, that was you. *Shocked face emoji*

Chapter 21

SEAN

"Tell me, what else do you need from me?"

Rob sits across from me at my dining room table. It's my day off, and thankfully, he was able to catch a flight, so we can discuss him becoming my agent.

He represents Shane and Mark, and I should have been working with him all along. It's one more thing I neglected to notice while my head was stuck in the clouds.

"Anything hiding in your closet I should know about? Birth parents, past acquaintances, addictions, anything that can be used to corroborate Morgan's claims or cause a new scandal?"

I spent the last thirty minutes telling him about my relationship with the Tigers and my sponsors, then diving into what went down with Morgan.

I shake my head. "No. Besides Morgan, I didn't really date, and one-night stands aren't my thing. I've never used drugs. I don't drink often, and my birth parents won't ever be an issue."

The pain of that statement still bleeds like a fresh wound. Rob helped Shane in the past with his convict birth father, but I won't have the same issue.

"I met my mom a few years ago, and there'll be no further communication, so…" I let it hang, ready to move on.

"And you and Ms. Parks are not in a romantic relationship?" Rob takes a cautious sip of his coffee.

I see his intention isn't to be invasive. But given I let Craig know way more about my personal life than I should have, I feel like setting some boundaries in this new professional relationship is essential.

"I'm not trying to be difficult, but I don't plan on discussing my personal relationships with anyone going forward. My personal decisions are my own, and I accept all responsibility for them. I won't have you speak for me regarding anything related to my private life. I hope you can respect that. I'm only looking for you to help me manage the business side of things."

He stares at me across the table. I'm guessing Rob to be in his late fifties. His short stature and small frame are hidden under an expensive suit, and his slicked-back dark gray hair resembles a luxury car salesman. If it weren't for Shane and Mark speaking highly of him and knowing what he's done for their careers, I'd question whether or not this is a good idea. I know he's good at what he does, so I'm going with it. I'll know what kind of man he is if he bites back at my stance.

"Are you sure you and Shane aren't blood-related? Anytime I ask him the most minute detail of what's going on with Maggie and the kids, I'm pretty sure he'd like to reach through the phone and strangle me."

He sets his mug down and smiles. "Sean, I don't care to know the specifics of who you're sleeping with or how you spend your time off the field. I do, however, care about how your actions make me look. I have a reputation to uphold, and I'm not wasting my time representing someone who'll piss away all my hard work."

He leans back in his chair, adjusting his blue tie. "I assume Ms. Parks isn't excited about being wrapped up in this situation. This event that the two of you are working on is a good idea. If nothing else, it shows people you're moving on and giving back in the process. Reaching out to foster families is perfect, and your history isn't something you should ever feel like you have to hide. You've come a long way and should be proud of that. You're an inspiration, really. So, keep moving in that direction, and we'll settle in fine together."

"Great. I don't have any intention of making waves anytime soon. All I want is a quiet, simple life playing the game I love as long as I can manage it."

"When is the event?"

"Three weeks. We still have details to work out, but registration is open. Families will come to the stadium to meet the team and stay for the concert. They'll also get tickets to the game the next day."

"Sounds like an amazing opportunity for some deserving people." He nods as if he's on board. "I'll be honest with you, though, about a couple of things. First, whether it's Ms. Parks or someone else, make sure the next person you get involved with is worth your time and someone you're willing to bank your reputation on. Another spin like this one, and it'll be difficult to come back from that."

He inhales through his nose and lets it out. "Second, I don't like what you told me about Craig referring to your age and the organization. He's been around a long time and is a weasel of the worst kind when he thinks things are slipping. If you're ok with it, I'll sniff around and see if there's anything we should be keeping tabs on."

Sneaky bastard. "Sure. That's probably good. I don't need to be blindsided again."

"Alright, then. I think we understand each other, and if you're good with it, we have a deal. I'll get my assistant to send the contract over first thing."

I stand, shaking his hand. I needed this to work out. "Thank you for coming all this way and agreeing to work with me."

"Ha. You boys are a dream compared to some of my other clients. For three guys who grew up the way you did, you should be making my life a nightmare, but you're all pretty good kids. Mark is questionable." I smile, and he slaps me on the back on the way to the door. "Keep your head up, keep working your way forward, and we'll get things back on track."

"Thank you." I reach for the door handle, opening it to a bright sunny day.

"If I didn't have to catch a flight back, I'd insist you play golf with me. It's too nice to be sitting on a plane."

I chuckle. "I'm not much of a golfer, so you'd be better off asking someone else."

"Well, what does a famous football player like yourself do on a day off like this?" He holds his arms out in the bright sun.

"I'm meeting Simmons at the children's hospital, hoping they might be excited about a visit."

Rob turns toward his rental. "Keep going, Sean. You and I are going to work just fine together."

I sit in the parking garage, waiting for Tyrell to text me he's here. I've never done something like this before. I'm a little nervous and unsure of what to expect.

I should have asked Andie or my contact, who arranged today's visit, for more details. The response I got was filled with blatant elation, and I hope the kids will be excited to see us.

It might be my best-kept secret, but I love kids. I've not spent much time around them, except a few visits to see my new nephew and Maggie's much younger siblings, but I love every second of it. They have a huge family, and I love when I get to be a part of it. It's like reliving a childhood I never had.

When I visit, the youngest and only girl paints my fingernails and pretends to do my hair. The boys are full of energy and fun-loving pranks. It all makes me wish for a family of my own someday.

If I can hang with them, I should do just fine here, right?

My phone buzzes with Tyrell's announcement that he's parking, so I climb out of my truck and exit the garage to meet him.

Standing just inside the revolving door, he grins like he's ready to put on a show for these kids.

He rubs his hands together. "Let's get this spreading cheer fest going."

We stop at the desk for directions to where we're meeting my contact. We pass an elevator, but I keep walking, eyeing the stairs.

"You still not over that little mishap? It's not likely to happen twice, you know."

"I'm good with the stairs," I say, pushing forward.

"Sure. I guess if I'm going to risk it, it'll be with my wife if you know what I mean." He waggles his eyebrow with a devilish grin.

"Seriously, I don't want to think about what you and your wife do…anywhere."

He laughs as we head to the stairs and climb. "You're just mad your lame ass didn't take advantage of being stuck in there with a beautiful woman."

"Why did I invite you?" I grumble.

"Because you know these kids will light up when they see the man who makes Tiger magic happen."

I can't help but chuckle as we cross into a brightly colored hallway lined with windows. Behind the doors stands a woman and gentleman in a long white coat waiting for us.

As we near, the man looks mildly familiar. Then, it hits me. *Oh, shit.*

The young woman beams at us. "Mr. Greyson. Mr. Simmons. Welcome. We're so excited to have you here today. I'm Susan Waters." She shakes my hand and then Tyrell's. "The children will be beside themselves to meet the two of you. We're so grateful you're taking the time." She gestures to the man next to her. "This is Dr. Taninbaugh, our Chief of Staff."

He sticks out his hand. "It's very nice to meet the both of you and very generous to spend time with our kids."

We shake hands, and I search his face for any sense of recognition, and I'm shocked to find none. I quickly wipe the confusion from my face, realizing this man has no idea who I am. To him, I'm just another good Samaritan showing up to bring smiles to these kids' faces.

The whole world thinks I'm sleeping with his daughter. Yet, he apparently has no idea. Relief washes over me. If I were him, I'd lay me out in this rainbow-colored hallway.

"We know your time is limited, so we'll let you get in there and give your attention to the kids. Most of them are already gathered in the common room, so if you head through these doors and down the hall, you'll pass the nurses' station. They can direct you to the room. If you need anything, they should be able to assist you." She smiles. "We really appreciate this. Please let me know if you have any questions or are interested in visiting again."

Dr. Taninbaugh's phone chimes. "I have to run, but please let us know if there's anything we can assist with. This is very gracious of you. Nice meeting you both."

He disappears down the hallway, and I'm left wondering about this man and his relationship with Andie. I already have a pretty good idea that Andie and her mother don't see eye to eye. Based on the benefit, that's likely putting it mildly. But her father not remembering me or knowing I'm reportedly involved with her is difficult to understand.

"Hey, you ready?" Tyrell bumps me on the shoulder, pulling me away from the questions rolling around in my head.

"Yeah. Let's get in there and see what kind of fun we can have."

We thank Susan, entering another hallway with walls covered in bright cartoon-like pictures that help pull your senses away from the sterile smell and environment. We stop at the nurses' station, and they direct us toward the common area. Halfway down the hall, we hear music and then a voice that I'm pretty sure I'd recognize anywhere.

"Sounds like the party started without us," Tyrell says as we step up to a wall of glass lining a large room filled with kids seated in a semicircle around Andie. A few parents sit nearby at wooden tables. Some kids are in bright-colored chairs in their pajamas, while others are in wheelchairs and gowns. IVs drip fluids as the sun shines through adjacent windows, illuminating the area and bringing a sense of the outdoors inside.

Andie smiles and laughs at something one of the kids said, her fingers moving delicately over the strings. She looks up, noticing us standing in the doorway. Her head tips to the side just slightly as she listens to the kids, her eyes flicking back to them.

Tyrell makes a humming sound. "Well, look who's here. What a coincidence?"

If we weren't standing outside a room filled with children, I'd smack him in the back of the head. "I didn't know she'd be here."

"Sure." His smirk is calculating, and I don't like it one bit.

Andie leans forward in her chair, whispering, and then points in our direction. Every head turns, and there's a hushed gasping sound followed by wide smiles that instantly make this worth the time on our day off.

We enter, and Andie introduces us. She puts her guitar to the side as we fold ourselves into the small chairs, the kids sitting quietly, looking at us with big eyes. Everyone is too shy to speak until a little boy asks if we're the real football players.

Tyrell throws a thumb in my direction. "I'm not sure about this guy, but I'm the one dancing in the end zone."

They giggle, and it gets us rolling. It's not long before we're moving around the room and getting down on our knees to take pictures and sign autographs. Tyrell has them grinning with elaborate stories that have them captivated.

I see Andie packing up her guitar, and I excuse myself, wanting to catch her before she leaves. I ignore Tyrell's evil eye as he re-enacts his most recent touchdown with a kid throwing him an invisible ball.

I cross the room to the corner where Andie is buckling the clasps on her guitar case. She's wearing a white thermal shirt and worn jeans that hug her perfectly, and my weak ass hormones recall the feeling of my hand squeezing her thigh. That is not something I should be thinking about right now or at all. Acknowledging that does nothing to prevent my temperature from rising as I approach her.

"Hey."

Her hair is pulled back in a ponytail, and she pushes a rogue curl behind her ear as she turns to face me.

"Are you coming over here to pay up?"

"We never agreed on terms." Thankfully. She kicked my butt in our first Words battle. She came up with words I didn't know existed in the English language. I would've accused her of cheating, except I looked them up. "I have no doubt that worked in my favor."

"Ha," she brags, her eyes glancing at the kids behind me who are cracking up at Tyrell's dramatics. "It's really nice of you guys to take the time to visit. They're going to talk about this for weeks."

"They're great kids." I turn to face them, watching a little boy pretending to lob a ball to Tyrell.

She moves a little closer to me, and her sweet scent, which I now know contains a hint of peppermint, wafts around me. "The best. You're good with them."

"You sound surprised."

"I am. I just didn't know there was all that smiling and laughter in there." She taps my chest with the back of her knuckle, and that tiny bit of contact shouldn't make me feel like I was hit with a shot of adrenaline. "I'm surprised to see you here. Didn't you just get back from…where were you?"

I look down at her, finding it interesting that she's following our games. "Houston."

"Huh. Well, thanks for making the time. It means the world to them." Her bright green eyes peer up at me. "I gotta get going."

"I met your dad out there," I blurt, wanting her to know just in case I completely misread the situation.

She exhales a long breath, her head falling to the side, and she scratches at her neck. I notice a tiny curl coiled at the base of her hairline, and I want to pull it and watch it bounce back. *What the hell am I doing? I'm not doing this.*

I should not be noticing Andie's impeccable ass or thinking about her thighs and how they fit in my hand. It should not feel like someone popped me with jumper cables from one small bare knuckle bumping my chest. I cannot be staring at curls, wanting to know just how soft they really are.

She halts my scolding mind. "I'm…going to guess he shook your hand and thanked you for coming." Her head falls forward as she kicks the toe of her black lace-up boot into the floor. Her tone is filled with sadness, and dammit, I don't like the tug it generates at the center of my chest.

It was one hug in a moment of emotional overload, and now my body is taking liberties like we're really doing the things people say we are. The joke's on my hormones. This woman barely even tolerates me.

I force myself to get it together. "Something like that. When I saw him, I expected something different than a handshake."

"Yeah, well, when this hospital consumes your whole life, not much of the outside world filters in. Anyone he works with would be too considerate to bring up his daughter's tabloid escapades."

Her shoulders sag with what looks like sadness, and there's a finger poking at that big muscle in my chest, wanting it to wake up and pay attention.

"Alright, kiddos." A nurse in blue scrubs walks into the room. "I hate to break up the party, but lunch is coming around, and it's time for vital checks."

There's a collective groan as kids turn toward the door. "Will you guys come to see our rooms?" One little girl asks as she's wheeled by.

"Sure," I say. "We'll make the rounds in a few minutes."

She grins as she's pushed out the door.

Tyrell joins us, and I suspect letting him anywhere near Andie will be a mistake, but it's too late.

"So I understand your elevator time with this ray of sunshine just keeps bringing you more joy."

Andie laughs. "Seems so. The stories just keep getting better."

"Tyrell, this is Andie." I give him a look, asking him to behave himself, which I know will be ignored.

He sticks out his hand. "It's nice to meet you, Andie." He's wearing a smug grin I'd love to wipe from his face.

"Your reenactment over there was uncanny," Andie says, referring to Tyrell's touchdown.

"You're a Tigers fan? Man, I knew I liked you."

"I'm only a fan of *some* Tigers." Her eyes roam to me briefly. "One of your running backs is looking tired and…old."

Tyrell bursts out laughing like it's the funniest thing he's ever heard. I could punch him.

"You know, he is pretty slow. We have to knock him around some to get him to step up and make a play."

I glare at him. I know exactly what he's doing, and it won't work. My body may be responding to Andie, but my mind knows there's no room in my life for a woman. I've been there and tried that, and it blew up in my face.

"We should probably make rounds and head out." I want to wrap this up before Tyrell takes things any further.

"You're putting on a concert at the event you two are working on?" Tyrell asks.

"Yeah, it's just me and a band. Nothing too exciting." Andie downplays it, but I've seen her with just a piano or guitar, and I know it will be unforgettable.

"Great. My wife will be the one in the front row pretending to be a backup singer. She's still talking about you singing the national anthem."

Andie smiles. "Awesome. I'm looking forward to it." She grabs the handle on her case and drapes her bag across her body, then turns to me. "I don't know if you saw it, but Miranda sent a list of questions we need to respond to. Let me know how you want to handle that."

I nod. "I'll take a look at it."

She looks between Tyrell and me as we follow her out into the hallway. "Thanks for coming today. Have fun checking out their rooms, but be careful. They might never let you leave." She smiles, her eyes shining as she turns away and walks in the opposite direction.

"Hmmmm," Tyrell hums.

"Don't even start," I grumble. "It's not happening."

"I don't know what, but something is happening, alright. You have your work cut out for you with that one."

"Nobody's working on anything." I turn, moving toward the rooms.

I hear him snicker behind me. Then his patronizing hand rests on my shoulder, and I'm tempted to slap it away.

"That woman is beautiful, smart, and there isn't an ounce of her that is interested in your good-looking, successful ass. She's perfect, and if you hang out in denial too long, you're going to miss your chance at snagging a woman who's actually worthy of being in your life."

"Simmons, you're getting on my last nerve."

"She's too good for you. You wouldn't stand a chance anyway."

I shake my head, unable to argue with that.

Chapter 22

SEAN

ANDIE: I can't meet today. Sorry.

ME: You ok? We only have a couple of weeks. We need to get back to Miranda.

ANDIE: Yeah, I know. Sorry.

ME: I have a game this weekend. Today is the only day I'm free.

ANDIE: I'm stuck at home today. I'll call later. Hopefully, we can handle it over the phone.

It's my day to sit on my couch, rest my body, and catch up on sports news. I was supposed to meet with Andie to finalize plans for the event in two weeks. But after her cryptic message, that's apparently not happening.

I hope she's ok. I'm sure she's fine, but if she wasn't, would she tell me?

I don't care. It's none of my business. Things come up, and she has a life. One that I'm not a part of, and that's how it will be.

I rest my head on the back of my couch, needing my mind to stop.

After running into her at the hospital, I put my traitorous hormones back in the box where they belong. All it took was another perusal of the stories and comments Morgan continues to spread to make me remember why I'll remain single and focus on playing football while I still can.

I know the day is coming when my body won't allow me to play the game my team and organization need me to play, but that day isn't today. So that's my main focus. That and getting my priorities realigned, which I'm making significant progress on.

I've removed much of the noise plaguing my life, and I'm beginning to settle into the stillness I've been craving–the calm, safe freedom of my own space.

My phone buzzes next to me, and I hope it's Andie. Besides finalizing the last-minute details, I need to tell her about a little thing Miranda is requesting. It's something I'm pretty sure Andie's not going to be excited about.

I flip my phone over, and my hope deflates. It's Rob.

"Hi, Rob."

"Hey, Sean. How are things?"

He and I are still getting to know each other, but he's been more helpful in the past few days than Craig was in a month. He's not someone I can read yet, but something about his tone has me bracing myself.

"I'm good. I'm having a rare quiet day today." I force myself to stay relaxed, hoping I'm misreading his tone.

"Well, that's good. I have some information for you that I'm not sure you'll like. I've been poking around and asking some questions. I'm hearing rumblings of a possible trade deal."

My stomach folds in on itself. *A trade? The Tigers want to trade me?*

I've been with the Tigers for the past four years. I have one more season on my contract. Then, I can evaluate my options or consider retiring if I'm ready, but I never imagined not finishing my career with this organization.

"What? They're talking about trading me? To where?" I feel betrayed and try to keep my emotions in check. I can't imagine starting with a new team and leaving all my teammates.

"I'm not sure. I'm hoping it's just rumors. Apparently, Craig was quietly shopping around. I don't know if that was on his own or if he had a conversation with the Tigers. As far as I can tell right now, the Tigers either aren't looking to trade, or they're keeping all talks behind closed doors."

There's silence on the line, but my head is beginning to pound with uncertainty. I was such an idiot to stick with that dick for so long.

"Sean, don't worry about this yet. Let me sort out fact or fiction."

"Ok." I take a deep breath and push it out. "Thanks. I appreciate you letting me know. Whatever you find out, I want to know right away."

"Will do. I'll be in touch. Hang in there."

Rob hangs up, and I squeeze my phone so tight I'm surprised it doesn't break. I can't even think about picking up my life and moving it somewhere else. It's not like I have a family or much of a life here besides the Tigers, but this is just...

I run my hand over my head as my body tenses with thoughts of being sent off to another team. *Why? Why would they do this? Why now?*

All this shit with Morgan and people looking at me like I'm the scum of the earth was one thing, but I never thought my team would kick me out for this. Something I didn't even fucking do.

I sit forward, resting my arms on my legs and letting my head fall into my hands. I try to breathe, closing my eyes so I can think clearly about what this will mean. A wave of nausea rolls through me as I consider being sent to a team looking to rebuild.

I can't sit here all day thinking about this and wondering if the inside of my organization is talking about trading me. I pace my living room, staring out at my backyard. I need something to do.

I look at my phone and back at Andie's messages. I think about texting her, but she said she's stuck at home. I contemplate it for only a second and then decide to screw it.

I grab my keys and head out to my truck, dialing Miranda's assistant.

"Hi. Yeah. It's Sean. I need a favor. Would you be able to pull an address for me?"

Chapter 23

ANDIE

I tiptoe from Axel's room, relieved to be able to put him down. The little booger fussed all night, and I'm pretty sure we only slept a total of four hours. I don't know if it's a cold, or teeth, or his apparent decision that I should hold him All. The. Time, but this is the first time I've been able to lay him down in his crib since yesterday afternoon.

I was supposed to meet Sean, but I knew that wasn't happening when Ax wouldn't even let Nora hold him without screaming. So here I am, still in my pjs at one in the afternoon, hurrying to shove dishes in the dishwasher, wipe down the counters, and get a load of laundry started before he wakes up again.

Every part of me wants to crawl into bed, but I know if I do that now, I'll never sleep tonight. I want to be working on the song that's started to come to life with Gem's exclusive wisdom about letting fear rule my life, but I'm not going to risk waking Ax up.

I give Snipe a long scratch behind the ear and drop a large scoop of food into his bowl as I leave the laundry room. Moving from one side of the main area to the other and back like a robot vacuum, I collect things as I go, ending up with a full load of misplaced things that need to go back to where they belong. For a single woman and a baby, we live like pigs.

I need to call Sean and get the remaining details of our event sorted out, but I need a minute to chill out. Once this event is over, it will be a relief. Then, we can both move on with our lives.

When he showed up at the hospital the other day, I was surprised to see him. The man I sat in the elevator with for two hours wouldn't have taken the time out of his precious schedule to do that. But the guy standing in the doorway of the common room filled with kids wasn't the same man. I watched him get down on the floor with the kids, smiling and laughing. It was nice to see him relaxed and having fun.

Sean is like a flower, unfolding bit by bit, but he's still a mystery. The way he hugged me in the conference room at the Tigers practice facility tells me his emotions run deep. I know there are deep wounds and scars, but he covers them well.

It's a funny thing. The more I learn about him, the more I wonder if he and I are really all that different. We're two people from completely different worlds but have wounds that bleed the same.

Just as I finish straightening, ready to make myself a cup of tea and warm myself in the ray of sunlight flooding the room, I hear tires on gravel.

My heart rate spikes at the possibility of it being my mother. I've been ignoring her calls, but I cannot handle a round with her today. I'll tap out at two seconds. I know it's not Nora, and Gem had plans this afternoon, so I'm praying someone made a wrong turn.

I peer out the window, expecting to see my mother and wondering if I can pretend I'm not home. I frown. Instead, I see a large black truck pull to a stop, and then… *What. In. The...*

I stand unmoving and watch Sean get out of his truck. He looks around as I wonder what in the hell he is doing here–at my house. Then, I look down, taking note of what I'm wearing. One of Josh's old Army t-shirts that's lost the hem around the neck and now hangs off my shoulder, pajama shorts, and purple knee-high socks with unicorns that Nora gave me for my birthday.

I push at my curls bound on top of my head. Seriously, someone should post a picture of this to set the world straight about the idea of Sean and me.

I cringe, trying to figure out what in the world I'm going to do. On the one hand, I could hide. On the other hand, Snipe will go ballistic at a strange male knocking on my door.

And time's up. Snipe growls at the sound of Sean approaching, and I shush him, hoping he doesn't bark and wake Ax. I really need Ax to sleep, so deciding to go with the 'who gives a shit' attitude and deal with it, I open the door as Sean climbs the steps.

His eyes grow wide with surprise, and he steps back as Snipe darts between us, barking in warning.

"Sniper," I whisper yell. "Calm. Down." I gesture, and he plops down but stays between Sean and me, his teeth bared as he growls.

Sean's wide gaze flicks between my dog and me and back again.

"Snipe," I say again in a calming tone. "Easy." He reluctantly eases himself to the porch floor but doesn't give Sean any space to approach.

Sean remains perfectly still, but his eyes roam over me quickly before meeting mine. I cross my arms and lean against the door. "What are you doing here?"

"Nice outfit," he says, but there's no feeling in it.

He looks…terrible. His short hair is mussed to one side, his eyes are red, and it's the first time I've seen him scruffy. His short whiskers are only a shade lighter than his blond hair, so they are barely there, but I see them. He's got on a hoodie and gym shorts, and that stoney look from the elevator has returned.

"Are you here as the fashion police or to tell me our affair is over?"

He ignores my flippant question as he glances around in all directions. "Can I come in? I…when I left home, I drove around to make sure no one followed me, but they're good at what they do."

I stare at him for a second, thinking about Ax. Letting Sean in is allowing him into a part of my life that's private, off limits, and I want it to remain that way. Axel is everything in the world to me. I know he didn't start this, but I want the negativity and the stories to stay far away from my baby.

"What are you doing here?" I ask again, noticing the cup of tea in his hand. *Well, crap. Can I send him away if he did something sweet?*

"I brought you this." He holds out the to-go cup, and the cool breeze catches the tea tag. "I thought maybe you were sick." His eyes roam over me again, and I feel very exposed. Now, I need him to go away.

"Thank you, but this really isn't a good time. I know you're busy, but…maybe we can meet up tomorrow, or I can call you later."

A little crease appears between his eyebrows, and then his blue eyes seem to take on some kind of understanding.

"Oh, I'm sorry. I didn't realize…you were busy."

It's my turn to frown. *What is he talking about? Oh. Oooohhhhh.* He thinks I have someone here. Well, I do, but definitely not in the way he's thinking. *Bugger.* Now, I have to decide if I'm going to let him in or just let him think I'm hooking up with someone for real…although it wouldn't really be for real.

He takes a tentative step up, keeping an eye on Snipe to hand me the tea. "Here. I'll just let you get back to it or…whatever." He suddenly appears drained and defeated, and he looked troubled to begin with. He turns and takes the first step down.

I take a breath and open the door wide, standing to the side. *Here goes nothing. I really hope I don't regret this.*

"Sean."

He turns to look over his shoulder, and it takes him a second to register the open door. "I thought–"

I cut him off. "Just…come inside."

I take a step back, gesturing for him to come in. Snipe hesitantly enters first, sticking close. Before stepping inside, Sean looks around again at the trees bordering my property and back toward the road. He stands just inside the door, surveying the open space that holds my kitchen, living room, and piano. He shoves his hands into his hoodie, facing me.

"I'm sorry. I called Miranda's assistant and got your address. I didn't mean to intrude or…overstep boundaries." He's stiff and uncomfortable–not the confident, easy-going guy I've seen recently. The man standing before me is not the guy I play Words with, and I wonder what's going on.

"Huh. Are you entitled to everyone's address or just mine?" I mean it as a joke, but he doesn't bite. His face is stoic, and his body is rigid.

"Are you ok?" I take a sip of the tea he brought me. It's peppermint with honey, just how I like it, and I'm surprised he remembered.

He shrugs his broad shoulders, not making eye contact, and that tells me whatever it is, he doesn't want to talk about it. I can respect that, but still, I'm wondering why he showed up at my house when we could have tried to work through Miranda's email over the phone.

"I thought maybe we could just knock out the last details quickly and get on with it, but if you have other things going on, then–"

I hold up my hand, stopping him. "It's fine, and you're…here, but I should probably warn you–"

I'm cut off by the coo coming through the baby monitor. *Great.*

Sean frowns. "What's that?"

Snipe hops up from where he was lying at my feet and trots down the short hallway to wait at Ax's door. More noises come through the monitor, and I move to snatch it off the counter, muting it.

"Andie, what was that?" He looks around like he's expecting something to pop out at him. "Andie…" The monitor pops on again with Ax's fussy grunts, and Sean just stares at me, his face morphing from confusion to…alarm. "What is that?" His agitation is growing, and I don't understand.

For some reason, I feel like I'm being interrogated in my own home, and the look of absolute horror on his face has me shooting from one to a hundred.

I cross my arms over my chest. "My son," I answer, trying to keep my temper in check.

"You have a son?" I'm not sure if that's a statement or a question, so I let it hang. "Andie, you have a son." I think he's saying it more to himself than to me, but my annoyance allowance has tipped over my maximum limit.

"Uh. I birthed him. I'm very well aware. Thank you."

"Shit, Andie." He rakes a hand over his head, looking like he might puke.

What in the hell is his problem? "Look, I don't know what your deal is, but I need to go get him."

He shoves his hands back into his front pocket. "Why didn't you tell me?" His voice is so soft, but it sends me to the moon.

"Oh, I'm sorry. I didn't realize having fictitious sexual relations with you required me to divulge all of my deepest and most precious personal details." I stare at him and the look of disbelief on his face. *What is his freaking problem?* Then, I think I understand.

"Wait. Waaaiiiitttt. Are you afraid people will think he's yours?" I spit it out like someone had just poured gasoline into my mouth.

"What?! No! Andie, no. Shit!" He moves to sit on the couch, putting his head in his hands.

"Go ahead and make yourself comfortable." I move toward the hallway and bedroom where Axel is crying. I don't know what Sean's problem is, but I'm about to kick his muscled ass out of my house.

I push the bedroom door open and lean over the crib's railing. "Hey, monster."

I pick Ax up and pull him to my chest, rocking back and forth. I need a minute to collect myself, or I might kill the big, bewildered football star sitting on my couch. I sing to him softly as I change his diaper, taking my time.

I hope this wasn't a mistake, letting Sean in. This is my life, and I don't need the drama that seems to follow him anywhere near here.

I thought maybe we were becoming friends, although I'd never tell him that, but now I'm seriously wondering if that's possible. The way he's acting is taking me straight back to Elevator Sean, and friendship with that guy is a big, fat HELL TO THE NO.

Chapter 24

SEAN

I'm trying to take some deep breaths, but a fat ass elephant is sitting on my chest. Coming here was a mistake. I should have just stayed home. But no, the need to get out of the house and the possibility of being traded depleted my common sense. Now, I'm here, unwelcome, only to discover that Andie has a baby.

This just makes it so much worse. Not only have I dragged her into this mess, but there's a child involved, and I don't know how to make this better. I didn't think Morgan and her lies could get worse, but this…I hate myself.

Andie should've never been wrapped up in this, let alone trying to keep her child safe and away from horrific tales being spun.

I know what this has done to my life with team management and my sponsors, but these were my choices. I spent time with Morgan and let her have a place in my life. Andie was just an innocent bystander, who I now know has a child and shouldn't have to worry about fending off made-up stories about her love life.

I hear Andie talking, and I lift my head.

"Alright, booger. That wasn't a very long nap." She walks back into the room, holding a baby, her guard dog trailing behind.

She sits on the other end of the couch, avoiding eye contact while she lays the baby against her chest. I have no idea how old he is, but he still looks tiny to me. He lifts his head when he notices me, his inquisitive blue eyes staring. I give her a few seconds, but Andie continues to ignore me.

"Andie." I try carefully, feeling like the biggest asshole in the entire world.

"If you say my name like that one more time, I will give Snipe the command, and he'll show you to the door."

"Say it like what?"

"Like…you're disappointed in me." She says it on an exhale, and I hear what sounds like hurt in her voice, which I don't understand, but it makes me feel horrible.

My whole body shifts to face her and that ridiculous statement. "Andie, I feel like the biggest jerk in the entire universe. I've been walking around for weeks, knowing just being near me for a few minutes turned your life into a nightmare, and that was enough to make me want to crawl into a hole and pile the dirt on top. I couldn't stand what people were saying and being unable to do anything about it or make any part of it better."

Her son fists the sleeve of her shirt and rests his head on her shoulder.

"This…you having a child only makes it so much worse. You shouldn't have had to deal with any of this, but you have a baby. What if someone follows you or they find out where you live and start parking outside your house like they do mine sometimes? What if they get pictures of you with him, and he becomes the new target? Andie…" I'm furious. My heart is pounding at the possibilities of how this could go.

I want to call Morgan and tell her this is done. Whatever she wants, however she wants to deface me, carry on. But not one more word about Andie. Not one more fucking word.

I run a hand over my face, trying to calm down. This whole situation needs to end.

"There's nothing we can do about it," she says softly. "He's my first priority." Her hand runs up his back and then down again.

"Andie, I'm so sorry."

"Stop." Her hand pushes toward me in a halting motion. "Don't apologize. You didn't do this."

"But it was my selfish decisions and the fact that I let myself get so far removed from what matters and what's really important that led to this happening. I was such a self-absorbed prick."

She gives me a raised brow side-eye. "I'm not going to argue with that." I sink down into the couch and stare at the ceiling. "Sean, all that may be true, but the reality is, your ex decided to sell a bunch of lies, not caring who she hurt in the process. You can't own that. We just have to figure out how best to live through it and make it to the other side. That's what we've been doing, and now that you know about Ax, it doesn't change that."

I turn my head toward her. "Ax?"

One side of her mouth turns upward. "Sean, meet Axel, my son. Ax, meet Sean, the mediocre football star your mommy is supposedly doing the dirty with."

A second ago, I was about to lose my shit, and then this woman goes and says something like that, and I instantly want to laugh. I wonder how she does it–remains light and grounded despite her circumstances. I envy that and could use a little of that in my life. Rather than sitting around hyperventilating, I need to focus on what I can control and move forward.

I peek at her out of the corner of my eye. "Doing the dirty? What are you, still in high school?"

She shrugs. "Well, we're not friends. The only thing that links us is the scandalous rumors about what we're doing behind closed doors."

"So you're saying we're non-friends with no benefits?" My lips tug upward, and it feels really good.

She grabs a pillow wedged between her and the arm of the couch and throws it at me. "Why are you still here? I'd think you'd be busy getting pampered or waited on or fawned over on your limited time off."

I slump into the couch even further, stretching out my legs, remembering why I came. We need to talk about the event, but I came because I needed a distraction, and I definitely got one.

I feel her eyes on me. "Go ahead, boyfriend, relax and make yourself comfortable."

I put my feet up on the small table in front of me, knowing it'll irritate her further. "Actually, I'm kind of taking a break from the superficial, self-indulgent kinds of things. I'm looking to do more meaningful things with my free time."

"Annnnndddd…sitting here with me qualifies as meaningful in your newly found sense of humility?"

I look around, trying to choose my words carefully. I don't know much about this woman, but I know she's different. I might even venture as far as special. For sure, she's nothing if not real, and it's a bit addicting.

She's been through a lot, and even though I'm not sure I can compare my life to hers, I can't help but feel we might have some things in common. I know she doesn't want to be my friend, but I could use a non-friend who doesn't give a shit about who I am or what I do. So it feels good to sit here and have her tell me straight-up what she thinks, holding nothing back. She has absolutely no idea how good it feels and how rare it is for me.

"Actually, yes. I wanted to check on you, but we need to finalize the event details. Now, I'm glad to know lowlife tabloid photographers aren't camping out and making your life hell."

She studies me for a long second, biting the corner of her bottom lip just barely before peeking down at Ax, who's fallen asleep against her. "I'm sorry you have to deal with that all the time. I know it comes with the territory, but it shouldn't have to."

"It doesn't bother me so much until it affects someone else." Silence fills the room, but there's no awkwardness. I figure this might be a good time to break some bad news to her. "I need to tell you about something."

Her head tips in my direction. "Is it going to make me want to kick you in the balls?"

"I hope not." I cringe at the thought. "Miranda stopped me the other day. Ed McNeil is throwing a party for the team and the organization. He's big on team bonding. He wants us to attend to help spread the word about the event." I put my hands behind my head, waiting for her to say no.

"So he wants us to talk it up to make him look good?"

I have to think about the question. I've known Ed since I started with the Tigers, and he's never struck me as that kind of person. "I don't think so. I've always considered him pretty generous. He loves outreach and likes to support when he can. I think this is his way of trying to get more of the team involved and those working behind the scenes to put the effort in to make it great."

I pause, my mind returning to the trade rumors, but I stop the thoughts. "Some of the guys have taken Morgan's side, but if the event gets Ed's endorsement, more of them will pay attention."

Andie's head rolls in my direction. "Seriously, your teammates think that Morgan's story is legit?"

I rub my temples. "Some of their wives and girlfriends are friends with her. It's what I get for trying to be discreet about our break up."

"It's a crock of poop. I don't know how anyone can believe those crocodile tears. I'm sorry. That really sucks."

"Yep." It really does.

She adjusts Ax's position. "What about your other friends?"

I let out a self-deprecating laugh. "What friends? I've recently discovered the people I was spending time with weren't even close to being my friends."

She eyes me briefly, but I can't look at her. I know how stupid I've been. Whatever look she has on her face, I don't want to see it.

"So you and I have to go together? Do you think that's a good idea? People will talk for sure."

"Andie, they're already talking. Some of them know Morgan made it all up, and they'll be at the event. The rest of the organization…" *Think I'm a lying, cheating bastard and want to trade me.* "Whoever is there will hopefully have a better understanding of why this is important. If we go together or separately or I go by myself…they've all already made up their mind about us anyway."

She kisses the baby's head. "People suck. I want this to be a success and for the families to feel honored. That's what's important. When is it?"

"Next week. I wasn't going this year, but I guess I am now." Not only because of this event but because my relationship with the Tigers may be on the line. I choose to keep that to myself. It doesn't affect Andie or the event, and for now, it's just more rumors circulating. "I feel like I owe Ed for being supportive and helping make it happen."

I hear her exhale. "Well, great. I guess I better find a dress."

The dog at Andie's feet pops up.

"What is he–"

"Shhhh," Andie hushes me as she carefully leans forward and gets up, walking to the window where the dog stands with his ears perked. "Nooooo," Andie spins back to me. "No. No, no, no, no, noooooo."

"What?" I sit forward. She spins back toward the window and then back to me, holding Ax tightly, but her face is pale. "Andie, what?" I start to stand, but she rushes my way.

"It's my mother. And don't even think about saying you're leaving now. You owe me. Here." She carefully lifts Ax away from her to hand him to me and commands her dog to stand down.

"Andie, no." I try to resist, but before I can, the baby is sliding from her arms to mine, and I have no freaking clue what's going on. I've only held one baby in my life, and that was months ago, for about two minutes. I have no idea what to do with this one.

"Just lay him on your chest and support him with your hands. Make him feel safe." She stands, looking down at herself and then back at me. "If I had earplugs, I'd give them to you." Her face falls, and she closes her eyes at the forceful knocks on the door. "Please try not to listen. This is going to be–"

Another round of quick knocks erupts as her dog growls, but she lets him. Andie walks to the door, slowly pulling it open. I'm not sure what this is about or what Andie is expecting, but I didn't like the look on her face or how she slumped her way to the door like she's readying herself for a beating.

I peek down at the warm, soft little body snuggled on my chest. His sleeping face is squished against me, and his long, dark eyelashes are pressed tightly together. If me holding him gives her comfort, I'll do the best I can. The not-listening thing isn't likely.

Just make him feel safe. I spread my hand over Ax's back and hold him against me a little tighter, hoping he stays asleep.

"Hello, Mother," Andie says, pulling the door open. Without being invited in, her mom steps into the house like she's a general invading.

"Andrea, I have tried to call you, and I am fed up with you not returning my calls." She stops when she sees me sitting on the couch. "What is this? What is he doing here? I thought you said this was all a misunderstanding." Her mom's eyes roam over me like I'm some kind of bacterial specimen.

Andie's posture stiffens as her dog moves to sit at her feet between the two of them. I like this dog.

"Oh, you know, he just stopped by for a quickie before his next game." I quietly clear my throat at her statement. Andie's eyes meet mine, and they're filled with fire.

"Andrea, is this amusing to you? Do you have any idea what people are saying? I have people calling and asking if this is true, that you and he…I'm spending my days trying to clear this up while you're here doing…whatever this is. This is going to stop. Look at you. You're a mess."

Andie puts her hands on her hips. "Is that all?" She looks around. "This is my house, and if I want to look like this or walk around butt naked, then that's exactly what I'm going to do. And, Mother, I'll do that in front of whoever I want."

Her mom's mouth falls open and then snaps shut. "Andrea, what is wrong with you? You're a mother now, and this is how you're behaving? You should be ashamed of yourself. This is not how you were raised."

I sit completely still, not to disturb the baby, but my body tenses with fury at how her mom is talking to her. If it weren't for Andie's request to hold Ax, I'd be off this couch and hauling this woman to her car by the pearls around her neck.

Andie's chest rises with a long inhale, and she releases it. "You're right, Mother. This is not how I was raised, but this is my life, and I get to decide how to live it."

Her mom scoffs. "Yes, well, I heard that when you ran off and married Josh. Look how that turned out for you. Here all alone, raising a baby. This isn't how it's supposed to be."

Andie looks in my direction for a long second, but she's not looking at me. She's looking at her son, and I can't stand the pain all over her face.

"You alright?" I whisper quietly. Her eyes rise to mine, locking there. She stares at me, bleeding wide open, but only for a second before she blinks it away. But I saw it. The grief is so raw and so evident I feel it wind its way through my chest. She nods, but it's so subtle I barely see it.

Her mom looks at me with disgust, but Andie's soft words pull her glaring eyes away.

"Don't talk to me about how this is supposed to be." Her voice is calm and quiet. Crushed. I see her swallow. "I am alone, which isn't how this is supposed to be. Nor was finding out I was pregnant and never even getting to tell my husband. Or lying in bed at night and wondering how in the world I would do this on my own. Or how about, Mother, driving myself to the hospital when I went into labor or that my own parents have never even acknowledged my son."

She takes a quick breath, her arms moving around herself and one hand curling over the center of her chest, where I feel it ache within my own. "None of this is the way it's *supposed* to be. So you may not like how I live or dress or who I spend time with, but you will *never* tell me how it's supposed to be when it comes to my son. Do you understand me?"

Her mom gathers her purse tighter, her eyes flicking to the baby in my arms and then back at Andie. "All this rebellion and lashing out, it's all going to catch up with you, and when it does, I just hope you haven't wasted all your opportunities to make some kind of life for yourself."

She turns and walks to the door without another word. Andie stands frozen in place for a whole minute, and I can only watch her. I didn't have parents or a family or anyone to call mine, and I always thought those who did were the luckiest people in the world. I thought they had no idea how good they had it. How blessed they were. I see now, very clearly, that some of those who had what I wished so deeply for were just as lonely as I was.

Andie eventually turns but doesn't look at me, her lips pushing to the side. "So, how much of that did you hear?"

"Every single word." There's not a chance I'm going to pretend.

She rubs her forehead. "Think it's possible you can forget all of it?"

"Nope. I couldn't even if I wanted to, and I don't."

Her eyes snap to mine, and then she walks and flops down on the couch, pulling a blanket off the back and wrapping it around herself.

"Want to talk about it?" I know she'll say no, but I want to offer.

"No. I'm sure the picture is pretty clear."

"We don't have to talk about it, but just so you know, I didn't like it. I don't know much about family dynamics, but I know that's not how it should be."

She bites her lip, thinking. "Thanks for holding Ax. I don't want him anywhere near that."

"I was scared shitless he was going to wake up."

She leans closer to look at him. "You want me to take him?"

I peek down at him. "Actually, no."

"Don't you need to get home and get your beauty rest or something? Or are you just going to sit around here all night waiting to witness more of the wreckage that is my life?" She tucks her legs up underneath her, sounding a little more like herself.

"Is that an invitation?"

She meets my eyes again with a hint of a smirk that makes me smile. Looking at her with this baby on my chest and everything that just happened, I can't imagine what it must be like raising a child alone. Again, I feel like I've been living in such a small world. My own little world where everything was fine and nothing else existed.

I must be staring because her smirk turns to a frown. "What?"

I shake my head. "Nothing, sorry."

She purses her lips. "If you have something to say, just say it. That's a benefit of us not being friends. You can say whatever you want, and if it sucks, I still won't like you anyway."

"So, not friends *with* benefits?" I just want to push her buttons.

"Ugh. You're annoying."

I chuckle. "Fine. If I can say anything I want, I just thought, I can't imagine going through all you have and raising a baby by myself." I try to find the right words. "It's just another reminder of how small of a world I've been living in."

She tips her head to the side like she's trying to see through what I said. I know she didn't want me to see and hear all that just went down, but I don't want her to be embarrassed or ashamed, so I'll expose a little of my own remorse.

"You weren't wrong that day in the elevator about me being shallow. I have been. I got so caught up, moving from one day to the next, doing what I was told, and keeping things simple I got lost. I've forgotten what the real world is like. People and the lives that they lead that don't look like mine. I should know better, given how I grew up."

I grimace, thinking about it. "Life might look perfect on a screen scrolling through pictures, but life isn't supposed to be like that. It's supposed to be messy and hard sometimes. It's taking me some time to get back to swimming in the deep, remembering what it feels like and how not to drown. This stuff with Morgan kind of gave me a shove, but even with all of that, it's nice to feel the difference."

Andie runs the edge of the blanket between her fingers. "With your life…it is so easy for that to happen. If I lived the life my mom wanted me to, I'd have been in the kiddy pool right there with you. Cut yourself a little slack. If you're not careful, it's so easy to step into a giant pile of crap and get lost in it. But it's the ones who find their way out, clean themselves off, who never make that mistake again."

"You think?" I hope she's right. Backsliding is a real fear, and I never want to find myself there again.

She nods. "If you finally realize how bad you stink, you'll never go back to that."

She rests her head back and stares at the ceiling before rolling her head towards me. She looks tired. More of her hair is spilling out from the top of her head, and her green eyes have dark circles underneath them. Yet, she's still beautiful.

"Do you ever feel like you just want to punch someone in the face?" Her face is so serious I bite my cheek to keep from smiling.

I don't have to think about it. "Most recently, about fifteen minutes ago."

She laughs. "She has that effect on people."

"Has it always been like that?" Now that we're talking about it, I can't help my curiosity.

She lets out a breath. "Pretty much. It wasn't as bad until I decided I should have a say in my own life." She eyes me, deciding if she wants to say more. "The shit really didn't hit the fan until I married Josh. I'm sure you've gathered he didn't meet their one-dimensional standards, but for me, he was the first person besides Gem to…see me. He didn't care that I could sing or that I was a Taninbaugh. He didn't push me to do or be anything I wasn't. He just loved…me."

She pulls the blanket up a little like she's revealing too much. "We got married, and that was really it. She said she hoped I'd come to my senses. She can't seem to understand that it's going to be a cold day in hell before that ever happens. I lived with Josh on base for a while, and being away made it easier. But when we decided I should come back to pursue my music more seriously, that's when she started to stick her nose in again. I think she thought I was back because things weren't good between Josh and me. Anyway, now I have Ax, and there's no way he's growing up like I did with all that pressure and feeling like he never measures up."

I give her a second to say more if she wants, but she doesn't. "You're incredibly brave. You know that, right?" I run a gentle hand down the baby's back, realizing I like the protective feeling of his little body next to mine. "Going through all that you have alone."

She lets out a breath. "In the moment, it's not brave. It's more like being scared to death and just doing what you have to do to make it through. But thank you for saying that. Something tells me you might know a little bit about that, too."

I don't look at her, knowing she's right. I do know what it is like to be so scared you just do whatever is necessary to make it to the next day.

She reaches over and runs a finger over her son's cheek. "If you really don't mind holding him for a bit, I'm going to go make a giant pan of nachos, and then we can knock this event stuff out. We didn't get much sleep last night. I wonder if he felt a cold chill in the air or the underground rumblings and knew the Dame of Narcissists was coming."

I laugh, and it feels so good. "I really don't mind, but nachos?"

"You don't like nachos?" She draws back like my question is offensive. "I knew I was a good judge of character. Who doesn't like nachos piled high with all of that spicy goodness? It's like a taco but so much better. It's also the best pigout food ever, and after that little showdown, I plan to eat on the couch with my hands like the unrefined woman I am."

"You add burping and farting to that, and you've got yourself the ultimate revenge." The sound of her laughter is like joy after a crappy day. "Nachos are fine. I'm just usually careful what I eat during the season."

She rolls her eyes. "Sean, you might just need to learn to live a little. You know, break the rules every now and then. You can eat and return to your finely tuned dietary restrictions tomorrow."

She throws the blanket down on the couch and goes into the kitchen. I hear the clang of the pan and the beeping of the oven, but as she works, she hums, and it's the most beautiful sound. I wonder if she hums all the time or even realizes she's doing it. I can imagine sitting here and watching her play the piano and sing all night.

I peek over my shoulder at her as she spreads chips over a cookie sheet. Her mom said that she looked like a mess, and she kind of does, but she looks like a hot mess, and I don't mean that in the terrible sense. Her bare shoulder hanging out of the collar of her shirt is sexy as hell, and her knee-high socks are ridiculous, but they're like a tease leading up to her bare thighs that are slender and defined. Those thighs I already know fit perfectly underneath my hand.

I should not be checking Andie out. I know this. She's incredibly beautiful, but her honest ability to be completely herself is freaking stunning. There's no facade or pretense. Her comfort and confidence in herself are intoxicating. The more I'm around her, the closer I want to be to her. She's refreshing and exhilarating and says she doesn't like me. I want to think about changing her opinion, but it's probably safer this way.

I came over here in a piss poor mood, and over the last hour, my entire attitude has changed. I brush my hand over Axel's head and realize I like it here. I like Andie and how she is with me, and even though I shouldn't be, I'm really happy I get to stay a little longer.

ME: I think I'm in deep shit.

SHANE: What kind? I don't have time to bail you out, and I'm getting too old to kick your ass.

ME: I think possibly, most definitely, the woman kind.
ME: It's not good.

SHANE: Shit.

ME: Yeah.

SHANE: Call Maggie.

Chapter 25

ANDIE

"Alright, let's run through the set list one more time, and then we'll make sure we're all set for rehearsal next week." I grab my binder, flipping through pages, and Jonesy does the same. "So after we welcome the families and introduce ourselves, we'll start with the first song."

"And you'll be introducing Greyson as your…?" Jonesy asks nonchalantly as he flips through.

Nora's snort from her perch on the couch has me wanting to whip my pen across the room at her.

"As my co-planner on this event." I try to sound as casual as possible because that's all he is.

Jonesy runs his hand over the plastic sheet cover of our setlist, smoothing it. "Hmmm. I heard the two of you had dinner together the other night. Here. Alone." He says 'alone' all deep and sexy like it was some romantic candlelit dinner.

I glare at Nora, who's rolling her lips to keep from laughing. "Yeah, we did. But clearly, *Nora* didn't mention that my mother came by. You can imagine how that went, so he stayed while I binged nachos and finalized details. It was sooooo romantic."

He lets out a soft, low whistle. "That sounds like a good time. He's a good man for sticking that out."

It's true. Sean sat there, and not once did he make me feel bad for how my mother acted. He was kind and thoughtful in asking me if I was ok right in the middle of her tirade, but it was his eyes. They held mine, and it was as if I could physically feel them reading me. In that moment, in the blink of an eye, I'm pretty sure he saw it all. Everything I'd never want him or anyone else to ever see. All of the holes burned into me time and time again for never being enough. For never measuring up and always ending up right back here. Alone.

But he never mentioned it. He held Ax tightly just like I asked him to, and funny enough, it seemed like he enjoyed it.

Seeing him with Ax snuggled up on his chest was something. There's no denying Sean is a very attractive man, but looking at him with my son sleeping soundly on his chest did something to my insides that I haven't felt in a really long time. Maybe ever, and that scares me a whole lot.

I never thought I could or would look at another man and feel anything like what I felt when I was with Josh. My heart belonged to him alone, but he's gone. My head knows this, but my heart wants to stay hidden. Locked up where it's safe.

Sitting on my couch, looking like a complete mess and giving Sean a hard time, was nice. It was easy and comfortable. Somehow, he seems to understand me in a way most don't.

It felt strangely natural to make dinner, feed Ax a bottle, and eat together, given how this all started and who I thought Sean was. After he left, I thought about what he said about getting caught up in all the pretension that constantly surrounds him. The fact that he was aware is one thing, but his taking action to change it tells me a lot about who he is and who he wants to be.

The thing is…even if I was ready to open myself up to someone again, when the event is over, Sean and I will go our separate ways. We live in two different worlds. He lives in the spotlight, and that's not a place I want to be.

I think sometimes people come into your life to simply help you get to the next phase. Maybe that's who Sean is for me. Someone who's helping me see that I don't have to be so afraid of the world that's waiting for me.

I run my finger down the setlist. "He was gracious. I owed him dinner after she treated him like he was part of a substandard species."

"He's an NFL star. What does she want? A foreign prince," Jonesy sneers.

"No, she wants Andie to marry a slimy surgeon of the worst kind, who can't keep his ding-a-ling from ding-donging more than one woman at a time." Nora just can't help herself. "Plus, he looks like he belongs in one of those ads for protein powder, although without any sort of muscles. So, like a really skinny weasel."

Jonesy chuckles and then turns more serious. "You know you deserve to be happy again, right? If Sean is a good guy, maybe you should consider giving him a chance."

"She's going to a party with him on Wednesday."

"Nora," I warn, but look at Jonesy's handsome, sweet face. "It's just…hard and scary. I have no idea how I'm supposed to know when I'm ready to think about it again."

"Maybe you should try *not* thinking about it." I wish I had his confidence. "No pressure. When you meet someone you want to spend time with, do it. When you're ready, it will happen naturally."

"Listen to you, Dr. Love," I tease. "You should start your own podcast. Nora can be your first guest since *she* hasn't had a date in at least three months," I say like it's a scandal. "She's so busy daydreaming about my love life she has no time for her own."

"It's not my fault I completely suck at dating. I meet a guy, instantly fall in love, and he never calls me again. I'm taking a break."

We laugh as we work through the setlist, making sure things are in order for our one and only rehearsal before the event.

When Jonesy has to leave, I walk him to the door, but he stops.

"I haven't been sure if I should bring this up, but we're partners, and you should know. I got a call from Mega. I know you met with Dirk to showcase some songs a couple of weeks ago, but he was pushing for information on you and Sean and wanted to know if I thought you'd be interested in signing with them."

"Why didn't he ask me himself when I was there?" I've known Dirk a long time, and he shouldn't be asking Jonesy when he can just ask me himself.

"Probably because he knew you'd say no. I didn't like how he was going about it, especially when I got the impression your tabloid debut is spurring his interest." Jonesy scratches his goateed chin. "My guess is he's trying to jump on the publicity and thinks if he can get you to sign, he's getting a bonus with what Sean can bring to the table."

I rub my forehead, feeling my agitation grow. "So now labels only want to work with me because they think Sean and I are a couple, and they can exploit that?"

He shrugs, his own irritation apparent. "All I know is this stuff with Sean has created a firestorm among our business contacts. Some are hesitant to work with you because of the cheating rumors, and it seems others think your current popularity is the perfect platform for sending you to the top. Sean is a bonus. You two could be the next 'it' couple."

"This makes me want to puke." My stomach rolls up in disgust. "This is what all my hard work has come to. They want to use a bunch of lies as a stepping stone to the stardom I've never wanted so they can make money." I push out a breath, needing a second. "I've worked with these guys for years. My songs are personal. They're a part of me, and I hand them over, letting someone else sing them because I don't want that life. It would kill me."

"I know," Jonesy says, and I know he understands.

"How am I supposed to sell my songs, our songs, to them when they only want to work with me because of who I might be sleeping with and what it will gain them? It's…gross. All of these jokers have known me long enough not to buy into it or at least respect me enough not to reduce me to a bunch of dollar signs."

"Then don't let them." Nora jumps in from the couch. "I wasn't eavesdropping. Or yeah, maybe I was, but I've been getting emails and phone calls. Certain labels want you, but I've been telling them no."

She scratches her head with her pen. "You two realize you don't need them, right? Stop selling your babies to these dirtbags and sell them yourself. Produce your own record and dictate your own tour schedule. Just a few shows. Ooooorrrr, start working with artists on your own. People know what you can do. You guys don't need them to act as your intermediary."

We stare at her, and she holds her hand up. "Ok, I'm out now. Just my two cents."

"It's not a bad idea," Jonesy shrugs.

"Yeah, but what about the royalties? We both need that."

"Not if we can sell enough on our own and prove that to other artists. It would be a risk but a start."

"I don't know." It would be a huge risk. Going out on our own means possibly failing, and I have to think about Ax.

Nora clears her throat, and I know she's got something else to add.

"Andie, your following skyrocketed when you sang the national anthem, and it's growing daily now that you're…whatevering with Sean. You put songs out there, and people are going to buy them. They want you, not someone else."

My gaze returns to Jonesy and his raised eyebrows as if trying to tell me it's true. "Let's make sure we think this through. Nora, you can work on telling us how far our reach would be, and maybe we can figure some numbers from there."

"Yes, ma'am," she sings sweetly.

I hug Jonesy goodbye with a million questions running through my head. This craziness with Sean just doesn't seem to end. The idea of singing my songs without being someone's property is appealing, but would it pay the bills? Would people buy what I have to offer if all they're getting is an unfiltered, raw, and painfully honest me?

I step out of the dressing room and spin.

"Sweet cheeks, are you trying to get the man to change his mind about being seen with you? If you're thinking that dress is a contender, we'll just run by the prison and ask for an orange jumpsuit."

I roll my eyes at Gem, seated in the dressing room with Ax on her lap. "Hmmm. I hadn't thought about getting Sean to change his mind, but now that you mention it…"

"Oh, pfft." I hear Gem tsk. "You're going, and you're going to make that man wish he really was sleeping with you and let everyone else know they messed with the wrong woman. Andie, there's no better revenge than showing up looking like an unaffected million bucks."

I unzip the ugly dress and drape it back on the hanger, although someone should put it out of its misery and burn it.

"How much longer do I have to do this? Can't I just wear one of the dresses I already have?"

"Not a chance. This calls for just the right dress, which must be jaw-dropping. You can't march your spectacular butt in there with all of these…fluffed and stuffed silicone Barbies looking like a tired breastfeeding hag."

"Why? I'm tired, and my boobs have seen better days. Although, your great-grandson has decided he's done with them. Thank goodness because I'm pretty sure my nipples wouldn't have survived." I zip up the last dress and step out.

One of Gem's penciled-in dark eyebrows arches up. "That, sugar butt, is going to make Sean want to do more than sleep with you."

"Oh, good grief. No one is trying to get Sean to think anything." I look down at the sleeveless black and white A-line dress. The solid black bodice is attached to a white pleated skirt. It is pretty and fits like it was made for me. Plus, black is my go-to color.

The other eyebrow goes up. "Why the hell not?! He's gorgeous, has a good heart, and…" She holds up her finger like this is the deciding point. "He sat through two of your mother's chastising sessions and once interrupted to ask if you're ok. What in the world are you waiting for?"

My mouth falls open, but I'm careful not to acknowledge the accuracy of her statements. They don't matter. Sean and I are working together. Although, his ability to remain unruffled by my mother's bullying is pretty damn attractive.

"Don't you and Nora have anything better to do than sit around gossiping about my life?"

"Andie, you know we don't. Besides, we're happy to thrive on your drama."

"I'm glad it's so entertaining." I turn back into the dressing room.

"I also heard about these labels wanting to cash in your newfound notoriety."

I tug my jeans back on. I'm pretty sure if I sneeze, this woman will know about it. The thing is, I really don't mind. She's always got my back and has the best advice.

"I also have to agree with Nora's advice for you and Jonesy to take matters into your own hands. Baby girl, you weren't meant to be a backup singer."

I slide the curtain open. "It's a big risk."

"But it's your music, and people want au-then-ti-ci-ty." She draws the word out. "They don't want this computer-generated garbage everyone knows would never survive unenhanced. You have a talent that is as rare as taut skin after sixty." I listen but busy myself collecting my things. She rests her hand on my arm to still me, forcing me to look at her. "There isn't much that compares to the simplicity of you and a piano or guitar. You have a gift. Just think about it."

I nod. I have been thinking about it. Working with Jonesy and being able to sing my own music would be a dream come true. It's when I look at Ax, the worry of failing calls long and hard.

I sit down beside her. "I'm thinking about it. It's a different kind of vulnerability, singing and selling myself. I don't need or even want the spotlight. I just want to be able to tell my stories. Sing them the way I hear them. I've had enough of people telling me who and what I should be."

She swings her arm around me and brings her cheek to mine. "People can't tell you who to be. They may want to, but it's a hell of a lot harder for them to speak when you're the one with the mic."

I lean into her familiar flowery scent and soft skin. With her, it feels so simple and safe. I want this. I want my music to be my own, not a hit that takes someone else to the top of the charts. I don't need to be at the top. I just want to share my stories in hopes they will help someone else.

"And I hate to break it to you, toots, but people are already watching your every move." She places Ax in my lap and pats my knee. "Now, let's go find some shoes to set that dress off."

I moan. "I have shoes."

She gives me the eye that says arguing is pointless. "Get your buns moving. Just any shoes won't do. The eye starts there, Andie, and travels up. You're going to this party, and my granddaughter is going to look like she's there to kick ass and take names."

Chapter 26

SEAN

My hotel room is silent, except for the buzz of the fan kicking on. I'm immensely familiar with quiet solitude. I like it. For a long time after leaving the group home, all I wanted was my own space and silence. Tonight, though, I'm itching for a distraction.

Our afternoon game tomorrow requires us to be here the night before, but more time with the team makes these trading rumors harder to bear. I want to know if they have validity, and Rob hasn't successfully pinpointed where they're coming from. He's hoping it's just more of the fallout from the firestorm Morgan created. I'd like to put my GM on the spot, but Rob advises I sit tight and see what he can casually squeeze out, not stirring up any ideas that don't exist.

My phone buzzes on the table beside me. Andie finally played a word. The smile creeping across my face at just the thought of her is dangerous. Thinking about Andie in any way other than my planning partner in this event will only hurt when it's all over.

The problem is I can't get sitting in her house, holding her baby, and listening to her hum and laugh out of my head. There hasn't been a time, maybe besides with my brothers, where I've felt completely relaxed and comfortable. My growing attraction to her brings about thoughts and feelings I've never experienced before.

The private things Andie said to her mom that night are stuck in my head, and I can't ignore them. I can't get over that her husband didn't know about Ax or that she had to drive herself to the hospital. That alone made me want to wrap my arms around her and hold her tight, knowing how terrifying all that must have been and how she faced it alone.

How her mom spoke to her makes anger spawn within me all over again. The more time I spend with Andie, the more I see what a kind and genuine person she is. She's rare and special, and I'm concerned when this event is over, I won't want to quit spending time with her. She's like a ray of sunshine in my artificially lit world.

While I stare at the Words board, trying to figure out my next play, Shane's name pops up, and I answer. "What's up, bro?"

"You just going to leave me hanging with the lady troubles?" His dry, grumbly tone is so familiar.

"You said to call Maggie."

"You haven't, so I assume that means you're in even deeper shit than you want to admit to someone intelligent enough to recognize it." *Damn.* I let that hang there because I'm pretty sure he's right. "So out with it, or I'll get Mark on the line, and he'll just nag you until he pisses you off enough you'll spill."

I groan and rest my head back against the headboard. Saying anything out loud feels like admitting something I'm not sure I'm ready for.

Shane huffs. "I don't have all day, so let me guess to get things moving. You're developing *feelings* for the woman you're not actually sleeping with."

"Shit, man. What's happened to you? You sound like a woman."

"I sleep next to one every night, and Liv is very sensitive. There's lots of sharing of feelings." He's trying to sound annoyed, but I know he's completely smitten with both ladies in his life.

I decide to try to carefully talk around this. "I don't know if feelings are the right word. I like her. I like being around her. She's…real, you know, and she couldn't care less about who I am."

"So, what's the problem?" Shane barks. "That can't be it, or you wouldn't sound like you're in an interrogation room without a lawyer." *Why does he have to know me so well?* "She's beautiful. I've seen pictures, but I know it's more than that. If that's all you were interested in, you would've stayed with Morgan." When I don't say anything, he all but yells at me. "Spit it out, or I'm calling Mark."

"Ugh. Fine. I like her…a lot. More than I should. She's beautiful and smart and so incredibly talented it's sick. She gives me more shit than I'll ever know what to do with, and when I'm with her, I can just be me." I pause, determining whether I want to tell him the next part. If it were Mark, he'd eat me alive, but I think Shane will get this. "She has a son. He's tiny, and the other night, I held him on my chest for an hour. I didn't hate it, man." *I liked it way more than I should.*

I give him a chance to say something, but when he remains quiet, I say the last thing that keeps floating through my mind. "The more I know about her, the more I want to know, and I already have a very good idea that she might be the strongest woman I've ever met. And you and Mark and I…we know what it means to survive."

I rub my head, feeling like a complete idiot waiting for him to respond. I wonder if the ridiculousness of it all has stunned my growly brother speechless.

When I'm ready to pull my phone away to make sure the line didn't drop, he speaks.

"I'm going to tell you something that I wouldn't tell anyone else, and if you ever repeat this, I will beat your ass." He pauses, letting out a breath, and I wait patiently, needing this to help me.

"When you meet someone who makes you laugh and drives you absolute bat shit crazy. Someone who makes your whole world better just by being near them, and when they're near, it takes every single ounce of your willpower to keep your hands off of them…That person who looks at you and sees nothing but the flawed person you are underneath and cares enough to stick around anyway because they think you're worth it. When you find that person, you do whatever is necessary to pull them in tight and pray that they never let go. I don't know anything, but I'm smart enough to know that feelings like that don't come around more than once if we're lucky."

Well, shit. I let out a long breath. "I feel like I'm insane for even thinking about her when I have so many things I need to work out. Rob's hearing rumors about a possible trade."

"First of all, love isn't convenient. It doesn't wait for you to be ready or come wrapped up in a nice bow." My tough-loving brother is back after that soft and sweet soliloquy. "Second, what the hell is this about a trade? Are the Tigers trading you? To whom?"

"I don't know. I'm not sure there's substance to the rumors. Rob is working on figuring that out without spooking them."

"You have a season left on your contract after this, right? That doesn't even make sense."

I roll my neck. "I know, man. I mean, there are my injuries, but I've had a great season overall so far. They may be looking to help the defense out, but trading me? With how Morgan spun all these stories...you know they expect us to lead a certain non-scandalous lifestyle. I don't think Ed McNeil believes what's being said, but you and I both know it's business. My face is plastered everywhere, and I'm being called every name under the sun. It isn't good for business."

"They'd be ridiculous to trade you unless they were getting a hell of a deal in return."

"You know as well as I do that if these rumors are true, I can't change a damn thing. I guess I'll play next season somewhere and decide if I'm done."

I can't see him, but I know he's thinking. "When you're done, you need to come coach with me."

I smile. "Well, keep a spot on the sideline warm for me."

"Sean," Shane says before I hang up.

"Yeah."

"You're not in deep shit with this woman. It sounds like it's a really good thing you've found there. Don't mess it up because you're afraid of some silly idea about timing or that you have to have everything in your life figured out. Part of being with someone is figuring all of that out together. She sounds like she might be a good person to help you do just that."

I push out a breath, thinking how, not that long ago, my growly brother didn't even believe in love. "Thanks. Hug Maggie and the kids for me. I can't wait to see you guys next week."

I hang up and toss the phone down. Seeing them at the event next week will make it all the more special.

I think about what he said. Andie's all of the things he described. He might be right about her being someone who can help me figure things out. The question is, is it possible I'm someone who could be all those things for her?

What I know is I may be hell-bent on trying because I already know when this event is over, I'm not going to want to let her go.

I throw caution to the wind and snatch my phone back up.

ME: Pick you up at 6 for the party.

ANDIE: I'll just meet you there.

ME: No. I'll pick you up.

ANDIE: Won't people think it's suspicious if we show up together?

ME: Maybe…I don't give a shit.

ANDIE: So we're going to an important party, not giving a shit? Just want to be sure I put on the right attitude.

ME: Isn't that your normal state of mind?

ANDIE: I didn't know if there was some kind of required fake personality disposition for entrance with the Tiger elite.

ME: Andie, you couldn't fake it if you tried.

ANDIE: You're right. Maybe I should stay home and far away so I don't offend anyone.

ME: Not a chance. I'll be there at 6.
ME: Never stop doing that…being real.

This woman. I think I'm going to have to figure out a way to keep her and quite possibly make her mine…in whatever way she'll have me.

Chapter 27

ANDIE

I stare in the mirror, smoothing my hands down my dress. It's been so long since I've had nerves like the one floating around in my belly that my nerves have nerves. I fiddle with my hair, tightening the clip I've used to pull it back and to the side, and then step into my shoes before I do one final glance over.

A whistle comes from the doorway, and I want to chuck something at Nora, but she's holding Ax.

"Hot mama. Sean will have to pick his jaw up off the porch floor."

I roll my eyes. "Why am I nervous?" I intend it to be rhetorical, but I know Nora will answer.

"Maybe because this is like a date with a very, very handsome man who'll be here any second."

"This isn't a date," I snap, but she's right. It does feel a little bit like a date, even though it's strictly professional.

"Maybe it should be." Nora raises and lowers one shoulder quickly, knowing better than to stick around for a retort.

I close my eyes, letting the swirling in my stomach do its thing. I can't even think about this being a date since I'm not sure how I'd feel about that. For one, I wouldn't be going out with Sean. *Wait, would I?* The things Gem said run through my brain like they're sprinting nowhere fast.

I let out a breath slowly. I can't think about a possible, likely never-happening date with Sean.

I hear Snipe bark, then Nora talking, and I know he's here. I want to stay in my room and hide, but that's who I'm trying not to be, so I pull up my brave girl panties and head out into the main room.

My heels click down the hall, and I see the instant Sean sees me. Just like Gem said, his ice-blue eyes start at the tips of my four-inch black and white heels until they gradually meet mine. There's a warmth that washes over me that is as uncomfortable as it is rejuvenating.

What in the hell is wrong with me? I should not be noticing Sean's lingering eyes. I don't care about his eyes or that they evidently like what they see.

"Hey." I squeak, apparently sixteen again, and the captain of the football team is picking me up. I never had that experience, but I imagine this is what it's like. I know before we step out the door, Nora's big mouth will make up for my lack of high school awkwardness.

"Hey." He smirks like my nerves are visible. That one dimple pops in to taunt me. He doesn't take his eyes off me, making it very hard not to blush, but I will not blush at Sean's long look. "You look…beautiful." His eyes roam over my face. "Are you ready?"

"Yes." I move to Nora, who's not even pretending to be anything but amused by this whole thing, and kiss Ax's chubby cheek. "Make sure he gets a bottle in an hour and then turn on his music. He should settle down quickly. He didn't have much of an afternoon nap."

"I got it. You two have a good time. Don't worry about us. We'll be here drinking our bottles and talking to Gem on Facetime." She holds up her root beer.

"You two seriously need to get a life." I grab my handbag off the counter and slip my phone inside.

"I'm thrilled to live vicariously through your salacious affairs."

I turn back to look at her. "Don't keep him up late snuggling."

"What mama doesn't know won't hurt her, will it, big guy?" she whispers to Ax. "Go stir up the rag mags so they can concoct some other fake news to entertain me and the rest of the world. Then we can give those label execs the big bird."

I meet Sean at the door, ignoring his frown. "Alright, let's do this."

Outside, he opens the passenger door of his truck for me, and I climb in, noticing his clean, crisp, manly scent fills the space. I miss that masculine smell, so I take a big whiff before he climbs in.

Ugh! Gem and Nora have put all this stuff in my head about Sean and dating. Now, I just inhaled his scent like I'm some kind of hormonally crazed woman.

He opens the door and climbs in while I want to open mine and throw myself out. I need to find the nearest tree and ram my head into it until all these bogus ideas about dating Sean spill out. I don't need to be dating anyone or thinking about dating at all.

I'm just going to a party with Sean to promote our event. That is all this is, and those two ladies who've filled my head with nonsense will suffer from lack of details tomorrow when I DON'T DIVULGE ANY.

I huff like it's decided a little too loudly, and Sean stops the truck at the end of the driveway. "Everything alright over there?"

"Uh. Yeah." I look at him in his crisp button-down shirt and charcoal gray pants. His clothes are tailored to fit him perfectly, and he looks like he belongs on the cover of a fashion magazine. His top button is undone, but the rest fits snugly, showing off his muscular build that I'm done paying any attention to now.

"Are you nervous?" His exotic blue eyes look slightly amused. "Just breathe, Andie." His voice is soft but demanding. He looks so calm and in control. I hate him.

"I am breathing." I try not to glare at his astute observation, but my weak facial muscles betray me. *Damn feminine traitors.*

"All these people can think whatever they want about what we're doing behind closed doors, but you and I know exactly what's up."

Do we? Because I'm feeling a hell of a lot like I'm all sorts of confused.

That strong masculine jaw mocks me, and I really consider asking him what exactly is up with the way he's looking at me. It seems like he knows something I don't, making me feel like my entire body is entering an inferno.

Like he can see straight through me, he reaches to push a curl out of my face, and I sit perfectly still and let him.

"Hey, it's just me. The guy you don't like very much."

The spot where his fingers brush against my skin prickles with life. I inhale and exhale, slowing my mind and body's roll. "If only these people knew just how much I don't like you."

He laughs, and I smile, feeling myself return from the brink of panic. He turns onto the road, and the only sound filling the space is the rumble of the engine. Although he doesn't seem to mind the silence, it's about to eat me alive.

The way Sean looks at me, and how he seems to see everything, I don't want him to. The way he smells and how good he looks. All that garbage Gem and Nora have been feeding me is just too freaking much, and I'm letting it get to me. Far inside my head, I jump in my seat when he speaks.

"Can I ask you a question?"

"Suuureee." Although, I'm not really sure at all.

He glances at me and smiles, and I want to tell him to wipe it off his pretty face. There's no room in here for that tonight.

"What Nora said about the label execs…I assume she was talking about record labels."

Business. I can talk business all night long, and that will put us right back on our strictly professional relationship.

"It seems some of the labels I work with want to sign me to capitalize on the publicity we've been sucked into."

That little crease between his eyes appears. "I don't understand."

"I met with a label a few weeks back to showcase some songs for a new artist. They spent the majority of my time there talking about you and me. I, of course, kept my answers vague, trying to move the meeting forward, but I should've known. Jonesy got a call from one of the execs wanting to know if he thought I'd be interested in signing with them."

He cuts in. "Why'd they call him?"

"That's what I wanted to know. They knew I'd say no. I think they hoped Jonesy would somehow convince me to take advantage of this *opportunity*."

"What opportunity?"

"The media spectacle that you and I have become. Good or bad, the press is all over us, and they see dollar signs attached to it. If I want to make it big, why not jump on this bandwagon and ride it into the sunset? You, big guy, are just an added bonus to the whole sweet deal."

He stops at a red light and turns toward me. "So you're saying they want to sign you because they can use the negative press to sell records?"

"Sean, you know as well as I do that some people don't care about what we are or aren't doing. If they can make a buck off of it, off of us, nothing else matters."

"I'm sorry, but that sounds messed up."

I laugh. "Uh, you think? Even worse is that I've worked with some of these guys for a long time. They know I won't sign, and I've made it clear. I didn't expect them to sink this low. I'm not sure I want to work with them anymore."

"So, what are you going to do?" he asks the question softly, like he's genuinely interested in my thoughts.

"Jonesy and I are thinking about branching out on our own. I'd get to sing my own songs and put out an album but not have to sacrifice myself in the process. I'd get to tell my own stories and have them be heard the way I wrote them." I pause. "If we're successful, maybe other artists would want to work with us."

"Are you going for it?"

I look out the window at the passing lights. "I'm thinking about it. It's a big risk, and I have Ax. No longer handing my songs over to others would be a real perk. I'd get to be in control. Nora thinks it's possible based on the following I've gained since singing the anthem, and you and I started our secret love affair."

Sean is quiet for a long minute, like he's taking it all in. "I'm really sorry about all of this."

I put my hand up to stop him. "Stop apologizing. You didn't do this. Any of it. Who knows, maybe this will be something else good that comes from it."

He glances at me again, and I can't read the look on his face. His blue eyes have a seriousness about them that's different, causing my lungs to momentarily malfunction.

His eyes return to the road, but their effect remains with me as I try to inhale.

"Can I ask you another question?" His voice is gentle. I raise my eyebrows, waiting. "Have you ever considered signing with a label?"

It's the question I've been asked a million times, like people asking why I'm not on the big stage selling millions of records and touring the world. Sean already knows I'm not interested in that life, so his question is more personal. The answer isn't necessarily short, so I weigh how much I want to tell him.

"There was a time when I was younger I thought that's what I wanted, or more that's what my mom wanted. It's funny, really. I'm pretty sure if she had her choice of talents to impose upon me, it would be something like Miss Tennessee or Best Society Matriarch, not music. Somehow, she miraculously embraced it and decided I should take it to a professional level."

"I always wrote music and played guitar, but I studied classical piano from a young age. Someone saw me play and got in touch with my mom. I was so close to signing a deal as a classical pianist. I was young. They liked how I looked, liked my edgy take on classical music, and thought they could sell me." I don't continue, thinking back to that time and how close I was to signing away my life.

Sean breaks into the flooding memories. "What happened?"

"At the last second, I saw what my life would become. Walking away was the best decision I ever made. It set my life off on a completely different course than where I could've been headed. I would've sold myself to a world I don't want to belong in."

I shrug. "That life isn't for me. People telling me who to be, what to look like, what kind of songs to write. I grew up with parents who wanted me to be someone else. It was enough. I just want to write and play music that comes from my soul. If I get to sing it myself, it'll be that much better."

"Good for you." His voice is soft and contemplative. "You should be proud to know who you are and what you want and not let anyone tell you otherwise."

I smile. "Yeah, well, even when I was slightly more agreeable, I still wasn't very good at having someone tell me what to do."

"I'm shocked. I would've never guessed that about you," he deadpans, parking in his designated parking spot at the stadium.

"So, we're still going with the 'not giving a shit' attitude, right, because schmoozing and falsities are not my forte?"

Sean laughs as he puts his hand on my headrest, angling his body towards me. "We're definitely going with that attitude. These people can say and think what they want, along with everyone else. We're here to solicit help in treating these kids and families to the best day."

I smile. Somewhere between my house and this parking spot, all my nerves have dissipated. Knowing that Sean and I are on the same page makes walking into the unknown of this party a lot easier. I can just be myself, which is good because being anyone else has never really been an option.

Stepping into the stadium feels surreal. The last time I was here, I was afraid and alone and got stuck in the elevator with the guy who's now escorting me through the halls. The very one I've been accused of sleeping with while he was committed to another.

When we come upon an elevator, we both look at each other. Sean cocks one blond eyebrow. "Stairs?"

I twist, taking in my surroundings. "Is this our elevator?"

He laughs as he keeps walking. "No, but I'm not risking it."

"You don't want to get stuck with me again, huh?" Those eyes, the color of the horizon on a warm summer day, move between mine, but he doesn't answer. "If we're going up twenty flights, you can wait for me at the top."

We climb. Fortunately, it doesn't involve me breaking a sweat. Through a set of metal doors, we arrive outside a large room that resembles the one for the meet and greet, only larger with a few high-top tables and chairs spread throughout. A bar is set up along one wall, and the food is arranged on long tables covered in white linens.

We stop just inside, and the party is alive with laughter. Groups are scattered about, and it doesn't take long for Mr. and Mrs. McNeil to approach and welcome us.

"Sean. Ms. Parks. We're so glad the two of you could make it." Ed offers his hand, and we exchange handshakes and pleasantries. "We're thrilled you're teaming up for the event next weekend. It sounds like what you've planned is going to be a real hit." The older man grins, and it seems genuine. "We hope to roll out the red carpet. What wonderful groups to support. Sean, I had no idea you grew up in foster care. This is a fantastic opportunity for these kids."

As if a current radiates from him, I feel Sean stiffen.

"Yes, sir. I'm looking forward to showing these kids a good time."

"It's a miraculous story," Mrs. McNeil chimes in. "You've made quite a life for yourself, given all you've been through. If you don't mind me asking, at what age did you enter the system?"

I can tell by the look on this woman's face she means no harm, and I don't know Sean well, but I suspect he's not interested in story time.

"I was a baby," he answers, keeping it short and sweet. Mrs. McNeil makes a quiet clucking sound of her tongue, pity filling her face, and I'm done with this.

"So," I jump in. "Mr. McNeil, I understand you know my Gemma."

He smiles, his bright white teeth matching his hair. "Yes. She's quite something, that woman. I was stunned to find out the two of you are related. I hope she'll be attending next weekend. It's been too long since we've seen each other."

"Oh, she'll be there. She's still a little perturbed I didn't invite her to hear me sing the anthem."

He laughs. "Oh, I heard. You never have to guess what that woman is thinking. She has a standing open invitation to all games going forward." His eyes roam the room like he's looking for someone. "Our granddaughter is around here somewhere. She's dying to meet you. She brought her guitar, hoping you'll sign it." Another couple walks in and catches his attention. "We're so glad to have you both here tonight. Thank you for coming. This is going to be a fantastic event. Grab a drink and enjoy yourselves."

They leave us to welcome others, and I survey the party as we inch further into the crowd. It's like walking into a Stepford community where the women mirror each other. The men are either obviously Sean's teammates or men who look like they belong in a high-rise office, telling someone to bring them coffee and connect their calls.

We make our way to the bar, and Sean orders two waters. I glance around, noticing it didn't take long for heads to turn our way and whispering to commence.

One of Sean's teammates approaches and sidles up the bar beside us, giving me the once-over. *Oh, please, buddy.* Interestingly, Sean must notice because he moves closer. My shoulder brushes his chest, but he doesn't move back an inch. *Hmmmm.* I'll have to dissect that little territorial display later.

"Well, this is going to be entertaining," the guy says, flagging the bartender. His tone is just a little too cocky for my liking.

"What's up, Charles?" Sean says, reaching around me to slap his hand.

Charles snickers. "I think I should be asking you. Look, I hate to be the one to tell you, but I drew the short straw. Morgan is here."

Sean's chest presses fully against me as I try to make sense of what this fool just said.

"Excuse me," I say, catching his attention. "Um, what did you just say?"

He straightens and looks from me to Sean. "She's here. One of the rookies brought her."

"You've got to be shitting me," Sean says as I look around, wanting to see the sick chick who has made our lives hell. All I see is Sean's friend Tyrell, with whom I assume is his wife, making a beeline for us.

"Dang, man. I can tell by that look you've already been warned." Tyrell and his wife encircle us. "I know you're both here to make sure next weekend is a success, but if you want to ditch, I'll do the best I can to spread the word and make sure the guys show up ready to party."

I move so that I can see Sean's face. His eyes are hard, his body is stiff as a board, and his chest looks like it's expanded three sizes with anger. He's about to explode. I know I'm unwilling to let this woman ruin one more thing, including getting these people to give their all next weekend for the families we've invited, but I'm not sure if Sean can handle being in the same room with the woman who used his trust against him.

I lean, now pressed against him, hoping for a semi-private exchange. His chin tips down, and his eyes meet mine.

"We still in the 'not giving a shit' zone?" I ask, needing confirmation.

He blinks twice slowly like he's trying to reel in his temper and comprehend what I said. Then, a small smirk crosses his lips. "Absolutely."

"Then she's the one who can leave." I grin, ready to take someone out, one person in particular. "We have work to do. So, let's get to it."

We're about to step away from the bar when Tyrell sticks his arm out, stopping Sean. "What's this I hear about a trade?" His voice is so soft I almost miss the question.

I look between the two of them, trying to figure out what they're talking about.

Sean rubs his temples. "I don't know." He keeps his voice low. "I'm hoping it's just rumors, but with all this…talk, you know it's bad for business. Plus, you know running backs are more dispensable."

Tyrell nods and rubs his chin like he understands but doesn't like it one bit. I want to know what this is about.

Sean's hand presses into the small of my back, and I take that as my cue to move on. I take a couple of steps forward but stop and turn to face him.

"What trade is he talking about?"

Sean's chest rises and falls with a deep breath. "There is a rumor the Tigers are looking to trade me."

I frown, not understanding. "What does that mean? Don't you have a contract or something?"

"Yeah, I have one more year, but that doesn't prevent them from trading me if it suits them or the team."

"Just like a piece of property." I glance around the room, taking it in. "If you only have a year left, why would they trade you?"

He shrugs. "My age. Too many injuries last season. Maybe they're looking to build up their defensive line. With only a season left, try to get a good trade deal while they can." He pauses. "Maybe too much bad press." He shakes his head. "It's business, and no one likes negative reviews on their product."

"Who makes that decision?" I whisper.

"The GM, coaches, the organization."

I look around the room at all these people who are a part of his everyday life. The people he works for and sacrifices his time and body for. The people he's been with for the past however many years. *What a crock!*

I don't know anything about football, but I know how highfalutin jerks act when things don't meet their stuffy, puffy standards.

"Sean, that's not right," I say, adding more force than I expected.

I think I see what might be a hint of a smile. "I know, but unfortunately, I can't do anything about it. If it's true, the best-case scenario is I might have a tiny bit of influence in where I end up."

I'm letting this all sink in when a couple of his teammates and their wives or girlfriends join us. Sean makes small talk about our plans for the event while my mind wanders through everything he just said. This professional football stuff is really just business. These guys are pawns in a game of chess. They strategize and negotiate in their quest to be the best, regardless of what it does to the person actually doing the job.

Sean's teammates move on, and we're left standing there just in time for Morgan to slither toward us from wherever she was hiding. She eyes us, and I can tell this woman has a spine, but it's likely made of some kind of generic material. Unfortunately for her, I'm familiar with her type. When she's smacked with the cold water of truth, we'll watch her shrivel.

Beside me, Sean is immovable. When I glance up at his face, it's like stone. This man could cut through steel with the fire blazing in his eyes.

She saunters over like she doesn't have a care in the world, stopping too close for her own good.

"Well, I guess I shouldn't be surprised to see you here together."

Neither Sean nor I say anything, and I wonder where the schmuck is who brought her. That guy has to be a real winner.

I'd wonder what Sean ever saw in this woman, but I already know. She's beautiful–long, dark, almost black hair, tan skin, immaculate makeup, and a body to match. She's the kind of beautiful you wonder if it's possible it's real. She and Sean looked amazing together. I also know it wasn't anything more than that, or we wouldn't be standing here right now.

She sets her cold, hard eyes on Sean. "How's the new life turning out?" Her eyes narrow, and she sounds amused. "I'd think you'd be a little more careful than to flaunt your little secret around the people who control your world." She glances around. "Oh, I forgot. You're moving on from football being your whole life."

"How much does it cost to sell your soul these days?" Sean asks so smoothly it almost gives me chills.

She ignores him and moves her eyes to me. "The whole sympathy card for your husband was a good play. I shouldn't have been surprised that Sean was the one to buy into it. Now, you think you can plan a pity party, and suddenly, everyone will forget what you've done." She scoffs. "You can try to deny it any which way you want."

I take just a little step forward, but I feel Sean's hand wrap around my elbow. I meet her glaring eyes and speak slowly and clearly.

"The difference between us is we have nothing to hide." I shrug. "Maybe half the people in this room believe you, and the other half think you're full of it. It doesn't make any difference to us. But for you, the truth makes all the difference in the world, doesn't it?" I slip my hand into Sean's, and without hesitation, he grips mine right back. "Good luck in life, Morgan. I hope you eventually find your way out of the misery you must live in."

I turn, pulling Sean along with me, ready to get away from the stench of her and her lies. We make it two steps, and I almost run right over a young girl who's staring at me with the biggest grin and starry eyes. She must be around fourteen, dressed entirely in black, and has pink stripes in her blond hair. A girl after my teenage heart.

"Ms. Parks. My grandpa said he thought you might be here tonight. I brought my guitar, and I was hoping you'd sign it."

All I can do is stare back at her, trying to reel myself in from the far edges of rage. I realize I'm still holding Sean's hand as her words start to come to me. I look up at him, and he's looking back at me with an intensity that makes my belly do a little flip. It's like a gymnast trying out a back handspring for the first time. I let go of his hand, turning back to the girl, needing a distraction.

"Yes, of course. I'd love to. Lead the way." I step away from Sean but peek at him over my shoulder as he stands there watching me with that look, and I'm not sure exactly what I see. Or maybe I do, and it's the kind of look that catches my breath and scares me a whole lot.

Chapter 28

SEAN

All I can do is stand like a damn fool, watching Andie as she makes her way across the room. I know I'm not the only one tracking her. Half the guys in this room are focused on the same thing I am. Only…I know exactly what's underneath her outward beauty, and I know what I want.

She steals a glance at me over her shoulder, and I want to smile. I want to tell her everything is ok because I have no doubt my face is giving me away. But all I can do is stare, thinking all the things a few weeks ago I wouldn't have dared let my thoughts go anywhere near.

Andie is always beautiful, but tonight, she's freaking stunning. When she came down the hallway at her house, I couldn't take my eyes off her. It doesn't matter what she's wearing. She has this way of always looking like herself, never using clothes as a way to morph into someone else. What I have, these chumps around me don't, is a vision of her relaxed and messy in purple knee-high socks and an old t-shirt. It's the Andie I prefer.

Her black and white dress and high heels are classy but with an edge and still completely her. Her soft dark curls are bound tonight instead of running wild, pulled to the side and draped over her shoulder.

Every time she's near me, I notice something new. The tiny scar just above her lip. The graceful soft curve of her neck and shoulders. The way her delicate necklace holding an 'A' charm dangles, falling just below her collarbone. Or how she didn't step away when I pressed my hand into the sensitive area of her lower back.

After Shane's rare poignant monologue, I'm allowing myself to take note of these minute details. I've even wondered how I might continue building a friendship with Andie after the event is over. After her eloquent response to Morgan's completely disrespectful and malicious comments, I'm not wondering. I'm fully in the needing zone. I have to figure out how to get her to let me stick around because I need her in my life.

Andie might be the most real, honest, kind, stubborn, and at times frustrating woman I've ever met. What I know is the more I'm around her, the more I want to be sure that I keep getting to be around her.

"Sean, it's good you're here." The Tigers GM, Doug, pulls me from my thoughts and my eyes away from Andie, who's at the other end of the room talking to Ed McNeil's granddaughter. "Sounds like things are coming together for next weekend. It's a good job sweeping the mess under the rug."

I've never had an issue with Doug or how he manages the team. I know this is all business to him. He's happy as long as things run smoothly and we're winning, but that comment has me clenching my fists. I'm not trying to hide anything. He's making it sound like this is just another publicity stunt, and it's all for show.

"It's a big deal to the kids and families attending. An opportunity they'd likely only dream of." I want to clarify exactly why Andie and I are doing this.

He slaps me on the back. "Well, I'm sure the press will eat it up. Postings on social media are receiving lots of attention."

I want to wipe the arrogant, smug look off his face, but I shove my fist in my pockets instead, turning to address him. "This is so much more than social media likes and good press. These kids live each day not knowing what the next will look like. Will they sleep in the same bed? Will they finally be placed in a home…with a family? Will they be safe, or do they need to fear what might happen to them in their new quarters?"

I take a breath, letting my words take root in his ignorance and insensitivity to what these kids and these families face daily.

"And the veterans and military families…some have been wounded or live with PTSD, knowing they'll never be the same. Their families live with that, too. Those with loved ones overseas never know when it might be the last time they speak with their husband, wife, or mom or dad. It's everyday life for them and a hardship you and I will never understand."

I look him in the eye. "This isn't about covering up anything. The few hours we're with these families next weekend is one hundred percent about them."

Doug nods, looking like he didn't care for my little speech, but I don't give a flying fuck. If he doesn't like the press I'm bringing, he can trade my ass and find someone willing to stroke his ego or make him look good.

"Well, I look forward to seeing how it goes. The sooner it's over, the sooner you can get back to your life and focus on what's important. All this stuff with Andie Parks is taking its toll, and she doesn't have as much to lose as you do. You'd be wise to steer clear after this." He smiles, slaps me on the back, and walks away.

I have to process what exactly he just said, and I'm about two seconds away from going after him when I'm stopped. It's likely good because my fist might have done the talking this time.

"Do I want to know what that was all about?" Tyrell's deep voice hits my ears from behind. "That looked…a little intense."

"Just making it clear what next weekend is really about. He had the idea that it's all covering my indiscretions." I survey the room, trying to find Andie, but I don't see her.

"How'd it go with Morgan? Don't think the whole room wasn't waiting for a catfight to break out."

"Really? Andie's way too cool to let Morgan get the best of her. She wished her luck finding her way out of her miserable life."

Tyrell's head rolls back, and laughter booms out of him. "She's something. My wife would've handed me her earrings and forced me to hold her back. Hair would've been flying everywhere."

Like her name conjures her up, Andie steps up beside me. "Have we met the requirement to be able to blow this pop stand?"

With her beside me, I toss my irritation and agitation from the last fifteen minutes overboard. Before I can tell her I'm ready to go, Tyrell's wife joins us in a tizzy.

"Hey, baby." Tyrell swings an arm out and pulls her close. "Where've you been?"

Her eyes dart around like she's hunting for someone. "I have no idea where that woman gets her nerve. Seriously, whoever brought her should be kicked off the team. I mean, who would do that? And she just won't quit running her mouth."

Tyrell groans, but she continues.

"She's over there licking her wounds and carrying on, but there are no tears. If she was smart, she'd at least go to the bar and squirt lemon juice in her eyes. Now, she's trying to convince everyone that Andie can't really sing. She said the whole thing was dubbed. Can you even believe it? What will it take for her to zip her double Botoxed lips?"

Andie shifts next to me, putting her hands on her hips, and I hear her suck in a breath and hold it. When she lets it out, she turns to face me. The calm, controlled Andie that addressed Morgan a bit ago is gone. Now replaced with the Andie, who looks like she's about to throw down.

Her fierce eyes hit mine. "You still good with not giving a shit, Pretty Boy?"

I smile. "Yep."

One side of her perfect mouth tugs upward. "The best way to kill a lie is with the truth." She leaves my side and disappears.

"What's she going to do?" Tyrell asks.

"Stab that lie right through the heart." I step away from them to find the perfect spot to stand back and watch.

I settle into a quiet space along the back wall. A second later, she's marching across the room with Mr. McNeil's granddaughter by her side, who's carrying a guitar. At the bar, Andie leans over to say something to the bartender before using a stool to give her the boost she needs to climb up and sit.

Crossing her legs, she gets comfortable before the girl hands her the guitar. As she strums a few chords, the room begins to take notice and quiets. She leans over to ask the girl something, then messes with the tuners and strums again while the girl sits beside her on a stool, starstruck.

When Andie appears to be satisfied, the melody of a song hushes the rest of the room. She clears her throat and finds me along the wall. The smirk that takes over her mouth makes mine tip upward. All eyes are on her.

"I thought I'd treat you all to a little musical snack." She smiles, but it doesn't reach her eyes like the one that appears when she's teasing me. "Sometimes the only thing you can do is show people who you are and hope they believe you." She turns to the girl and winks.

Andie's fingers work together in rhythm with the guitar, and a song takes form. Her voice starts out soft and gentle, but when she hits the chorus, there isn't a person in the world who could ever say this woman can't sing.

I listen to every word, knowing it comes from her soul. She sings about being called a rebel and being afraid. She says she was covered in lies and hidden from the truth.

As I listen, so much of this song speaks to me. It could have been written for me. Standing in this room with these people who only want one thing from me–to perform. What's left of me when it's over is up to me. If I let them, they'll take it all, and I'd be left with nothing resembling the man I want to be.

Andie's voice pushes through my thoughts as she sings about being dragged through hell, but it only making us stronger. She talks about wearing our scars and calls me out. "*People can talk, but Pretty Boy, they'll never know.*" Her eyes meet mine as she tells me she can't teach me how to live, but she'll fight when I'm standing on the ledge.

It's exactly what she's doing. Even now, in this room full of people judging her and thinking the absolute worst, she's standing up for herself. She's living and speaking her truth, regardless of what anyone thinks or says–no matter how many people in this room would like to see her crumble and fall.

When the final chord fades, half the people clap, holler, and whistle. She only climbs down and hands back the guitar. She hugs the girl, saying a few words before heading straight for me.

"Nicely put," I say as she stops before me, a small smile on her lips. "I especially liked the mention."

She bows her head as if saying, 'You're welcome.'

"Want to get out of here? Tacos on the way home are my treat."

Her eyes widen, a grin replacing her smile, and it's the real deal. "Heck, yeah."

"After wading through the muck of Morgan's lies, I think this might be the best taco I've ever eaten in my life. I bet this is what the woman who swam the English Channel felt like. I bet she thought about her favorite food the entire time she was in the water."

Andie sits in the passenger seat of my truck with her legs crossed, lifting her taco to her mouth to take another bite. "If I ever get stuck on an island, someone needs to make sure there's a taco stand."

"You're ridiculous. No one could or should eat tacos every day." I take a bite of my own taco.

She raises and lowers one shoulder. "Well, good thing I don't like you. I really don't care what you think. I'll eat tacos as much as I want, and if you judge me, well then, that sounds like a personal problem to me."

She takes another bite, talking around the food in her mouth. "When I was pregnant with Ax, I couldn't stand anything spicy. I seriously cried about it one night. It was like all the good things in life were gone. Alcohol, sleeping, walking without feeling like I was going to pee my pants, nachos…"

I stare out my window, imagining all of the things that probably made her cry during that time, and it causes a dull ache in my chest. All of the things she went through, things no one should have to go through, and she did it alone. I'm very familiar with the feeling, but finding out she was pregnant after losing her husband and not having the support of her family had to be traumatic and extremely scary.

She crumples her wrapper, tosses it into the bag, and turns in her seat to face me. "Can I ask you a question?"

Her voice is soft, and I know this isn't some flippant question to give me a hard time. I've only known Andie a little while, but I know her well enough to know this is a personal question I may not want to answer. It doesn't mean I won't, but there are certain things I just don't talk about.

I finish chewing and toss my own wrapper. "Do I have the option not to answer it?" I try to cast some light on whatever is coming.

I feel her eyes roaming over me as I take a drink. "Sure."

"Ok, then." I glance at her, bracing myself against my seat for whatever she wants to know.

"You said tonight that you entered the system as a baby." She pauses for just a second before asking her question. "Do you know anything about your parents?"

My instincts weren't wrong. This is at the top of the list of things I don't like or want to talk about. A couple of years ago, it would've been an easy answer. 'No' is a quick response, but now that's not the truth.

I keep my eyes averted, knowing I can't and won't lie to her. I also know telling her would be ok. I know it wouldn't change our non-friendship, and I'm pretty sure she wouldn't look at me differently because of it.

Tonight, when Mrs. McNeil started giving me the pity face, I know Andie saw it too and changed the subject. How many people would recognize that, and if they did, be sensitive enough to step in rather than stand there waiting for the answer themselves?

I screw that cap on my water bottle, deciding I can trust her. "There are a lot of days that I wish the answer to that question were no, that I don't know anything about them. The truth is, I don't know much, but enough."

I see her shift in her seat out of the corner of my eye like she's settling in, all ears.

"A few years back, I hired someone to see what they could find out about my parents. The investigator was able to track down my birth mother. I contacted her and asked her if it was possible to meet. I flew to where she lives, and we met at a coffee shop. I had a lot of questions and was finally able to look into the eyes of the person who birthed me. I wanted to know if I looked like her or if she ever thought about me. I wanted to know why I ended up in the foster system, and I hoped maybe whatever put me there could be the past, and we could get to know each other."

I inhale and let out a long breath, needing to keep the rest short and to the point. "It's not what happened. We only met that one time. She'd been assaulted and couldn't keep me. She surrendered me at the hospital after I was born, thinking I'd be adopted. She was devastated when I told her that never happened. She was sorry. She told me a little bit about herself and her life. She has a husband and children and felt it was best if we didn't form a relationship. I've respected that and haven't contacted her since."

Done telling my little story, I'm met with silence, so I risk a glance at Andie, feeling the force of her stare. She's frowning, her eyes set on my face. There's not an ounce of pity or apology. They're fierce and…protective. Something about them stirs a longing inside me that I'm not sure I've ever felt before, and the ache runs deep into my bones.

"You know that there's not a single part of any of that's reflected in you, right?" I stare at her, thinking about it, and when I don't answer immediately, she pushes harder. "Sean, you know that, right?"

Do I know that? I don't think I've ever asked myself the question, but maybe that's part of why it was so important to me to gain everyone's approval–for people to stroke my ego and tell me how great I am. I wanted to fit in and feel valued. I wanted to know that there was some amount of good in me, but it was all bullshit. I surrounded myself with people that didn't know me and didn't care to. All they wanted was Sean Greyson, the football star, and to ride on my hard work and drive. I let myself believe *things* made me worth something. They gave me value and made me wanted, despite my ugly beginning.

I answer honestly. "I think maybe I'm starting to see that. It's hard to know that's where I started. That my existence was the result of something so evil. Then going from home to home, never wanted long enough to have anything or anyone that lasted." I let out a slow, steady breath, needing it to release the tightness in my chest. "Sometimes all of it is hard to stomach, to wonder why it had to be that way. But my brothers and I, we made it. I do know that. We didn't get to where we are for nothing."

"That's for damn sure." She says it so adamantly it makes the corner of my mouth turn up slightly.

"Careful, I might think you care a little bit," I tease, wanting to move on and not dive into this any further. I've learned wallowing in questions I'll never have the answer to gets me nowhere but stuck in a big pit of pain and misery.

She rolls her eyes. "Ha. Not a chance." She turns, staring out the window, contemplating something. "I think about Ax and wonder what questions he'll have about Josh. All the things he'll wonder but never know."

"At least he has you to tell him all the things you do know." She doesn't look at me, but I know she hears me. "Can I ask you something now?"

She turns to look at me. "I guess it's only fair, but I also reserve the right not to answer."

"Fair enough." This question has been one I've wanted to ask for a while but never felt it was appropriate. Knowing she's a Taninbaugh and her parents' expectations and now understanding she was close to signing with a record label, my curiosity has gotten the best of me. "How and when did you and Josh meet?"

She laughs, but I have no idea what's funny about the question. "There are a million things I thought you'd ask, but I wasn't expecting that."

"Well, you can answer those, too, if you want."

"Haha. In your dreams." She smooths her hands down the front of her dress, resting her hands in her lap. "I actually met him the night I turned twenty-one. Some friend convinced me to do the whole bar thing, which isn't my scene. I was bored out of my mind, and he asked to buy me a drink, but I refused. He was on leave and out with his buddies. He didn't know who I was, who my family was, that I had anything to do with music, and he just talked to me."

She runs her finger over the seam on my truck seat completely in her head like she's reliving the memory. "We talked all night until he had to help his drunk friends out of the bar. After that, he went back to base, and we kept in contact. The next time I saw him, he asked me to marry him, and I said yes. I knew my parents would flip, and they did, but for the first time in my life, I felt like I was free. I left any thoughts of music behind and moved to base with him until the longing to get back to it took over, and he convinced me to come back and work on selling my songs."

I understand the feeling of finally being free and the call to do what you love. "The distance must have been hard."

"It was. Every time he came back, it was like we had to start all over again. Not that we didn't know each other. It was just hard to do life together when we were so used to doing it apart. He was military for life. He loved it. His guys were his family, and it would've been tough with Ax."

She peeks at me before looking away like she's determining if she wants to say more. "I wouldn't change a single thing, but the twenty-one-year-old me didn't think about what that life looked like. I just jumped in, not fully understanding or thinking about the future. We didn't have the kind of relationship or connection other couples have. We were two people living separate lives. I was still…alone." She shakes her head, a faint smile tugging at her lips like she's pulling herself back from a pool of vulnerability. "I don't know if that makes sense."

I nod slowly, suspecting she just trusted me with her admission. "It does. I'm not sure anyone thinks about all the future could hold unless it's a dream, and even then, it doesn't always turn out the way we imagined. We ignore the negative and focus on the here and now. It's easier. Plus, if we didn't, we might never move from where we're at."

"Yeah, I think you're right about that."

I cough. "Wait, did you just say I'm right? I need to write this down somewhere. It's definitely a moment to document in our no-benefits non-friendship."

She swats my arm with the back of her hand. "You should because it's never going to happen again." Laughing, I start my truck and put it in gear. "Thanks for the tacos. Although, you better watch out. It's now two weeks in a row your cheat meal consisted of the ingredients that should make the world go round. Pretty soon, you might have an addiction problem on your hands, and if the press got a hold of something like that, the Tigers are sure to trade your slow, old ass."

I can't help but laugh again, but her comment brings me back to what Doug said tonight and stirs the taco in my gut. He thinks, or maybe demands, that Andie and I steer clear of each other after the event is over next weekend. But if I have it my way, I hope to see her more. He said I have way more to lose than she does, which is one hundred percent false. We've both lost, but what I've gained is already a thousand times worth it.

Andie said earlier that singing her own music and producing her own records would be another good thing that comes out of this. I want to ask her if she thinks there's any chance she and I could be something else amazing that might come from this, too.

Chapter 29

ANDIE

ME: Let's do it.

JONESY: It's about time. Yeah, man. I'm ready.

ME: Whatever we need to do, I'm in.

JONESY: Let's start with your new song.
JONESY: And let's have Nora get some footage of us in the studio.

ME: I don't want to screw this up for you.

JONESY: Andie, the screw is just about to come loose. Wait until you see when it does.
JONESY: When do you want to get started? I'll reserve a studio.

ME: I'm ready when you are, but we have to rehearse for next weekend first.
ME: See you soon.

After singing for the last thirty minutes, I chug some water to moisten my dry, overworked throat. Our set list for next weekend covers an hour, so we're halfway through and sounding pretty good.

It's been a long time since I've sung with a band. I actually prefer the raw sound of just me and a piano or an acoustic guitar, but this is really fun. Being on stage next weekend with Jonesy and the girls, along with the drummer and guitarist Jonesy enlisted, will be a blast.

A car door slams and Nora walks into Jonesy's man-caved garage with her large bag in tow.

"Alright, people, your videographer has arrived. Tell me where to set up and your best angle. I need to send the video to Miranda."

"How do you always have so much energy?" I take a sip of my water, wondering if I ever had as much energy as Nora does.

"I drank a Monster on the way here. Plus, I don't have a kid. Those little things suck the life right out of you. I've watched my sister slowly turn into a zombie."

"How's Gem?" I know the two of them are in constant communication. They are like the *Golden Girls* of separate generations, and it's a good thing there are only two of them, or the entire world would be set afire with their antics.

"Spicy as usual. You'll have to watch her around those players next weekend. She has favorites, you know."

I laugh. "She'll give those big boys a run for their money. Now, because she's in love with Sean, she's their biggest fangirl. They won't know what to do when she hits the field and tells them how they should be doing things."

Jonesy plops down in the seat next to me. "Should we tell her?"

"Tell her what?" Nora's eyes bug out.

"Nah. Let's just wait a little while. We don't need to–"

"Tell me what?" She's practically bouncing.

Jonesy puts her out of her misery. "Andie finally agreed to put a record together with me."

"WHAT?!" Nora's mouth hangs open. Then she's screaming, jumping, and hugging me. "Oh my gosh! Why didn't you tell me immediately?" She moves over to kiss Jonesy on the cheek and squeezes his neck. "You guys. You're going to kill this. The music world isn't going to know what hit them. You're doing it, and you're doing it your way." She beams like a proud mama.

She moves over to hug me again, and I hug her back. It feels really good to be moving in this direction, and I hope she's right. I hope we can put my music out there, and it will move people. I want it to help them, whatever they're going through, or make them sing and dance on their best and worst days.

She pulls out her phone and starts tapping away.

"What are you doing?" I laugh.

She looks at me guilty. "Nothing."

"Nora Renee, tell me right now, or you're fired."

She looks at her phone and then back at me. "Juuuuussssttt texting Gem because we had a bet. I thought you'd keep playing it safe, and she said I had mush for brains if I thought that."

Jonesy laughs. "I don't know how anyone keeps up with you ladies. It's too much." He bumps my shoulder. "You ready to hit the second set?"

"Yeah." I pull my phone out of my pocket, seeing a Words notification that Sean played a word. I shoot him a text.

ME: Where are you?

SEAN: On a plane getting ready to take off.

ME: For where?

SEAN: You already know. I know you track the schedule.

ME: Oh, you're on the plane with the team. I thought they left your sorry butt behind this week.

SEAN: Lady, they want to score touchdowns.

SEAN: Now, play your word so I can triple-word score your losing ass.

ME: Sorry, I'm at rehearsal while you're being pampered on your private jet. Later, sucka.

"Awwwwweeee, look at that flirty smirk," Nora says in a sing-song voice. "If I were a betting woman, which I totally am, I'd bet a McDonald's Happy Meal that our sweet but mostly sassy soon-to-be rockstar is texting the sexy, gorgeous football player."

If I wasn't afraid of breaking my phone, I'd throw it at her, but then she might see she's right. Yes, I'm texting him, but I haven't talked to him since the party last week. *Wait, why am I defending myself to…myself?*

When he dropped me off that night, after I'd gotten a shower and tucked myself in bed, I thought about what he told me about his birth parents. I knew by the way he wouldn't look at me and kept fiddling with the cap on his water bottle, he didn't want to talk about it. I also know that there's a very real and very deep pain that resides within him from not only being given up but also from finding out that he was the result of a horrifyingly traumatic event.

When I asked him if he knew that horror was not reflected in him, I didn't like his hesitant answer. I wanted to hold that pretty face and strong jaw in my hands and make him hear me until he believed it. No one should have to live thinking they're only the consequence of a vile act.

The many layers of Sean continue to reveal themselves. All of that stone I saw at first is being chipped away shard by shard, leaving a man who is soft and tender and fun. I see a man who doesn't take himself all that seriously but also one who honors right and good and just. An image of him hanging out on my couch with Axel on his chest skirts through my mind, causing a warming sensation I really want to ignore.

When he told me about the rumors of him possibly being traded, it made me want to kick every one of those suit-wearing pricks at the party in the balls. If it's because of what his ex is saying, it's such a slap in the face.

He told me it's business, and part of me understands that, especially with how the labels came chasing me. But in the time I've known Sean, I know how much he gives and sacrifices for the team. How can they just toss him out because some chick decided she wanted to get back at him? Where is the team in that, the camaraderie, the loyalty?

I heard the hurt in Sean's voice when he told me about the possible trade, and I saw him roll back his shoulders and stiffen as he talked to a guy at the party who I have to assume is the team's GM. Only a GM, who holds the lives of his players in his hands, would look like a slimeball. I don't know what they said to each other, but the feelings of betrayal were clear, and I can only sympathize with him.

Nora sits down next to me, pulling me from my thoughts. "Soooooooo, what made you do it?"

"Do what?" I ask, still trying to pull my brain back from thoughts of Sean possibly being traded.

"Decide to make an album on your own. Andie, this is amazing. You have no idea how many people want this. When we announce it, it's going to blow up."

I weigh my head from side to side. "At the Tigers party, when I heard that Sean's crazy ex was telling everyone I couldn't sing, I'd just had it. I'm tired of giving away my soul searching and pain for someone else to deliver to the world. If I'm going through it, I want to sing it my way."

Nora grins. "I still can't believe you sat on the bar and sang. You were like one of those lounge singers."

Jonesy chuckles from behind his phone.

"What are you laughing at?" I kick his shin.

"I can see it. You sprawled out on top of the piano, singing your heart out for all those giants." He starts singing *My Heart Will Go On,* his pitch high but still on key.

"Whatever." I shove his shoulder. "There wasn't anywhere else to sit, and I needed those people to pay attention."

Jonesy stifles his laughter. "Did it work?"

"You know it did. I know you both wish you could've been there. You'd be even more jealous to know Sean bought me tacos after my little moment of truth."

Nora gasps. "Hold the freaking phone. He bought you tacos afterward?"

Crap. Why did my mouth let that out of the bag? Now, she'll think we're going to get married.

I shrug, making it clear it was no big deal. "Yeah. He drove through, bought us tacos, and we ate them in the parking lot.

"When's the wedding? Seriously. You sat in his truck and had a taco picnic," she whines like it's the most romantic thing she's ever heard.

"Nora, you've lost your ever-loving mind. That man owed me. I spent the evening in a room full of millionaires who try to get a ball down the field for a living. They looked at me like I was standing there naked, thinking Sean and I were getting jiggy with it. Even those who'd never admit it."

"Then," I stick my pointer finger in the air for emphasis, "I not only came face to face with the woman who's caused me to become the most hated woman in Tennessee or possibly, America, for having counterfeit relations with their famed football star, but I also had to hear about her telling people that I. CANNOT. SING." I growl-yell the last part because it is the worst. "If that was not taco-worthy, I don't know what is." I get up, putting a period on this conversation.

I look at Jonesy, who's snickering. "Are you ready to get back to work?"

"I have to admit, Andie, that is pretty romantic. The man bought you tacos because he knows you love them."

"Ugh." Part of me wants to smile because it's true. Sean did it just for me, but my lips stay put. "If you're both done gushing all over Sean, I'm ready to sing."

Jonesy stands, moving to sit at his keyboard. I pick up my set list, and we get back to it.

I sing, but my mind is elsewhere. It's back with Sean in his truck. I went into that night freaking out that it would feel like a date with all the prep talk from Gem and Nora. I didn't know if I was ready for anything to even remotely resemble a date. It scares me to think I might be.

Spending that evening with Sean felt date-like, and it's strange to admit that with him, it didn't feel all that frightening. In fact, it was easy and kind of nice. Maybe too easy and too nice. Now, what scares the absolute crap out of me is that I might even be willing to someday do it again…with him.

Chapter 30

SEAN

The plane touches down, and I check my phone, hoping to see that Andie played her word. Nothing but a missed call from Mark.

I grab my duffle and toss it over my shoulder. We won, but I'm ready to be home.

These trade rumors are weighing on me and my relationship with the team. I need to call Rob first thing in the morning and find out what he knows. He needs to get a handle on whether or not this is legit. The longer I'm in the dark, the harder it is for me to work for a team evaluating my worth.

In my truck, I dial Mark.

"Hey, man. Good game today," he says, picking up. "That catch was ridiculous. I have no idea how you held onto the ball."

"Me either. It was so cold I couldn't feel my fingers. My ass will be on the couch tomorrow watching you, so play smart. I'm not interested in bad TV."

Mark is the starting quarterback for the New York Liberties. Despite having a recurring shoulder injury, he's one of the best quarterbacks in the entire league. The press wants you to believe he has the ego to match, but Mark is like me, a victim of people putting together an image that doesn't represent reality.

"I always play smart. Why do you think we're leading the division?"

"Defense is kicking ass."

He laughs. "My bye week is early, so I'm coming to see you. I need a break from the city, and Shane said he's heading your way for your big event."

"So, I'm second string?" I tease.

"Nah, man, but Shane and Maggie have the kids, so they win every time. I also thought about hitting Cole up to have a little fun in the sun, but…" He doesn't finish his statement, and I may be crazy, but something in his tone sounds off.

Cole Matthews, Maggie's oldest brother, was a first-round draft pick and is the starting quarterback for the Miami Stingrays.

"Fine. You can stay with me, but you have to clean up after yourself. I'm swamped next weekend with the event and the game, but I'll get you a pass."

"Does this mean I get to meet the elevator girl you've been secretly sleeping…working with?"

"Not if I can help it."

Mark is an obnoxious flirt, and I don't need him anywhere near Andie.

"It's like that, is it? Are you worried? Something you want to tell me before I jump to my own conclusions and then confirm for myself?"

I groan. "No. I'm not telling you anything. There's nothing to tell. Even if there was, I wouldn't tell you. You can't keep your big mouth shut."

He laughs. "Oh, there's definitely something to tell, but I'll let it go. I'll know exactly what's up next weekend. I already know Andie Parks is insanely gorgeous, and you're not blind. All that natural beauty, curly hair, and spunk. That voice that makes the hairs on the back of my neck stand up."

I know he's trying to get a rise out of me, but I can't even think about Andie's voice making the hairs on anyone's neck do anything. I want to inject cement into Mark's ears so he can never hear her voice again.

When I don't respond, he continues, poking and prodding.

"I can't wait to meet her and get to know her myself. We should invite her to come over and hang out and–"

"Mark, if you want to stay here and not be smothered in your sleep, shut up." He laughs, but it's not his usual unhindered, carefree, contagious laugh, which makes it almost impossible not to laugh with him, even at your own expense. "You need to take it easy. She lost her husband, and she…"

I hesitate telling Mark about Axel, not because he'll think it's a big deal. He'll just know that if anything is going on between Andie and me, it's not just for fun. "She has a son."

He's quiet on the other end of the line, and I think he's processing that revelation. "Huh. First Shane, and now you." He's uncharacteristically soft and gentle.

It wasn't the response I expected. I wonder what the hell is up with him.

He clears his throat. "So, you're even more into her than I thought." I don't answer, and he continues. "What are you going to do if you're traded? You shouldn't start something you'll just have to walk away from. It sounds like she's already been through enough."

I bristle. I know very clearly what Andie's already been through. I grip my steering wheel, wanting to roll down my window, and toss my phone out, hoping I'll run over it. Everything is piling up, and the pressure is too much to bear. I feel like I might snap.

"I don't have a freaking clue what I'm going to do. I have no idea if I'll even be here tomorrow. I could get a call tonight and be on a plane tomorrow, and then, you're right, I'll just have to walk away because Andie has been through enough."

I let that hang there as I try to breathe through my anger.

"Listen, I know this sucks, but like it or not, it's what we signed up for. We fought and worked our asses off for this job and life. I'm not saying it's right, but if you care about this woman, which, given your tone, I suspect you do, you need to think about this. Don't get caught up in something that could make things worse."

I want to jump through the phone and rip his head off. Instead, I take a deep breath, trying to reel myself in. I know he isn't trying to be a prick. He's only looking out for me. But the thought of saying goodbye to Andie permanently has my stomach falling to the floorboard. It's selfish, but I don't want to.

I pull into my garage and let my head fall back on the headrest, trying to prevent myself from melting into a pile of angry defeat. "All of this is so messed up. I just want to live my life. I want the Tigers to make a decision and just get on with it." I pause, thinking of Andie. "I want everyone to leave Andie alone and let me..." *Figure this out with her.*

"I know, man. I know this has all taken its toll. Maybe just give it a little time. Let Morgan move on to trying to ruin someone else's life. Get some distance there. See what the Tigers are going to do. If you care about Andie, you need to put her first."

He doesn't understand putting her first means telling her goodbye, and I don't know if I can do that. Shane said to hold on tight and not let go. I'm so freaking confused.

"Just be careful. Be smart."

My loud, dramatic, and annoying brother is sensitive and thoughtful. *What's happening to my life?*

I know he's trying to help, but my temper is blazing while my burst of hope is being trampled. I was letting myself want this one thing. Maybe it was too much to hope for. It's too much of a good thing to let myself think I might actually be able to have her.

We hang up, and inside my house, nightlights provide a faint glow that matches my gloomy mood. Dark, with only a glimmer of light that at any moment could go out.

I head straight to my room, then into my sauna, and while I let the steam work on my sore body, I think about all that Mark and Shane said. I feel like someone may as well rip me in half. I'd never want to hurt Andie, and with this trade looming, that might be exactly what I end up doing if I'm not careful.

I rest my head against the wall, and salty sweat stings my eyes. If it's best for me to step away, we'll do the event next weekend, and then she can get back to her life, and I'll try to go on with mine.

That thought is like a kick in the stomach, making me get up and hit the shower. I sit in bed, staring at my phone. Andie still hasn't played her word. It's ridiculous, but if she plays her word, it gives me hope she's thought of me too. It's stupid, juvenile, and even girly, but I don't care.

After next weekend, I have no idea what will happen. The trade deadline is approaching, and maybe I'll be moving. Maybe I won't ever see her again. Maybe it's what she wants, but it's not what I want.

I don't want to lose Andie. Her honesty and candidness. She makes me feel normal and alive and accepts nothing but the real me. The Sean

Greyson who grew up in the system with nothing and no one and somehow made it here.

It's selfish, but I've never met someone like her. I want to be the one she lets in. The one who gets to know what goes on inside her head, all the things she hides so damn well.

I cave and send her a message. If I want to know what she's thinking, I have to take a risk and try to find out. If next weekend is goodbye, I'll have to let it be.

ME: How was rehearsal? You ready for next weekend?

After fifteen minutes, I'm certain she isn't going to respond, but my phone buzzes. Thankfully, no one can see the smile it brings to my mopey face.

ANDIE: We're ready. How was the game?

ME: We won. So good.

ANDIE: Any news about the trade?

After talking to Mark, this trade suddenly seems like it could cost me a lot more than my comfort and team. I want to know what she thinks will happen after the event. Will this be it? Is she ready to move on with her life without the cloud of constant drama that seems to follow me?

ME: If I ask you something, will you promise to tell me the truth?

I see three dots, but they disappear. I'm expecting a smart-ass reply, but after a few minutes, there's nothing. I tip my head back toward the ceiling, and it hits my headboard. *This is nuts.* I'm nuts for thinking she and I can ever be anything other than co-event planners. Then my phone rings.

"Hey." I don't even try to disguise my surprise. I wish I were sitting on her couch so I could read her face.

"So that's a stupid question. I have no reason not to tell you the truth. What's this about?"

My heart starts to race, and I chicken out. "Why haven't you played your word?"

She knows I'm a chicken-shit but lets it go. "I'm…working on it. I'm taking my time, making you sweat a little."

My body relaxes, and the corners of my mouth creep upward. "Maybe you just need to surrender this round."

"Ha. Not a chance. Who in the hell do you think I am?"

I know exactly who she is, and I don't want this to end. I'm not ready for her to tell me good luck with my life.

When I don't bite back, her tone softens.

"Sean?"

"Yeah." I try to clear my head.

"What's going on with you?"

"Nothing. I…" I rub my temples. I don't know what to say.

"Who's messing with your head?" Her tone is suddenly irritated.

"No one. It's nothing, just…next weekend and so many people will be watching us. These trade rumors are gaining attention, and I'm just waiting for the call at any moment. I don't know if the organization is waiting to see what happens with the event or if it even has to do with what Morgan said about us." I roll my neck, trying not to let myself tense again.

"Next weekend will come and go, and people will forget about us." I want to ask if she'll forget about *us*, but my tongue is glued to the top of my mouth. "What happens if they trade you?"

"It's starting over with a new team, a new organization, and having to leave my guys." I don't want to start over somewhere. I want to finish out my contract and figure out what's next. "All of this stuff is becoming too much. I can't focus with all the noise. It's too loud, and the last thing I need is for it to affect my game."

She's quiet, and I wonder if I've spilled too much.

"We'll get through next weekend, and then that will be over." She needs to quit using words like 'we' and 'us' because I like the sound, and it feels lasting. "Then all your focus can return to playing. Maybe then those trade rumors will die, too."

I don't say anything because I don't want next weekend to be over if that means I can't talk to her and see her anymore.

"Sean, it's all going to be ok."

"Then why do I feel like I'm standing on a ledge, and someone is about to jump out and push me off?"

She laughs, and it's like joy to my sad soul. "Because you've had some shitty days. But after the storm, there are rainbows and sunshine."

I've gone from darkness to light before, so I believe her. I just want to know that when the storm finally stops, it doesn't mean she'll step out from underneath the umbrella and be gone.

Chapter 31

ANDIE

I lift my face to the sun and close my eyes. The blue sky is filled with fluffy white clouds, and even though there's a chill in the air, warmth radiates through me.

The outfit I chose for today is perfect–my black leather jacket over a crop top, high-waisted leather leggings, and black lace-up boots that hit just above the ankle. I've even gone with a more dramatic eye of purples and gray with some black liner, and I can feel it shimmering in the sun.

Enjoying the heat enveloping my body, I can't help but think about Josh and wonder what he would think about all of this. What would he say?

I know he'd be proud. He'd want to meet these families, and then he'd laugh and carry on bringing smiles to their faces. He'd be honored these veterans are getting to be a part of something so special.

But I know he'd also tell me it's time to let go.

I keep my eyes closed, breathing through the burn in my throat and the well of tears collecting under my eyelids. Not completely. Pieces of him will remain tucked inside me always. But over the past few months, since I stood on a platform in the middle of this exact field, hearing him tell me he loves me one last time, I've found myself able to see life on the other side. I've somehow climbed my way out of the devastation and utter despair.

I've started living again, and day by day, it's as if my heart is being stitched back together, one tattered piece to another. It's like it's started beating again. Maybe to a different rhythm, but it's coming back to life, revived and renewed.

I'm not sure if it was by chance or divine intervention, but this mess with Sean has shown me that life goes on with or without us. No matter how hard we try to hide, we eventually have to open the door and step back into the light, or we'll die, too.

We weren't meant to stay in the dark forever, no matter how badly we may want to. It becomes safe and comforting, but it only feels that way because we think nothing can reach us there.

The truth is, even if we can't see it, the light is still there, waiting for us to return. Whether we want to or not, we have to crack the door, step out, and feel the sun on our faces to be reminded that there's still goodness waiting for us.

"Are you praying or tanning your face?"

My eyes pop open as Gem slips her arm around me. It's familiar and comforting.

"Just thinking." I rest my head on her shoulder. "Last time I was here, it was very different."

"How so?" She rests her head against mine, and her soft, floral scent wafts around me in the breeze.

"Every part of me wanted to run home where I was safe and comfortable. I didn't think I was ready for anything to change. Today, it doesn't feel quite so scary, like…I'm starting to discover this new part of myself I've never known before. It's still scary but also exciting."

My Gem holds me tighter. "I'm really proud of you, sweet cheeks. You're one brave girl."

We stand there together as people mill around us. The band is setting up the equipment on stage, and team members are filling tables with Tiger memorabilia, food, and drinks.

"What happens when this thing is over?" Gems asks quietly.

"I start working on my album and hope people like what I have to offer."

She shifts a little. "Andie, that's not what I mean. What happens after this event?"

I frown. Gem never calls me Andie. If she does, it means I'm on her shit list. "I don't know what you're asking me."

"With Sean, baby girl. What happens with Sean?"

I haven't seen Sean yet today, and I'm anxious to see him after our last conversation. Something was going on with him underneath our little chat the other night, and I'm curious to know what it was.

"I don't know. It's probably best if we just go back to living our lives." I pause, waiting for her retort, but she says nothing. "The other night, he texted me and asked if I promised to tell him the truth if he asked me something, but…we never got to whatever it was."

"Hmmm."

"Sean is…different from any man I've known. There's a lot underneath that pretty face and all that muscle, but we live in two very different worlds. All that's happened is everything I've wanted to avoid and a big part of why I've never signed with a label."

"Sometimes the things we think we don't want are exactly what we need. That man, this ugly misunderstanding, helped you find your way out of the hole you'd fallen into."

I sag a little, not wanting to admit she might be right.

"You know I wouldn't say this if I didn't mean it, but I want you to hear me." She turns to face me. "Things like getting trapped in an elevator and being thrown together in a mess of tabloid paraphernalia aren't coincidental. Sean gave you a nudge on a day when you wanted to fall apart for a reason. He's been right by your side, climbing through this pile of horse manure when he didn't have to. So many other men in his position wouldn't have cared in the least how this affected you. He's worked with you, helped you, and put a sparkle back in your eye that hasn't been there for a very long time."

Her soft, wrinkled hands cup my face. "This doesn't have to be the end of it, but you have to be willing to put yourself out there and quit giving him a hard time long enough to let him know you want that."

A knot forms in my stomach, along with a rippling wave of anticipation. I'm not sure what I want. Suddenly, there's a pressure building, and it's uncomfortable.

"Gem, I don't even know if he wants that."

"Oh, pfft! Are you blind? No man would do any of those things just because. Besides, he hasn't been able to keep his eyes off you since he got here." I frown and start looking around, but Gem nudges me. "Good night! You're going to cause yourself whiplash. Have I not taught you anything in all these years? Be subtle, my girl."

She straightens her black coat. "Just make sure you don't accidentally end something that has the potential to be magnificent."

"Hey, hey, ladies. Let me get your pic."

Nora interrupts us from behind. I had to get here early for a sound check, so she brought Ax, who's currently strapped to her front in a carrier with a stocking cap that looks like a tiger.

"Wait." I move toward her. "I want Ax in the picture." She helps me get him out, and I kiss his growing cheeks. "Hey, monster." I lift his chubby little body in the air.

Gem and I squeeze together, and Nora snaps a picture. "Hold it," Nora orders, waving someone over. "Oh, come on. You're used to having your face plastered everywhere."

I look over my shoulder, and she's talking to Sean. Gem winks at me, and I see the mischief in her eyes has returned.

Sean's big body settles next to me. "Hey."

"Hey." I take a breath, feeling my nerve endings prickle as his large hand wraps around my side, and the warmth of one finger presses against a sliver of bare skin at my waist. That one tiny point of contact creates a zing that claws its way through my entire body, and it's ridiculous.

As Nora encourages us to smile, he pulls me just a little tighter, and the pressure of his hand increases. Not only do I not mind it, it's a feeling I've wondered if I'd ever have again. I'm just not sure if I should be having them with Sean.

Nora snaps a couple of pictures and smiles as she checks them. Gem leaves with a flourish, off to make the rounds and let everyone know she's here.

"Are you alright with him for a few minutes?" Nora gestures to Ax. "I'm going to go take pictures of the band setting up. We'll get all of you before you start."

"Sure," I say as she scurries away like a mouse in a wide open space, and Sean and I are left alone.

"Are you ready for today?" He surveys the field that's slowly filling with people. "Miranda said the families are starting to arrive."

It's strange standing on this field with him and being in such a different place than before. Instead of pads, a helmet, and that stoic face, he's in a Tigers long-sleeved shirt and black athletic pants. He's no longer the nameless stuck-up football star. He's become…my friend. Someone I care about and root for.

"Yes. I'm excited to meet them and hope to see a ton of smiles." Around us, Sean's teammates gather and talk, with Gem now interjecting herself into their circles. "It's nice your teammates showed up. These kids are going to have the best day."

"I hope so." He breathes out and turns his attention back to me. "I'm sorry about the other night…," he starts but doesn't finish.

I meet his eyes, searching. He looks tired and unsure, which isn't like him. "Are you alright?"

He nods, but I'm not convinced. "I'm glad you brought him." He tugs on the ear of Ax's hat before dropping his hand to his side. "The hat is great." He smiles at Ax, but it's not the real deal. This one took work.

I bump his shoulder. "Hang tough and keep going. It'll all work out. I've learned recently that sometimes even disasters can be beautiful."

Those clear blue eyes hit mine with an intensity that has my cheeks heating, and a flash of his touch runs straight through me. I shiver.

"That so?" The question is simple, but there's an underlying importance to it that makes me smile.

Before I can respond, he's almost taken down by a little girl with braided pigtails. "Sean, Shaney told me we're going to meet some kids today and show them how to play football."

He scoops the little girl up and holds her at his side. "How did you sneak in here? I've been watching for you." He tickles her, and she giggles and then sets her eyes on me.

"You're very pretty. Are you Sean's girlfriend? Maggie said he needs a nice girl who doesn't talk shit about him."

I laugh, and Sean groans. "I'm not, but I definitely think Maggie is right."

"I don't think you're supposed to say bad words," Sean whispers in her ear as a large, good-looking, and very intimidating man steps up beside him with two boys.

The man, who I assume is "Shaney" slaps Sean on the back, and they hug, but it's more than one of those friendly man hugs. I have to assume this is one of his brothers. When they're done, Sean bumps fists with the boys before turning back to me.

"Andie, this is my brother Shane, and this is Liv, Garrett, and this jokester is Teddy." He ruffles the younger boy's dark hair as he squirms.

All their eyes land on me. "Nice to meet you all."

"Who's this guy?" Shane asks, raising one of Ax's arms.

"This is my son, Axel. He's playing drums today."

"He's too little to play drums," Liv laughs. "He should come play with Aiden when Maggie is done breastfeeding him. She's over there keeping her bits covered." Liv points in the direction of some chairs.

"Liv," Shane warns.

"Do you breastfeed Axel?" she asks.

"Alright, you little interrogator," Sean interjects. "I think it's time for you all to go find a football so we're ready when the kids make it down to the field."

"We've been watching you, and we know your routes," Teddy says. "Hope you can keep up."

"I don't know. He's getting pretty old and looking a little tired these days," I say, like I have any idea what I'm talking about. "My money's on you guys."

Shane laughs, and his face relaxes. I wonder if his other brother has the same tough, serious look. Growing up in foster care would harden you.

Shane slaps him on the back and calls the kids away as he wanders to where people are gathering.

"I better see if Jonesy is all set and then find Nora. Do you want me to come find you when we're ready to welcome everyone?"

"Sure." He takes a step back.

"Have fun today," I command, knowing we likely won't see much of each other. Given everything, it's probably for the best.

"You too." He turns but stops, turning back, hesitating. "Can we talk after today?" I frown, not exactly sure what he's asking. "I mean, I still have to beat you in Words, so…"

I smile. "Never going to happen. You might as well give up now, loser."

He smirks, and for the first time today, it's legit. "Nah, I don't give up. I know how to work hard for what I want."

My stomach squeezes tight with something that feels a whole lot like a swarm of anticipation, and it kind of freaks me out…in a really good way.

"Well, good luck. I've never been one not to put up a fight when someone sets a challenge in front of me."

He laughs as he turns and walks away.

I watch him for just a second, trying to understand exactly what just went down, but then I turn to go find Nora. Whatever happens now will happen.

After today, we'll see where Sean and I end up. If I think about it too much, I'll run in the other direction. For today, I'm just going to let it be and do what I came to do. Help these amazing families have the best day.

"I can't even tell you how amazing this is." A woman grips her husband's hand, who's in a wheelchair. "We are the biggest Tiger fans, and to get an opportunity to do this...we saw you sing the national anthem, and your story resonated with us. I didn't think he was going to make it." A tear falls down her cheek, and I lean to hug her.

I've been doing a lot of hugging over the past half an hour. Families are scattered about, talking to players while kids toss footballs back and forth. Smiling faces are everywhere. People are laughing and having a wonderful time, with a few tears mixed in. This is exactly what Sean and I hoped it would be.

"It's a real honor you were able to join us and all these other families." I take a step back, needing to get myself ready to sing. "Make sure you get autographs and pictures with all of these big guys, and I hope you can make it to the game tomorrow."

I've been inching my way from one family to another, trying to find Nora to hand Ax off. I finally see a clear path, but I'm stopped by Gem and the McNeils. They're chatting with the same guy I saw corner Sean at the party. The one who I assume is the team's General Manager.

"Andie." Mr. McNeil beckons me. "Let me see that young man. Gemma has been gushing about how handsome he is."

I stop and turn Axel to give them a good look at my little guy. "This is Axel."

"Awe. Look at him." Mrs. McNeil reaches for his hand. "He's just adorable."

"This is your son?" the maybe GM asks. Today instead of the slimeball suit, he's wearing a team pullover. His long perusal tells me my instincts about him aren't wrong.

"Yes." I hold Ax a little higher and kiss his cheek, ignoring the discomfort in my belly.

"Andie, I don't know if you've met, but this is Doug Miller, our General Manager," Mr. McNeil says.

"Nice to meet you," I respond as the guy's calculating eyes run over me.

"You too," he returns, but it feels fake. "You and Sean have quite the turnout. Unfortunately, such a scandal had to exist to make this happen. Today needs to put that all to rest, and everyone can get back to business."

"Well, I'm certain business around here was never interrupted over poor acting and a wounded ego." Gem looks the tool dead in the eye before turning to Mr. McNeil. "Besides, anyone who makes decisions based on what that woman said is a clown." She turns to me. "I think we should go find Nora. It's time to get this show on the road."

We turn, and I hear Gem mumble under her breath. "Shove his head up his tight–"

I laugh, listening to her go on about Doug. When we find Nora, I leave Ax and Gem with her to babysit so I can join Jonesy and the rest of the band, but like he was watching me, Doug stops me.

"Andie," he says like he knows me. "I know this may be a personal question…your son…" He crosses his arms over his chest. "Is he, you know?"

I frown, wanting to understand if he's asking me what I think he's asking me.

"I've been told your relationship with Sean is strictly professional, and there's no merit to Morgan's claims." His eyes travel away, then harden as they zero back in on me. "I'm concerned we have more of a problem here than we realized."

I stiffen. "What problem would that be?"

Doug lets out a snotty chuckle like I'm slow. He rests his hands on his hips like he's choosing his words carefully. I know they're going to send me into a rage, regardless.

"Look, whatever arrangement you and Sean have is your business, but we don't need the press getting hold of any information about a baby. I'm sure you understand what that would mean." My fist wants to make contact with his face. "It'd be best for everyone if you make sure the wrong people don't get wind of him. This needs to be over, and Sean needs to focus on his job. We don't need any more problems."

I stare at him, trying to figure out who he thinks he is. He takes a small step closer.

"I'm not sure if you understand, but Sean's career is on the line. That won't work out so well for you in the long run, if you know what I mean."

I roll my shoulders back and match his stance, trying not to hurt him. "What I understand is you seem to think Sean and I care about what conclusions people may draw. This is my life. It's his life, and we have to deal with people like you trying to manipulate situations to cover your ass. That baby is *my* son, and not you or anyone else will tell me how to handle anything when it comes to him. If you have an issue, take it up with Sean. I don't work for you, and even if I liked you, I still wouldn't do what you're suggesting."

I turn and walk away, wondering if Sean knew anything about this. Did he know Doug or someone else would have an issue with Ax? My mind is spinning when I'm supposed to remember the words to songs in just a few minutes.

I don't want to make things worse, and I definitely don't want Ax to be the next target, but I couldn't let that asshole tell me to hide my son. I also wasn't going to let him think he could dictate what happens with Sean and me. He may have leverage with Sean, but I don't give a damn what he says.

I climb the stairs and find Jonesy.

"You alright?" he asks while I stand there, trying to collect myself back from the brink of kneeing someone in the balls.

"Yeah. Some dick just tried to tell me I should hide Ax."

"What?!" Jonesy's face scrunches into a look of disbelief. "Who?"

"The team's GM."

Jonesy searches the crowd like he wants to know who he is. "Does Sean know about this?"

"If he doesn't, I have no doubt he's about to find out." I look at the crowd gathering around, having the best time. I don't see Sean.

"Do you think you should give him a heads up? This is no joke."

"Maybe. I'm just really tired of all this." I let out a long, calming breath. "I have to find him anyway so that we can welcome everyone. Are we all set here?"

He nods. "We're ready when you are."

Oh, I'm ready, and then I'm ready to be done. "I'll find Sean so we can get things moving and kick off the first set."

"Try to have fun. This is for you, too." He grins, making me smile, but I'd really like to punch something.

I search the crowd for Sean, spotting him off to the side, taking a picture with a child. I don't want to add to his stress, but his GM just hit a nerve, and I'm over all of it.

I'm certain what I said didn't go over well, and I probably just made things a whole lot worse for Sean, but what was I supposed to do? I won't do anything different with Ax. He's here, and he's staying. If Sean can't handle that, then after today, we'll say goodbye and go on with our lives.

Chapter 32

SEAN

I pull my arm back and release a ball. Twenty yards away, a kid with a big toothless grin catches it. He brings his arm back and uses his entire body to launch it back to me. Kids are everywhere, running, playing, and laughing as my teammates do the same thing, stopping to take pictures and sign jerseys.

"Alright, I'm taking names. Who's on the list, and where do I start?" Maggie steps up next to me with Aiden over her shoulder. "I've heard too many things lately that are really pissing me off, and I don't care what Shane says. It's my business, and I'm at your disposal for a limited time only. Shane's busy with kids so now's our chance. He can't stop me."

I smile and reach over to hug her tight. This woman has become the sister I never had.

"Hey, I'm so glad you guys could make it." I toss the ball back to the kid waiting on me.

"You hanging in there?" she asks, rocking side to side.

"This helps." I glance around, noting all of the smiling faces.

"Shane told me about these preposterous trade rumors. What are they thinking? They seriously can't be legit or about this BS your ex is trying to sell."

I shrug. "Rob's working on it, but my GM doesn't like the negative press. Defense is lacking, so maybe this would be an effort to beef up for next season."

Maggie blows air between her lips. "Trading you for defense would be a mistake. You don't trade someone who gets the ball into the endzone."

"Yeah, well, I guess I'll find out soon enough. The deadline is nearing, and chatter is picking up. They have to know the rumors exist, and they're not doing anything to dispel them. At this point, besides leaving my team, I'm not sure I care. I don't want to be a part of an organization that isn't going to stand by me or thinks I'm disposable."

Maggie nods like she understands and then turns in a circle, looking at the crowd. "Sean, this is amazing. Shane and I've talked to so many families, and these kids are having the time of their lives. You did an awesome job."

"Just wait until Andie starts singing. It's only going to get better."

"Where is that hot little thing? I haven't met her yet, and I need to know who you've been *hanging* out with." She raises and lowers her eyebrows.

I know exactly where she is, but I'm not giving that away. I haven't been able to keep my eyes from drifting in her direction every chance I get.

When my hand unintentionally found that sliver of bare skin earlier, it took everything in me not to let my hand linger there. It was all by accident, but that small skin-on-skin contact lit up my entire body like it had scored the winning touchdown at the Super Bowl.

My physical attraction is intense, but the reality is, it's everything else that Andie is that has me wanting to hold on to her when this is over.

"She's making sure things are set with the band."

"I heard she brought her little guy, and I need to introduce Aiden. They could be best buds."

I roll my eyes. "We're just friends."

Maggie pushes her lips to one side. "You know Shane was pretty slow regarding matters of the heart, but I know better with you." She rests her hand on my arm, stopping me from throwing the ball so I'll look at her. "If there's something there, this other stuff doesn't matter. Don't be afraid to take a chance. The job will work itself out. Love doesn't knock on our door every day. If you have feelings, swing that baby wide open and see what happens."

She squeezes my arms before walking away. I toss the ball back and then let my eyes roam the field, searching for Andie again. She's talking to another family and leans in to give a woman a hug. I want to believe that everything will work out, but it feels like, at any moment, everything is going to come tumbling down.

When I spoke with Rob last, he said the rumors seemed legit. He's ready to meet with the organization and start the conversation, but I asked him to wait until after this event.

Seeing Andie this morning made all my worries disappear for those few minutes. When Nora took a picture, having her tucked against my side, I felt secure and wanted to stay exactly like that for the rest of the day. It was calming for all the uncertainty stirring inside me.

That's the thing about Andie. I never have to guess what I'm going to get. I always just get her. She's unchanging and strong and brave, and it's contagious. I want to absorb everything she is. In my world, I've become addicted to the authenticity and genuineness she lives by.

She gave me a hard time about calling her after this event. I hope that maybe I'm not the only one who feels something shifting between us. Even if that's true, my life brings constant attention and time away. She may not want any part of it. The first kept her from signing with a label, and she told me how difficult it was for her and Josh to be apart. These things will only worsen if I'm traded.

I want to do what Maggie said. I want to say screw it and see what Andie and I could be, but it feels like one wrong move and she'll disappear. I only know bits about what she went through losing her husband, but I've noticed her hesitancy and shyness, and I respect that it takes time. I won't push her. I don't want to do anything that will cause me to lose the person who has become my best friend over these past months.

"Well, well, if it isn't Mr. Scandalous."

I turn as Mark steps next to me. The kid I've been tossing the ball with eyes grow wide at the sight of him, and I hand over the ball so he can throw it back.

"Hey, bro." I hug and release him in time to catch the ball.

"Nice thing you got going on here. I just saw Shane and the kids. They're getting teams together for a game."

The kid I've been playing catch with approaches wanting a picture with Mark. After a few clicks and an autograph, he runs off to find his foster family.

"I can't even imagine what it would have been like to do this when we were being held captive. You and Andie did a hell of a job making dreams come true." He sounds somber and reflective.

I'm not sure what's going on, but this is the same tone I heard on the phone, and it's not his usual annoyingly sarcastic and boisterous self. Over these next few days, I'll have to get to the bottom of it.

"I'm glad schedules worked out, and you could be here. These kids are going to attack you any minute."

He laughs. "Why do you think it took me so long to get over here? I thought I was going to get sacked on the way in." He slaps me on the back. "Be careful what you wish for, though. You're stuck with me this week. I hope you have my pass for the game tomorrow. I'm ready to sit back and watch your ass get tackled in real life. It's been a while."

"Hey." Andie's voice catches my attention. "Are you ready to officially welcome everyone? We need to start the first set so things wrap up on time."

Her head tips up, and her green eyes are even brighter today with the purple eye makeup she's wearing.

"You must be the elevator girl that hates his guts," Mark interrupts. "I've seen the pictures, but he didn't tell me they don't even come close to the real deal." His slick smile appears, and I want to slap him upside the head. "I'm Mark, this idiot's brother from some other mother." Rather than being normal and holding out his hand, he moves in to hug her. I want to kill him.

Mark is a habitual flirt and only becomes more exaggerated when he wants to drive Shane and me absolutely insane.

Holding on to her tight because he knows it makes me want to punch him, he fake whispers, "I'll have you know that I'm much better at keeping a low profile if you're tired of all the drama and turmoil that follows this guy around."

Usually, I don't think twice about Mark's fictitious playboy persona, but today, I want to mess up his styled dark hair and wipe that smug-ass look off his olive-toned face. I mouth, 'I'll kill you,' but that only makes him grin.

Andie laughs, but it's out of kindness, which has my lips turning upward. "Something tells me that you keeping a low profile would be like asking a monkey to stop climbing trees."

He pretends to stab himself in the chest. "You wound me. Stunningly beautiful and witty. I bet the press didn't know what they were doing messing with you."

"Yeah, well, they don't really care as long as they make money." She forces a smile. "It's nice meeting you, but we've got to get started."

"I'm here for the next few days, so I hope I see you again. If you're coming to the game tomorrow, come find me." He winks, and I want to groan but hold it in. "We'll hang out, and I'll give you all the goods on this one."

"That would be fun, but I won't be here." She turns to me. "You ready, Pretty Boy?" Her tone is tight and quipped.

Mark snickers. "Pretty Boy."

I shoot him a glare and follow Andie, wondering what's up with her. Something tells me it's not nerves.

"What's wrong?"

She doesn't break her stride heading toward the stage. "I need to talk to you."

That's never a good statement, and my stomach squeezes into a knot, falling to the ground somewhere behind me as I try to keep up with her.

"Can you stop and tell me what's going on?" She's like a woman on a mission, dodging people to get to the stage. "Andie." I wrap my hand around her elbow, but she resists and keeps moving.

"Just hold your horses. I'm not doing this out here." She charges forward, taking us around the back of the stage, and finally stops. Her eyes are focused on the ground, her hands in her coat pockets, and I don't like it. A loose curl falls in her face, and I fight the urge to push it away.

I take a tiny step forward. "Tell me what's going on."

Her shoulders slump. "I did something you might not like, or at least, it's probably not going to do you any favors."

My brows pinch together, and the space where my stomach used to be aches. "Ok."

She kicks the ground with the toe of her boot. "I was trying to find Nora earlier when Mr. and Mrs. McNeil stopped me wanting to meet Ax. Your GM was there."

I try to remain relaxed, but every muscle starts to contract, that ache growing heated. I know I won't like what's going to come out of her mouth.

"He's an arrogant jerk, in case you didn't know. He pretended to be all friendly, then followed me. He asked me, or maybe he assumed…Ax is yours." She pauses. "Apparently, he's a problem, and he doesn't care what our arrangement is, but there can't be any reports about a baby."

"That son of a bitch." I run a hand over my face.

"Sean." She waits for me to look at her. "Do I need to worry about this? Are you worried people will talk about Axel…or that they'll think he's yours?"

The pain in her eyes stabs me straight through the chest. I don't even have to think about it.

"No. I told you that before, and I meant it. Andie, I don't want any more of this to hurt you. It's absurd to even think about it, but we both know practicality doesn't factor into what these bottom feeders will report on. They don't care who they hurt, the cost, or whether or not an innocent child is harmed in the process."

She swallows hard. I want to step into her and pull her close, but I force myself to stay put.

"He's my life," she whispers. "I won't hide my son, but I will protect him. So, I won't parade him around giving these predators an opportunity."

She sucks in a breath and pushes it out like she's collecting herself, and I can barely stand it. I want to hold her and tell her it will all be ok, but I can't. I don't know that it will be, and it's killing me.

She pulls herself up and meets my eyes. "I…I've spent some time hiding from things and can't do that anymore. I pray if people find out I'm a mother, they won't use that to make headlines, but like you said, they don't care. You and I can't control what lowlifes will do."

"I couldn't stand it if that ever happens."

"You didn't do this, Sean, and I'm not going to live my life worried that someone might say you're Ax's father. That could happen today or six months from now, regardless of what you and I do or don't do. I'd do anything to protect him, but he's also my son, not something to hide."

Her confident words help ease the fury raging through me. "It's only Tiger PR here. No, outside reporters, but are you sure you aren't worried?

That's not why you didn't tell me about Ax? When this is over, I can make a statement or…"

I hear her inhale and exhale, and I'm not sure if she's pissed or just thinking. "Sean, I didn't tell you about Ax because it was none of your business. He's not my little secret."

I hear anger and hurt, and I don't like it. "I didn't mean–" I start, but she cuts me off.

Her tone is soft, but there's an edge to it. "My own parents have never met my son. They've never asked about him, called him by his name, held him, and made him feel safe…like you did." She pauses, the rawness of her words and the tears she's determined not to let fall, kick me straight in the throat. "He is the best, most important thing in my life. I won't let them or anyone else hurt him or make him feel inferior. I trusted you enough to let you into my house. You held my son."

I suck in a breath, needing it. "You can trust me now." I want her to know it and believe it.

"What happens if they say he's yours and this whole thing starts over but worse?" She's putting me on the spot and has every right to.

In this, I'm surprised to find I have no fear or hesitation.

"Then you and I do whatever necessary to keep him safe and away from it."

Her eyes flick between mine, searching. "Ok."

"Ok?" I need to know that this conversation is closed. I can't stand being worried she'll end up hating me, which could happen at any moment. Given my history, I'm very familiar with people walking me to the door and closing it.

She bites her lip. "He said your career is on the line."

A string of curse words hovers on the edge of my lips, but I hold them back. "What did you tell him?"

"I'm sorry, but I couldn't–"

I cut her off, needing to know what she told him before I go find this fucking asshole and tell him how this will be. "Andie, what did you tell him?"

She pushes her lips to the side, her eyes drifting away from me, and it's only then that I feel slightly better, knowing she let him have it.

"I told him you and I don't care what other people think. I said if he has an issue, to take it up with you."

I rest my hands on my hips and let out a long breath, trying really hard to keep from smiling. "Is that all?"

Her cute face scrunches up. "Why are you smiling? This isn't funny."

"Actually, it is. You told him exactly what I would have, but you were nicer. I don't care if they trade me. I'm so sorry you had to deal with all of this."

"Seriously, you aren't mad? I didn't make it clear that Ax isn't yours and…I know this only makes it harder for you. What if he uses this against you?"

I grab her hand, and I don't even care. She doesn't pull away. "Andie, you're right. It's our lives. It's my job, but it won't be my entire life. Doug is going to hate to hear that."

Her eyes drop to the ground. "I told him I didn't work for him and that even if I liked him, I wouldn't do it."

"Is that all now? Does he have a black eye?"

"I definitely thought about kneeing him in the balls, but I thought I'd let Gem have the satisfaction. She is turning eighty soon. It'll be my gift."

I laugh, and it feels so good even though I should be worried about what's coming. I can't believe Doug would do this or think I'm the kind of man who would hide a child, one he thinks is mine.

She pulls her hand back and sticks it in her pocket, my momentary joy turning sour. "Look, I should've probably been a little gentler in responding. I don't want to go another round with all of this, and Ax can't be involved. This all needs to stop." She shakes her head. "I won't hide Ax, but after we welcome everyone, I'll keep to myself."

"Andie–"

She holds up her hand to stop me. "This is your job, and a lot of people are counting on you. Your team, your fans, all these kids who now believe they can be you one day. What Doug is suggesting isn't right, but what you do matters to all these people."

A growing sense of doom fills my empty space inside, and my heart rate picks up speed as my palms start to sweat.

"Andie, I don't want this organization or anyone else to tell me how to live my life. I did that, and look where it got me. In the tabloids because I trusted someone I shouldn't have. I'm tied to an organization that doesn't trust or value me for anything other than what I can do on the field. Evidently, even that doesn't matter anymore."

I hang my head, needing to calm the blood racing through my body with the fear of her walking away from me. "It shouldn't be like this. I can't go back to pretending nothing mattered. I was numb and lost and wrapped up in bullshit. I let everything important just fall away, and now…" *I'm going to lose my closest friend.*

She tips her head to the side. "Let's just get through today without new targets being painted on our backs. Hopefully, the damage is minimal, and you can figure out what's really going on, and I won't be a factor."

How did things turn so quickly? I rub my temples, trying to figure out how to tell her that won't work.

"There you guys are." Jonesy interrupts from the stage. "Miranda is on the hunt. We've got to start now."

"Ok," Andie says and then turns back to me. "Let's do this, and then you have time to figure things out. This will be over."

"I don't want this to be over." That damn elephant is squatting on my chest again, and the last thing I want to do is stand on this stage and pretend everything is fine.

Andie grabs my hand. "Don't let those bastards ruin one more thing. Just give it all a little time. Things will work themselves out."

I want to believe her, but besides football, that's not how my life works. It's probably why I let myself get lost in the first place.

The drum sets the beat of the next song, mimicking the pounding in my head. The crowd before me is singing and dancing, while it's all I can do to keep myself planted here instead of finding Doug and getting myself into a hell of a lot more trouble than I'm already in.

"Not only is she a smoke show, but I could handle listening to her sing me to sleep every night." Mark slides up next to me, Shane with him.

"Not right now, Mark," I warn.

"What's with the scowl and bad attitude?" Shane grumbles quietly, although, with the music, I'm certain no one can hear him.

I don't want to get into it. I'm one spark away from blowing my lid, and Doug is still loitering. I need time to figure out how best to handle him.

My eyes wander to Andie, beautiful as ever up on stage, and I want nothing more than to pull her off of there and make her promise not to let this ruin our non-friendship.

When I don't say anything, Shane pushes. "You want to tell us what happened, or do we need to guess?"

"Man, she dumped you today? That's harsh, but maybe it's for the best." Mark shrugs like this is some kind of joke, and my face must morph into full-on rage because Shane's hand grips my shoulder.

"What happened?" Shane's voice is low and calm.

I take a step back, needing not to be touched. I'm hot, someone's taking a sledgehammer to my head, and I may need an oxygen cannula.

"My GM cornered Andie. He asked her if Axel is mine and told her to hide him. He said my career is on the line."

"Damn." Mark rubs his chin. "I didn't see that coming. What are you going to do?"

"He's not going to do anything," Shane says coolly. "What did Andie tell him?"

"She told him we don't give a shit what he thinks." I'm trying hard to keep my temper in check, but every moment that goes by, I'm one step closer to losing it.

"Is that how you feel?" Shane's eyes move around us like he's ensuring our conversation is private.

"What do you think?" I bite at him, but he takes it. "He's a baby. He comes first, and there's no way in hell I'd ask her to hide him." Mark remains quiet, which is for the best. Shane, Mark, and I have had enough squabbles in the past for him to remember we have no problem taking our anger out on each other. "She said she's going to lay low and let me get this figured out."

"Maybe that's for the best."

My head snaps in Shane's direction. This is not what I expect from him. I know with one hundred percent certainty if this were Maggie and the kids, he'd be throwing punches and asking questions later.

He holds up his hand. "Look, I know that's not what you want to hear, but you need to take a minute and think this all through, not just for you, but for her."

He sounds like Andie, and it makes me want to stomp out of here and go to my quiet house where I can think.

"This isn't right, any of it. I shouldn't feel like I'm being chastised for something I didn't even do. I come here every day giving it my all, thinking this organization is ready to be rid of me because of a bunch of bullshit. Now, they want to throw their weight around to ensure an innocent baby doesn't create headaches for them. I can't do this."

I take a step away, but Shane stops me.

"Just listen. This is complete bullshit. You and Andie shouldn't have to explain anything to anyone. Unfortunately, you still have one season left on your contract, and it might be best for everyone if you let this play out. Get Rob in there and get the conversation going. If they're going to use this to excuse trading you, you want to be as much a part of those negotiations as you can be."

He pauses, making me look at him. "If Andie is who you think she is, she's not going anywhere. Take a minute. Not everyone walks away. Trust me."

I close my eyes, wanting to believe him. It's easy for him to say it now, but before Maggie, he didn't believe in love or people sticking around. He was a loner and planned to be forever.

I nod, having to trust him. There's nothing else I can do. "I have to find Miranda and see how she wants to wrap things up. Then, I need to get out of here."

"I'll find you before we go," Shane says, releasing my shoulder.

I wander toward that stage, needing to find Miranda without running into Doug. Thankfully, she's easy to spot among some of my teammates and gives me orders on what will happen once Andie wraps up.

I see Nora with Ax strapped to her, wearing tiny hearing protection over his ears, and sound asleep. I find a place to the side to stay out of the way and get some space, feeling sucker-punched at how this day has turned out.

This is not how it should be. This is not how I want my life to be. I won't be controlled and manipulated to fit into a world I'm not sure I want to belong to anymore.

"Hey, handsome." Lost in my head, I miss Gemma moving in beside me. Her tone is soft over the music and similar to Andie's when her guard is down. "You know that saying when life gives you lemons? It's complete horse shit."

She lets that hang in the air, her attention on Andie belting out a song from behind the piano.

"When life starts to jerk us around like we're on one of those carnival rides operated by hard criminals…" Out of the corner of my eye, I see her finger move in a circular motion. "We can either let them continue to take us for a ride or decide we've had enough."

When I remain silent, her head swivels in my direction, and I feel her wise eyes on me.

"Do you understand what I'm saying?" she asks, seemingly not expecting an answer because she continues. "You must know a whole lot about not having things turn out and the universe treating you as its dumping ground, but things are different now. You're different. You've fought, worked hard, and won."

I scoff, and it's sarcastic. "I'm not sure I've won anything at this point."

She turns toward me, resting her hand on my arm. "Young man, you have what so many strive for, and few ever achieve. Fame, fortune, and most importantly, a platform. You have a whole city of people who believe in you. A team that calls you theirs. You have brothers and a family I've met today who stand by you."

She pauses. "These people wouldn't have anything if you boys didn't show up here every day and make their incapable asses look good. If they want to let you go, let them. Take your talent and your good heart somewhere it's appreciated. You aren't that little boy anymore. People will only shove you around until they realize you'll knock them on their sorry behind."

She raises one eyebrow, and a smirk crosses her mouth. "I'm just a woman who's seen a whole lot of life, and I don't presume to know anything about this world that you live in or the pressures that come with it, but I do know a little something about small men in fine suits trying to bully their way through life. They don't like pushback. Use what you worked so hard for, Sean."

"And that one up there," she gestures to the stage. "If you let her, she'll run so fast you won't catch her. Something started in that elevator and on this field that brought her back to life. I suspect the same might be said for you. Don't let the temporary dictate the future. If you want her, make sure she knows you're not going anywhere. Give her a chance to do the same."

She pats my arm twice and then steps away. "Oh, and Sean, consider this your invitation to my birthday party. I don't accept declines. It's not a game day, so there are no excuses."

She walks away, and I try to let all she said sink in as Andie hits the final note and thanks everyone for coming. I pull myself away from my angry sulking and make my way through the crowd to shake hands and bump fists with the families and kids one last time.

It takes an hour, but the field finally starts to clear while the band packs up their equipment. I have no idea what to say, but I need to find Andie and see if I can get a clue as to what happens now. Part of me doesn't want to know.

I think about what Gemma said about not letting her push me away and wonder if that's what she's doing. Is she pushing me away, protecting herself from me, or from the potential backlash of us and now Ax?

My head throbs, and my body aches as I search for her amongst the workers cleaning up the field and getting things in order for tomorrow's game. I eventually spot her talking to Miranda and head in their direction.

"Sean, this was amazing," Miranda beams as I step into their conversation. "I was just telling Andie not only did these kids and families have the best day, but I think we might have actually turned the ship around for you two. Social media is screaming with positivity, and fans love the two of you."

I try to act like I care, but I can only look at Andie. "That's great." I can't even muster fake enthusiasm.

"Well, I need to pack up," Andie says. "Please let me know if there's any way I can help in the future." She tells Miranda, her statement sounding so final it punctures a deep scarred wound.

"Of course. You're gaining quite the following here at the stadium, so I'm sure I'll be in touch." Miranda steps away, rushing off to direct workers moving the remaining team souvenirs.

Andie stays put, but her eyes are everywhere but me. "I think today was a success. Good work."

"Don't say it like that."

I see her stiffen. "Like what?"

"Like this was only some stunt. You and I both know it wasn't."

She shoves her hands in her pockets. "Sean, I don't know what to say. I do know we probably shouldn't be seen arguing in the middle of the field."

I can't withhold my sarcastic scoff. "Since when do you care who sees you arguing with me?"

She tips her head to the side, her eyes finally meeting mine and filled with an irritation that matches my own. "Maybe since it's become abundantly clear that you live in a world that doesn't have room for ordinary people with real lives and real backgrounds and real…" She doesn't finish.

"That's not fair, Andie."

She holds out her arms but not exaggerating so she doesn't draw attention. "Look around, Sean. These guys, your team, they're your friends. They live in the same world you do. Your brothers, both of them, same world. All of these people meet the acceptable standard." She shrugs. "I don't, and I don't want to."

I see exactly what she's doing here, and it's pissing me off. Andie doesn't give a shit what other people want or think, and this is her running, pushing. Gemma called this.

It's been a long time since I had to fight for what I wanted, but I haven't forgotten how. Andie is about to find that out.

I take a step closer, but not so close I invade her space. I speak calmly and clearly, letting her know I mean every word.

"This place and these people may be my world, but it is no longer my entire world. Andie, there's no standard you fit into. No box. No category. You are an outlier, and these people have no idea what to do with you."

I feel myself start to relax just a little, knowing exactly what's going to happen. "I'm going to get to the bottom of this stuff with Doug, the trade, and anything else loitering out there. I'm going to play this game I love, wherever that is. When I step off the field, it's my time, my life, and I get to decide what to do with it."

She bites her lower lip. "I hope it all turns out the way you want." Her eyes move to the stage. "I need to go help pack up."

Her stubborn ass is making this so difficult. "It will because I know what's important now. I have to go too. My brothers are waiting." She nods once and takes a step back. "I'll call you."

She stops her retreat. "No. Figure out your life."

She says it like it's final, but that little two-letter word coming out of her mouth is like pouring gasoline on a fire.

"I'll see you soon, Andie." I take a couple of steps away, but she doesn't move, her beautiful green eyes almost disappearing as her lids close halfway over them.

"Sean, I don't like people who don't listen."

"I know. You don't like me anyway, so I don't really care." I turn, not giving her a chance to respond.

I'm going to find my brothers and figure out what in the hell to do about Doug, this team, the trade, and whatever else is going on that I don't know about. Then, I'm going to call Andie and make damn clear I'm not going anywhere. I need her in my life. I don't care in what capacity. She's dead wrong about not meeting the standard of the type of person acceptable in my life. Hell, she set the new bar.

Chapter 33

ANDIE

"Are you going to answer that?"

My phone buzzes on the table in front of me. I flip it over to see the caller and set it back down. "No."

Jonesy clears his throat and hits the button to play back what we just recorded. My phone buzzes again, just once. I don't need to look at it, but Jonesy raises his eyebrows.

"You sure you don't need to get that?"

"Yeah."

He hits the button, and my song stops playing as he swivels his chair in my direction, leaning back so far the chair looks like it might tip over. "Are you avoiding him?"

"I don't know what you're talking about." I lean back in my own chair, crossing my arms over my chest.

It's been three days since the event, and Sean is calling. Again. He told me he would, and he has, despite me telling him not to.

I don't know what to say. He looked pitiful and frustrated and like he was about to lose his lunch right there on the field, but I'm not interested in more drama or ruining the career he's worked so hard for.

I know it's immature to avoid him, but he needs to figure out his life, and I need to get back to mine. Dictators run his life, and there's no room for anything other than football. His GM made that clear.

What started out as two hours in an elevator became a horrific nightmare. One we're both more than ready to put behind us. We helped each other through it and used it to do something amazing for some incredible people. Now, maybe it's time for our dreadful adventure to come to a close and move on.

Jonesy taps a pen against his lips. "Andie, I've known you long enough to know something is going on, and I'm smart enough to guess it has to do with Sean and what happened at the event. If that man is calling you, you can't avoid him forever."

I roll my eyes. "You sound like Nora and Gem. Please tell me you haven't joined their sewing circle."

He laughs. "Not yet, although they're highly entertaining."

I flip my phone over and look at it.

SEAN: How long is the blackout going to last? I'm going to keep calling.

I meet Jonesy's expecting eyes. "I'm not avoiding him. I just don't know what to say yet. This whole thing has been…too much. It's constant drama and worry. I can't live like that. He needs to get stuff sorted out with his management and know what's happening with the possible trade. I need to not be a part of that…at least until things settle down."

He twists the chair from side to side, studying his hands. "So, you can't be friends until then?"

I rub my face. "I don't even know if we're friends."

It's a lie. I know we're friends. Actually, he's become my closest friend outside of Nora. I've even shared things with him that I haven't admitted to anyone. I'm fairly certain he's done the same, but maybe that's because it was safe. There was no pretense or misconception that we were anything other than what we were. Just two people caught up in a lie, trying to make the best of it.

There wasn't a single thing between Sean and me that was fake or dishonest. There's never been a reason for it. The whole world thought we were sleeping together, but we relied on each other, dealt with the consequences, and unbeknownst to all those people, we became friends of the truest kind.

Jonesy picks at a fingernail. "Want to know what I think?"

"Do I have a choice?"

"Nah. All of what you said might be true, but good friends don't come along every day, nor do relationships. They can suck and are hard work. That's why we fight to make the good ones last." His chair squeaks as he leans forward, resting his arms on his knees. "Think you might be scared there's possibly a little more going on here than friends, and you're pushing him away?"

"I'm not pushing him away." *Nuts. I might be. Crap.*

His head falls to the side, and his eyes peek out from under his eyelids. "Andie, even a blind person could see what's happening between the two of you. You guys developed your own team of two. You're partners, battling the rest of the world. You sure you want to give that up?"

I wipe my clammy palms on my jeans, scared to really sort through this. "I'm not pushing him away. I'm just…being careful." I pick at the fringe on my jeans. "I was all in from the moment I met Josh. I didn't take even a second to think about what his life and commitment to the military meant to me. It didn't matter. I loved him, and his commitment became my commitment."

I pull a strand loose and wrap it around my finger. "Jonesy, I have no idea what I'm ready for or not ready for. I have no idea what I'm doing, and on top of that, Sean is in a mess. I won't get in the middle of something again if I don't know I can sustain it. His life belongs to football. He could be traded any moment, and then he's gone." I debate whether to state the last of it, but Jonesy's empathic eyes pull it out of me. "These guys get hurt all the time."

He's quiet as he watches me, and I squirm under his close examination.

"Is this about him or you?" He challenges softly. "It sounds to me like he's going through hell and might need a friend. A real friend. I know Nora and Gemma are putting pressure on you, but you don't have to be anything else. If you ever want to cross that bridge, it's up to you when and how far you go. No one gets to decide that but you, and from what I know, Sean's not pushing for anything more. Give him a chance. You could use another friend. This shit is exhausting." He grins, and I bite my lip to try to prevent mine. "What's the worst that can happen? You're already sleeping with him."

I toss my pen at him, and he catches it. "Is our therapy session done?"

"Yes. The hourly rate here is too expensive, and we need to finish this song."

He rolls the chair back toward the soundboard and hits the button. My voice fills the room while I think about what he said.

I might be hiding. I don't know what I feel for Sean, and I'm not sure I want to find out. Or maybe I'm just really scared I feel more than I might be ready for. But then I think about what Gem told me about not letting fear keep me from the possibility of love, and it makes me want to kick myself.

Sean's never been anything but honest with me. If I'm going to take a chance, he might be one worth the risk. Especially when I'm not even sure I like his pretty boy football-playing ass.

Chapter 34

SEAN

I stare at my phone like somehow it will make her name appear. This is day four of Andie avoiding me, and I'm over it.

Mark is in my kitchen singing *Free Falling* and making a giant mess according to the banging and clanging mixed with his horrible voice.

"Do you have any cornstarch?" he hollers.

"Do I look like Martha Stewart?"

"Quit watching your phone like it might jump up and dance. Get your ass in here and help me cook. It's my last night, and I'm making dinner. I'm sick of eating that tasteless garbage we've eaten the past few nights."

I toss my phone on the couch and pull my sore body up to help him, even though I don't want to.

After the game last weekend, I had Monday off, and we spent it binging a series and playing video games while we both avoided talking. I'm trying to deal with my issues, and Mark is clearly dismissing his. I spent the rest of the days at the facility, and tomorrow, Rob is meeting with Tigers to get answers. I want to know what they're looking to get for me and from whom.

After talking with Shane and Mark, I've made sure to steer clear of Doug and let Rob handle this. Approaching him myself won't do me any favors, and I just need to know where I stand.

I've tried to call Andie just like I told her I would, but so far, she's not answering. If Mark weren't here, I'd be tempted to just show up at her house and make her talk to me.

I know she doesn't want to be in the middle of whatever happens with me and the Tigers, but whether she meant to or not, it tells me that she cares, so I'm not giving up. At least not until she tells me she wants me to leave her alone, and I believe her.

I step into the kitchen, immediately wanting to turn around. "What in the hell are you doing in here?" There is shit EVERYWHERE.

Mark looks up from what I assume is a recipe. "I'm cooking, jackass. What does it look like I'm doing?"

"It looks like a toddler went on a rampage and emptied every cabinet, drawer, and the entire flipping pantry."

"That's ridiculous. I've discovered your kitchen and pantry are seriously lacking. This chicken marsala will likely taste like shit because I've had to sub half the ingredients." He points a spatula at me. "I don't even care how bad it tastes, I've put up with your temperamental ass all week, and you're eating it."

I pull out a stool at the island, trying to ignore the mess and sarcasm. All week, I've had to watch him try to pretend he's fine, and I'm sick of asking him if he's ok. He's like a woman. Stomps around, clammed up, making it clear he's not ok but never wanting to talk about it.

I'm ready for this drama queen to go back to New York. "My temperamental ass? You're like a freaking hormonal woman." I speak in a high tone. "I'm fine. Stomp, stomp, stomp. Slam. Everything is fine."

Tipping a pan over chicken breast, he stops mid-pour. "Me? I'm like a woman? For days, you've been staring at your phone like a teenage girl waiting for her boyfriend to call."

"Look, she matters to me, and I don't know what in the hell is going on. I know you think this is stupid, but I'm not like you. I don't want to run from party to party, wanting the world to believe I'm doing just fine. I got lost in that, but I won't again. I made a huge mistake with Morgan, and I'm paying for it in more ways than one. Andie has been the best thing that has happened in my life in years. No, probably ever, and I don't care what you think. I'm not going to just let her walk away without a fight."

I take a breath. I hadn't intended to say all of that, but damn, it felt good.

Mark stares at me, the pot still in his hand. He slowly pours the rest of the sauce on the chicken and then turns to set the pot back on the stove before facing me again.

"I was wrong." His voice is soft and quiet.

"What?!" I bark back, not expecting that from him.

"I was wrong." He steps back and leans against the counter, crossing his arms. "What I said on the phone about laying low with Andie and her son, I was wrong." He rubs his unusually scruffy face. "I was probably also wrong about what I said the other day. I don't think you should just give her space."

What. The. Hell? Mark never admits to being wrong, even when Google clearly proves it. "What are you saying?"

"I'm saying I…was…wrong," he says slowly like I'm an idiot. "I saw the two of you together. I've been here the last few days watching you sulk like a sad puppy, and it reminds me of how I've felt for the last eight years without Lex."

Ahhh. Now we're getting somewhere. Mark's first and only love, Lex, is getting married. If I wasn't so distracted, I could've guessed this.

"You sit by your phone waiting for her to call?" I ask, hoping to make this easier on him.

"No, dumbass, but if I thought there was a chance in hell she'd call, I'd freaking do nothing else just to be sure I didn't miss it. You care about Andie. I've never seen you look at a woman, any woman, like that."

"Like what?"

"Like you wanted to take her right there on the field but also…like she's the one you can't afford to be without. Bro, that doesn't happen every day. Plus, I've seen you mope around here waiting for her to call, and no man gets his panties all in a bunch unless she really matters."

"She won't call me back, though. I can't make her give this a chance or see what we can be. She doesn't want any part of this life, and I can't blame her. It's brought her nothing but trouble."

"It brought her you."

I run a hand over my face. "I'm not sure that's enough. She lost her husband. Lived apart from him. What I have to offer isn't much better. We get hurt every day. I may be moving. I don't even know if pushing her to talk to me is fair."

Mark raises his shoulders. "It's just talking. I saw how she was with you. You need that in your life, especially now. You won't push her for something she's not ready for, but we don't give up on friends. We have so few. Don't give up. Trust me, you don't want to regret letting something amazing slip away."

"What are you going to do?" I understand now how much he's hurting.

His eyes drift to the floor as his arms cross over his chest like he's protecting himself. "I have no idea. Not much I can do. She's getting married. I want her to be happy. So damn happy, but I want her to realize she can only be happy with me."

"It's been eight years, man," I cringe.

He runs a hand through his hair and holds it there. "I know, but until that ring is on her finger, I have hope. I have to. It won't matter how many years go by. I have to believe what Lex and I had was the whole package. I don't know what happened, and I'll probably never know, but that hope is what's been getting me by. In a few weeks, I guess I'll have to figure something else out."

I ask a question I'm not sure I should, but given his openness and honesty with me, I'm going for it. "Have you ever thought about going back and talking to her?"

Mark stares at me like I have two heads. "Uh, yes. Pretty much every day."

"Then why haven't you?"

He blows out a breath. "Because there's a very real chance it won't make one bit of difference, and I'll have to live the rest of my life knowing I'd made it all up in my head, and it's really over."

"But aren't you going to find that out when she gets married anyway?"

"Yeah, but at least then I don't have to look into her eyes. I don't think I could walk away again."

"Shit, bro." I put my head in my hands. "When did we turn into these guys?"

"It's all Shane's fault. He started this looking all in love and happy." I chuckle. "I need a beer," he says, moving to the fridge. "You're going to call her tonight and figure this shit out so that at least one of us can have hope."

I laugh. "You've got weeks. You might think about doing something with it. I can't stand spending any more time with you like this." I point at him. "You all pouty and pissy is just…gross and annoying as hell."

"Whatever, you're getting a home-cooked meal out of it. It might taste like ass, but it was made with love, and you're going to think of me when you heat up leftovers."

Chapter 35

ANDIE

I kiss Ax's head, carefully laying him down in his crib. I watch him breathe and run my finger over his soft, chubby cheek. His dark hair is barely long enough to show some curl, and it makes me so happy.

My phone rings in the other room, and I quickly move to pull the door almost closed. I reach for my phone on my bed, hoping it's Sean. It's time to be a big girl and get this conversation over with. I don't know what that conversation is precisely, but I know it involves talking.

Like I conjured him up with my thoughts, it's him.

"What are you doing?" I have no idea where to start, so I jump right in.

"Calling you." His voice is soft and unsure, and I don't like that's where we are, and I know it's my fault.

"Whhhhhyyyyy?" I draw it out in tease.

"Beeeeecaaaauuuuse I don't know why I'm not supposed to call you."

I can almost see that pretty boy face brightening with that response. "Ummmm, maybe because I could jeopardize your career."

"I'm not accepting that. I don't care what other people want or what they say, and that includes Doug. We're the 'not giving a shit' team, remember?" He's right. We are that team. "Listening to what other people think and want got me into trouble. When I'm on the job, that's one thing. Off the field, that's not happening anymore."

"Sean, this is everything you've worked for." I hear him push out a breath. "You have your life, and I have mine with Ax."

"We're friends, Andie. They can't tell me who I can be friends with."

"We're not friends. We worked together, and now it's done." I try to say it with conviction, but I'm pretty sure I failed.

"I know we're not friends, and you don't like me all that much, but Andie, you're one of the few real things in my life. You are real with me."

"At all."

"What?"

"I don't like you at all." I clarify, teasing him.

"I know, but I like you, and you are my friend. Not Doug or anyone else is going to tell me otherwise."

"Sean, I don't give two diddly dos about what that jerk says. This isn't about him. It's about you. It's about what you've worked for and everything you've overcome to get where you are. That shouldn't be taken away over a bunch of lies. You can't just throw that away for something silly like this. You're doing the thing you love with a team that depends on you. It's not just about you and me."

"Andie–"

I cut him off. "Pretty Boy, you really want to be friends with someone who doesn't like you so bad that you're willing to get traded because of it? To start over with a new team in a new city? To possibly lose the thing you fought tooth and nail for when you had nothing else?"

"Andie, if they trade me, it's not because of you, and even if it was…I'd pick you."

Oh bugger. He had to go there. "I don't want you to lose anything because of me."

"First of all, none of this has anything to do with you. I'm pretty sure whatever is going to happen with the Tigers is probably already decided. My agent is meeting with them tomorrow. He's also making it clear that my personal choices outside of my contract are off-limits to them. If they don't like it, it's too damn bad. They can ship me off to another team."

"Will you promise me something?" No matter what Sean and I ever end up being, I can't be the reason everything he's worked for falls apart.

"I need to know what it is. I'm not into breaking promises."

The man has to make this difficult. "Fine. I want you to promise me that if I'm a factor in you not staying with the Tigers, you won't let me be. We can't be friends if it's like that. You need to put your job first, and we'll give it time and see where it all settles."

"So, we are friends. Friends with no benefits."

I know he's smiling. I groan. "We're maybe friends. It's still up in the air."

"Hey, it's progress."

"You are such a loser."

He laughs, and it's a nice sound. The anxiety I had about this conversation has totally dissolved.

"You need to promise me," I say, meaning it.

"All I can promise is that if you come up as part of that conversation, you and I will talk about it, but I don't plan on you being any part of any conversation having to do with me and football."

"I don't know if I like the sound of that." I'm starting to see Sean has a stubborn side, and I don't think I hate it.

"Tough. It's the only thing I'll promise."

"Fine. Stubborn ass."

"You know I've been called a whole lot worse lately, so I'll take it."

I bite my lip, fighting a smile. "You suck, but I hope the meeting goes well and you get to stay with your team."

"I'll let you know." His voice is soft and gentle and stirs something in my belly.

"Ok."

We hang up, and I flop back on my bed. I don't know what I'm doing or what is going on, but I like it, and at the same time, I'm terrified out of my mind.

I pull a pillow over my face. I'm going to be brave. I'm going to be patient with myself and with Sean as he figures this out, and I'm going to take this one call at a time.

Crap. Who am I kidding? I'm going to freak the hell out because caring even the tiniest bit about this man is opening up my heart to get broken all over again, and I don't know if I can withstand that.

Chapter 36

SEAN

"What *exactly* does that mean?"

Rob stands next to me in a quiet hallway of the practice facility. "It means they're looking at their options. They're shopping you around to see who's interested and what they can get in return. With next season being your last under contract, they're getting creative. This stuff with Morgan probably didn't help, but they're anticipating other organizations actively pursuing you next year anyway."

He pauses as someone passes. "They're looking toward next season. They have confidence in the second-string running backs, but the defense needs a significant boost, and they know they're losing Gibbons. You're marketable. If they can get a good deal and you're likely gone anyway, they're evaluating all options."

I rub a hand over my face. "Who's showing interest?"

"So far, Houston, Phoenix, and Miami…Seattle hasn't gotten back to them. If you have a preference, you need to tell me. Cole is in Miami, but they're rebuilding." He lets out a breath. "Doug said he'd be in touch. You'll be the first to know, but we need to be proactive here. This is business, but they respect you and what you've done for this team."

It sure as hell doesn't feel like it. "I don't know what I want."

Rob leans back against the wall. "If we play this right, you might have a better chance at a division title or maybe even the Super Bowl. Think about it. Get back to me quickly with your thoughts."

I nod. I don't know what to think. I don't know what I want, and my head is spinning.

"They're impressed with the attention the event got and the fan responses. You did a good thing there. Other teams are paying attention and would be excited to bring that kind of positivity and community involvement to their organization."

He slaps my shoulder. "You and Andie are on everyone's radar."

"She stays out of this," I demand.

"Understood. Doug understands that, too. I made that very clear."

"You and I both know I have little say in this." I rub my neck. "I won't fight to stay with an organization that's done with me. I want a cohesive team with loyal management. Maybe see if you can find out what's going on with these teams and see who's a real candidate." I let out a breath while my stomach pitches upward with all the uncertainty. It's like living on borrowed time.

Rob steps away. "I'll be in touch. If we can get ahead of this, we may even have some bartering power." He shakes my hand. "Sit tight. Try not to stress about this. You've got a lot to offer, and the Tigers know what they might be giving up."

In the weight room, I try to release my anxiety and prepare for tomorrow's game. My focus is shot, and I need to get it back. There's nothing worse than stepping out onto the field when my head isn't in the right place. It's careless and dangerous.

At home, I dial Mark and Shane, needing their encouragement and advice. Sitting around doing nothing, waiting for the gavel to drop, is a massive distraction I can't afford.

I scroll through the list Rob sent me with teams showing interest. "I just sent it to you," I tell them.

"What are your thoughts?" Shane asks.

"I don't know. Miami sounds interesting. Cole is there, but their offense is struggling. I'm not sure I have years of rebuilding left in me."

"Houston is a mess. I'd steer clear of that if you can help it," Mark says quickly. "But Arizona's got a pretty good thing going on, plus I'm a free agent after this season, and Arizona's on my list. They're interested, but I'm sure they'll wait and see how my surgery turns out and if my shoulder heals. It'd be like old times."

"I'd pay to see you two playing together," Shane laughs. "If you have time, you should catch up with Cole. He has some work ahead of him and could use some help."

"What's happening with Andie? Is she a factor?"

Mark asks the question I've tried not to think about. I promised her she wouldn't be, but how could she not be?

I've never met anyone like her or felt the things I feel when I'm with her. I don't want to screw it up, but moving and spending most of my time away might be exactly what happens. She did that with Josh, and I know she's not looking to do it again. If a trade goes through, I don't have a choice.

"She doesn't want to be a factor in my career decisions. I'm not sure I like that idea, but we all know I won't have any say in this." It's as honest as I can be.

"You're right. With the trade deadline looming, you'll likely not have a say or time to sort anything out, but if you do have any sway, you need to be ready. Figure out which of these teams is most likely to get you where you want to be. Do you want a chance at the Super Bowl, or do you want to be closer to Andie? Only you can decide that."

Shane makes it sound so easy. I know he knows it's not. He gave up an opportunity for a head coach position because he wasn't willing to leave Maggie and the kids. It's not the same. Shane and Maggie were married. I don't even know if Andie wants anything other than us not being friends.

"All you can do is wait and see what happens," Mark says, sounding sympathetic. "I know it sounds cliché, but if you and Andie are supposed to be, it will work out. She won't walk away simply because you're forced to another team. You can't change this. She'll understand that."

I want to believe that's true, but Mark doesn't know Andie's past, all she's faced, and her desire to protect herself. I can't give her any more reasons to run from me, or she'll disappear.

"You can't let this mess with your head," Shane's tone is demanding. "Play the game and keep Andie in the loop. I know it's not the same, but I didn't tell Maggie about the interview at Ohio State. That was a mistake."

"Yes, sir."

We hang up, and I have to get ready for another phone call. This time, it's a meeting with one of my sponsors. So far, my potential move to another team hasn't been an issue. Really, all these guys want to talk about is Andie and me. Some are interested in featuring us together, which is a hell NO.

This trade is coming. I don't want to go, but I'm not sure I want to stay with the Tigers after what Doug tried to pull with Andie. If I decide to play another couple of years, maybe moving teams now is the way to go. The deadline is approaching. I need to talk to Andie and tell her it's likely that I'll be moving within that time.

I'm worried this will be the final thing she uses to push me away, but like Mark said, I can't change it. If I'm traded, I'll have to go. All I can hope is that she'll understand and not use it as one more reason why we won't work.

The uncertainty of how she'll respond has a pit growing in my stomach. It's a real possibility this will all end before she even gives me a chance. Figuring out how to make this all work seems like an overwhelming challenge, but walking away from Andie completely isn't even an option I'm willing to consider.

I take a deep breath, resting on my couch. I have to try to do what Rob said. I need to sit tight and let this play out. If I move to a different team, it'll suck, but I've done it before and can do it again. The problem is, this time, there's a beautiful, stubborn, curly-haired woman I'd really like to make sure doesn't tell me goodbye in the process.

The vice around my chest wall twists a little tighter. Standing in front of my locker, I stretch my arms overhead and to the side, needing it to ease. The idea of putting on my pads with the added pressure and restriction is daunting.

I've tried to prepare for what's waiting for me on the field, but my thoughts are scrambled and messy. I couldn't stand to listen to my pregame playlist of *Happy* on repeat today. The thought of that song is like a fist around my stomach. I rest my head against my hand, trying to pull in air.

I haven't talked to Andie about my conversation with Rob. I can't handle her pushback. I can't fight one more fight right now, even though a battle sits before me out on the field.

Talking to Shane and Mark hasn't helped. What I really want is to hear Andie's voice and have her give me shit because, on some level, it makes me feel like everything might actually be ok. It reminds me that this is just a job, and when I walk out of here, there are more important things waiting.

The problem is, besides my brothers and Maggie and the kids, I don't know if there is anything else. I don't know what will happen with Andie. I don't know if she'll continue to push me away and eventually be successful.

"Hey, man. You alright?" Tyrell leans up against the side of my locker.

"Yeah. Just thinking." I swallow down the bile choking me.

"Something you need to get off your chest before we go out there?" He points to his head. "This needs to be here."

I nod, knowing he's right. "I can't turn my brain off."

"This about the rumors?"

I shrug. "Which ones?"

"Any of them?"

"How about all of them?" I try to smile, but I do a shit job of it.

"One play at a time, man. That's all you can do today. Leave tomorrow in here. You're a good man, Sean. You'll end up on top of all of this." He punches my shoulder. "Now, let's bring in a win and show these sissies what we're made of."

I tighten my pads and pull my jersey over. I only have a minute before Coach comes in, but I grab my phone, not stopping to think about it, and dial Andie.

The longer it rings, the harder my heart beats in my chest. I need hope that something else exists beyond this. I've never wanted anything else, and now I need something. I need her. Her voicemail picks up, and her voice is strong in telling me to leave a message. I close my eyes and breathe, trying to swallow down my fear.

"Hey, I'm about to head into the tunnel, but I hoped to catch you. I met with Rob and…I know I haven't called. I kept my promise, but I wanted to tell you about it. Anyway, I've got to go. I'll call you later."

I hang up, my eyes still closed. I lean over, resting my arms on my locker, trying to breathe around the obstruction in my throat. I spent the past few years living a different life. It was easier living in a superficial world based on a well-groomed image and only living for the game. The weather was beautiful there every day, but it wasn't real.

Life is hard, tiresome, and scary. I spent my childhood knowing only those things. I escaped for a while, but it left me lonely, isolated, and in the end, afraid. All of these things will work themselves out, just like they did when I turned eighteen and I was set free. Today is hard, but I know that at some point, tomorrow won't be.

I suck in a deep breath, only having that to hold on to. I shove it all to the side and grab my helmet, readying myself to join my team in the tunnel. As agitated and exhausted as I feel, it's better than not feeling anything at all. I'll tackle one play at a time and see where I end up. Hopefully, wherever that is, I won't be back to lonely and scared. I've had enough of that to last a lifetime.

Chapter 37

ANDIE

"What are you doing?"

Nora is sprawled out on the floor, scrolling her iPad and looking at table settings.

She peeks at me over her shoulder. "Gem asked me to help her plan her party, so I was putting together some table-setting ideas. She said she wants simple and classic."

My eyes switch to Gem, who's holding Ax, but has her attention pasted to the Tigers game. "Seriously, all of a sudden, you want to have some fancy party. Since when do you celebrate getting older?"

"Sweet cheeks, eighty is a milestone. I look damn good for a new decade, so I've decided it should be recognized."

"And what kind of party are the two of you planning?"

Gem raises her nose slightly. "Just a small dinner with close family and friends."

I squint my eyes at her suspiciously. This woman either goes grand or goes home. "Simple and small. What's up with you?"

"When was the last time I planned a party? It's been ages, and it seems about time. Eighty is a rite of passage. Besides, I can throw a small dinner party for no reason at all if I want to, but this seems like an excellent reason. You and Ax are the first guests on the list."

"Who else is coming?" At least two names on that list will make me wince.

"Baby girl, you're going to have to deal with them for the rest of your life, so you might as well get used to it."

I groan. This woman tries every ounce of my patience. "I think you and I are going to have to take a break until this shindig is over."

"Oh, put your big girl panties on. They'll be on their best behavior. It's at the house and not on your mother's turf."

Nora snorts, and I glare at her. "Are you going to be there, Miss Manners?"

"No, sorry. I have to watch my niece and nephews. My sister and her husband are going away."

I rest my head against the chair, trying to refocus on the game instead of thinking about having to be civil with my mother for an entire evening. This will be the first time we'll be in the same room. Axel, me, and them. I'm going to be consumed by dread until it's over.

The game is in the second quarter, and Sean is in. The ball is snapped, handed off to him, and he takes off, only making it a couple of yards before he's tackled. The camera gets a close-up of his handsome face as he squirts water in his mouth. I've been wondering how the meeting went with his agent, but I'm giving him space to sort things out.

"How did the recording go?" Gem turns Ax to face her while he tries to wiggle free. My little guy is working on crawling and wants to be down on the floor, seeing what he can get into.

"Jonesy and I spent an afternoon in the studio. I think we're set on the first song. We're trying to keep it as clean as possible. Just me and the piano."

"I can't wait to hear it," Nora says, still scrolling. "After I posted some of the footage from the event, people are dying for more. They're loving the acoustic sound."

"Well, Jonesy is working his magic, so hopefully, that's exactly what they'll get, but even better."

I watch as Sean jogs back onto the field. If he knew I was watching his game, he'd have that subtle, cute smirk I need to ignore. I finally had to fess up to being friends, but the man doesn't need to know I only watch these games because of him.

The ball is snapped to the quarterback, and number twenty-four takes off down the middle, hooking to the right, and catches the ball just as a player from the other team slams into his side. He goes down hard. I have no idea why this game is appealing, yet here I am watching.

My eyes stay on the screen as Sean lies there. It takes exactly one second for my heart to launch into a sprint. "Why isn't he getting up?"

Nora's head snaps up, and then she's upright. The three of us stare at the screen as he lies there. I can't even hear the commentators. All I can do is watch as people from the sideline jog out and kneel next to him.

"Why isn't he getting up?" I ask again, standing and stepping closer to the screen as if it will make him move. A sour taste fills my mouth as my heart pounds in my ears. I place my hand over my stomach, needing comfort.

I try to focus on the voices coming through the speakers and make sense of what they're saying, but everything is muffled as I watch Sean's unmoving form lay sprawled out on the field.

"He's moving, honey." Gem moves beside me, one arm pulling me close. "See his feet."

He bends one of his legs. It doesn't do much to lessen my anxiety. I need him to get up and these cameras to show me his face.

I wait for what seems like an hour, my body shivering with sweat, and he eventually sits. The damn station cuts to a commercial.

"Wait. What are they going to do?" I turn to Gem as panic fully takes over when I can no longer see him.

I feel so stupid, not knowing what they'll do with him. We stand there, the minutes ticking by, waiting for the game coverage to return. When it finally does, it's replay after replay of the hit, which I can't stand to watch as the commentators talk about concussion protocol. Sean is taken into a tent on the sideline, and minutes later, we watch him leave the field on the back of a golf cart.

I spin, the taste of my lunch returning to my mouth. "What now? Where is he going?"

Gem drops her arm from around me. "I don't know."

Nora pipes in with her iPad in hand to inform us that depending on the severity of the concussion, he may have to go to the hospital for scans and observations. When she starts talking about the protocol in place, I stop listening.

I'm helpless, and it drives me crazy. "How do I find out if he's ok or what's going on?" I ask the room like someone has a magic answer.

The game goes on as I stand there, trying to think of what I can do to find out something. There's no one to text but him, and I know he doesn't have his phone.

"This may not be a likable option, but give it a little time, and we'll see if your dad knows anything. He'll be able to find out if he's at the hospital." I nod at Gem's suggestion.

In the kitchen, I grab my phone, willing Sean to call me and tell me he's ok, knowing it's wishful thinking. When I pick it up, I see I have a missed call and voicemail from him, and I frown, looking at the time. It was from an hour and a half ago.

My shaky hands press the phone to my ear, listening, and his voice sounds…sad. I'm pissed I missed it and wonder what it was really about. *Shit!* I toss it down and pick it back up, needing to do something.

ME: Please let me know you're ok.

We watch the rest of the game, listening for information, the commentators providing none. All I can think is the last time something bad happened to someone I cared about, I didn't even get a chance to say goodbye. That reality is causing a recurring sinking feeling in my gut that I can't even begin to acknowledge.

After a few hours, when I can't stand it any longer, I call my dad, and surprisingly he answers. Fifteen minutes later, I know Sean's been admitted to the hospital. My dad relays the few details he's able to find out, including the room number Sean's been assigned, all without any questions.

I throw on some jeans and a shirt, leaving Ax with Nora while trying to assure myself that my maybe friend is going to be ok.

Chapter 38

SEAN

The nurse leaves the room, following the doctor who reviewed my results. It's finally quiet, although now I'm only left with my thoughts, which immediately turn to Andie.

I wonder if she was watching and if she saw what happened. *Did she get my message or try to call me back?* I need my phone, but who knows how long it'll take someone to bring my stuff from the locker room.

Blacking out on the field wasn't part of the plan today. I flinch at the thought of her seeing what happened. For once, I really hope she wasn't watching. Of all things, this is not what I need right now.

I knew I wasn't in the right headspace stepping out on the field today, but this was just a bad hit. No one's fault, but it doesn't change the fact that Andie didn't need to see it. It would scare anyone, but for Andie, I'm certain it'll bring about a reality she never wants to relive.

Gemma told me she's scared and will run if I let her. This just gave her a perfect reason to run fast and far. I try to think of how to get her number, but my brain won't work. The pounding is so intense vomit rolls up my throat with force, but given I've done that multiple times already, I swallow it down.

I work to push myself to sit up, but that only makes my head feel like it might explode, so I rest back again. I squint as the sliver of light filtering in from the door widens and brightens slightly.

As if she knew I needed her, Andie slips just inside. I'm so happy to see her, it causes a different kind of burn to creep up my throat. My whole body relaxes knowing she's here and I can talk to her. I can see her face and tell her I'm ok.

She remains in the dim light, her hair pulled back. I can barely make out her eyes as they trace over me.

"Come here," I whisper because any louder, I might actually puke. She shakes her head. "Andie, come here."

Her voice is soft and weak. "No."

I take in a slow breath, knowing this shook her, and that's exactly what I was afraid of.

"Please," I beg softly.

"I just wanted to make sure you're ok. Are you?" She doesn't move an inch.

"Yes. I have a concussion, but I'm fine. I have to stay for observation but will be out in the morning."

She looks down at the floor, closing her eyes. "Good."

"It's the only time I wished you weren't watching." That earns me a fleeting smile, and a flicker of hope ignites that this didn't just ruin everything.

"I'm sorry I missed your call."

"I wanted to hear your voice." I stare at her, wanting so badly to eat up the distance that's growing between us. "Please come here."

She meets my eyes. "I can't. I can't do this. I'm sorry."

She starts backing out of the doorway. "Andie. Please, I can't get up," I beg again, but she's gone.

I clench my jaw, wanting to scream and throw something, but my head won't allow it. *FUUUUCCKKKKKK!!!* I rake my hands through my hair, and the shot of pain through my head is so intense I may black out again. I lay with my eyes closed with so much frustration that my body won't let me run after her.

I take some slow, steady breaths, needing the pain to stop and my temper to cool. The physical pain lessens, but a deep burning ache scorches the hope I desperately need.

A subtle sniff has my eyes popping open. Andie stands next to me, tears running down her face.

"I don't like you."

I let out a breath. "Ok."

"You just keep being…you and made me care. I don't want to. I don't want to care about you, you big jerk."

I grab her hand and hold it against my chest. "I know. Come here."

She shakes her head. "No. Why can't you just go back to being the self-centered butthead I sat in the elevator with?"

I try to smile, feeling her coming within reach. "I let you believe something that wasn't true. I won't lie to you." She stares at me. "I called you before the game because I wanted to talk to you, to hear your voice. I can't focus with all of the noise, and you…ground me. You remind me that some things are real when everything else feels so messed up."

I pull her gently, and she sits on the bed facing me. I want to hug her and hold her close, but all of her guards are up, and I won't push her.

"I don't want this. I don't want to worry every minute. I can't do that again. I don't want all of the drama and spotlight. I don't want to care about you. I don't want to see you get hurt like this or worse. I know all of this is your life, but…"

I know I have to tread very lightly here. There's a canyon growing between us. She's standing on one side, and I'm on the other. If I push, she'll turn and run, and I won't be able to get to her.

"I know, but I'm selfish. I want you here. I don't want to lose you. Besides my brothers, you are the only person who–"

She pulls her hand away. "Don't say things like that. This…you and me. We don't work."

I try to be firm and not let my panic show. "Don't pull away from me. Don't hide, Andie. I'm right here. Take a chance. I won't let you down. I can't say I won't get hurt or bad things won't happen. No one can. But I can tell you *I* won't hurt you."

She starts to stand, and I tug her back.

"I have to go. Nora is watching Ax, and she can't stay."

I pull her to me again, and she comes willingly, resting her head against my chest. I try to push down the fear that when she walks out the door, she'll be gone…for good.

"Stay. Not right now, but stay with me. I need you." I sound pathetic, and I don't care. I've spent too many years alone and afraid to care anymore.

When she doesn't say anything, I lift her head and cradle her face, forcing her to look at me. "When I get out of here tomorrow, I'm coming to see you."

She lets out a shaky breath. "Sean…please don't."

"I'm coming to see you. Ok?" I want to pull her a few inches closer and press my lips to hers to seal the deal, but I know I can't.

She stares at me for a few long moments before she nods. "Ok. I still might not like you very much."

"Well, at least I've moved up from not liking me at all to not much." I earn the tiniest, saddest smile. I want to wrap my arms around her and keep her with me. If she's here, she's safe and won't disappear. "Go. I'll see you tomorrow."

She stands and moves toward the door, turning to look at me one more time before pulling it closed. I just need to get through tonight so I can take a chance at rediscovering my hope tomorrow.

Chapter 39

ANDIE

My eyes trace the path of a raindrop as it slides down my window, disappearing as it hits the ledge. The pitter-patter of the soft rain is welcomed company. It echoes the grief and fear I've held onto so tightly and might finally be too heavy to carry any longer.

With my fingers resting on the keys of my piano, my heart and head are at war. Sometimes, it seems like they're fighting the same battle. Other times, it's as if they're opponents, ripping each other apart. I'm confused and unsure, and it's all Sean Greyson's fault.

I wanted to stay in bed and hide today, maybe forever, where it's safe and warm, and there's nothing to fear. Instead, I sit here, standing on what feels like the precipice of defining the rest of my life.

He told me he was coming today. I want to pack up and hide out at Gem's, so there's no chance of being here when he shows up. But I've planted myself here, waiting, and it's pure torture.

The little beads of sweat underneath my fingertips, the nervous beat of my heart, and the roll of my stomach are daring me to stay and face him. I want to see him, to know again that he's ok, and that little fact has me calling my punk of an internal dialog's bluff.

Seeing Sean lay in the middle of the field and not get up had me reliving the worst day of my life over again and again. Only this time, I had to sit by and watch. I had to wonder if he would be ok, which was maybe even worse. The relief I felt seeing him only made the fear and the need to avoid it come roaring back to life in full force.

Once I knew he was ok, I left his hospital room, letting that fear guide my feet. I wanted to hit the hallway running, but I only got as far as the next door, realizing everything in me wanted to crawl into bed with him just so I could continue proving to myself that he was really all right. To hear him breathe, feel his warmth, and remind myself that this is not the same.

My relationship with Josh was hedged by constant worry, and I'm terrified to go back to anything resembling that. Living each day wondering if the person you love, the one you build your life with and around, will be there at the end of it.

So, I sit here, having to decide if I'm going to let fear win, keeping me from living and loving, or take the chance Sean asked me to…and stay. Stay and wait for him. Stay and keep my friend. Stay for the possibility of what might be.

I don't know what I feel for Sean. All I know is watching him lay on that field looking lifeless, and having no way to get to him shoved me down a path, and I'm uncertain where I'm headed. It's brighter and hopeful but none less scary. There's the risk of thorns and roots, stumbling, and wrong turns with dire consequences.

When I left his hospital room, I had every intention of turning back down the same familiar, safe way I'd come. But I carried myself back in there, my heart kicking and screaming, begging me not to.

My head knows Sean's career and life don't compare to what Josh dedicated himself to, but the worry remains alive. Bad things still happen. People still disappear. Love sometimes doesn't last. And despite all the warning bells blaring in my head, I stayed.

I wanted my heart to follow my brain. I wanted it to listen and remember the bad, the pain, the heartbreak, and the devastation. I wanted it to be ok to tell him goodbye and good luck. I wanted to convince him that our lives are too different and that we don't work.

But lying there, my head on his chest, was the safest I've felt in a very long time. It was then that my heart started to overtake the forces of my brain.

Sean was right when he said we can't promise never to get hurt or that bad things won't happen. But when they do happen to you, you know the possibility exists. It's that possibility that makes me want to hunker down somewhere deep and dark and stay there until he gets tired of trying to find me.

The thing is, what really scares me is that I don't want him to get tired, to give up. I want him to push and keep trying and not let me go back there. He says he needs me, and no matter how much I don't want to, I think I might need him too.

If I didn't, this would be so much easier. I could continue to walk my safe, comfortable, easy path. I wouldn't have to risk a new one, and my heart and my head could shut the hell up.

That's not the kind of person I want to be. It's not who I am. I don't want to live hiding in the past because I'm afraid of what the future might bring. I want to take a chance, and despite the fear and possibility of all that could go wrong, I want to take it with Sean.

He asked me to stay with him, not run and hide. I'm trying really hard. I'm trying to be brave, and I'm doing it for me, Ax, and Gem…and for Sean.

Gem is right. We weren't meant to live this life alone. He and I have both had enough of that.

So, I watch the rain, keeping my butt planted on this bench, hoping to hear the crunch of gravel and be reminded that he's ok and safe. After all, he's taking the same chance on me, I'm trying so desperately to let myself take on him.

I hope somewhere along the way, I might figure out where I'm going. And when I do, it'll be somewhere far better than where I've been.

Chapter 40

SEAN

It's been two hours since I stepped out of the Uber and climbed into my truck at the stadium. I collected my stuff from my locker and sped home to shower. Now, I'm two miles from Andie's house.

I should be thinking about the concussion protocol and when I'll be released or possibly traded, but all I can do is wonder what I'll find when I knock on Andie's door.

Will she be there? Will she let me in or turn me away? Did what happened yesterday change everything, and she'll tell me goodbye?

I asked her to stay, to give us a chance, and ever since she left my hospital room yesterday, I've thought about this moment. As much as I want to believe she'll be there, that she'll let me in, tease me, and give me shit for getting hurt yesterday, my past experiences tell me it's all wishful thinking.

Outside of my brothers, people only want Sean Greyson, the football player. They don't want the man who likes calm and quiet, the one who came from the foster system and overcame it. To them, all of that is insignificant and unnecessary, but not to Andie. Not since the day I met her has she ignored me. She called me out. She's pushed me and helped me find my way back.

Not once has she pitied me or made me feel less than. She's never looked at me as anything other than Sean. Me, as a whole person, not just the man in the helmet with a big paycheck. I'm scared to knock on her door and find out one more time that I'm not worth it.

My tires hit the gravel of her driveway, and my hands tighten around the steering wheel. I hold my breath as my chest feels like it's caving in.

Since I stepped out of the group home when I was eighteen, fear hasn't had a place in my life. I had nothing to lose and the whole world to gain. As I throw my truck into park, fear rolls through me. It's uncomfortable and foreign, but it hasn't been so long I've forgotten what to do about it.

I push my door open and step out. It's the only way. The fear of rejection will only last until I knock and find out what's on the other side.

I climb the steps to the soft, smooth tones of the piano. There's relief in knowing she's here. As I get closer, Sniper barks, and the music stops. I knock softly, not knowing if Ax is sleeping.

The door swings open, and Andie is holding the little man on her hip, Sniper by her side.

Like an idiot, I just stand there, trying to read her. She's wearing a sweatshirt and jeans. Her hair is bound in a low ponytail, with curls falling around her face. Her eyes are tired.

"Hey." Ax twists in her arms to see who she's talking to.

"Hey." My stomach clenches tight with anticipation.

Then, the most amazing thing happens. Her perfect lips turn upward into a smile, and she moves to the side to let me in.

She closes the door, and we're like two people who've never met.

I detest the awkwardness and squash it immediately. "I'm sorry–"

I don't have time to get a third word out because she steps into me, sliding her free arm around my middle and hugging me tight. I don't hesitate, pulling her close and wrapping her up just as tight.

"Don't apologize. That sucks," she says into my chest. "Unless you did that on purpose, and in that case, you can haul yourself right back to your truck." I laugh, and it's like food to my weary soul. "You scared me," she whispers, and Ax squirms between us.

"I know. I'm sorry. I hate that I scared you. I didn't have my phone."

She pulls away and takes a step back to look up at me. "How's your thick head?"

"Thick?" I cock an eyebrow just slightly, so stupidly happy she's teasing me.

She shrugs one shoulder. "I could've said suffocatingly big head."

I glare. "My doctor said I have a pretty brain."

She glares. "Is that so?" Ax squeals, blowing spit bubbles and bouncing his legs. She moves into the room and sits on the floor where toys are scattered. I follow, sitting on the couch. "How long until you get to play again? I read there's some sort of process you have to follow."

"I have to rest. Then I'll be evaluated and released for light training before I can get back on the field."

"At least they take it seriously," she says softly, keeping her eyes on her son.

I rest back on the couch and rub a hand over my face. "Andie, I'm really sorry. That doesn't happen often. It was a bad hit, and even if I'd been completely on my game, it would've been the same."

"What do you mean if you'd been on your game?" She turns toward me, frowning, and it's filled with concern.

I kick my feet out in front of me, watching Ax move from sitting to his belly and trying to inch himself closer to the ball. "Look at him." I point. "When did this start?"

She pats his butt as he grunts. "Last week. Once he gets it, I'm in trouble. He's going to be into everything." She watches him work, but then her eyes move back to me. "What happened?"

I knew better than to try to distract her. "I've been having trouble focusing. Meeting with Rob the other day only made it worse."

Andie pulls a toy closer to Ax to give him a break. "What did he say?"

I rub my unshaven jaw. "It's not a rumor. The Tigers are looking to see what they can get for me. It doesn't sound like it has to do with what Morgan pulled. I think they're using that, but it's more that I only have next season left on my contract. They think I'll be shopping, but they are running out of time. The trade cut-off is approaching, so if they're going to make a move, it's got to be coming. They're looking for a deal to strengthen the defensive line or beef up the team."

I pause as Andie tries to process. "The other running backs are solid, but our defense is lacking, and they know other teams will see me as a valuable asset. They want to get out of me what they can before I'm gone."

"What do you want?"

"I don't know." I rest my hands behind my head. It still aches, but at least it's tolerable. "I thought I'd fulfill my contract and then decide what

I want to do. If I want to play or if I'm ready to retire and figure out what's next. After these past few months, though…I don't know."

I don't want to talk to Andie about the possibility of leaving, but there's a significant chance I will be, and I won't keep that from her.

"I told Rob to see if he can find out who's really interested. I want to know what the real possibilities are and get a feel for where I might end up. If we are ahead of it, maybe I'll have a small amount of influence."

She bites her lip, her eyes focused on a toy ball in her hand. "Sometimes change is necessary."

I can't read her tone, and I don't like it. "Tell me what you're thinking."

Her eyes snap to mine. "I was thinking you're really good at what you do, and you're going to find a team that needs and values what you have to offer. It's all going to work out, maybe better than you imagine."

Her tone is soft and sweet, making kissing her all I can think about. Knowing she is nowhere near ready for that, I deflect.

"You think I'm really good?"

The color of her green eyes deepens, and she chucks the bouncy ball at me, hitting me in the head.

"Oooowww." I fake, rubbing the side of my head.

Her hand flies to her mouth to cover her laugh as she crawls on her knees over to me. "Oh my gosh, I'm so sorry. Do you think you need another scan?" she laughs.

"Yes, probably. I'll have to call my team doctors and tell them I've had another head injury. I'll be out for the rest of the season. What team is going to want me now?"

She leans forward, resting her hand on the side of my face where she hit me, trying not to laugh, but it isn't working. "Is your head ok?"

It still hurts, but it's not from the ball. Her hand is soft and warm. I want to turn my head and kiss the underside of her wrist, but I resist. Her smile, laughter, and nearness make everything better. She smells so good, like mint and flowers. I want to pull her into my lap and keep her there so she can tell me again that everything will work out. When she says it, it's easier to believe.

I smile, her eyes lingering on my face as her thumb moves over my scruffy cheek. "If I say no, can I hang out with you and Ax and order food or something? I haven't eaten since yesterday."

Her eyes grow wide. "Are you kidding? Yes, what do you want? I can make you something, or we can order, but getting delivered here will take a while."

"I don't care. Anything is fine."

She rolls her eyes. "Yeah, right. Clean eating is not my specialty, but if you watch Ax, I'll make something."

She starts to move away, but I grab her wrist. Her eyes inspect my hand, wrapped loosely around her arm.

"Thank you." I hold her there. "For caring about me and letting me stay."

She smiles and pats my knee. "Sean, we might be sort of friends, and I might care a little but don't think for one second it means I like you."

I groan and let my head fall back as she stands. "All that much, Andie. You don't like me all that much. Remember."

She laughs, and I find a spot on the floor with Ax, so thankful she let me in. She didn't tell me to go away or try to convince me we won't work. Hope is blooming inside me like a freaking bouquet, and given the past couple of weeks, it feels like I'm coming back to life.

Ax inches toward me, one chubby hand grabbing my pants to tug himself closer. I scoop him up and set him on my lap.

"Hey, partner. We've got to get you on those hands and knees so you can drive your mom crazy. What do you think about that?"

"Sean, he doesn't need any help. If you want to stick around, you can keep those ideas and comments to yourself."

I hold Ax up so he can stand. She doesn't even know the ideas I have. All of them involve me sticking around for a long time.

Chapter 41

ANDIE

It's night three of Sean hanging out at my house. It's been different. Instead of eating at the counter and walking around in a t-shirt and underwear, I've had to put on legit clothes, and there's been someone to have an actual conversation with. It's been really…nice.

Tonight, he brought dinner, and Ax is in his highchair throwing peas and carrots on the floor with Snipe at our feet, eating his fill.

"How was your time at the studio today?" Sean takes another bite of his steamed vegetables.

"It was good. We wrapped up the second song, and Nora's been teasing about a release," I shrug. "We'll see if people care."

His hand halts with his fork halfway to his mouth. "People already care. I'm not sure if you're aware, but not only are people shipping us, I get a hundred comments a day about how beautiful your voice is and asking where they can find your music."

"Shipping us?"

"Andie, you've lived in a hole too long."

I smile wistfully like I'm reliving fond memories. "Yes, but it's safe and cozy and warm."

"You're ridiculous. It means they want us to be in a relationship."

I scoff. "Oh, now they do. After calling us every name in the book for supposedly sleeping together, now they really want us to. Isn't that just the way the crappy world works."

Sean laughs, and it's beautiful. There's a rare sighting of that cute little dimple.

Something has happened, spending these past few nights with Sean. Our time together has always been pretty easy. Even stuck in the elevator, when I thought he was a stuck-up jackass, it was easy. But something in the air is slowly shifting. I can feel it like when you know it's going to rain.

A lot of me is terrified, and the other part is curious. I'm no dummy. I've seen the way Sean looks at me sometimes. It started at the event when he asked if he could call me, and it happened the other night when he held my wrist. Last night, when I joined him on the couch, him on one end and me on the other, and my legs stretched out toward him, his hand found its way around my calf. All of it is inching toward something. All of it is incredibly scary.

Josh was my one and only. He's all I've known. I thought he was my forever, even though we spent more time apart than we did together. In all of this, I feel naive and inadequate. Then, add in the uncertainty of what I'm ready for, and it equals a crapload of nervous suspense.

Sean is patient and kind. He's treading lightly, which only makes me like him that much more.

I get up from the table to throw away my trash. "What did you do today? Get a massage again."

I'm so freaking jealous of his regular massages. He looks all pretty, while I look like a homeless old hag most of the time. I haven't had a massage since I was nineteen when my mom took me for my birthday. Even then, it wasn't that enjoyable. I had to hear about Brice and his medical school applications and how wonderful he was the entire time. It was not relaxing.

"No. I talked with Rob. He said the Tigers are in negotiation with a couple of teams, and I have to wait and see if any of them come to an agreement. We're talking with a potential sponsor and reviewing a contract."

I grab a washcloth and wipe Ax's hands off. "What sponsor? Anti-fungal cream to take care of your terrible case of athlete's foot."

"Ok, smart ass. First of all, I don't have foot fungus issues. Second, I try to only take on sponsors of stuff I actually use, like gear and certain sports drinks or protein bars."

I pull Ax from the high chair and carry him to the living room, where his toys are, while Sean takes care of his trash. It's so easy and natural.

I settle Ax on the floor, pulling his toys from the basket, and he gets to work trying to inch and roll himself around. I flop on the couch, and Sean sits beside me, not leaving much space between us. Snipe, the traitor, lies down at his feet.

"Do you care if I stream the Colorado State game? My brother, Shane, is the defensive coach."

I shake my head and hand him the control. "He's the big, good-looking guy with all the kids?"

Sean's head swivels in my direction. "Good-looking?"

I smirk. "Yes. He's very handsome. His wife is really nice, too, and their kids are adorable."

Sean makes a noise in his throat. "He's a quiet, grumpy pain in the ass."

I want to pick at the hint of jealousy, but I don't. "So, how did your brothers become brothers?" I ask carefully, knowing he doesn't like to talk about his past.

He messes around with his phone and the remote until the game appears on the screen. "We ended up in a group home and stuck together. We played high school football and somehow ended up being good enough to get picked up by colleges. We didn't have anything else to do, so all we did was play ball."

"Did you all end up in foster care when you were babies?"

He fidgets with the control but still answers. "Shane's mom disappeared when he was five, and Mark was removed from his home when he was eight."

I let my shoulder rest against his solid arm. I didn't grow up in the most loving home, but I had a home and was safe. I hate thinking about what his life might have been like.

He focuses on the game, so I change the subject. "When do you get to play again?"

"I meet with the team doctors tomorrow. Hopefully, I'll be cleared for some light training. Maybe another week, and I'll be fully cleared, but then it's bye week, and I'll be off. I should definitely be good after that. What about you? What do you have going on?"

I blow out a breath. "Jonesy's set up more time in the studio, and Ax has his nine-month checkup. I should schedule some therapy sessions for a party I'm required to attend. Get a head start, you know?"

"A party? Whose party?" he asks, and I lean over to roll a toy to Ax.

"Apparently, Gem has decided getting older is a reason to celebrate rather than be ignored and dismissed."

He bumps my arm. "Funny thing, I was invited to this party."

I turn my whole body towards him. "What?"

"Gemma invited me and said that under no circumstances would I be excused from attending. I don't take that woman's threats lightly."

I scowl. "That sneaky old biddy. I knew she was up to something. This is just…" I let my head fall on the back of the couch. I've been dreading this party, and now it's just gotten a hundred times worse.

"Hey." Sean squeezes my knee. "What's wrong?"

"Um…spending the evening in the same room as my mother with whoever else is there is bad enough, but now, assuming you're not going to risk getting raked over the coals by my grandmother, you're going to get a front-row seat to the most uncomfortable and likely humiliating interaction of my life."

His hand slides higher on my thigh, comforting my growing anxiety. "Why?" His voice is gentle and soothing.

I peek at him from the corner of my eye. "You've kind of met my mother. I'm sure you have an idea. Plus…" I roll my head towards him. "I'm taking Ax. Maybe I shouldn't, but it's Gem's birthday, and he's my life. If they don't want to acknowledge him, that's their problem. It's embarrassing and–"

"Hey." He swings his arm up on the couch behind me so he can turn toward me. "I don't want you to ever be embarrassed about anything with me." I search his way too handsome face and see his honesty. "If you really don't want me to go, I'll risk Gemma's wrath."

That's not what I want. I know Sean would never judge me because of my parents' actions. He showed me that the day my mom showed up here, and he interrupted her verbal beat down to ask if I was ok. I know how they'll ignore Axel and try to make me feel small for the decisions I've made. Her behavior is inconceivable, and it's embarrassing.

I know Gem has good intentions and thinks getting them in the same room with Ax will change things. I know she probably invited Sean, thinking it would help me, but this is not how I want it to be. I don't need her meddling with my parents or with Sean.

I grab his hand off the couch behind me and hold it. His fingers are rough with callouses, and there are a few small scrapes across his knuckles. "I want you to go, but I don't want you to go because Gem invited you." I look at him, and all that goodness underneath the muscle. "I want you to go with me. It's going to suck and be really hard, and I'm absolutely dreading it, but if you're there, it won't be so bad."

He laces his fingers with mine. "Then I'll be there."

"She's not going to be nice," I warn.

He smiles, pulling me closer, and I curl into him and rest my head on his chest. "I'm not afraid of bullies. I've dealt with my fair share."

"Will you beat her up when she starts rambling on about all my poor life choices and how it's time for me to get my life together before it's too late?" His arm comes around me, his hand spreading across on my hip. He feels safe and warm and smells so freaking good. A smell I'm becoming more and more familiar with, and I like it so much.

"I don't hit women, but I certainly won't stand for her talking to you even close to the way she did that day she was here or ignoring Ax."

"If it weren't Gem, I wouldn't be going."

"It won't be so bad. We'll get tacos afterward."

I smile against him. "Really?"

His fingers press into my hip, holding me tighter. "It's all going to be alright. You don't have to deal with them alone this time."

I don't have to do it alone this time. I can't remember the last time that was true, and it feels really, really good.

Chapter 42

ANDIE

Nora's newly dyed fuchsia hair makes her light brown eyes look like little golden rings, and those rings dance around the small space, afraid to look at me.

We're meeting at the coffee shop to finalize our marketing plan for my album release. But first, I need to address these secret party plans with Gem.

"Nora, I want to know what you were thinking when you decided not to talk her out of this. This is going to be an absolute nightmare, and now Sean will be witness to it."

"But now he's going because you want him to, not because Gem threatened him," she points out delicately like it changes everything.

I roll my eyes. "Yes, I want him there, but it doesn't change that this didn't have to happen. I need to figure things out with Sean all on my own. I don't need Gem or you sticking your noses in, and she knows there's no making things better with my parents."

She straightens in the chair across from me. "She's just trying to help. Gem knows your mom is a narcissistic twit, and your dad is uninvolved and aloof. She has her own issues with them, but she doesn't want you to be alone when she's not here anymore."

I look at her. "I am alone. They made that choice when it was their way or the highway. No cozy little dinner is going to fix that." I try to stay calm, but this attempt to smooth things over is eating me alive.

Nora takes a sip of her drink. "Andie, I'm sorry. I was just trying to help Gem. We both just want to see you happy."

I inhale and let it out. "Do you know how long I tried to make them happy? Even when I did what they wanted, it wasn't enough."

"I know. Is it bad to hope this time it might be different? At least Sean will be there." She peeks at me from under her eyelashes. I toss my straw wrapper at her, and she tries to dodge it like it's a rock.

"There's always hope," I grumble. "But I think that hope should be placed in me not punching someone before the night ends."

Nora laughs. "Man, I really wish I was going to be there. I'd like to see Sean hold his woman back."

I groan. "His woman?"

"Yes, don't even try to tell me you aren't digging him. He's been over every night this week. You'll miss him when he's cleared to play again."

I don't want to think about it because the truth is, I will miss him. "Yeah, well, he'll probably attend this party and decide his drama is nothing compared to mine and give me the big 'peace out.'"

"Nah. That man is so into you." She rummages through her purse, pulling out her phone. "It's nice to see, you know." Her eyes meet mine. "You look happy. I think he has a lot to do with that, and it's really nice."

I can't help my smile but try to hide it by getting back to work. "Jonesy and I have time in the studio the next two days, and then–"

Nora gasps. "No way!" She squeals and starts waving her phone around.

"What?" I watch her wiggle around, about to fall off her chair. "What's your problem?"

She stops moving, her eyes wide as she pushes her glasses up her nose. "You aren't going to believe this. You just got an email. The FlyOver wants you to perform ahead of your release date."

"What?!" I need her to tell me again. The FlyOver is one of the most well-known little cafes where some of the biggest singers and songwriters have been discovered. Only the elite get invited to perform at The FlyOver.

"Andie, they want you for a whole evening. Can you believe it?! This is amazing!"

"How do they even know about me?" Years ago, I went to some open mic nights, where I was noticed by some of the labels, but this is completely different.

"I don't know." Nora is tapping away on her phone. "Maybe all this stuff with Sean or the event. Maybe they've seen what I've posted about you releasing an album."

"What are you doing?" Her fingers keep moving, and I'm starting to freak out.

"I'm texting Jonesy. He's going to be your second. Then I'm emailing them back a giant YES!" She squeals, and I laugh.

I cannot believe it. I pull out my phone, my fingers flying over the screen as my heart races in disbelief.

ME: Something just happened.

SEAN: Are you ok?

ME: YES!

SEAN: Can you tell me what it is so I'll quit worrying?

ME: I just got the MOST AMAZING news.

SEAN: Am I to assume by the all caps this is a really big deal?

ME: Only like the most amazing thing ever. I'll tell you later.

SEAN: I have to wait?

ME: Uh… YES!!!

SEAN: Not cool, Andie. What is it you tell me, you suck?

SEAN: Yeah, you suck.

Nora jumps out of her chair to hug me. "Andie, this is so amazing. Jonesy is blowing up my phone. This is incredible."

My eyes burn, and my throat suddenly feels dry. I can't even believe it. I'm going to sing my songs at The FlyOver. *How is this even real?*

"Just wait until you tell Gem and Sean. They both have to be there."

I hug her, knowing I absolutely want Sean to be there, but I also know that depending on things, he may not be able to be. He may not even be living here then, and that thought tames my excitement. So many times in my life, I've had to do big things on my own, and I don't want this to be another one.

"Yeah. I think I'll save this news for Gem's big day."

Nora gives me a look. "She's going to be pissed you didn't tell her right away."

"Too bad. She's the one throwing this party, so she's just going to have to wait." And I'm going to have to wait and hope that Sean will be able to be there because I really want him to be.

Chapter 43

ANDIE

"Give me that young man."

We just set foot inside Gem's large entryway, and she's tugging Ax out of my arms. This grand house is as familiar to me as my own. It's where I felt most at home as a child. Tonight, I should be comforted by the familiarity and memories, but the stirring of worry inside me is overriding it all.

"Happy Birthday." I lean in to hug her and then shrug out of my coat.

"Thank you, sweet girl. Where's the other handsome fellow whose attendance I require?"

I squint at her. "So, were you going to tell me you invited him or just let it be a surprise?" She kisses Ax's cheek, ignoring me. "I can invite anyone I want to my party. I was hoping he'd be coming with you."

"I don't need you meddling," I say sweetly.

She raises an eyebrow, giving me a look that makes my cheeks heat. "So I heard."

"He's coming. He had a meeting."

I wish he was here. I've been on edge all day and just need this night to be over. The cold, crisp air outside matches the icy layers of my inner turmoil, and I'd so much rather be home, warm and hanging out on my couch, but here I am.

We move into the dining room, where the table is set, and Ax's highchair is at the far corner of the table. As I move around, I feel like there should be background music playing soft and low where you know that any moment the foretold catastrophe will strike.

"Who's all coming?"

"Oh, you know, your parents, Gerald and his wife, Bev, and John–"

I stop her. "You invited Bev and John?" Brice's grandparents have been family friends forever. They're nice people, but somehow, Brice turned out to be an egotistical prick.

"Yes, but don't worry. I wouldn't invite that little slime bucket to eat with the dogs."

I run a hand over the corner of the table to smooth the white linen tablecloth. "You know that you can't fix things with Mom and Dad. It just is what it is. I can't and won't ever be what she wants. Until she accepts that there's no point in trying."

Gem hands Ax back to me and then grabs my face with both hands. They're warm and soft and only mildly comforting tonight.

"I know they aren't easy, and your mother pushes tolerance boundaries like it's her job. Her ideas and plans for you are absurd, but baby girl, we only get one family if we're lucky." She releases my face and reaches for her drink on the table.

"You know she's going to be terrible to Sean." My mother can't see anything beyond the circle she's formed around her.

Gem pats my arm. "I strongly suspect he can take care of himself."

She goes to move away, and I tug her back. "I want to tell you something before others get here." Her eyes go wide, and both eyebrows shoot up. "I've been asked to play at The FlyOver."

Her arms jet outward, her drink sloshing as she comes for me, wrapping me up. "Andie, I'm so proud of you. You better believe my still tight butt will be at a front table, letting everyone know they've been missing out this whole time." She squeezes me tighter. "It's about time, sweetheart."

The doorbell rings, and she steps back, looking at me, beaming before moving toward the entryway.

"Gem, there's an eerie stillness in the air. Please don't open that door. I'm pretty sure the weatherman predicted we might get a taste of what hell is like tonight."

Gem waves a hand, dismissing my warning. I hold Ax tighter as I hear voices, and I wonder if I could go hide out in the kitchen and pretend to help. Before I can make my escape, Gerald and his wife enter. I'm caught.

Here goes nothing.

Twenty minutes later, I'm standing in the living room talking to Gerald and his wife while my mom and dad stand on the opposite side, occupying themselves with Bev and John.

My parents greeted me with a swift mock hug and a brief interaction with Ax. All of which lacked any sort of real affection, and then they moved on. Gem is floating around handing out drinks, and the doorbell rings again.

She winks at me. "Andie, would you please get that? I need to check on dinner in the kitchen." She scurries away like she knows it will calm me to see Sean.

I excuse myself and move quickly to the door with Ax in tow. So ready for him to be here, I swing open the door, but of course, it's not him.

"Well, Andie, it's been a while." Brice smiles like the Cheshire Cat, and I want to punch him directly in his scumsucking face.

"You weren't invited." I really want to slam the door closed on his douchey ass.

"You are mistaken. Your mother told me you were celebrating Gemma's eightieth birthday this evening and was certain I wouldn't want to miss it."

It's possible flames are shooting from my ears. Of course, my mother would invite him, even though this is not her party or house. Her level of entitlement never ceases to amaze me.

Brice steps through the doorway a little too close when I don't move out of the way in time. I close the door and turn to see his eyes scan over my body even though I'm holding Ax. I seriously want to puke. My plain black dress, tights, and heels are nothing to ogle over.

"So, this is the little GI Joe." He sticks out his hand like he's going to touch Ax, but I take a step back.

"Don't touch him."

Gem strolls into the foyer, and her surprise morphs into loathing. "What in the hell are you doing here?"

"Oh, Brice, you made it." My mother comes in gloating like she's the hostess with the mostest.

"Hello, Donna." Brice leans in to kiss her cheek. "It was so nice of you to ask me to join you for this wonderful celebration."

"You can take your fake–" Gem is cut off by the doorbell.

My ability to be polite has left the station. I open the door. Sean stands strong and handsome, staring back at me, and I could hug him. So, I do.

I step out to meet him, throwing my free arm around his middle and squeezing Ax between us where I know he's safe. Sean doesn't hesitate to hug me back. He pulls me close, his thick arms wrapping us up as he leans down to whisper, "That bad already?"

I pull back and smile, but his arms stay locked tight for just a moment before letting me go and stepping in.

"Hey, handsome, you're just in time for the show." Gem squeezes his arm and takes his coat as my mom leads Brice into the living room.

"What's he doing here?" Sean whispers, clearly remembering him from the benefit. Ax jibber jabbers, recognizing Sean as his big hand takes hold of the small, chubby one.

"My mother invited him."

"I'm sorry I'm late. My meeting ran long. You ok?" His blue eyes are full of sincerity and concern, and I like him so much for it.

I raise and lower one shoulder. "I'm just really ready for tacos."

He laughs softly, and I grab his hand, feeling like I'm leading him to the wolves, but his hand around mine is the comfort I've been looking for. I have no doubt Sean can take care of himself, but my mother can be vicious, and he's just too good to have to deal with that.

We stand off to the side, but it only takes a second for my mom to approach, and here's where it begins.

"Andrea, may I speak with you for a moment?" She eyes Sean and then focuses back on me. "In private."

"Actually, I think I'm fine right here." If I'm going to make it, I can't handle one of her beatdowns, so I'm going to keep myself planted beside Sean.

She fidgets with her pearls and looks around. "I don't understand what's going on here."

I shift Ax to my other hip, and he grabs a handful of my hair. "What is it that you don't understand?"

"This?" She waggles her finger between Sean and I.

"Uh…it's pretty clear, I think." I don't even try to hide my annoyance. "This is Sean Greyson. The man I was supposedly sleeping with. Now, he's here with me. See, crystal clear."

"Andrea, this is unacceptable. This, whatever it is, can't be serious. Brice has been patient, and it's time–"

As if she knows, Gem taps her ring against her glass and tells us that dinner is ready to be served. I grab Sean's hand again and tug him toward the dining room, not caring to finish that conversation.

While everyone decides on seats, surprisingly, my dad takes a moment to shake Sean's hand and welcomes him, telling him it's nice to see him again. I would be shocked, but this is very characteristic of my father. He's completely detached and indifferent to pretty much everything unless it has to do with his job. It's how it's always been.

Everyone sits while I put Ax in his high chair and dump a few puffs on his tray.

Sean waits for me to sit and then moves his chair closer to mine, making me smile. My parents sit across from us, with Bev and John next to them. Gerald and his wife are on the other side of Sean and me.

Gem glowers at Brice as she tosses a plate and silverware down in front of him at the end and far away from me.

"So, Andrea," Bev leans forward. "This is the first time we're meeting your little one. What's his name?"

Before I can respond, my mother jumps in. "His name is AJ. He's going to grow into such a strong young man."

I feel Sean's arm press into mine like a checking point.

"Actually," I address Bev, ignoring my mom. "His name is Axel Joshua."

Bev smiles.

"But AJ is such a stronger, more suitable name." My mom tosses it out like she has a say.

"Dinner will be out in just a minute," Gem incepts. "I'm so happy you could all join me this evening. It's been such a long time since I've entertained. I hope we can all enjoy ourselves and remember another decade simply means I have so many more things to be grateful for." She turns and runs a hand over Ax's head, giving me an apologetic smile.

I try for a reassuring one, but it's difficult.

The food is served, and Gerald keeps Sean busy talking all things football while my parents talk hospital and country club with Bev, John, and Brice.

When a lull in conversation takes over, Brice makes it an opportunity to be a jackass.

"So, Sean, rumors are you haven't been cutting it, and there's talk about you being traded before the season is over. Surely, that's putting a strain on…things. When are you leaving?"

Sean rests back in his seat and swings his arm over the back of my chair, his hand wrapping around my shoulder. "Clearly, you don't understand much about the game or how these organizations work. My stats are as competitive as they can get. You can put stock in whatever rumors you want, but everything else that may or may not be going on or how anything or anyone is affected is confidential."

I bite my lip to prevent my grin, but it's quickly squashed as Brice presses on.

"The benefit you and Andie put together was really something. I didn't know you were a foster kid. It's interesting that's one story that hasn't been shared."

Sean sets his fork down. "It's not a story that needs to be shared. It's not a secret, but my childhood is just that, mine."

"Don't you think your fans would love to hear the story about a boy overcoming hardship and difficulty making it to the pros? I mean, all those years, you had to go through some pretty tough stuff."

I feel Sean stiffen, his fingers pressing into my skin.

"I've never pretended my life was easy," he says quietly. "It's just not anyone's business what I have or haven't been through."

Brice leans back in his chair. "Actually, I'm not sure I agree. You get paid to plow over other men for a living. Men in your line of work can be known for their erratic behavior, and with your background, I'm not sure I'd be real comfortable with you spending time with–"

I cut him off right there. "Brice, no one is ever comfortable even when you're fifty yards away. What would be interesting is to talk about how many times you've been caught with your pants down. Shall we discuss how many of those women were married, or should we skip those for the sake of time?"

Sean's leg rests against mine, and it's calming, protective, and reminds me that I'm not alone.

"Andrea," my mother gasps. "What is wrong with you?"

Ax smacks his tray, and I hand him part of a roll to gnaw on.

"What's wrong with me? Are you serious because I can't tell?" *I can't deal with her. I just. Freaking. Can't.*

"Brice has been nothing but sincere and kind and has waited around for you to get your life together and see what is right in front of you."

I let my head fall back to look at the ceiling rather than her. "What's right in front of me? Him?" I point at Brice, not giving a single crap. "That's what you want for me. A man who doesn't understand boundaries and can't keep his pants zipped." I look at John and Bev apologetically, but the truth is the truth, and seriously, how can they not know?

"Andrea, I'm certain you're mistaken. This is completely inappropriate."

Blood pounds in my ears. I might go ballistic, but Sean's large hand moves gently to my thigh. It's only enough of a distraction to reel in my temper slightly.

"Oh, right. Just like I was mistaken when the label executive you arranged a meeting with slipped his hand up my skirt and invited me to escort him upstairs. I might have only been seventeen, but I'm not sure you can misunderstand a grotesque gesture like that, or maybe you just wanted me to ignore it."

Sean's hand tightens around my thigh, and I quickly slip mine underneath his to interlace our fingers, needing strength and confidence. His hold is gentle but firm, and it's everything I need.

I stare at my mother. "That's what you want, right? Be a good girl. Marry the man who looks the part but can't keep his hands to himself."

"Andrea, this is enough," she hisses at me.

"You're right. It is enough." I move to pull Ax from his seat.

"I don't know why you have to be like this." She shakes her head. "You are so obstinate. Why do you continually choose to do everything you can to destroy your life? We've given you everything, and you're just throwing it away."

"Donna," my dad says quietly, trying to step in.

I hold Ax to my chest. "It's too bad that you're so stuck in your own world that you can't even see that you're the one that's doing the destroying."

"All I've ever wanted for you was a good life," she glares, her hands fisted on the table.

Ax starts to fuss, and I bounce, holding him close. "No, you've wanted me to have your life. That's not what I want. I'm not you. I never have been. When are you going to see that?"

"You don't have any idea what you want," she spats. "You run around thinking your choices don't affect anyone or have any kind of consequences?"

I see red and suck in a breath as Sean's chair slides back like he's done here.

"Come on. We're leaving." His tone is fierce, and it's clear he's not asking.

"You don't think I understand consequences? Are you for real?" I feel myself coming undone and need to get out of here. I stand.

"It's time to go," Sean states, slipping his arm around me.

"Oh, I see. You're going to run away," she spits. "After everything we've done for you."

"Donna," my dad says again, but she continues.

Her face is red, and she's unphased. "After everything we've given you. We took you in and–"

"Donna!" My dad's hand comes down on the table, and Ax jumps in my arms and begins to cry.

Sean's fingers press into my side like he's trying to pull me away, but I can't move. I'm frozen in place. Stuck. The silence beyond Ax's whimpers is deafening.

"What did you just say?" I speak calmly while my heart pounds so hard I feel it crack as it bangs against my ribcage.

She drops her head, unwilling to look at me. I turn to Sean, handing him Ax. My hands shake so badly, I'm afraid I might drop him. He takes him, but his free arm stays around me tight, supporting me.

My dad's chin remains tucked, his eyes on the table. I turn to Gem. Her moist eyes tell me exactly what my mother said.

I drop my head into my hands. "I'm such an idiot. How did I not see this?" My head snaps up, finding Gem. "How could you have not told me? All this time…" My throat begins to swell shut as more tears gather in her eyes, but I ignore them.

Sean's hand grips my waist and tries to pull me closer, but I resist.

I look at my dad, waiting for him to man up. "I'm not yours, am I?" He doesn't respond, his eyes returning to the plate in front of him.

I let out a defeated laugh, waking the stillness. I wait for my mother's eyes to meet mine. "I'm very sorry you didn't get what you paid for. At least now we don't have to pretend there will ever come a time that I'll be good enough."

I move my chair out of the way and leave the room, frantically grabbing my stuff in the foyer. Sean joins me, trying to help gather my coat, Ax's car seat, and diaper bag while giving me the space I need.

I quickly have it all together, and I'm out the door, Sean on my heels. When we get to my car, he helps me load Ax and then stands there. I can't look at him. I can't do anything.

He reaches for me, but I step back, my body shaking. "I'm sorry. I just…I need a minute."

"Andie, tell me what I can do. Tell me what you need. Anything." He says it so softly, like he's being tortured.

"I just…need a minute," I repeat, feeling the world spin around me like I'm in another dimension. "Just give me a minute, ok?" I rub my temples, knowing any moment, I'm going to lose it.

"Ok." He takes a tentative step away, so unsure.

I can't look at him, or I'll break into a thousand pieces. I climb in my car, start it, and drive.

Chapter 44

ANDIE

Still in my dress and tights, I stand in the middle of my living room, staring into nothing. Thankfully, Ax fell asleep in the car, exhausted from the evening, and I was able to lay him down for the night. Now, the darkness is my only comfort in the swirl of my downward spiral.

My mother's words spin around in my head like they're on repeat. "*We took you in.*"

I can't move. I can't speak. It's as if all of my senses have shut down, and there's no sensation other than to stand here and try to let those four simple words take root and fully register their deep meaning. It's as if everything finally makes sense, and nothing makes sense at all.

I have a thousand questions, but none I can formulate. All I can wonder is how I didn't see this. The constant disconnect, the lack of bonding and loving embraces, the unending desire for me to be something or someone I know now I could never be. I was placed into shoes I was never, ever going to be able to fill.

I sink down to the cold, hard floor, and it presses into my knees as impossibility and understanding collide. I never even stood a chance, but that doesn't stop the flood of grief and heartache for all the years I tried so hard to be enough. The pressure I felt as a child to measure up, to be the little girl and daughter she demanded I be. All of the time, the self-sacrifice, and the heartbreak, existing in a world that was never meant for me.

Warm tears seep through my fingers as sobs erupt from my gut and force their way to the surface.

All I've ever wanted was to be loved unconditionally. To be seen and accepted for exactly who I am, with no expectations or demands attached. To be seen as the girl, the young woman, and now the woman I've become, despite the pressures of never meeting their high standards.

It's all been a lie. Every single little bit, and for what? To live a life filled with unceasing disappointment and resentment? Always trying to find a middle ground and hoping somehow it would be enough to win their support and affection. Their wanting, desire, and expectations for me to be someone that would never exist. The conflict of it all…was for nothing.

Everything I thought to be true is gone. I fought so hard to just be accepted. It was a battle I should've never had to fight in the first place. All I wanted was to belong. To be included and not set apart, but the reality is I didn't belong there, and I don't belong to them. I was just a placeholder for the one who was supposed to be.

Crumpled on the floor, I swipe my snot with my wrist. Snipe nuzzles my side with his wet nose and soft whimpers, trying to bring comfort I don't have space for as betrayal and complete awareness take over.

My chest heaves with hiccups as I try to pull in air. Gem knew all this time how hard I tried and the pain I carried of never being good enough.

How could she keep this from me? The one person who I've always counted on to just love me. To hold my hand and hold me up when the rest of the world left.

How could she look me in the eye and not tell me the single most important piece of information? The one thing that changes everything. To not give me the peace of knowing there wasn't something wrong with me. I'd simply been misplaced.

I don't know how long I lay there cold, damp, and shivering, but eventually, exhaustion pulls me under as I cry myself to sleep.

I wake to the still darkness and muffled sounds of Snipe's snores. My entire body aches, which is minimal compared to the searing pain in my chest.

I slowly pull myself from the ground and carry myself down the hall to peek in on Ax. A new burn forms in my throat as fresh tears drip down my cheeks at the sight of his innocent little face. A love for him stabbing me clear through. One I've never known. I force my body across the hall to my bedroom. I strip down to my bra and panties, pull on an old t-shirt, and crawl under the covers.

My puffy eyes sting as they drift closed. I surrender, wanting so much to feel the relief that seemingly should come with this revelation. The freedom of finally being off the hook, no longer tied to a life that doesn't fit.

But as I lay lost and alone, not having a clue where I go from here, a shifting begins in my core that I know will grip me tight and pull me under if I allow it.

With dawn comes the soft murmurs and coos from next door. I pry open my swollen, crust-filled eyes and haul myself to Ax's room, unable to care about anything other than him. I lift him and hold him tight to my chest, hoping to find comfort and rest in his scent and closeness.

I change his diaper and take him to the kitchen for a bottle. Through the swollen slits of my eyes, I watch the sun rise as he drinks, snuggling him so tight.

Another day comes forth, bright and shiny and new, but there's nothing bright and shiny within me. Anger and hurt swirl with the wounds of betrayal and dishonesty.

I can only wonder how things would've been different if I had only known. If I'd had the chance to understand. Would it have made a difference? Maybe it would've changed everything. Maybe, just maybe, I wouldn't be so afraid that I'll never find my place. I wouldn't fear there will never be a person who will see me and won't turn and leave because there's something or someone more fitting, more important. Maybe I'd believe I might actually be enough for someone.

Even with Josh, I quickly learned I came second to the job. I never resented him for it. It was his life, his dream, and he sacrificed everything for it. It was what he was made for, and because I loved him, it was my sacrifice as well.

But I've spent my whole life trying to fill a role that wasn't designed for me, never feeling at home or like I belonged, and now I'm afraid I'll never know what that might feel like.

Ax starts sucking air, and I pull the bottle from his mouth. I take it to the sink and drop it on top of yesterday's dishes. Finding the diaper bag by the door, I search for my phone, guessing there's at least a message from Sean.

His plea for some way to help last night almost pushed me over the edge. I can't talk to him. He's the only person uninvolved, and I want to keep him there. Safe and untainted by the grief and anger that overwhelms me.

I don't want him to see me this way. Broken and weak. And just like last night, I know he might be the only person who understands in a way no one else could. Right now, that understanding seems more than I can bear.

After digging around, I find the cold metal object, not wanting to look at it.

SEAN: Please message me or call me.
SEAN: I just need to know you're ok.

NORA: How did the party go?

I toss my phone on the table and cross the space to set Ax down, surrounding him with toys. I let Snipe out and sit on the floor with Ax, wanting to forget the world.

I need time and space to figure out how I'm supposed to start over once again. Only this time, I have Ax, and there isn't a single person who will ever again tell me how I should live my life.

I hear my phone chime from the table, but I don't get up to check it. Whoever it is will have to wait.

Chapter 45

SEAN

"What's up, man? You going to be good to go after bye week?"

I set the weight bar back in the rack and sit up to slap Charles' hand. "Yes, sir. I just got full clearance, so I'll be back on the field after next week."

"Yeah, man. We've missed you around here. Tyrell is like a lost puppy. He's going to be a mess if a trade goes through."

Word has gotten out about the trade, and it's not making anything easier. Social media is lit up with speculation about where I might be headed, only making it more difficult to sit back and wait.

The latest word from Rob is Arizona is a strong possibility, and I can't complain. The team ranks high in their division but is hurting due to injuries. If I'm handed off, there are definitely worse teams to join.

I've played with some of the guys in Arizona before. Besides moving and getting used to new coaching and management, I hope whatever team I join will be welcoming and the transition as smooth as possible.

The bigger issue is a beautiful green-eyed woman who's becoming increasingly important to me, and making sure she knows that is something I have to figure out.

"It'll suck to leave all of you guys, especially mid-season."

Today, it's even harder to think about leaving Andie. After last night, I'm worried about her. I know she was stressed about going to the party and facing her parents, but her mom's backhanded admittance that she was adopted tore her in two. I felt it in the way her body sagged into mine. It was as if she'd literally been punched in the gut.

I can only imagine what she's feeling. She's already been through so much. I don't want her to face this alone. I want her to know she has me, but she's not letting me in. She's keeping me far away. I'll let her be, but not for long.

"Yeah, well, at least Morgan has finally seemed to move on and is leaving you alone." I ignore his comment. I don't give a shit about Morgan and whatever the hell she's doing now. He smiles. "Have a good week off." Charles holds out his hand, and I extend mine.

"Thanks, man. You too."

He moves to another area of the weight room where some other guys are working out. I grab my phone, hoping Andie responded to my texts, and quickly find she hasn't.

I didn't sleep much last night with flashes of the look on her face as she stood before me, completely devastated. It took everything in me not to haul her away from there, keeping her close and safe.

I wanted to wrap her up and make everything better, but she asked for time, so I'm trying to be respectful of that. The problem is I'm worried, knowing she must feel betrayed by one of the most important people in her life.

I have no doubt her heart is breaking all over again, and keeping my distance is the absolute last thing I want to do. I'm falling for this woman, and it scares the shit out of me. I want to be there for her, and I want her to know that she can count on me, but how can I do that when I'm likely moving to another state and possibly to the other side of the country? I don't want to be one more person who lets her down.

I finish up in the weight room, and on my way out of the practice facility, I send another text, hoping she'll respond and give me a chance to show her that I'm here.

> ME: Andie, please. Text me and tell me you're ok. I'm worried about you. I'm not going to stop, so text me back.

Chapter 46

SEAN

I've given her two days. Two whole days, and I'm done waiting. She may think she wants to be alone. She might want to push me away, but I'm here and not going anywhere.

I don't know what's happening with her family or if this trade will screw everything up. I don't know if I'm going to walk away from all of this with a broken heart of my own, but what I've learned these past months is that when you find something real, someone who makes you feel alive and like going on without them isn't even a possibility, you fight.

So that's what I'm going to do. I'm going to fight for Andie, and I'm going to show her when she's weak, I'll be just fine fighting alone for the both of us.

I knock on her door for the third time, listening to Sniper's muffled growl, which lets me know she's given him the command not to bark. I know she's in there, and she's about to see a whole new side of me if she doesn't open this damn door.

I've given her days to call or text me back. Time's up.

"Andie, open the door, or I'll introduce you to my breaking and entering skills I'm not all that proud of but come in handy when necessary. You have thirty seconds. One, two, three, four…"

If that beautiful little smart ass doesn't make me wait every one of those thirty seconds before unlocking the door and then *not* opening it.

I twist the knob and push it open to find her retreating down the short hallway, her long dark curls hanging down her back. Looking around, there are dishes and bottles piled in the sink. The garbage can is overflowing, and Snipe sits at my feet, staring up at me like he's happy to see that someone is here to help.

"Need to go out, boy?" I give his head a rub. By his wagging tail, I assume it's a 'hell yes, let me out of here,' so I open the front door, and he darts out.

I stand staring down the hallway, and if this woman thinks she can hide from me in her bedroom, she has another thing coming. I would much prefer to go in there invited and under entirely different circumstances, but desperate times call for putting those thoughts and feelings aside. She will never admit it, but she needs me, and I already know I need her.

I walk down the hallway and peer into the room I assume is Ax's. From the cracked door, I can see just enough to know that he's asleep in his crib.

I brace myself to face Andie's wrath as I move to her doorway. Her door is wide open, but the room is dim from the curtains being drawn closed. I can make out her form where she's curled up under the covers. Her hair is sprawled out on the pillow, and she's facing away from me.

I step into her room, and it smells like her. Mint and flowers. I inhale, wanting everything I own to smell just like this. Her room is tidy, which is a relief, given the state of the rest of the house. I walk to her side of the bed and sit on the edge. She doesn't move, and I push the hair out of her face.

Her eyes are red and puffy, which confirms the past few days have been hell, but I'm here now, and she's not going through this alone.

"I need you to get up," I speak softly, carefully, knowing this will be a battle or more like a world war. She doesn't move or open her eyes. "Andie, I need you to get up. I'm going to go deal with the mess in the other room, and you're going to shower and then pack."

That has her eyes cracking open just slightly. "Can you please just leave me alone?"

"No." I'm sure to be clear and concise. "Funny thing, I have this week off, and you and Ax and I are going to hang out...the whole time."

"Sean, if you don't get out of my house, I'm going to...I'll tell Snipe that special word, and you will have a whole different use for this week."

I hear her sniff, and her nose is all stuffed up. "Snipe and I are becoming buddies, and once I tell him we're leaving the dungeon for the week, that special word won't mean a thing when it comes to me. Now, come on, get up."

"Leave me alone, Sean. Go find some other pity project for your time off."

I'm not going to lie. That stung a little, but it tells me how much she's hurting, and everything in me wants to make it better. What I know is what she's doing won't stop the hurt.

"Andie, I'm going to count to ten, and if you don't get up and get in the shower, I will gladly haul you in there and help you do it. I'm not scared, I'm not shy, and you kind of smell." I won't admit that even though she might not have showered in days, she still smells so freaking good.

She doesn't move, and I start counting again. "One, two, three, four, five–"

She flops on her back and throws the covers off. Her eyes are wild. Her t-shirt is twisted around her and reveals some very tiny, very tight shorts that, under ordinary circumstances, she'd likely never let me see.

"Sean, get out of my room, get out of my house, and leave me alone."

"Ten." I stand and scoop her up in my arms, but to my surprise, she doesn't fight me. I don't know if she's stunned or in shock that I actually did it, but I stand there with her in my arms, and it only takes a second before I hear her sniff and then relax, maybe finally giving up the fight.

I sit back down on the bed as her sniffs turn into sobs, and I just hold her, letting her get it out. She buries her face in my chest, gripping my shirt. I think about the pain she's faced in her life, and it's not the same as mine, but yet so very familiar. I hold her tighter, pressing my lips to the top of her head.

"Why? Why would they keep this from me? All this time." She swallows, trying to catch her breath. "All these years. It's all been a lie." After a minute, she pulls back. I push the sticky, damp strands of hair out of her face. "I've spent my whole life trying to measure up, trying to somehow be what they wanted me to be without sacrificing every piece of myself."

I look into her eyes, and what I see breaks my heart. Loneliness, devastation, and so much grief. So many years of isolation and never feeling loved.

"I tried for so long to be what they wanted me to be and felt like no matter what I did, I was never going to be good enough." Her lips curve up just slightly into a defeated smile. "It was all for nothing. I always wondered why I couldn't just be what they wanted or why they couldn't just love me…the way I am." Her head drops. "All this time…I've never belonged there."

I place my hands on her face, my palms smearing her tears. "I'm so sorry, Andie. I'm sorry they lied to you. I'm sorry you were ever made to feel like you weren't enough. That you had to try to mold yourself to meet their ideas. But you knew exactly who you were and fought for yourself, for what you wanted, who you wanted to be, knowing exactly who you are. Andie, you have no idea how extraordinary you are."

Tears trail down her cheeks, and I push them away with my thumbs. "Don't ever again let anyone make you feel like you aren't enough. Do you hear me? Never again. You don't belong there anymore."

Her lip quivers, and more tears spill over. "I don't know where I belong. Every time I think I've found my home, my place, it just gets ripped away."

I pull her to me, my lips brushing against her forehead, and hold her until she quiets. I understand that fear better than she'll ever know.

We sit there, her in my lap, against my chest, and tucked into me for a long time. So long, I wonder if she's finally succumbed to her exhaustion.

I tip my head down and see her eyes are open, staring into space. "Hey. Come with me. Get away from all this, and come be with me."

Her nod is so subtle I barely noticed it, but then she moves off me, walks into the bathroom, and closes the door. I sit there for just a second, missing her. If I didn't know I was in deep before, I know now. I have a mountain to climb, and it likely won't be easy, but not much in my life has been, so I'm up for the challenge.

I let Snipe in and get to work cleaning and straightening the kitchen, praying that these next few days will show her that she belongs somewhere and that somewhere is with me.

Chapter 47

ANDIE

Darkness has become my friend. I think there's a song about that, and I strum my guitar softly, playing the tune as I recall it. I think it's the first time in days my lips have tipped upward even a millimeter, and my tarnished spirit seems to peek its head out of the depths of despair.

I sit on Sean's large sectional in his large house, staring out at the blackness of his yard beyond his large screened-in porch. It's only for the numerous nightlights spread around the massive room that I can see anything, but the soft glow is calming and warm, like little votives lighting the night.

When Sean showed up yesterday, every part of me wanted to shove him far away and make him leave, but he lifted me in his arms, and that's all it took for me to come undone. I clung to him and didn't want to let go. I let myself spill everything, and when I was finished, I still wanted him to hold me. He's solid, gentle, and, surprisingly, the safest place to fall apart.

I didn't even hesitate when he told me to come with him. Running away might be something I'm experienced in, but this is what I needed, and here is where I want to be…with him.

We've had a quiet day, Sean giving me the space he somehow knows I need. He helped me with Ax and took Snipe for a much-needed run. Then he laid on the floor playing with Ax all afternoon, and seeing the two of them started to warm my cold, wounded soul.

Sean is so comfortable with him. It's almost shocking, given that he hasn't been around babies. It was a sight that made me wonder again what was so wrong with me that my own parents never did that.

Here I sit, still looking for understanding, one that I'm not sure I'll ever have. I strum chords, waiting for something to strike, when I see a shadow and hear the click of Snipe's nails. My traitorous dog has made himself at home here with Sean and follows him everywhere.

The couch sinks down next to me.

"Hey." Sean's soft voice interrupts the quiet. "Don't stop on my account. It's beautiful."

I get back to it, but it only takes a minute or two before the inevitable frustration kicks in. Usually, when I'm lost or confused or hurting, music is where I find solace, but tonight, it's not giving me the answers I want and need.

I set my guitar on the couch next to me and pull my knees to my chest. "I don't know how I'm supposed to get over this, to move past it." I set my chin on my knees.

Sean's large body stretches out next to me, his ankles crossed and propped on the table in front of us.

"I'm not sure you need to, at least not yet. Give yourself some time and let this settle in a little. You don't have to do anything right now. You've given them years. I think it's ok to take a little time."

"I have so many questions, but I'm so angry I can't even begin formulating them."

"I'm sure." The tenderness of his voice makes it hard to suck back a new wave of emotions.

"The worst of it is Gem not telling me. How could she not tell me something like this? I trusted her with everything." Just the thought of it brings tears to my eyes.

"I know." Sean's arm comes around me as if he understands the stabbing pain in my chest. "It wasn't hers to tell, though. No matter how much she may have wanted to, it wasn't her place to tell you." His warm hand spreads around my side. "I don't know much about families and that kind of love, but Andie, it's clear to me that woman would do anything for you. It's never mattered to her, not one bit. You've been hers all along."

I taste the salt of a single tear as it hits my lips, and I lean against him, trying to hear what he's saying and believe it, but the wound is so raw. He pulls me into his chest and wraps his other arm around me, holding me tight.

We sit in the semi-dark for a while, the silence falling around us, and rather than being uncomfortable, it's soothing. Sean's warm body is comforting, and the rhythm of his slow breaths is relaxing.

"You have a very nice house." I need to talk and think about something else for a while. "The view is amazing. Where's the giant pool and the servant staff?"

"No pool. Just a hot tub."

"Huh. Do you sit in it often? Is that good for your body after games?"

I feel his chin tip down like he's looking at me, probably surprised by my shift in thoughts. "The hot tub and sauna are must-haves. Sometimes, after games, I feel like I've been hit by a truck. It helps with the soreness."

"Mmm. Sounds nice."

"It is. You know what else it's good for?" There's a hint of mischievousness in his voice.

"What?" I ask, not sure I'm ready for his answer.

"Internal wounds."

I don't know what I was expecting, but that was not it.

I lift my head slightly. "Really?"

"Yep." His reply is quick, and then the football player comes out, and he's got me over his shoulder and carrying me out onto the porch.

"Sean, don't even think about it."

"I'm way past thinking about it and have moved on to the doing part."

"Sean." He pushes open the porch door, and the bite of the cold air stings my skin. "Put me down or–"

"Not happening, Andie. You've needed this for the past three days. I don't know why I didn't think of it sooner. You're lucky I don't have a pool." He marches on, and I hear him flip a switch and push the top back, exposing half of the hot tub. Steam billows around us as he lowers me to the edge of the hot tub but doesn't let me go.

His hands stay firmly on my waist as he surrounds me. I drag my eyes up to his, peeking at him from underneath my eyelashes, a little intimidated about what I might find there.

He's zeroed in on me. I'm not in the hot water, but heat consumes me.

I clear my throat. "Seriously, I'm fully clothed." That might be a slight exaggeration. I'm wearing shorts and a sweatshirt.

"You can take off whatever you want." His eyes are intense, but a smirk appears on his lip–lips that are very close to mine.

I bite mine, trying to figure out exactly what's going on here. A second ago, I was inside, tending to my fresh wounds. Now I'm sitting here on the edge of…something, with a very pretty, very sexy football player. One I'm beginning to realize I like way more than I probably should.

I let out a breath. My emotions are one hundred and fifty percent messed up and will likely never return to any sort of normal. This isn't helping.

"Turn around," I tell him, trying to sound annoyed.

It takes a second, but his big hands release me, and without stepping away, he turns his back to me. I flip my sweatshirt over my head and thank goodness I have a decent full-coverage bra on. I swing my legs over and sink down into the water.

"You in?" He doesn't move.

"Yes, sergeant."

I hear the porch door open and close, and he disappears. The big shit all but dumps me in here and then leaves me for some ax murder to find. That would be on par with the way things are going. Oh well, I guess I'll take my chances.

I sink down a little further. The warmth and the bubbles are pretty fantastic. The glow of the tub lights illuminates the area, but I rest my head back, watching my breath meet the cold air and dissipate into the clear sky above. I'm in desperate need of all of my thoughts and feelings to fade into the black abyss.

Another minute goes by, and I hear the door again. Sean appears with two towels, and…he's in swim trunks and shirtless. The man with the beautiful face does not need a body that does the face justice, but of course, he does.

Each and every muscle is perfectly defined and cut–his arms, shoulders, chest, and stomach. He's not muscular in a meathead kind of way, but his body is chiseled, showing the dedication and hard work that makes him excel at his job.

A smile creeps across his lips as I meet his eyes like he is very much aware of my thoughts, and then he slips down into the water across from me with a splash.

"I thought you left me out here for the wolves and escaped convicts."

"Nah. I think you've had enough for a few days." His light blue eyes sparkle from the reflection of the lit water.

"I think I've had enough to last me the rest of my life." I tip my head back again and relax in the water.

"I'd say that's probably true."

I run my finger over the top of the water, feeling the bubbles. "How about you? Have you had enough to last you a lifetime?"

He's quiet, and I know he's probably uncomfortable that I switch the topic to him and his life, but I know he can handle it. I also know that at every turn, Sean is surprising me. Never in a million years would I have thought I'd be staying in his house, sitting in a hot tub, letting him see me at my worst, but here I am.

The more I'm around Sean, the more I want to know him, and the more I like him. And I'm beginning to really, really like him in a way I wasn't sure I'd ever care about a man again.

"I'd say I've had my fair share, but unfortunately, we don't get to choose. I learned that a long time ago."

I take another risk, pushing where I know he doesn't want to go, but I want him to trust me enough to take me there, even if it's just a little. "What was it like moving from home to home?"

I hear him pull in a breath and let it out. I'm certain he's deciding what he wants to share.

"It was…horrible, terrifying. I wouldn't wish that on any child. Some homes were ok, others weren't. The group home was at least consistent, and then I had Shane and Mark and football."

"That's when you started playing?" I move my hands back and forth, pushing the hot water around.

"It was the best, most acceptable way for the three of us to take out our pent-up aggression and actually use it for good. Somehow, we got into a camp with one of the best players in the NFL at the time, or maybe ever. It got us started. Then, a man who volunteered at the home would come and work with us. He helped us get on the high school team. If we weren't in school, we had a football in our hands."

"It's miraculous, you know that? The three of you. You're three miracles walking around in a world that did you so wrong, but you've all turned it into something so great."

"They have. I kind of pissed it all away for a while, looking for value and attention in all the wrong places."

I flick water at him, making him look at me. "You're not now. You caught yourself. There's strength and character in that. So many people would've just kept walking the bright, superficially lit path because it's so much easier. It feels good and looks a whole lot like happiness."

"Yeah, well, you see, I got stuck in the elevator with this little smart mouth that told me I was shallow and pretentious. I couldn't go on ignoring it after that."

"Huh, that's interesting." I bring my finger to my lips, tapping. "You see, I was stuck in an elevator once with a guy who, I'm pretty sure, after we were rescued, stood on the sidelines and dared me to sing."

He flicks water at me this time, his small smile warming me. "It's funny how things turn out sometimes."

Something stirs low in my belly. It's as if something is awakening, stretching, and it has me holding my breath. At this very moment, a big part of me wants to glide across the water and close the space between us to find out what it would be like to press my lips to his. But the other very real part of me is utterly terrified.

It's been a long time since I let a man in like that, and before him, there wasn't anyone. I don't want to lose whatever this is with Sean, but I'm also finding it difficult not to want more. To explore whatever is happening and find out all it could be.

When I married Josh, I thought it would be forever, that he'd be the only man–always. But these feelings surfacing with Sean are new all over again, or maybe new for the first time. I'm not sure, and it scares me. I don't know what to do with them or even if I should do anything about them.

The problem is when he pulls me close or tells me the exact thing that I need to hear and says things like I'm not alone anymore, I want to believe him. I want to hold on to him tightly and not let him go. I want to be brave and let that be true, believing that neither of us has to be alone anymore.

I release a long, slow breath. *This is the last freaking thing I need to think about right now.*

I avert my eyes from his heated stare and the ideas swimming in my head about what could be. I need a minute or maybe two to think about this and all the other things swirling within me.

Having an unusual loss for words, I smile back, wanting to believe that things really do turn out sometimes, and not only that, but when they do, they actually last.

Chapter 48

SEAN

"That isn't even a word."

"The hell it isn't," I challenge.

Andie's lips pull to the side, studying the few letters she has left in front of her. Her hair is spilling out of the top of her head, and one lonely curl hangs just to the side of her face. She picks up one of her letters and chucks it at me, hitting me square in the chest.

"You suck, you know that? I can't believe you think you can win with that."

"Want me to get my phone, and we can look it up?"

She rolls her eyes and huffs as the corners of her perfect lips curve upward ever so slightly. There she is. My girl. She's finally coming back to me.

These past few days, I've seen her slowly climb out of the despair and heartbreak she'd been drowning in. Her strength and resiliency inspire me, but if I have any say in it, no one will ever break her heart or hurt her again.

When I showed up at her house and asked her to come with me, I knew I had feelings for Andie. Strong feelings. But having her and Ax here in my house has shown me that this is how I want it to be. Always. There's no going back to a life without her, and I'm terrified that if this trade goes through, I'm going to have to figure out how to.

There hasn't been a time in my life where I've spent this much time with someone outside of Shane and Mark. Waking to the sound of Andie singing to Ax, laying on the floor watching him learn how to crawl, sitting with her at night as she strums her guitar, talking about nothing and anything. It's been the absolute best time of my life.

I don't want it to end.

There have been moments over these past days where I've felt like she might be ready to explore more between us, and it all started in the hot tub. Andie's eyes told me she was thinking exactly what I was thinking, but yet neither of us moved. I don't want to push her too far or too fast, especially right now, but it's becoming increasingly hard to ignore it.

The question is, what do I do about it?

She picks up her remaining three tiles and throws them at me.

"You're a sore loser."

She stands, her hands on her hips, taking offense to my comment. "You're the loser." She grabs her mug, moving toward the kitchen, and I pick up the letters she pelted at me. "You big, fat cheater."

"Baby, you and I both know I don't cheat."

In my peripheral, I see her stop dead in her tracks. At the pace of a sloth, I force myself to meet her gaze, knowing what I might find there and wondering if I can ignore it.

Those vibrant green eyes stare into mine, and there's a level of intensity in them I've not seen before. One that stirs the fire in my belly that's been blazing for a while, but I know if I make any move, it will spook her, so I keep my ass right where it is on the edge of the couch.

She doesn't move, just stares at me, into me, and I need to know what she's thinking because she's a risk worth taking.

I give her a second, but just one. "Come here," I say, and a few moments pass before she shakes her head. "Andie, come here." I'm trying really hard to be patient, but she's making it difficult.

"No."

I detest that word, especially coming out of her beautiful mouth.

"Andie, I need you to come here. If you don't, I'll come over there, and even if you run, I will find you."

I watch her contemplate it, and then, knowing I mean every word, she hesitantly walks in my direction. I push the gameboard out of the way, and she sits in front of me on the coffee table. Her shorts ride high, revealing those thighs I've thought way too much about over these past few days. Her oversized sweatshirt hangs off her shoulder, and it's like a tease that might actually drive me insane.

I search her eyes, wanting to see everything. "Tell me what you're thinking." I see so much, but I need to be sure.

"No."

There's that damn word again. I move closer, needing her to understand that I'm not going to let this go. I'm not going to let her go. I rest my hands on her bare knees, and she watches as I run my thumbs over them.

"Tell me exactly what you were thinking over there." I tip my head to where she was standing.

"I don't want to."

Her eyes haven't moved from my hands, but I watch her face. "Why?"

It's such a simple question, but I know this answer is profound. I can feel it. I know what I want and have a pretty good idea of what Andie wants, but there's no stepping over that line until I know she's good and ready. She's so damn beautiful and so scared, she may not even know what's happening here or what she wants, and I'll wait as long as it takes.

Her fingertips meet mine and linger just a second before she pulls them away like they've burned her.

"I'm scared."

Now, we're getting somewhere. "Of what?"

Her eyes flick up to mine and then disappear, and it might be my imagination, but I think she's breathing faster. I wrap my fingers around the back of her knees and tug, pulling her just a little closer. I need her to feel safe.

"Hey. Look at me." I see the effort it takes for her to drag her eyes to mine. "There's nothing to be scared of."

She laughs softly. "Funny, I feel like I have a whole lot to be scared of."

"Andie…" I try, but she cuts me off.

"I was thinking I wanted to try something, but I'm…terrified."

"Of what?"

She closes her eyes, and her chest rises and falls with a deep breath. "What if…it…feels different? What if…*I*…feel different?" She peeks at me, and I see a shyness that's rare. "Or maybe worse, what if it's…better?"

I cup her face, knowing she's sorting through the guilt of moving on and that whatever has been building between us is different, new, and possibly even more.

"Don't punish yourself for something you had no say in. Life is supposed to keep moving. We're supposed to keep going. In order to do that, we have to risk it sometimes to see what might be there waiting for us."

I take a breath, needing her to hear me and know she has nothing to be afraid of or feel guilty for. "It's going to be different and new, but it doesn't have to be better or worse." I run my thumb over her cheek, needing her to trust me. "He and I are two completely different people."

Her eyes flick between mine so fast, thinking, searching, contemplating. Then she's leaning in. I don't move. I don't even blink, letting her decide.

Her fingers run along my jaw softly, tentatively. After a moment, they press into my skin with more force, tugging me closer and letting her lips brush against mine so gently. She pulls back just slightly, searching me again, before kissing me, holding her lips to mine longer this time. Her lips move over mine carefully, hesitantly, and then she tilts her head, inviting me in.

I've waited patiently long enough, and I take it. I pull her onto my lap, diving in like I've been dying to. My hands find her hair, and her head moves one way and mine the other. Her sweet, smart mouth tastes even better than I imagined–peppermint and honey.

Her body molds into mine. Her soft skin under my hands is like silk, and they're becoming greedier by the second. I grip her thighs, resting on either side of mine, needing grounding.

Her hands slide around to the short hair at the back of my neck, holding me to her like she can't get close enough. I let her lead and explore, wanting this to last. Nothing about this feels clumsy or new. It feels like it was always meant to be.

She slows, barely giving us room to catch our breath, but I take advantage and find her neck, trailing kisses from the tender skin just below her ear down to her collarbone. A soft feminine hum comes from her throat, generating a riot between my willpower and my desire to have her. My meter of self-control escalates to a brand-new level.

She leans against me, her body flush with mine as she places lasting kisses along my jaw until she finds my mouth once more. Her lips part, and our tongues meet again, slowly, delicately, this time, as my hands glide up her thighs and over her hips, finding the hem of her shirt. My eager fingers relish the soft, tender skin at her waist, but I force them to stay put, seeking no further.

Andie pulls her mouth away but kisses me softly once more before letting her head fall to my shoulder and nuzzle into my neck. Her hands slide around my back, holding me so tight, like she's afraid I'll disappear. She places a single kiss on the sensitive skin under my jaw, and I wrap my arms around her, holding her to me.

We sit like that for a long time, and everything in me begs to ask what she's thinking and feeling, but with her body relaxed against mine, holding me tight, it tells me everything I need to know.

The stillness surrounds us for so long that I think she's fallen asleep. I'd be happy to sit just like this for the rest of the night, but as soon as I think it, I hear a whisper.

"Good news, I still don't like you."

Chapter 49

ANDIE

What. In. The. Hell? What in the freaking hell did I do?

I pull a pan from the cabinet and set it on the stove, making a louder clang than expected. I have enough nervous energy this morning to power an entire city.

I grab an applesauce pouch from the counter, open it, and hand it to Ax, who's patiently waiting in his highchair like he knows I'm a frazzled ball of nerves.

I turn back to the stove and stand there, trying to remember what I was doing with the pan, but all I can think is that I kissed Sean last night. I kissed him, aaannnnndddd it wasn't just a kiss. It was a bunch of kisses with a little sprinkle of make-out, and it was fan-freaking-tastic.

I'm not sure what I was expecting. Maybe that it would feel rushed, or awkward, or clumsy. Maybe I expected it to be terrible, or that I wouldn't feel anything, or it would change things between us and not in a good way. But shit! I wasn't expecting to spend the entire night reliving every single moment of those kisses, his hands, his strong body, and needing it to happen again…like right now.

I've gone from standing at the start line, hesitant and scared, to full-on sprinting to the finish line, and I need to chill the heck out.

"What are you doing?"

I spin, probably looking like the Tasmanian Devil. Sean is standing at the edge of the kitchen, staring at me. He's wearing a T-shirt with the sleeves cut off and is open down the sides. His cut and defined arm muscles are on full display, his face is a touch red, and beads of sweat cover his brow.

He frowns and pulls up the hem of his shirt to wipe his face, giving me a full view of his abs that look like his own personal washboard.

Nope. Nope. Not going there. Crap. STOP!

I spin back around, not needing any more fuel for the fire burning through my entire body. Sean is beautiful but sweaty, messy Sean is damn sexy, and that version of him is not what I need right now.

Nope. Nope. Nope. Noooopppppe. Nope. I bet he still smells good. Shit!

"I'm making breakfast, I think." I rest my hand on my forehead like it will help me get my thoughts under control, but the only thing it does is make me feel like a complete idiot.

Cool, just be cool. Everything is fine. I'm fine. Sean is FINE. It's all fine. I'm just going to take one thing at a time.

I start moving around the kitchen like I know what I'm doing, but I'm completely lost. I have no idea what I'm doing, and Sean comes into my space, and that's not going to help. I need him to get out of here so I can't see him or smell him or have any reminder of what happened last night.

As I flit around like an absolute basket case, I feel his eyes tracking me. He's doing that thing like he's Superman and has the power to turn me into a pane of glass and see everything I don't want him to. Then he steps in my way, boxing me in with his arm and keeping me between him and the counter. He bends down so we're eye to eye.

"Don't freak out. Everything is fine."

Damn him. Those baby blues are too sweet and kind. The light scruff over his strong jaw is too tempting and only adds to the appeal of his too-pretty face–the face I want to grab and kiss and make out with for maybe the next hour or two. *Shit!*

"Right," I say softly, calmly. "Everything is fine. Just…freaking…fine," I let out slowly, trying really hard not to breathe him in or pull him to me and kiss his face off.

"We don't have to–"

"I want to do it again." I blurt, watching his eyes grow wide. "Like right now, or I'm going to lose my ever-loving mind. I don't know what I was expecting, but I feel like I'm losing my shit, and all I can think about is how amazing your lips felt on mine and your hands and your…"

His sly, cocky grin stops my insane rant.

"Don't." I poke a finger in his chest and then really wish I hadn't touched him. "Don't even look at me with that self-confident smug-ass smile."

He raises to his full height and slips his hands around my waist, moving me towards the other end of the kitchen. When he gets me there, he lifts me, setting me on the counter. He stands between my legs and pushes his hands into my crazy hair.

"What are you doing?" It comes out as a whisper because my lungs are no longer working properly, and my heart races like I'm climbing to the crest of a roller coaster, anticipating the free fall.

His mouth hovers over my ear. "It's my turn to try something, and Ax needs to be over there."

Oh, good night. Someone help me.

I go limp in his hands as he places the tenderest kiss on my forehead and then proceeds down the side of my temple to my cheek. He takes his sweet ass time, but it feels so good, and I was right. Sweaty Sean smells just as amazing.

He makes his way down my neck and back up, finding the corner of my mouth before pulling back just an inch, and his eyes are filled with fire. He tilts my head to just the right angle, that cocky, smug smirk returning, and he will never know what a player he really is.

His lips meet mine, hot and hard, and I taste the salt of his sweat mixed with whatever fruity sports drink he had. He kisses me, still taking his time, but there's also an urgency to it. This is the closeness I've been longing for since last night.

I slide my hands inside his damp shirt, allowing my fingers to trace the lines of each of his muscles. When I drag my nails back down his back, a groan escapes from him, bringing forth a smile he kisses away immediately.

His hands move from the mess of my tangled hair to grip my hips, pulling me closer. I wrap my arms around his neck, holding him to me, needing him close. I bite one lip playfully, and he dives back in, crushing his mouth to mine, and there's a wakening inside me that is more than physical desire.

Sean's strong fingers glide up my body until they grace my neck as he slows our kisses and gives us enough room to breathe. He doesn't move away even an inch but holds me close and secure, making me feel safe and cared for.

I try to process all that I'm feeling. What is painfully clear is that for the first time in my life, I'm uninhibited by anyone and anything. Free to experience exactly what I'm feeling without having to make excuses or, explain it or sacrifice a single thing.

He rests his forehead against mine. He never asked me for anything other than friendship, and it was *me* whom he wanted to be friends with. He didn't want some made-up version or desired me to be someone else. There was no list of required conditions.

His strength, patience, and vulnerability with me make me nervous to let this moment end. Our time here, away from the world. Here, it's just the two of us figuring out what this means and what we want it to be.

I don't know what Sean wants this to be, but his gentleness and tender care tells me it's more than fooling around and testing the waters. He's considerate and tentative, stepping into this with me instead of pushing or pulling. I have no doubt he's being cautious with his own heart.

I bring my chin up to kiss his jaw and then rest my head against his shoulder, wrapping my arms around his neck, needing to hold on tight just a few moments longer. Loving Sean wasn't part of the plan, but I think it's quite possible I do, and it's a kind of love that's new for me. One that's founded on friendship, honesty, and selflessness, and there's a growing fear inside me that this, too, won't last.

A vibration erupts between us, forcing me to let him go. He reaches into his pocket and pulls out his phone to look at it.

"I'm sorry. It's Rob. I have to take this."

I nod, but he holds my chin and kisses me softly one more time before stepping away. I hear him greet Rob as he retreats down the hallway. I hop off the counter to get back to whatever I was doing before, trying to remember my name and not worry about whatever this call might be about.

I pull eggs from the refrigerator and scramble some on the stove, then place a pile on Ax's tray while the anticipation of what might be and the worry about what might not war within me. The one calming thought revolving around me is knowing that Sean is as trustworthy as the sun.

He came for me and brought me here. He waited until I was ready to make any move beyond non-friends. He kissed me and held me, safe and secure. His steadiness and reassurance are something I can lean on, and I know he won't let me down.

The problem is, I'm not ready to say goodbye and let go of the possibility. He's the unexpected gift that I never saw coming. He's become my truest friend, and I'd rather have Sean distantly than not at all.

Distance is hard. I've done that before and never thought I'd consider doing it again. This is not the same, and I know that, but just like muscle memory, the sadness and nerves are as real as ever.

Even if I could get past the distance, would Sean even want that? Every bit of his life is likely to be consumed by this move, and I can't expect him to have time to figure out whatever this is with me.

I put some eggs and toast on a plate and sit at the counter next to Ax, pushing them around rather than eating. Anxiety gnaws away at me while I wait for Sean to return.

Eventually, I clean up the mess and take Ax to get him changed and dressed. I leave him in the Pack N Play with some toys while I shower and dress, knowing I need to get in touch with Nora and Jonesy and, at some point, return to real life.

As I stand looking in the mirror, getting back to life is the last thing I want to do. I want to stay here with Sean and figure out where this might be going, worrying about real life later. There's a pit in my stomach telling me that isn't going to happen, and life will catch up to me much sooner than I'm ready for.

Chapter 50

SEAN

"So that's it then?"

I've been on the phone with Rob for the past hour, going over the details of the trade. Me for draft picks and some money. Six years with the Tigers, and this is it.

"They'll be sending a private jet for you, and I'll get my assistant on lining up movers, along with a realtor on both ends if that's what you want. Just tell me what you need, Sean. I know this is happening quickly, but they need you on the field in two days. They're not interested in losing their standing."

"I understand."

My stomach sinks with thoughts of explaining this to Andie. The guilt I feel over moving forward with her and now having to tell her I'm leaving is killing me. The last thing I want to do is hurt her or leave her any more confused or conflicted with everything she's dealing with.

"I'll see you in a few days in Phoenix," Rob says, pulling me from the dread rolling around in my gut.

I thank him, hanging up and trying to figure out what to say to Andie to make sure she knows I'm not going anywhere. I need her to know this doesn't mean I'm leaving her. The problem is, that's what she's used to. She's not used to people fighting for her, but I will.

Needing a few minutes, I shower and then go in search of her. I find Ax in his playpen and hear the shower running, so I lift him out and take him into the living room. The idea of leaving these two is like being torn right down my middle.

I don't want to go, but I can't stay. Football isn't just my job. I love it. It gave me life and hope when I didn't have anything else that could. It's just not everything to me anymore.

I sit on the floor, setting Ax between my legs, and he quickly tries to climb over my thigh to get to Snipe. I tug him back, tickling his sides, and a giggle erupts from his belly.

The sound lifts my spirit from the bottom of a pit, and I do it again just to hear him laugh. I hold him above my head, pretending he's an airplane, realizing how much I'll miss this.

I'm not just going to miss Andie. After these past few days, Ax has become my little buddy. I'll miss my time on the floor with him, watching him try to figure out how to maneuver his little body. Having him look or reach for me or holding him while he sleeps.

As a boy, my whole life was moving and starting over. I became good at remaining unattached to people and things, never knowing when it would be my time to go. Maybe for the first time, I find that despite the potential pain and heartbreak, I don't want to do that anymore. I might have to move, but I don't want to move on.

Andie steps into the room and smiles at Ax and me, but it doesn't reach her eyes. She sits on the couch adjacent to me, tucking her legs underneath her and curling up like she's guarding herself. There's already a distance between us, and I hate it. I'd like to go right back to what we were doing before the phone call and forget all of this, but I can't.

"Come over here." With Ax still above me, I gesture with my head to the spot on the floor next to me.

She doesn't react immediately like she has to think about it. Her sluggish movement tells me she's bracing herself, or maybe shielding herself, from what she suspects is coming.

She scoots down next to me. I set Ax down in front of us, pulling a toy piano close to him, and he starts pounding away.

"What did Rob have to say?" Her question is soft, like she doesn't really want me to answer.

I decide it's best to just rip the Band-Aid off. "The Tigers traded me. I have some calls to make and things to sort out this afternoon, but I leave early tomorrow morning. I have to get to work immediately. My first game is next week."

"Where?"

I slide my hand into hers, needing her to know this is not the end. "Phoenix. It's a good team and a supportive organization, so not a bad deal."

She nods, lacing her fingers through mine, bringing me a small amount of comfort. "Is it bad that I'm happy you won't be working with Doug the Dick anymore?"

I wrap my arm around her and pull her to my chest, kissing her forehead. Her sassy mouth is everything I need. This woman is something else, and I don't know how this will work, but it has to because there isn't a chance in hell I'm giving her up.

I flip the switch, and the night lights flick to life, accompanying the dim wall lamp beside my bed. Cool, crisp air bites my skin as I crack the window, but it's refreshing and helps calm my anxiety about all the changes I'm facing.

I spent the afternoon going back and forth with Rob's assistant, making arrangements for my transfer and move. It wasn't how I wanted to spend my last bit of time with Andie, but it had to be done.

The sounds of her strumming on her guitar while Ax slept and I made phone calls filtered through the house. It's just one more thing I'm going to miss. I could get used to hearing her sing, play, and work out lyrics. Listening to her would never get tiresome. Her voice is the most beautiful sound. The song she's working on is raw and emotional, and I won't be here for its progress.

My phone buzzes on the nightstand.

MARK: Can't wait to face off in AZ. I'll be seeing you soon, bro. Congrats.

News of the trade hit hard and fast. New teammates are welcoming me, and former ones are sending me on with best wishes. Tyrell is pissed, but he'll get over it. The worst is not even having a chance to tell my team goodbye. All of the chatter matters, but as I sit waiting for Andie to put Ax down for the night, all I really care about is making sure she knows that I'm still here.

Like she knows I'm thinking about her, she appears in my doorway. She's wearing a cropped white t-shirt with Rock n Roll in pink letters scrolled across it, black leggings, and brightly striped socks pulled up to her shins. Her hair spills all around her, and I try to cement the vision in my mind, needing to take it with me.

She bites her bottom lip. "Can I come in?"

"Uh. Yeah," I tease like it's a ridiculous question.

She crawls up on the bed and stretches her legs out next to mine, resting against the headboard. "It's strange that you're leaving tomorrow. Just like that."

"I know." I try to read her tone, but I can't. "It's unfair, but unfortunately, it's how it works."

She runs her finger over the stitching in my quilt. "Can I ask you something?"

"You can ask me anything." I set my phone on the nightstand.

She crosses her ankles. "What happens now?" She pauses, letting the question hang there for a second. "I mean…with us. I know this wasn't planned or expected. I don't want what happened with my parents or everything that's going on to make you feel like you've committed to something you'd rather just be free of when you get on the plane."

I choose my words carefully, needing her to see. "I don't want anything to change. I know I'm leaving, and it's completely selfish of me to ask you to give me a chance, but I want one. I don't know how often I'll be able to come back before the end of the season, but I want to come back. I want to be with you."

"I don't want to be something that hangs over your head or be a distraction. It's important you're focused, and I imagine you won't have a lot of free time."

I grab her hand, lacing her fingers with mine and bringing them to my chest. "This is important. I made a mistake, thinking football and fame were everything. I thought it gave me value and made me worthy, but…I know now that there's so much more. None of it even matters if I lose what's really important."

She rests her head on my shoulder. "I don't want anything to change either, but I've done the distance thing before. Even though it was to a greater extent, it was really difficult. You and I, we're just–"

I cut her off, unable to stand her going any further. "This isn't the same. There are no scheduled phone calls or limits. You can call me whenever you want. I'm going to talk to you all the time, and when I can, I'll come to see you." I pause for a moment, hesitant with my next words. "I know it may be difficult, but you and Ax can come to see me as often as you want. I might even give you passes to the game."

Her head pops up, surprise written all over her face before her eyebrows pinch together.

"What's wrong?" I see her wheels churning.

"If I were to ever step out on a field with you, we'll create a firestorm all over again."

"Maybe. Or maybe by now, you and I are old news. Either way, I don't give a shit what anyone thinks or says or writes. It's you and me and no one else."

"I'm not going to pretend that doesn't worry me."

I squeeze her hand. "I know. It's up to you how we do this. I'm perfectly fine keeping things just between us, but I'm also happy to take a picture right now of you in my bed and blast it everywhere."

She shoves me, laughing. When it's quiet again, she shivers. "Do you have a window open?"

"Yeah. I like the fresh air. Are you cold?" I wrap an arm around her, and she brings her knees to her chest, leaning into me.

"Can I ask you another question?" The pad of her pointer finger runs over my knuckle and back again.

"Andie, stop asking me that."

Her voice is soft and gentle. "What's with all of the nightlights?"

This is not what I was expecting. My eyes dart to the two nightlights, one on either side of the room. The dozen or so placed around the house are familiar to me, so I didn't even think about her noticing. No one ever has.

I'm not embarrassed, but talking about this brings an amount of anxiety and memories I like to avoid. Being a full-grown man and still afraid of the dark is not common and not something I like to admit, but with Andie, I'm willing to lay my masculine guard down and explain.

"I don't like the dark. At least not pitch black. I can't sleep like that. It feels…confining, and if I wake up in complete darkness, sometimes I panic."

"How come?" Her arm moves over my stomach to my side, like a hug, and it helps lessen the strap pulling tight around my chest.

I pull in a breath and let it out, attempting to ease my fight or flight response activating with memories. "One of the foster homes I was in, they locked me in the basement; no light, no windows–it was complete darkness. I never knew how long I'd be there or if they'd ever come back. I think sometimes it was hours or sometimes longer. Sometimes, I'd be so scared I'd wear myself out with fear and panic and fall asleep. When I'd wake up…"

My skin prickles, my heart pounds, and every muscle contracts with stepping back to that time.

"I wasn't in that home too long, but it was long enough. Eventually, I got smart and started keeping things in my pocket to try to pick the lock. I never got it, but it gave me something to do, to focus on."

"Sean." She exhales my name like it pains her.

"I can assure you, I'm excellent at picking locks now." I try to lighten it up and slow my body's response down, but the reality is it still gets to me. "I don't like the dark, closed, tight spaces or rooms without windows."

"Is that why the window is open?"

I nod, and she snuggles into my chest further, but then her head pops up, and she pulls away, her eyes wide.

"The elevator."

I thought I might lose my shit that day, and my intense meltdown would be blasted worldwide.

A weak smile creeps across my face. "I scrolled my phone, counted the carpet tiles, tried to count my breaths, wiggled each toe individually in my shoes, sent text messages–"

She cuts me off like she's panicked. "And that worked?!"

I shake my head and take her face into my hands. "Then you started talking and giving the most shit I've ever gotten in my life." I pull her closer. "You…just you…made everything ok."

Her head tips to the side as understanding registers. "And when they opened those doors, you took off like a bat out of hell. I thought you were just being a jerk."

I smile. "I was an asshole, but it wasn't on purpose."

"Sean...I had no idea. I'm sorry. I was...if I–"

I cut her off with my lips, holding it for just a second. "I would've never wanted you to know. I liked how you treated me. Like I was just some guy."

Her perfectly kissable lips turn upward. "You know I'm never ever going to stop giving you shit."

I wrap one arm around her waist and haul her onto my lap. She laughs, and the weight of ten rhinos lifts off my chest. I brush the curls out of her face. "I don't want you to ever stop."

Her eyes flick between mine rapidly, and she leans forward, pulling my face to hers. Our mouths meet, and my hands slide up her thighs. It only takes a second before she lifts her shirt over her head to reveal a purple lace bra, and the beauty of her is stunning.

She kisses me again, but it feels frantic and rushed. I want Andie, all of her, but not like this. Not because she knows I'm leaving and is afraid I won't come back. Not when I have to drop her off to face the devastation of finding out she was adopted, and I can't be here to hold her hand through it.

I kiss her until the desperation calms and then pull back, holding her face. It's filled with question and worry and need. I need her more than I want her at this moment.

"Hey." I kiss her cheek, keeping her close. "You have no idea how much I want you right now." I bring her forehead to mine. "But, baby, not like this. Not when you're scared that this is it. That I'm going to disappear, and this is our only chance." I kiss her. "It's not. I don't care what I have to do to make this work."

"Aren't you scared?"

Her lips run along my jaw and down my neck. This might be the hardest thing I've ever done in my life.

I push out a long breath, and she pulls away to meet my eyes. "I'm scared shitless to leave you. I'm terrified I'm going to get on that plane, and you'll feel like I left you. That eventually you'll realize you're better off without the spotlight and drama."

I hold her tighter. "I'm scared the most real, most perfect thing I've ever had in my life will vanish the minute I set foot on that plane, and I won't be able to get back to find you."

I close my eyes, just admitting my biggest fear. "But you are more important to me than this. I'm not about to screw this up and risk the chance you might ever think this was all I wanted." I brush my lips against her cheek. "Believe me, Andie, this is taking every single selfless fiber of my being."

"I wouldn't think that." She moves to sit next to me again but keeps one leg over mine. "And I'm not going to think I'm better off." I slip my arm around her. "Can I… at least stay in here with you tonight?" Her shyness is cute.

"I don't want you to go anywhere. Tomorrow is going to come too soon." I scoot down, and she rests her head on my chest.

"I'm not ready for you to leave."

"Me either." That is the understatement of the century.

"I'm not sure I'm ready to see your pretty boy face all over my feed again, only wearing black and yellow." I hear the smile in her voice. "I wonder if Arizona knows what a slow-ass old man they're getting?"

I tickle her ribs, and she wiggles and laughs, and it's the best sound in the entire world. It sounds like hope and peace and possibility. It might even sound just a little like love.

Chapter 51

ANDIE

Sean sets Ax's car seat base and diaper bag next to the door. I shiver from the cold air, but my insides are trembling with the anticipation of goodbye.

Waking up next to him this morning was the most comforting feeling in the entire world, making this all that much harder. For the first time in so long, I don't feel alone, but like I have a partner. Someone who's fighting for the same thing I am. Someone I can rely on and trust. A man I want the very best for and who deserves it.

But now, after just a few short days, I have to say goodbye to the person who's become my best friend. The one, I'm pretty sure, holds my tattered and torn heart in his hands. I don't want to let him go, but I also can't wait to see him soar, showing everyone exactly who he is and what he's made of.

I watch him look around, making sure he brought everything in. Never in a million years did I think I'd be here…with him.

He crouches down and runs a hand over the top of Ax's sleepy head. Then he stands tall and strong and freaking handsome as ever, but I see the anxiety running through him. I don't want to make this any harder.

He reaches for me, and I go willingly as he wraps me up. The warmth of his strong body consumes me, and he rests his chin on the top of my head.

"I'll text you when I land, but I probably won't be able to call until tonight. Ok?" I nod against his muscular chest.

"This just really sucks. Can't you just call and tell them you're going to be a little late?"

He laughs. "I wish."

"Huh. You have kind of a crappy job. You know that?" I tease, knowing this is what he loves.

"This is definitely a shitty part." His arms cinch me in a little tighter like he, too, doesn't want to let go. "But now, it's even worse."

"Why's that?" I bite my lip, hoping the pain will ease the burning in my throat.

"I don't want to sleep alone anymore. You with me in the dark is so much less scary."

I move to peer up at him, resting my chin on his chest, begging the tears to stay locked behind the tear duct dam. "Don't say that."

His lips press against my forehead. "This doesn't change anything. I have to go, but I'll be back."

"I just wish you didn't have to go right now."

"Me too. You have no idea." He kisses me slowly and sweetly and then hugs me tight one more time before opening the door and stepping out onto the porch, where Snipe waits to be let in. "Keep these two safe, boy." He scratches his head before Snipe darts inside.

He steps away, but I tug on his arm, stopping him. "Don't get your big muscled behind kicked out there, old man."

His head falls back, and he groans, making me grin. "What's it matter to you? You don't even like me."

I raise and lower my shoulder, releasing his arm. "I can't have the press thinking I was sleeping with some loser."

He turns and walks away, leaving me there on the porch. "Don't forget, Andie, I don't give a shit about what the press thinks."

I smile, moving back inside and closing the door, hoping this might just be ok. I scoop Ax out of his seat but stand, listening to the crunching sound of Sean's tires fade as he hurries to catch his plane.

I survey our bags and all the things that need to be put away so I can get back to my life. I pull in a breath and hold it, not wanting to get back to it. Nothing is the same. I don't want to face all I left when Sean took me away from here.

The burn in my throat returns with a vengeance. I swallow, trying really hard to relieve it, but it's not working, and tears fill my eyes. I might have run away with Sean if he'd asked me to. It would have been easier than having to finally accept my reality.

The family I thought I had isn't really mine at all. My parents aren't really my parents, and I have no idea where I came from. I feel lost and alone, and I really just want Sean to come back.

I push out a breath and swipe at the single tear I allow to fall. The hardest part will be facing Gem. She's the one person I've always counted on to tell me nothing but the truth. It's the thing that hurts the most, but I need to talk to her. Maybe, just not yet.

I put Ax on my hip and carry him to the kitchen to fill up my kettle and get to work putting things away. I turn the burner on and kiss his cheek.

"One thing at a time, monster. That's what we're going to do." I blink, needing the tears to stay at bay.

First, I'm going to drink some tea and try not to miss Sean. *Yeah, not happening.* Then, I'll put some of our stuff away. After that, I might think about who I want to talk to…if anybody.

"This is incredible." Nora's eyes are wide, her mouth gaping open. "Andie, I'm so sorry. I can't even…this is just… What now? What are you going to do?"

I sit curled up on one end of the couch and Nora on the other, both of us lounging and trying to make sense of it all. Sean moving to another state far away, needing to talk to Gem, and the thought of approaching my parents for information are overwhelming my emotional capacity. I'd really rather shove it all in a box and wrap it up to open at a later date, or maybe never.

"I don't know." I steal a little more of the blanket spread across the two of us. "This may sound weird, but I'm not sure I want to do anything. I mean…I have questions about where exactly I came from, but then I think, what good will it do? It won't change anything. I guess I'll talk to them when I'm ready. For now, I just need time and a hell of a lot of space."

Nora nods, her bright pink bun bouncing back and forth. She pushes her glasses up her nose. "What about Gem? Are you going to talk to her?"

The question is tentative, fully aware of the excruciating pain I feel that she didn't tell me.

I've thought a lot about what Sean said about it not being Gem's place to tell me, and even though it totally sucks, he's right. This was not her story to tell. He's also right that she's always been my Gem. She has loved me fully and unconditionally.

"It hurts, but I think I understand her not telling me. She's giving me time, but I need to talk to her."

Silence falls around us, along with the night, except for Snipe rolling and snorting on the floor.

"What about Sean?" Another soft-spoken question and one that fills my belly with flutters and has me blinking back tears at the same time.

"He's…completely unexpected, and I have no idea what to do about it. These past couple of months with him, it's like I've felt myself slowly come back to life. Where the numbness was, there are a whole bunch of new sensations. Excitement and terror. Joy and impatience. I feel so safe and secure when I'm with him, but now he's gone."

I leave it there because what else is there to say. I don't know what happens now other than to wait and see. I have to be patient while he gets settled in Phoenix and with his new team. I just don't know how this will work, but I really want it to.

I can't talk about Sean, so I change the subject. "You and I need to get back to work. Jonesy's set up more studio time, and we need to start promoting."

Nora's head falls to the side with annoyance that I'm not giving her more about Sean and me. "How many more songs do you have to record? I thought I'd come into the studio the next time and take some videos to post. People love the teasers, and preorders spike every time we give them a little taste of what's coming."

"We have two more, but I have something new I've been working on."

One pierced eyebrow raises. "Is it about him or them?"

I smile, knowing it's just about me, and she knows it too.

My phone buzzes next to me, and I see a Words notification that a new game has been started. It buzzes again.

SEAN: I win. You come see me. You win. Name your worst.

My heart does a little jig at the thought of seeing him, but I quickly pull the rug out from under it. I love the idea of visiting him, but hauling a baby back and forth halfway across the country seems intimidating. There's also the little fact of knowing that once I was there with him, I might not want to come home.

What am I thinking? I need to get my life back in order and finish this album. I need to talk to Sean and figure out if this is going to work with him there and me here.

We've only known each other a few months, and half of that time, I wasn't even sure I liked him. But I like him now. I more than like him, and figuring that out and then telling him goodbye seems all too familiar. I'm just waiting for him to slowly fade into his new life and forget about me. It's only been a few hours, but so far, he hasn't, and I'm afraid to let myself believe that what he and I have found in each other is something long-lasting.

I weigh my options, trying to determine if I'm going to counter his wager. Sean has skills at Words, and with what's at stake, I know he'll have every intention of winning. I might even want to let him.

Nora clears her throat, eyeing me with a smirk. "You know I've never been to Arizona. I wonder if the male population in the desert is more open to love at first date."

I give her side eye with a large dose of deadpan. "I don't think that's legal in any state."

She throws a pillow at me, and it bounces off and falls to the floor. "Maybe you should wipe that sappy smile off your face and just go get your man. Then I'll have an excuse to find out for myself."

"First, he's not my man. We're…seeing where this goes." I say he's not, but I think I really want him to be mine and that thought has my stomach rolling itself up into a ball.

A gurgling sound comes from her throat. "Oh, please. You can live in whatever village of denial you'd like. That man got under your thick-as-steel skin the second you started your elevator smackdown."

I think about what Sean told me about how I distracted him, and a warm sensation washes over my body, spiking goosebumps. The thought of him still being afraid of the dark and tight spaces and how sleeping with him made it easier makes me want to go to the airport and get on a plane to show him that he doesn't have to be afraid ever again.

Ugh. There I go again. I need to get back to making sure I can support Ax, which means getting back to work and real life. My mind wanders to Gem again. A big step towards that is talking to her.

I let Sean's message hang while I figure out what I want in return, and instead of responding, I message Gem.

ME: I'm ready to talk.

Chapter 52

ANDIE

"Shhhhhh."

I bounce, holding Ax's head to my shoulder. The little daredevil's arms couldn't keep up with his legs, and he face-planted the hard floor. Not helping is the fact that he's completely exhausted from refusing to nap this afternoon.

I spent most of the day in the studio, finishing up two songs, and I played my work-in-progress for Jonesy, which he insists will become the final track on the album.

Nora stopped by to get some footage to share on social media, and over the past couple of weeks, pre-orders have skyrocketed. We're down to one more scheduled day in the studio, and if I can sort out the kinks in my song, tomorrow will be a wrap. Then, Jonesy will be set to work his magic.

Ax's body relaxes against me as his cries turn to fuss, and I try to peek at the goose egg on his forehead. His little spill is an unfortunate distraction while we wait for Gem, who should be here any minute. I'm not nervous. I'm just ready to put this behind us and move forward.

After texting her yesterday, she replied immediately, like she'd been waiting with her phone in her hand. I have no doubt these past days have been torture for her, but her patience is only proof of her love and how much she understands me.

My brief but sweet phone conversation with Sean last night reminded me that despite circumstances, we need to hold on tight to the people who show us time and again that we're valued and loved. Those who show up when everything around us is falling apart, and we end up at the bottom of the pit.

My front door flies open like a gust of hysteria just blew in, and Ax jumps in my arms. Wide-eyed and alarmed, I stare at my grandmother, who is silhouetted by the setting sun and looks like a freaking mess.

Her hair is mildly kept, tied up in a scarf. She has no makeup on, and her signature red lips are pale. There's no spicy gusto to her sad state, and the woman standing before me is in some kind of matching cotton suit like it was pulled from a closet at a retirement community. Gem is wearing SWEAT–PANTS.

I'm so alarmed at the sight I've turned mute. There's nothing wrong with these matching sets, but my Gem wouldn't be caught dead in one. My Gem would strut around butt naked before she would don such an appalling use of soft pastel textile.

My mouth overrides my brain. "Are you wearing a…sweatsuit?"

She steps in, shoving the door shut behind her, and then places her hands on her hips. "Sweet cheeks, if I had to wait one more agonizing minute for you to ring me, I'm pretty sure I would have resorted to a muumuu, having given up entirely on ever needing to look respectable again."

She stares at me, her eyes brimming with tears. "Life without you…" She shakes her head. "Looks a hell of a lot like sweatpants and garbage bags made out of fabric with a slit. Neither is tolerable, and one more hour of this, and I might have lit myself on fire."

I smile, tipping my head to the side. "Is there really a need for such dramatics?"

She walks straight to me and hugs me like she hasn't seen me in decades.

"Andie, there has never been a single second since you were put into my arms that you were not my granddaughter. You belong to me. You are a Taninbaugh through and through, and if there was ever a soul on this earth that was made for mine, baby girl, it was yours."

She pulls away and holds my face as Ax blows spit bubbles of delight. "I'm so sorry for what you've had to deal with in your life, for not knowing, not understanding, and I have no doubt you have a million questions, but I hope you've never had to wonder how very much I love you."

I hug her again, tears filling my eyes. "I know." I choke out through my constricted airway. "I know."

"I need to know you forgive me. I couldn't tell you, Andie. Maybe it was wrong." Her eyes draw shut, and she inhales, taking a moment to collect herself. "I don't know. All I've done for these past days is wonder, but all I come back to is that your parents needed to be the ones to explain, to tell you."

"Do you know anything about my birth parents?"

It's a question I've pondered the value of over the past few days. I've thought a hundred times about Sean's meeting with his birth mom and how it was just one more rejection he didn't need. One more heartbreak he could've done without, but maybe in it, there was a sort of closure. Or perhaps it was just more pain added to the already overwhelming pile.

Ax leans for her, and I hand him over. We both move onto the couch, and Gem smothers him like she thought she might never see him again.

"I know it was a closed adoption. There was no communication between your parents and your birth mother."

I nod, letting that information settle in. "So much makes sense now, and then sometimes I feel like nothing makes sense at all. If they wanted a child badly enough to adopt, why couldn't they just love me?"

Gem takes a steadying breath. I'm not used to seeing her emotionally frazzled.

"I think they think giving you their world is loving you." She kisses Ax's head. "Ever since your father was a young man, he could see nothing beyond becoming a leading physician, and he's helped so many people, but that doesn't mean I haven't seen how he's neglected you. He's my son, and that's not easy to admit. And your mother, well, I don't know. She and I have never seen eye to eye, but I think it's possible she could never let go of the idea that you would be what she always imagined you to be…just like her. Someone she could relate to and understand."

She pauses, letting that tidbit hang in the air. "I'm not making excuses for her behavior or the pain she's caused you, but I've lived long enough to know that each and every person walks around wounded and scarred from the battles they've faced, and very often, we'll never know what they've seen or been through."

My mind flashes to the nightlights that flickered throughout Sean's house and how I would've never imagined and still maybe don't know everything he's survived. It makes me want to hold him, to tell him how much I care about him and how proud I am of everything he's become despite life beating him down.

"I'm so glad he came for you." This woman's ability to follow my thoughts is frightening. I rest back, squinting at her. "I have no doubt he had to carry you out of here kicking and screaming."

"Were you stalking me?"

"Oh, pfft. Only tracking your phone, sweetheart. I could kiss that man for getting you out of here. I see he's in Phoenix." She raises one very faint, thin eyebrow.

"It happened fast. He left yesterday morning."

"Anything happen I should know about?" Heat rises from the depths of my toes, making its way through my body, and I have no doubt she sees it. "That young man looks good in yellow and black. It's a real shame he's out there all by himself, trying to sort things out in a new city with a new team."

"He's really busy, Gem. He's playing this weekend."

She turns Ax to face her as he tries to shove a textured ball in his mouth. "It's a big deal for him to step out on a new field, in new colors, with new guys, and there won't be anyone in those stands for him. Seems a real shame."

I let my head fall to the back of the couch. "You're laying it on a little thick, aren't you?"

She shifts, directing herself towards me and looking more like my Gem. "He's good for you, Andie. He cares about you enough to stand by you and up for you, and he came here unafraid and determined not to let you hurt alone. It's rare, sweet girl. It takes bravery and balls to do that."

I groan, not wanting to think how right she is. He's done all that for me.

"Take it from a lonely old woman. Sometimes we have to be brave and ballsy, too, and go after the things we want."

"So, I just take Ax and travel across the country for a weekend?" I know it sounds pathetic and like a massive excuse, and maybe it is. It's a huge risk. It's putting my heart fully on the line once again. What if Sean changes his mind and I'm not what he wants after all?

"Who says it should only be for a weekend?" This woman says it so casually, like I'm making much of nothing.

"Just like that? Only after a couple months?"

Both eyebrows lift along with one thin, bony shoulder. "Why not? What do you want, Andie?" Here she goes, calling me by my name. "Are you going to sit here and tell me it's not him?"

"What about the album? Nora and Jonesy?" I'm not going to mention Nora's on board to travel. "What about you?!"

Her eyes move to me, unimpressed with every excuse. "I imagine there are studios out there or that you could come back when you need to, and, honey, I'm perfectly capable of getting on a plane. The warm sun and dry air would do my spry bones some good."

"So just pick up and go? Leave everything behind?" I'm exasperated with the pressure of this sudden life-altering decision.

Both her shoulders shrug this time. "Is he worth it?"

Damn her and her questions. I don't even have to think about it. He's so worth it, but the idea of going after what I want scares me to no end. Maybe that's the point.

"My girl, you've spent enough time waiting for things to happen or life to change. It's time to live your life for no one else but you. We only get one, so you need to make damn sure you're living it."

"Hi."

"Hey." His voice is the one I've longed to hear all day.

"How was it today?"

"Excruciating. My body is tired, but my brain is in overdrive, trying to learn all the plays and get used to a different system and dynamics. I spent thirty minutes in the sauna, and my body is still tight and stressed."

He sounds worn out and worn down. It makes me wonder what he's holding back.

"How are the guys? If you can believe social media, Kings fans are stoked about you joining the team." The news of Sean joining the Arizona Kingsnakes is everywhere. Tigers fans are outraged at his departure, but Kings fans are excitedly lighting up the web at his arrival.

I will never tell him, but I've watched every single one of his interviews a hundred times just to see his face and hear his voice.

"They've been great and are helping me get adjusted. There's one guy who seems to be a bit of a hothead, but that's nothing new. How did your conversation with Gem go?"

His quick change of subject only makes me more suspicious. Her comments about going after what I want stir up a flock of butterflies, or more like fire-breathing dragons, in my stomach, causing a rush of heat and chills to mingle over my body. I shiver. Gem's right. It's time for me to live my life for me.

Sean has shown up and stood up for me time and again. I wonder if I'm brave enough to step out there for him. I could continue to try to lie to myself, but I already know he's what I want. Going after Sean also means being on display for all to see. I'm not sure I'll ever be ready for that, but given how this whole thing started, I know I'll never deal with any of it alone.

"It was good. She blew in like a miserably depressed whirlwind and looked a complete mess." I can't help but smile thinking about it and her solid, warm hug.

"You're lucky, Andie. That woman loves you." His tone is so soft it causes my heart to squeeze in my chest.

"I really am." I bite my lip, knowing what I'm contemplating and also fully aware that there's no way I'm letting him in on my newest dilemma.

We fall silent while my mind spins with the wonder of actually doing it.

"You haven't played a word yet or accepted the bet," Sean says, pulling me out of my nervous pondering. The mischievousness in his tone is alluring, and it's like he's snapping out of his funk.

"Listen, loser. I'm still contemplating. You can't rush a bet. I've got to make sure that when I win, I get exactly what I want."

"Is that so?" His voice is low and sexy, and this distance is completely unacceptable.

"Yep." I pop the 'p.' "So you, Pretty Boy, are just going to have to wait. Now, tell me about the game this weekend. It's possible I might be busy, but if my plans don't pan out, I might watch, and I'm not at all interested in seeing this new running back get his ass drug up and down the field by some mediocre low-standing team."

"Andie." I don't even have to see him to know those lips I really wish I were kissing are turning upward.

"What?" I play dumb.

"You're ridiculous."

I scoff. "Whatever, I'm just unwilling to waste my time unless I know what I'm getting."

"I miss you," he says gently, that hint of sadness returning, and it's killing me.

"It's possible I might miss you a little, but don't let that go to your head. It's volatile."

"I would never. How's my buddy?"

"You might have to send us a miniature helmet. He pissed the floor off today, and it bit him. He's getting a little big for his britches."

"Awe, man. He's such a tough little guy. He needs one of those things you put them in with wheels so that boy can get where he needs to go."

"Right. That's just what he needs." I know Sean is trying, but I can hear the uneasy tension in his voice. "You're tough too, you know that? I know all this hasn't been easy, but it'll get better."

"Think so?" He sounds doubtful.

Those damn dragons take flight again, spewing fire as I think about buying a plane ticket. The uncertainty in his voice makes it clear to me that, for once, someone needs to show up for him, and I want it to be me.

"Yeah, I have a pretty good feeling about it."

Chapter 53

SEAN

I lug the big box inside my rental and set it up against the wall in one of the spare bedrooms. I'm tired, every inch of my body aches, and the only thing I want to do is sleep, but sleep hasn't been coming easy.

Ever since Rob called about the trade, I feel like I've been tossed into a tornado and spit out the other side. My heart is missing, left behind in Nashville. Talking to Andie on the phone isn't enough. I hate walking around like a lonely old sap, especially when loneliness has been a constant companion, like an invisible defect I was born with.

All I've ever wanted was to be understood and accepted, to be seen as more than the pitiful kid raised by the system and valued as a person beyond the guy in the jersey. I've wanted to be loved. Really loved. The kind that doesn't turn me away or only sees me as a social stepping stone with a dollar sign attached.

There hasn't been a single time Andie has treated me in any way other than as just a man–one who started out alone and frightened and made it to the other side. She may not know it, but she's the first person outside my brothers to show me what that kind of love feels like, and it goes so far beyond that. She hasn't said it, but I know whether she likes me or not, she cares about me, and that's way more than I've ever had before.

I make my way down the hallway and into my new space, which contains the kitchen and living room. The white walls, vaulted ceiling, and sliding glass windows leading out to the pool make the large open area light and bright. All of it is a drastic contrast to my former home, which was painted in dark hues and settled in the woods.

I don't mind the brightness and the warm air, but I miss the peace I'd recently found just before I had to uproot my life and enter the unknown once again.

My phone buzzes on the counter, and I reach for it, hoping it's Andie, but it's just Shane.

"Hey, bro."

"How's your mind? You ready for the game?"

Shane's bluntness and concern is evident. He knows precisely the stress and anxiety of this kind of move. There's a whole lot more involved than putting on a new jersey, but I have no doubt this phone call is more about who I left behind.

"I guess we'll find out. I've got most of the plays down. The coaches have been great, and I can already tell the team works like a well-oiled machine. Kenny's great, and I think we'll work well together. We just need a little time to work on cues."

Kenny, the Kings quarterback, is a veteran and has taken me under his wing. We've not played together before, but working with someone experienced and comfortable in his role makes this kind of quick change easier to adapt to.

"I wish we could be at the game. You being a King was not something I ever thought I'd see. Maggie is losing her shit over this. Her crazy sixth sense is predicting you're going to help get these boys to the Super Bowl."

Not so long ago, a shot at a Super Bowl ring would have been my sole focus, and this trade would have been welcomed. It would have been an easy transition because nothing else mattered, but everything has changed. I've changed, and it hurts like hell to finally see what's right in front of me, but it's still out of reach. The whole world. The real deal. What was within my grasp now feels like it's being tugged away, and there isn't a single thing I can do to keep it from disappearing.

"I feel lucky to have ended up here, but the timing couldn't have been worse." The line goes quiet, and I know this is the real reason he called.

"How did you leave things?" Shane's soft question is like a punch in the stomach.

I'm not sure I even know how to answer. I told Andie nothing was changing, but over the past four days, it's completely apparent everything has changed. Our short phone conversations are not the same as sitting with her, looking into her eyes, and knowing what she's thinking.

She'd just let down her guard with me, but last night on the phone, when all of the sass came out, I couldn't help but feel like the vulnerable Andie, the one she finally let me see, was gone. It was like a stab in the gut. I don't want to lose the trust and closeness we gained with the physical distance between us.

"I'm not really sure. I mean...I told her I didn't want this move to change anything, but how could it not?"

I try to sort out if I want to say more and then decide if I'm going to be honest, Shane is the one to do it with.

"She got some difficult news right before I left, and it was torture leaving her to deal with it on her own. The last thing she needs is to be alone."

"Sounds like you're in deep shit."

I run a hand over my face, knowing that doesn't quite do my feelings justice.

"Andie's husband had a dog. When I booked this rental, I made sure dogs are allowed because I know she'd never leave him. He's easily the smartest dog I've ever seen, and by some miracle, he started to warm up to me. In some dream world, I see her and Ax here with me. That dog, too."

"Damn."

I rest my forehead on the cold, hard countertop, knowing I need to get a grip on reality before I lose my mind further.

I hit the speaker button but keep my head down. "You know how Maggie sees through everything…your past, football, money, fame, and sees you inside of it all? That's Andie. She sees me, just me. I've never once had that, but her life is in Nashville, and we're only halfway through the season. Can I really just show up a couple months from now for a few weeks and try to make up for lost time, then turn around and leave again?"

"You didn't have a choice in this. I'm sure she understands that."

"Neither did her husband. She's not interested in going there again."

I remember Andie telling me exactly how hard it was to live separate lives and then reconnect for the short time he was on leave.

"I don't know what military life is like, but this isn't the same."

"Yeah, well, I keep trying to tell myself that, but I wouldn't blame her if she doesn't see it that way." I take a breath to reel in my growing fear and frustration. "The selfish man in me wants to beg her to come so I can be sure I don't lose her. I don't want her to go on with her life and find someone better to spend her time with because I'm never there."

I bump my head against the hard surface of the counter, hoping to knock some kind of realistic sense into it. "Her life is there. She has a son, a career, and friends. I can't compete with that, and I shouldn't."

"You can't give up, Sean." Shane's voice has that coaching tone to it. "When you meet the person that makes you feel the way you just described, giving up isn't an option. You talk to her, and you fight."

"Since when are you a picture of optimism?" I don't even try to hide my annoyance.

"Since Maggie showed me that sometimes people stay. Even when it's hard and complicated and totally messed up, sometimes we actually matter to someone else enough that they hold on to us when we are scared shitless and think it's better to just let go before they do. Don't be that guy. Call Mark and ask him how life is going. He'll tell you to man up and do whatever you need to keep her."

I don't need to call Mark. We've already had that heart-to-heart, and I don't need to hear his sad, dismal story again.

"Take it one day at a time. Right now, you need to be focused on the game. Go out on that field and get down to business. Then, you can worry about how to make this work."

"Alright, if I have to listen to your quiet and stoic ass be upbeat and positive one more second, I'm going to want to shove toothpicks through my eardrums."

The sound of a rare laugh comes through my speaker. "I'll be watching when I'm not coaching. Good luck tomorrow. When you put that helmet on, your mind needs to be on that field, nowhere else. You got it?"

"Yeah. I got it, coach."

"Sean." His tone is a bit softer. "Love sticks around. Give it a chance to before you convince yourself it won't."

He hangs up, and I look around my empty rental, knowing he's right…about all of it. I need to get my head straight and down to business.

Once tomorrow is over, I'll fight distance to make sure it doesn't destroy the very best thing that's ever happened to me.

I drag myself to the bedroom. The issue is I have to sleep, but when I close my eyes, I only see Andie's beautiful face standing in my doorway. It's what I want for the rest of my life, but every past experience screams and hollers that it's never going to happen.

Chapter 54

ANDIE

The smell of exhaust and diesel wafts around me as an inaudible voice crackles over the intercom. I stand next to the town car parked against the curb in the departure lane. The evening air is chilly as dusk is just starting to settle in.

Ax is strapped to my chest, content chewing on a toy. There's a cart piled high with two large suitcases, a car seat, a stroller, my guitar, and everything I will hopefully need, while Sniper sits with his vest on patiently awaiting orders to proceed inside.

"This is a horrible idea." I put a hand on my forehead, trying to regain my sanity. I let out a cackle of nerves, needing a paper bag before I hyperventilate. "I'm just going to show up there and…this is ridiculous. Just put everything back in the car."

Snipe's head whips in the car's direction, but he stays put.

Nora slides one strap of the diaper bag over my shoulder and then the other one. "We've been over this. It's time, Andie. You need to go after what you want. No more hiding. No more wasting time."

"What if he doesn't have room for us?"

She moves to stand in front of me, her shoulders slumped, looking at me over the rim of her glasses. "He has a house. After tonight, you're going to stay there with him, and he's going to be so happy to see you. In fact, he's going to be so elated you're not only going to stay with him, but you're going to be staying with him…in his room."

A devilish smirk moves across her face, and I want to smack it away for her and Gem encouraging me to do this.

I've completely lost my mind.

I don't know what I was thinking. I got off the phone with Sean last night, and after hearing his sad, lonely, and downtrodden tone, I booked a plane ticket without thinking it through.

Now, I'm standing outside of the airport with a cart piled high with all of my stuff, about to make either the worst or maybe best decision of my life.

Crap! What the hell was I thinking?

I spin back to Nora. "What about finishing the album?"

Ignoring my panic, she grabs the last bag and throws it on top of the pile.

"You're finished, Andie. Jonesy is all set. He'll be sending files for you to listen to. I'm rolling with promotions and preorders, which are fantastic. This is going to be so big, Andie, and you're going to sit back and watch from Phoenix. No offense, but we don't need you for this part."

I huff. "This is my album, Nora. It's my first time putting myself out there, and I can't mess it up."

She grabs my face. "It'll be perfect. Everything is going to be fine. That big dreamy hunk needs you out there, and Andie, you need him. So quit stalling and get in there. Get on that plane and go be happy."

I try to swallow the growing lump in my throat. Nora starts blinking really fast, and I don't need her tears right now.

She smiles, pulling me into a hug and squishing Ax between us. "Go be so freaking happy. Walk on sunshine and write sappy love songs that drive us sad, lonely singles crazy with jealousy." Her tone softens. "There's no one that deserves it more than you. And Sean deserves it, too."

I hug her as tightly as possible, swallowing down my tears.

"I'm coming to visit as soon as you want me to, and I'll stay however long you want or maybe longer. Gem's already looking at long-term rentals."

I laugh, running a finger under my eyes as my Gem comes strutting down the sidewalk with a young airline employee in tow.

"Break it up, you two. She needs to get her buns in there, or she'll miss her flight."

Gem directs the kid, showing him what needs to be checked and demanding he line up someone to help me once I land in Phoenix.

Nora's smiling eyes meet mine at Gem's assertive dictation. When she's done, the kid looks dazed and overwhelmed but is shocked back to life when she hands him a generous tip with a wink.

She swiftly wraps her arms around me. "It's time, baby girl. I'll see you in a couple weeks."

"Oh, really. I heard you're already looking for a rental."

She doesn't meet my eyes. "I'm just doing a little shopping." She kisses Ax's head, and a faint red lip print remains. "You call me as soon as you get settled in your hotel and make sure you line up a car to take you to the game tomorrow. I'll send you the information Ed McNeil sent me to get you into the stadium, and someone will be there with your field pass."

I nod as my stomach flip-flops with the thought of surprising Sean. "I still can't believe he was able to get me a ticket."

She rolls her eyes. "Honey, that man only had to make a phone call. He hated to see Sean leave, and he adores you, so this was an easy favor. Besides, he owed me one."

I hug her. "Are you sure I'm doing the right thing? This is really big, Gem." I hug her tighter, choking on air. "I'm terrified," I whisper because any louder, and my anxiety will consume me.

She pulls back, holding my face in her hands. "Nothing. Absolutely nothing in this life ever worth having comes without fear. You are the bravest person I know. You love him, and he needs to know that. It's time. It's time for you to stop fighting the world and just go for it."

I bite my lip, hiding a teary smile. She's right. It's time. *I can do this.* I can go for it because I know at the end of this Sean will be there. Even though I might be more terrified than I've ever been in my entire life, I somehow know it's all going to turn out ok.

I nod to the kid, and he pushes the cart toward the sliding doors as Ax, Snipe, and I follow. I turn for one last look over my shoulder at Gem and Nora standing there, arms linked with giant, smug grins on both of their faces.

I take a deep breath and hold it, trying to strangle my fear and suppress my tears. One lonely droplet escapes as I walk toward what I really hope is the rest of my life.

Chapter 55

SEAN

"Greyson. First game as a King. Let's go!"

One of my new teammates slaps me on the back as he walks past while I tighten the straps on my shoulder pads.

The last thing I want right now is more pressure surrounding my rib cage. Droplets of sweat cover my brow as my stomach clenches uncomfortably tight, working itself back into my esophagus. My nerves are so far on edge that if I don't get out on the field soon, they'll start flinging off one by one, and I'll end up hanging over the toilet again.

My mind is swimming through the sludge of too many thoughts and emotions. I've tried everything since last night to get focused, but every time I'm almost there, her name pops into my head like a mallet to a gong.

I tried calling last night, needing to hear her voice and have her tease me like only she does. It's calming and a reminder that she hasn't left me yet, but she didn't answer and hasn't called me back.

I keep trying to tell myself it doesn't mean anything. Then, the past rears its ugly head to remind me that hope is fleeting, and I should see it as a giant yellow caution sign to plan for the worst.

I pull on my jersey, the number twenty-four my only familiar comfort. It's been my number since the beginning, and I was fortunate to be able to keep it. Grabbing my helmet, I join my new team as they file onto the field for pregame drills.

I find my trainer and space, ignoring the roaring fans. I run a couple routes, trying to get used to the feel of the turf under my cleats and making sure I can gain traction. I pause to catch my breath, feeling the warm sun on my face and the cool breeze against my sweat.

I stop and pull my helmet off, taking a moment to close my eyes and ready myself to do what I was brought here to do. I think about what Shane said. It's game time, and this is what I love. So, I'll play this game and then do whatever I have to afterward to ensure I don't lose Andie.

I take some deep breaths, working to clear my head of all the noise and remove the hand that's been around my neck all morning. The beat of *Happy* fills my mind, and a smile wants to tug at my lips, but that grip on my throat chokes it out.

Someone bumps my shoulder, and my eyes pop open.

"You ready to take this down the field?" Kenny stands next to me with the football in his hand.

I force a smile. "That's why I'm here."

"Good. That's what I want to hear." He laughs. "I guess we're going to be hanging out." I frown as he tosses the ball in the air and catches it. "My wife is over there making plans with your girlfriend." He bumps my shoulder and steps away while I try to process what he just said. "I'm glad you're here, Greyson."

I don't move, terrified to let myself hope…

I spin, looking along the roped-off edges of the endzone where family and friends wait, certain he's mistaken. But then…I see her. In that instant, all the emotions swarming me let loose. My eyes blur, and I can't make her out as I start jogging.

My body lightens with relief. My stomach no longer clenched tight with sickness, balloons with joy and excitement as my throat itches and burns.

I approach her, my helmet in hand, seeing the moment she notices me. Her sunglasses hide her eyes until she pushes them up on her head, holding back her mass of dark curls. She's wearing a Kings shirt under her leather jacket, jeans that hug her perfect legs, and black lace-up boots. It's my girl.

She takes her turn up to the rope, meeting me with Ax on her hip, who's wearing a very tiny jersey with my number on it. It's a declaration I wasn't sure I'd ever see.

She smiles, but it's filled with nerves, and it takes everything in me not to grab her and haul her to my side.

My throat is so thick I try to swallow, but it's painful. "You…came. You're here."

She bites her bottom lip. I know how big of a step this is for her. She's putting herself out there for me. What she might not understand yet is that we're going to show the world what real love looks like.

"Yeah. I'm here."

I want so badly to reach for her, pull her close, and breathe her in to be certain this is real.

I take a shaky breath. "Are you ready for this?" I need her to be sure. I already know the cameras all around us are snapping away.

She shakes her head, her eyes moving to the ground. "I don't know." Then, her chin tips up to meet my eyes as she steps closer. "But, if I'm going to do this, you're the only one I want to do it with. Are we still not giving a shit?"

I can't control my wide-ass grin. I move in, bringing my forehead to hers and my free hand up to cup her face. Breath enters my lungs for the first time since I left her standing on her porch.

"Always. You have no idea how happy I am to see you. You're the only one I want here. The only one I *need* to be here."

That itching sensation returns to my throat, along with some extra water in my eyes.

I know she sees it when she gives my chest a little shove. "Well, that's good because I'm not going through some crazy public breakup."

I frown. "No?"

"No. There's no elevator, but I think you really are stuck with me now."

I pull back, running my hand over Ax's head. I've missed the little guy like crazy. "We'll see how long I can stand you. It'll be tough, but I'm willing to challenge myself."

She grins this time. "I still don't like you."

"I know."

She takes a small step forward, pushing into me just slightly as her eyes flick between mine. "Be careful, ok?"

"Ok," I whisper, leaning my head down to brush my lips against the corner of her mouth. "I'll do my best. I love you."

I step back and turn around, giving her time to let that sink in. I'm so ready to play this game. It's been so long since I've felt this kind of energy, and after we win, I'm going to find my girl and show her just how much I love her. Maybe there will be cameras. Maybe there won't. I don't give two shits.

"Hey, twenty-four."

I hear that voice behind me, the one I want to hear for the rest of my life, and I turn in her direction.

"You suck."

Her voice cracks, and those green eyes are glistening with tears. I grin. As much as I want to kiss that teary glare right off her face and tell her a hundred times more how much I love her, she's going to have to watch this game first.

Chapter 56

ANDIE

He thinks he can tell me he loves me and then just walk away. In what world did he think that was a good idea?

As I stand here waiting for his broad frame to appear, all I can think about is how he played this dangerous game, and I didn't even get the chance to say it back. His punk-ass is about to get a piece of my mind.

I roll the stroller gently back and forth, trying to soothe Ax to sleep amidst the celebratory chatter of the team's family and friends. This booger is so past exhaustion he's close to losing it. Traveling and then sleeping in a new place, along with the time change, has left him a fussy mess. If Sean doesn't get his tail out here soon, I might be right there with him.

Waiting, I text Gem, knowing she and Nora are together after watching the game. They've been blowing up my phone, demanding a play-by-play, and I'm having so much fun torturing them with the bare minimum. I put my phone back in the diaper bag as players finally start to filter out. It's only a minute before Sean's strong form comes into view.

Watching him stride toward me on the field today, I'm pretty certain my heart skipped with joy, and every single bit of worry and doubt vanished. He looked in shock, and the second tears formed in his eyes, I thought I might lose it right there on the field like some kind of blubbering fool. I kept it under control, but then he had to go and tell me he loved me, sending me over the emotional edge.

This time his face is set in pure determination, and there's a level of heat to it that has me wobbling just a little. I tighten my grip on the stroller as he drops his duffle bag next to me, then sweeps me up, bringing me level with him.

His crystal blue eyes are shimmering with tears, and all my frustration takes flight. I wrap my arms around his neck and hold him so tight. This is what I've needed and longed for.

"I can't believe you're here." His voice is muffled through my hair. "I've missed you so much. Seeing you…I thought I was losing my mind."

I smile, breathing in his clean scent that smells like home. "I missed you, too." I squeeze him tighter, having needed this since he left. "Are you allowed to get out of here yet? Ax isn't going to last much longer without a bed. He hasn't slept much."

He sets me down but doesn't release me like he's still trying to convince himself this is real. I grin, which causes his grip to loosen.

"Yes."

I push the stroller as he collects his bag and takes my hand to lead us out of the mob of people. A couple of his new teammates offer congratulations on his first win with the Kings, but Sean keeps us moving forward until we're free.

"When did you get here?" he asks quietly as we wind our way out of the stadium.

"I flew in last night."

His head turns in my direction. "You were here last night?"

I bite my lip. "I didn't want to be a distraction." His head tips back toward the ceiling as we walk, like he's annoyed by my statement. I want to push his buttons. "Can you give me a ride to my hotel, or should I get an Uber?"

He tugs me to a stop. "When you didn't answer last night and then didn't call me back, I thought…" He doesn't finish his statement, but I can see all over his face what he thought, and I will my lips not to turn upward. "I'll take you to your hotel to get your stuff." His tone is firm and absolute. I like it.

I want to ask him if he's sure about that and if that offer is valid for more than a night or two, but my racing heart overrides my brain. "Ok." It's all I can get out as he links his fingers with mine and leads me forward again.

The fear of this decision had receded, but the nerves of going home with him and telling him I want to stay are alive and kicking to the perfect beat of a snare drum.

The stark contrast between Sean's rental and his home back in Nashville matches my emotional state. On the one hand, I can't wait to kiss his face off. On the other hand, I'm on the verge of losing my cookies.

I stay just inside the door, inhaling and exhaling like I'm some kind of yogi while Sean hauls the last of my stuff into the house. Snipe and I must be on the same page. His loud snorts and incessant sniffing fill the room as he proceeds to investigate every inch of this new space, ensuring it's safe and sound. Ax's dead weight in my arms and his face nuzzled in my neck is the only thing mildly comforting.

Sean's eyes were filled with both delight and confusion when he saw Snipe waiting in the hotel room for us, and despite all sound reasoning, my big fat mouth remained sealed shut. I don't know why I'm so nervous, but my stomach is twisting and turning while my heart races wildly with the realization that I actually did this.

I've played it safe for so long, living one day to the next, just letting life happen. I wasn't actively participating but simply watching it pass by. The idea that I flew across the country planning to tell Sean that I'm moving in has me turning into a complete nutjob.

I don't want to waste any more of my life hiding from the things I want or being separated from the person I want to be with, but what if this is crazy? What if he's not ready for me to invade his space and life?

I knew stepping on the field today would put me front and center with Sean. If I learned anything from the whole fiasco with his ex, it's that as long as I have him by my side, everything will be alright. But telling him I'm here and planning on staying is a mammoth-sized leap into unknown territory.

He told me he loves me, but that doesn't mean he's ready to live with me or build a life with me and Ax.

I rock back and forth subconsciously as sweat collects under my armpits, and I start to feel a little woozy. I just need to spit it out and hope I'm not rushing things.

He huffs behind me, setting my second overstuffed and overweight suitcase and guitar inside the door before closing it.

"Babies require an exorbitant amount of stuff." He rests his hands on his hips, and then his brow furrows while his eyes roam the room. "What's wrong?"

My pulse rushes in my ears, and it's suddenly hard to breathe. *What in the hell is wrong with me? Just say it.*

I try to pull in a little air. "So, about all my stuff…" My voice is breathy and not at all my own.

He steps closer, concern taking over his handsome face. His eyes search mine as he waits patiently.

"I was hoping Ax and I could stay…for a while, but if that's an issue, or this is moving too fast, or it's too soon, and you need time to settle in, then…"

His head cocks to the side just a quarter of an inch. "What?"

Snipe's nails click against the tile floor as he re-enters the kitchen, coming to sit at my feet. I have no doubt he's sensing my freak-out. I just have to get this out. *Shit, breathe.*

I inhale long and slow, then push it out quickly. "I'm not going back. I don't know how it will all work, but I want to be here…with you. I don't want to waste time or try to pretend that distance is somehow going to work because the truth is, I did that, and it pretty much sucked all the time. I don't want to do that again, and…I don't want to be away from you. I want to see where this goes…here…with you."

I bite my lip, trying really hard to pull myself together while Sean just stands there dumbfounded, and I don't have any idea how to interpret that. I probably need to stop now, but given that he's staring at me, I keep going.

"If this is a problem or it's too much too fast or–"

"Andie, stop." His voice is soft but demanding, and he moves closer, grabbing my free hand and pulling me along with him.

"That's all you're going to say," I babble as he tugs me to the other side of the room. "What are you doing?"

I shift Ax a little, trying not to jostle him as Sean leads me down the hallway and to the first door on the right. He opens it and steps inside, the only light coming from a small nightlight.

It takes a second for my eyes to adjust, but along the wall stands…a crib. The mattress tucked inside is covered with a sheet with little guitars all over it.

It's my turn to frown as my mind spins with wonder. All of my anxiety suddenly evaporates, and an overwhelming sense of astonishment washes over me.

"Sean…" I'm stunned, speechless.

His fingers lace with mine, and when I look up at him, there's a shyness that is both new and cute as hell.

"I want you here, both of you. Always. You being here is everything I wanted but was too afraid to ask for."

I swallow what feels like a tennis ball and blink back the tears burning in my eyes. I move to gently lay Ax down in the crib, still trying to process this gift. I run a hand over his head, then return to Sean, pressing up on my tiptoes to wrap my arms around his neck and loving him so much my entire body lights with electricity that's painfully alive and completely new. His strong arms come around my middle, holding me just as tightly.

We stay like that for a minute, maybe two, and then he lifts me one-armed and carries me out of the room, pulling the door slightly closed behind us. In the dimly lit hallway, he sets me down but doesn't let go.

"I don't want you to ever question again where you belong because it's right here," he taps his chest, "with me."

I press back up to my tiptoes and crush my mouth to his. His light scruff brushes against my face as my mouth moves over his. His hands grip my hips, guiding me until my back presses up against the wall. Those large hands glide from my hips up the sides of my body until they push into my hair, and he takes charge, angling my head, slowly deepening our kiss.

His scent, his warmth, his security, and love surround me, and there's nothing more I want in this world. He said this is where I belong, and he's absolutely right.

Needing air, he releases my mouth, pressing kisses down the side of my neck to my collarbone, and a soft whimper escapes me. One large hand grabs the back of my thigh, hoisting me up, and I wrap my legs around him.

He finds my mouth again as he carries me down the remainder of the hallway and enters another room on the opposite side. He kisses me once more before releasing my legs and setting me on the edge of the bed. His bedroom holds the soft glow of the nightlights on each wall.

Sean moves to his knees in front of me, his hand cupping my cheek. "I want you, and I want us forever. I love you, and I love Ax. I've never in my life said those words to anyone. Before you, I didn't understand what they meant, but I do now, and you coming here…" He pulls in a breath. "Andie, it means everything to me."

I pull his face to mine, kissing him softly, my lips brushing over his. "Having you so far away wasn't working so well for me. I was worried you might get your ass pummeled, and I wouldn't be here."

He pushes me back on the bed, and his massive body hovers over mine. "I've missed your smart mouth."

"Yeah, well, I will never forgive you for what you pulled today." I slide my hands under the soft fabric of his t-shirt and let my fingers linger over the defined ridges of his muscles.

His lips move over my cheek to the sensitive skin just below my ear. "I have no idea what you're talking about."

I tug his shirt upward, and he moves just enough to pull it off in one swift masculine motion, his warm skin exposed.

"You know exactly what I'm talking about, you big shit." His hands find the hem of my shirt and graze the tender skin of my stomach teasingly, causing my sharp inhale. I can barely make out his smug grin. "If you ever do that to me again and then walk away without letting me say it back, you can be certain that it'll be a cold day in hell before I will ever like you."

Sean braces himself on his forearms, looking down at me. His blue eyes flick between mine, holding an intensity filled with longing for both me and the words he's probably never been told.

I move my arms between us, my thumbs running over his jaw. "I love you." He blinks, letting the words sink in. "I love you so much," I whisper again, needing him to hear it. He blinks some more. "Do you have any idea how incredibly beautiful you are?"

That has his lips turning upward ever so slightly, but he doesn't move. When he does finally speak, his voice is rough and ragged and sexy as hell.

"I'm hanging on by a very thin strand here, and I need you to tell me if you aren't ready for this. I will wait however long is necessary, and nothing will change." He brushes my curls away from my face.

Staring up at him, I see everything that he is. Gentle. Kind. Loving. Courageous. Strong. Mine.

He's mine. He's my home. My place. My safe and secure.

"There isn't a place in this world where I feel safer and more loved than when I'm with you. I hauled my baby and my stuff halfway across the country for this. For you. For us. I don't need to wait. I don't want to."

His lips move hungrily over mine again as his hands tug at my shirt, pulling it up over my head. His eyes move over me, and passion and desire reflect back. But also love for me, just as I am.

His bare chest rests on mine, and my hands slide up his back, pulling him to me. This. This is where I always want to be. It's where I'm meant to be.

He trails kisses down to my shoulder as his fingers toy with the lace around my ribs.

"Sean, just so we're clear," I whisper. "I may love you, but liking you is still very much up in the air."

His kisses abruptly stop. His hands slide down my arms to my wrists as he holds them, and I lay perfectly still beneath him.

"What's it going to take? Huh?" His eyes bore into mine.

"Hmmmm," I tease. "I'm going to have to think about it. It might take a bit."

"Really? How long?" He glares, those enchanting blue eyes slowly disappearing.

"Well, I'm thinking forever." I grin.

He grins back. "Excellent. Then I've got plenty of time to change your mind."

Chapter 57

SEAN

I wake to the sound of soft coos coming through the baby monitor, which instantly brings a smile to my face. I lie staring up at the ceiling, wondering if this can possibly be real, terrified that at any moment, I'm going to find out it's all a dream.

Andie's warm hand runs across my bare chest, stirring me from my anxious thoughts and confirming my unbelievable reality. I didn't even know it was possible to feel like this. To be so full of joy and happiness that you might literally burst.

I pull her closer, pressing a kiss to the top of her head and breathing in her minty, flowery scent. When she told me she loved me last night, I needed a second to be sure I heard her correctly.

Love hasn't been a part of my life. My life has been a function of survival and keeping my emotions tucked away so as not to be disturbed. But for the first time, I have someone who loves me completely.

I've never known what this feels like, and it's so overwhelmingly good it hurts for all the years I've missed this. What I know is there won't be a single moment I'll take for granted.

A squeal, followed by a fit of spitting, erupts, and I hear Snipe leave the bedroom and prance down the hall.

Andie moans and stretches next to me before placing a kiss on my chest. Her bright green eyes peer up at me. She smiles and buries her face.

With one arm around her, I pull her on top of me, and her quiet laughter fills the room this time.

"Good morning." She crosses her arms on my chest and rests her chin on them.

"Morning."

Her curls are everywhere, and her small frame is warm and soft on top of me. I link my arms around her to hold her there. She inches slightly forward to press a subtle kiss to my lips, but then she bites my bottom lip playfully, and a groan erupts from my throat.

I roll, flipping us over and sending her to her back. I kiss her mouth, neck, and shoulder, taking my time.

"Aren't you football players supposed to play it cool during the season?"

"Baby, I've played it *cool* enough seasons. You're here, and it would be impossible not to–"

She laughs and writhes as I run my hand from her ankle all the way up her thigh and over her hip. I've learned that Andie is incredibly ticklish, and I love it so freaking much. It's my non-verbal way to match her constant verbal shit-giving attacks.

"Stttoooooppp," she whines.

I halt my torture, pinning both her hands over her head. "Do you have any idea how insanely beautiful you are?"

Her sleepy green eyes narrow. "Are you stealing my line, Pretty Boy?"

"It's not a line if it's a fact. That day in the elevator, I thought you were the most beautiful woman I'd ever seen."

"You're out of your mind. You looked at me like I was some ragamuffin who wandered into the stadium looking for a hot meal."

I lean down to brush my lips over hers. "You are soooo wrong." I find her neck. "You had on those tight holey jeans and that black rocker chick shirt that hung off your shoulder. When your eyes hit mine as you started to give me shit for the very first time, they took on a vibrancy that is completely unique to you. Never having experienced someone like you before, I'm pretty damn sure I started having heart palpitations which didn't do my panicking ass any favors."

She tries to move her hands, but I don't let them go, lacing my fingers through hers.

"Listen, loser, don't think just because you've got me in your bed and whispering sweet things like how beautiful I am will cause me to be nice to you."

I run my lips over her jaw. "I don't ever want you to be nice to me."

She grins as another round of baby babble comes from the monitor. "Now, if we're adding *not* playing it cool to our mutually agreed to list, then we're going to have to continue this later. Ax won't patiently wait for food much longer."

I kiss her one more time and roll off her, letting her climb out of bed to get Ax. I feel like the luckiest man alive, and I've done nothing to deserve it, but I'll take it. All of it.

I shower quickly and pull on some shorts.

"You have got to be kidding me!"

I hear Andie as I make my way down the hallway to the kitchen. She stands at the counter in one of my t-shirts, and I'm ready to throw her over my shoulder and carry her right back to bed. *Damn.*

Ax sits on the island countertop in front of her, pushing cereal around with his finger. When he notices me, he grins, and drool runs out of his mouth as he claps his hands.

Andie turns in my direction. "You have to see what Nora sent me."

I can tell she's completely annoyed, holding out her phone. I take it, and not surprisingly, there's a picture of Andie and me from the game yesterday. My forehead is pressed to hers, and her hand rests on my chest. The headline reads, *Parks Shows Support for Our New Favorite King.*

Andie stands waiting while I read. "Seriously. After all we've been through, this is the best they can do. Where's the claim to our innocence? Or at least a note about us clawing our way back from the gates of hell."

"You know, if it weren't for that mess, we might not be here." Her head falls to the side like she sees my point. "At least the comments directed at us are positive, and people wish us well this time."

She scoffs. "Nora said my album pre-orders went up ten percent overnight."

"That's amazing. What about finishing your album?"

I move around the kitchen, pulling things out for breakfast, noting we need to order groceries. Glancing at Ax as he shoves a fist full of Cheerios in his mouth, we also need a highchair and likely a bunch of other stuff that I have no idea we need.

Andie rests her arms on the counter around Ax and spoon-feeds him some oatmeal. "I wrapped up a recording a couple of days ago. Jonesy is working on cleaning up each track. If he thinks I need to re-record anything, I'll either have to go back or see if I can find a studio here. We're trying to keep it pretty raw, so hopefully, what we already have will work."

I set a pan on the stove and pull eggs from the refrigerator along with the ingredients for my morning protein smoothie. Besides knowing that Andie plans to stay for a while, we haven't discussed any of the logistics or exactly how long 'a while' might be.

I'm hesitant to ask my next question. I know what I want her answer to be, but I'm nervous her response won't match. I turn toward her, halting my progress on breakfast.

"When you said last night you plan on staying for a while, what exactly does a while mean?"

Her hand stops scraping the oatmeal remnants from the bowl, and she turns to look at me, her brows scrunched together.

"I mean…I want you here as long as you want to be here, but I know you have a life back…" My heart has suddenly kicked into high gear, and I'm a blubbering fool who can't formulate sentences.

"Sean." Andie sets the empty bowl down, her tone calm but cautious. "I was hoping we could stay, like, for good." I'm pretty sure my heart skips a couple of beats to get back into a normal rhythm, or its new normal filled with complete elation. "I want to be here with you or wherever you are. I know this is fast, but I'm kind of tired of sitting by while life goes on. I want to live it…with you."

I don't even care that a sappy, love-struck grin covers my face, ear to ear. "Good answer. What about your house and all of your stuff?"

She laughs, feeding Ax the last bite while I crack eggs.

"Well, Nora said she would line up movers for me when we're ready. We need our clothes, all Ax's stuff, my piano, and other equipment. I think I'll keep my house. I have to go back for my album release. Hopefully, you'll be able to go with me." She says the last part hesitantly, like she's the unsure one now.

"When my season is over, I'm going wherever you're going."

It's her turn to grin, and I realize eventually, we'll get this all figured out.

"I'm listing my house for sale, so keeping yours makes sense. Do you think you can wait a couple weeks for your stuff so we can look at houses here? It doesn't make sense to move it twice."

When I don't get a response, I glance at her over my shoulder, and she's staring at me. "What?"

"You want us to look at houses?"

"Yes. This place is nice, but it's a short-term rental and too small. I was thinking we'll buy a piano and whatever other equipment you need. We can even talk about building a studio. Plus, I don't like that there's no barrier to the pool with Ax, and Snipe needs a yard. We need space for Gem." I watch as tears fill her eyes. "Baby, what's wrong?" I turn the burner off, leaving the mostly cooked eggs to pull her to me.

Her arms come around my middle, and her face presses into my chest. I worry I said something wrong as I hear her sniff and feel her squeeze me tighter.

"I've never…" she sniffs. "I've never had anyone think of me and care for me the way you do. You…the crib, the pool, and a yard for Snipe." She pulls away to look up at me, a tear running down her cheek. "You want to get a house with space for Gem."

I brush her tears away with my thumb. "Andie, I love you and Ax so much. From now on, this is how it's going to be. You and I are figuring everything out together, and nothing comes before that. Ok?"

She nods, wiping the tears away. "I love you too." She rests her head on my chest again. "Gem's already looking at rentals."

I chuckle. "Really?"

"Yeah, and Nora is coming out as soon as we're ready for her. She's going out of her mind this morning, along with all of your fans, at the pictures of us."

"She can come out as soon as you want her to. I'm off today, but my days are long. I'll spend a lot of time at the practice facility, and then when I get home, I'll sit in the sauna for a while. I'll be gone some nights for games, or I'll be home really late." She doesn't let me go. "I know this isn't ideal–"

She cuts me off. "Sean, this is your job. I just want to be with you as much as I can be."

"When the season ends, we can do whatever you want."

She tips her head up, resting her chin on my chest, a smirk forming on her lips. "Really? Because I seem to recall that you wagered that I would visit you if you won the next Words game. Now that you got something even better without even having to win, I feel like that's grounds for me getting whatever I want right now."

"Huh. I think you should get whatever you would have wagered at the time."

Her lips push to the side like she's evaluating my logic. "Ok. I don't mind that idea."

"Sooooo, what were you going to bet?"

She wraps her arms around me tighter, linking them. "I want you to come with me when I perform at The FlyOver."

"You're performing at The FlyOver? When did that happen?"

She nods. "When my album releases. I didn't get a chance to tell you before everything happened."

"Andie, that's amazing. Of course, I'll be there. I wouldn't be anywhere else." I kiss the top of her head, hugging her.

"It won't be until after the season ends, so maybe we can stay for a bit." Her face tips down. "At some point, I have to talk to my parents, and I'd really like you to be with me."

I find her hands and link them with mine. "We'll work through all of that together. Everything's going to be alright."

She pushes up to her toes and kisses me softly. "I love you."

"I know."

She kisses me again and then puts an arm around Ax, who's been busy pushing his cereal off the counter and watching Snipe try to catch it.

We eat breakfast together, and while Andie showers and dresses, Ax and I take Snipe for a walk and then find a spot on a rug to spread out some of his toys. Andie gets busy ordering groceries and urgent necessities while I start perusing homes for sale.

As Ax naps on my chest, we sit on the couch, looking at a couple of homes the realtor sent me. Andie's guitar sits across her lap, and her gentle strumming and quiet singing fills the house.

This is the only thing I want for the rest of my life. I didn't know such a life existed, but if this can be mine, I'll spend every day trying to be worthy of it.

Chapter 58

ANDIE

NORA: What kind of clothes do I need to bring?

ME: Ones that cover your body. Comfort is optional.

NORA: What if I want to go on a date?

ME: Definitely all the clothes, then.

NORA: You're no fun.
NORA: Should I bring something extra revealing to wear to the games to fit in?

ME: Go to bed. I'll see you in a few days.

NORA: SEE YOU IN A FEW DAYS!!

The security alarm beeps and Snipe dashes out of the room. The alarm is disarmed, and I know he's home. It's late, and I'm so tired, but waiting up for him is one of my favorite things because I actually have someone to wait up for. Just so happens he's also my favorite person.

I hear his keys hit the counter. I know he'll go to the refrigerator to grab a bottle of water before carefully checking on Ax and finally making his way to me. Snipe's nails click in the background as he follows Sean from one stop to the next. Eventually, those footsteps and that tap, tap, tapping get closer.

"Hi." He stands in the doorway looking tired and beat up, but his face brightens, and his lips turn upward. He played in Texas this afternoon and won, keeping the Kings winning streak going. The amount I've learned about football these past months is almost miraculous. I've learned to enjoy it despite constantly worrying he'll get hurt.

"Hey. You look like you need about two hours in the hot tub and eighteen hours of sleep."

He drops his bag by the closet. "Yes, to both, but the only thing I want to do is shower and crawl in bed with you."

I smile. "If it were earlier, I'd make a smart-ass comment, but I'm too tired, so hurry up. I'm cold, and we both need to sleep."

Instead of heading into the bathroom, he comes around to my side of the bed, and using his finger to tip my chin up, he leans down to kiss me, taking his time. This…I'll take this forever.

I push at his chest. "Go take a shower. Then I have good news for you."

One eyebrow shoots up. "Really? How about the news, then the shower?"

"Come on, loser, what kind of game do you think we're playing? I'll hold it over your head so you'll hurry your fine-muscled butt into the shower and get back out here quickly."

"Fine-muscled butt?" He turns toward the bathroom.

"Oh, for real. Don't even pretend you don't know you have the most magnificent butt. It might even be better than that pretty face of yours."

"I thought your smart mouth was shut down for the night?" He pulls his shirt over his head and tosses it into the basket.

"Yeah, well, you woke her up with that kiss. It's your fault."

I hear the shower turn on and return to my Words game against Gem. She's kicking my tail this time, and I've tried for the past half hour to hit a triple-word score, but I'm stuck. The stakes are high. If I win this round, she's coming to stay for two months and make rounds to the playoff games with me.

Somehow, I think she'll be making the trip regardless. Nora let it slip, probably on purpose, that Gem lined up a six-month rental. With Sean being gone so much, having them here will be nice.

After ten minutes, I toss my phone on the nightstand as Sean climbs into bed.

"Alright, I want this good news."

I turn my lamp off, pulling the covers up over me as I scoot over to plaster myself against him. The nightlights flick to life, bringing our room a soft, warm glow.

Since the first night I slept in his bed, I've become addicted to everything about it. The dim light. His giant, fantastic bed. The feel of his big body next to mine and the safety and security that comes with it that I've never had before. I've spent too many nights afraid and alone to ever want to do it again.

I rest my head on his chest, and his arm automatically comes around me as I flip one leg over his. "First, I want to hear about the game. How was it really?"

"I got my ass drug down the field, but winning felt great. We had to work for it, which makes it all the more rewarding. Their defense was all over me."

"I saw. I didn't like it." His lips press against my forehead. "Gem was blowing up my phone the whole game, cursing like a sailor every time you got tackled. I don't think we should let her attend games when she arrives. She's likely to get kicked out."

He laughs. "Having you ladies at my game means the world to me. I've never had that before."

I smile. "I definitely like it much better when I can be there."

"I want you at the playoff games. Leading the division gives us home-field advantage, but if we have to travel, I still want you there."

I prop my chin on his chest. "We'll figure it out. I want to be there, too."

I shift to press my lips to his before returning to my comfortable position. "So, you want to hear the good news?"

"Yes. Quickly before I fall asleep."

"Actually, I have two pieces of good news. First, Jonesy finished up the last song, and I have an album release date, and I'm scheduled at The FlyOver."

"When is it?"

"Even better news, it's after the season ends."

His arms squeeze me. "I can't wait to hear you sing all of your songs. Although, I really like it when I just catch you playing and singing when you think no one's paying attention."

"Yeah? Most of the time, I'm just messing around."

"Well, it sounds like professional messing around, and I like that nobody gets to hear that but me. It's incredible when you play the classical stuff on the piano."

"Hmmm. Sometimes, it's just good to go back to the basics and know I can still do it."

Sean yawns. "You said there were two pieces of good news."

"Oh yeah. Are you ready for this?" I prop myself up on my elbow so I can see him. "The realtor called. The house that we wanted in Scottsdale came through. It's ours."

We've been looking at houses because trying to live without my stuff has been difficult. Most of Sean's things are in storage, and even though Sean and I aren't on hold, it feels like we're still waiting for it all to come together. This house is the final step, and I can't wait.

"When can we close?"

"The sellers are already out, so the sooner, the better for them. I was thinking with Nora here, maybe we could make it happen if you're ok with that. She's packed all my things that need to be moved, and Gem said she'll let movers in and give directions whenever we're ready."

"Let's do it then. I'm ready to get out of here and have you and Ax settled before things really pick up."

"Yeah?" This doing-life thing with Sean is so surreal to me. Whenever I think about all of the decisions I used to have to make alone, like buying a house, dealing with car issues, or having a baby, I'm so grateful for his support. It's the small things you take for granted unless you've never had them.

"Yeah. I want us in our own house as soon as possible. We'll be here at least through next season, so the sooner, the better."

"It may sound weird, but I like making these kinds of decisions with you. When I learned that I was pregnant with Ax, all of a sudden, decisions had to be made. I wanted a house for us. I needed to find a doctor I was comfortable with delivering him. I needed to find a pediatrician and decide if I was freezing the umbilical cord. All the most important decisions I'll ever make. I was terrified to make the wrong one. I laid in bed at night praying I wouldn't screw it up."

My stomach still pinches at the thought of all those nights I lay there, scared, and with no one to talk to or help me.

I link my fingers with his. "Buying a house is not the same as having a baby, but it's still a big decision, and it's been really nice doing it with you."

"You don't have to do any of that stuff alone anymore. You and Ax and I are a family. We're going to do all of the life things together."

I rest my head on his chest with the comfort of this truth overwhelming me. I'm so thankful that I made it here, that I took one step at a time, climbing out of despair and into a happiness I'm only just beginning to discover.

Epilogue

Two Months Later

ANDIE

I use my hand to shield my eyes from the bright lights to survey the small crowd gathered in the confined space. The FlyOver is packed. Every table is filled, and Gem and Nora sit at a table in the front, beaming like two idiots. Jonesy sits on a stool to my right, a guitar resting on his leg.

"Thank you so much for joining me tonight. This is a dream come true. You know…it feels like not that long ago, I sat up here on an open mic night, just needing one person to hear my song. Never in a million years would I have thought I'd be playing a whole album's worth of songs for you. I'm truly honored to have been asked here tonight."

I set my guitar on the stand next to me. "I have one final song I'd like to share. So, if you'll indulge me, it's something new."

A round of soft applause fills the space as I move to sit behind the piano. I search the back wall until I find Sean. He's standing in the back, rocking a sleepy Ax high on his chest.

I adjust the mic before I play a chord lightly. "This song is incredibly personal. I wrote it late one night after getting some difficult news." I find Sean again. "And amid my heartbreak, someone came in, scooped me up, held me, and didn't let go. He's held my hand every day since."

I sing of walking in the dark, knowing everything will be ok as long as he's by my side. I tell him I need him to hold me, keep me, and never let go. It doesn't matter what happens or what life may bring. I'll ride with him until the end.

I hit the final chord and let it ring out as people stand and applaud. I press my hands to my chest, thanking them, but I look for the one I need, like my soul needs music.

His spot along the wall is now empty, and as I search, my eyes snag on a couple in the far back corner. My breath catches in my throat as my parents stand, eyes trained on me.

I shake myself loose from the shock, joining Jonesy on the side of the small stage where Sean is waiting for me. I walk straight into his free arm.

"I'm so proud of you." He kisses me and hugs me so tightly that my entire body relaxes into him. Home. He is my home. "Baby, I will ride with you anytime, anywhere, forever." I lean back to see his face. "I'm never letting go."

"I love you." The idea of forever with him sounds perfect to me.

Sean kisses my forehead and leaves me to chat with his former teammate, Tyrell, and his wife while I spend the next hour greeting and talking with friends and acquaintances. Jonesy and I speak with a few people from the industry. Eventually, I make it to Gem and Nora's table, who sit relaxed with drinks in their hand.

"Take a seat, sweet cheeks. You earned it up there. There wasn't a dry eye in the house with some of those songs." Gem takes a sip of her drink. I search for Sean and spot him talking to the McNeils. "I told everyone here that you're about to blow the top right off the charts."

"Gem. You didn't."

She scoffs. "You bet your sweet ass I did."

Nora's head falls back as she laughs. "She did, and they all kept saying how they begged you to sign with them. They still want you to. I told them they could send a formal offer."

I roll my eyes. "You two need to be separated."

"Not a chance. We're coming back to Scottsdale as soon as business settles down." Nora surveys the room, leaning in and resting her arms on the table. "Did you know your parents are here?"

"I have no idea how they got in."

I hear Gem clear her throat. "Avoidance is for sissies. Baby girl, you have nothing to be afraid of."

I search the room again, and an ugly churning rises in my stomach. My eyes drift around the dim space just in time to see my parents slip out the door. It's been an emotional night, and seeing their backs as they leave fills me with equal parts relief and sorrow. I wonder why they were here, but I'm grateful they gave me space and didn't use it as an opportunity to dampen this night.

I know I need to speak with them, and I have a mountain of questions I'd like answers to, but none of them can erase the years of pain and heartache. A little longer won't change anything.

For the first time, there's peace within me concerning my parents. The constant pressure and battle to stay true to myself while also trying to please them is gone. Things with them will fall wherever they may, and that's a really nice place to be.

I pull myself up out of the chair, wanting to find Sean. I wander the room and find him tucked in a corner, chatting with Jonesy.

"I couldn't stand to watch you lose the Super Bowl." Jonesy slaps Sean on the shoulder. "Man, I had to turn it off. If the Kings have you all next season, hopefully, you'll be able to change the outcome next year."

"Our quarterback is retiring, which will stir things up a bit," Sean replies as I slide my arm around him. "Joining the Kings has brought about some of the best changes in my life, though." He glances down at me, his handsome face smiling. "Winning the Super Bowl would be great, but I already have everything that really matters."

Jonesy grins. "You two are sickening, but I'm glad it all worked out. Hanging out with her all depressed and moody and sad was a lot of work, but it sure made for some damn good music. Y'all need to keep the drama going so we can get started on the next album."

Sean laughs as I glare at one of my best friends. "Maybe I'm ready to make happy, joyful music."

Jonesy rolls his eyes. "The day I hear you write happy music…Andie, that will be the day."

I give him a gentle shove as I move to hug him. "You are the best, you know that. It doesn't matter what kind of music I write. You'll make it sound incredible, and it's our music. Our next album is going to rock."

"You just keep writing, and I'll make it shine." He hugs me again. "Alright, I'll see you two before you head home," Jonesy says, stepping away.

I hug Sean tight again and spot Gem across the room, staring at me. She winks, and that devilish smirk on her face says everything. That woman. I smile, finally feeling like everything might actually be ok. More than ok. It's more than I could have ever dreamed.

"Sounds like you and I just need to create a new scandal so I can write more songs."

Sean laughs. "You're ridiculous. Are you ready to go home? This kid is getting really heavy."

I wrap my arms around his waist, pressing my face to his warm chest. "Yes. Can we stop for tacos?"

"Of course."

I grin up at him, wondering how in the world I got here. "Pretty Boy, if I ever start to like you, we're going to have a real problem on our hands."

I push up to my toes to kiss him, taking his hand to gather my things.

"Well, we better make sure that never happens, then."

I laugh, so ready to go home with my guys.

SEAN

"What exactly are we doing? I really need to pack. I'm ready to go home."

I lead Andie through the Tigers stadium, where kids are registering to participate in a sports clinic.

"I told Ed last night we'd stop by if we could. I owe him for getting you a pass to my first Kings game."

I drop Andie's hand as my heart starts pounding in my chest. I've thought about this since the day she showed up in Arizona, taking a chance on me. Beads of sweat are starting to break out on my forehead, and my hands are clammy. It has less to do with what I'm about to do and more about where I'm doing it.

"Does it feel weird being back here?" Her voice is so cool and casual it's only mildly calming my impending anxiety attack.

I take a steadying breath. "A little."

"Are you alright?" She turns in my direction, and the fists punching my lungs pause momentarily.

"Yeah. It's just..." I reach for her hand again as we round the corner to our destination. I tug her to a stop and hit the button.

"What are you doing?" Her furrowed brow has turned to concern. "Are you for real?" She looks around. "Wait, is this our elevator? We're not going in there. You hate elevators. Where are the stairs?"

She tries to let go of my hand in search of the stairs, but I hold her there, trying to keep it together.

"It'll be fine. It's just two floors. Ten seconds. I can handle it. The stairs to get down to the tunnel are–"

I can handle it. I can do this. I have Andie. I let out a long, slow breath.

"Sean, you're an elite athlete. I think we can handle a short walk."

She tries to tug away again, but I wrap my hands around her waist. "I'll be fine." I tip my head in the direction of the opening elevator doors. "For old-time sake. Plus," I try to say confidently, though I feel anything but, "I have you."

She stares at me like I'm out of my mind. "Really? You want to go in there?"

I nod, forcing a smile to reassure her and myself. Before I determine this is a dumbass idea, I pull her into the elevator with me, hit the button for the lower level, and back us up to the wall. She comes willingly and rests her body up against mine, linking her arms around my neck.

The doors close, and I bring my forehead to hers as the elevator starts to move.

"Are you ok? I can feel your heart pounding," she whispers as if not to make this worse.

"As long as I have you."

She presses up to her tiptoes and nuzzles into my neck as the elevator dings, moving past the first floor. Blood pulses in my ears as I try to do what I came to do.

"You know, the last time I was in here, it changed my life forever."

"Oh yeah?" I feel her lips press against the side of my neck.

"Yeah. I walked out of here feeling like I was shoved off the ledge I'd been standing on, and it had nothing to do with this elevator." The elevator dings again, and the doors open. She tries to take a step back, but

I hold her there. "I didn't know it then, but sitting in this elevator with you was the best thing that could have ever happened to me."

The doors close again, and Andie turns to look at them and then back at me. "You don't want to get out of here?"

"I do, but not yet." My racing heart has calmed, and all I can see is her. Her brilliant green eyes search mine. "Andie, you stirred something inside me that day, and I haven't been the same since. Running into you after that was a gift, a second chance for me to realize that you are exactly what I needed and everything that was missing in my life."

She stares up at me, her head falling slightly to the side.

"You very quickly became my best friend, and then, not long after that, I fell ridiculously and hopelessly in love with you." Her perfect lips turn upward, and it's as if my nerves snap off and fall to the floor one by one. "You already know I'm spending the rest of my life with you, but I would really like to do that as your husband. I want you to be my wife. I want to continue to build our life together with Ax. I want to make more babies with you, however many you want. I want to laugh and joke, fight and make up, and have you give me shit every single day for the rest of our lives."

I reach into my pocket and pull out the princess-cut onyx stone surrounded by diamonds. Her eyes grow wide, and I release her to get down on my knee.

"Don't." She stops me. "Nope. Just..." She lifts my hand to look at the ring, looks up at me, and then back at the ring. "You..."

My heart starts picking up pace again, and I break out in a cold sweat. Suddenly, I need air, but before I can move to hit the button, Andie grabs me and kisses me like...everything in the world disappears but the warmth of her mouth on mine. Her hands are on the sides of my face, holding me so close and kissing me like she needs to be sure this is real and taking every advantage of it.

My heart and body begin to take on a different need, and I relax into the feel of her pressed up against me. In an instant, I have her up against the side wall, my hands tangled in her wild hair, and I'm oblivious to anything except Andie. I lift her up, guiding her legs around me. I kiss her like my life depends on it because if I stop, I might suffocate in this tiny box.

There's a noise and a rush of cool air behind me. I slowly pull away and turn to find two dudes standing outside the elevator, staring at us.

Andie laughs, resting her head against my shoulder as I slowly set her down. She adjusts her shirt.

"Sorry, we just need one more minute," she tells them as the doors close again, hiding their smug smirks.

She grabs both of my hands and holds them. "Sitting in this elevator with you for those two hours helped me see that I still had a life to live. I'd been hiding in the dark, letting life pass me by, thinking somehow it would get better. Eventually, the light would just spill in, and everything would be ok. That light never came." She shakes her head. "But I stood on that podium afraid to sing, that if I let go, there'd be nothing left. Then, I saw you, and you gave me the courage I needed. I didn't even like you."

Tears gather in her eyes, and she looks down at our hands. "Sean, from that day, you haven't left me alone. You just kept appearing, each time pulling me just a little bit more back out into the light. You were trustworthy and kind, and I think without me even realizing it, you not only stole my heart, but you mended it. I didn't know if I could love someone again, but this, you and me...I love you so much. You don't even have to ask. I want nothing more than to be your wife. I would marry you this very minute. I want everything you said and only with you."

I gather her back up and lift her, kissing her again. I only let it linger a second or two before I set her back down, placing the ring on her finger and then pressing the button to open the doors.

"Sorry, but my limit in this space has hit the max."

Andie laughs, and we step out into the fluorescently lit tunnel. I rest against the wall, taking some slow breaths, happy to be out in the wide open.

Andie leans against the wall next to me. "If those dudes recognized you, it'll be blasted everywhere that we got caught making out in an elevator."

"They're lucky we were just making out." She swats my arm. "It may not seem like it, but I'm so freaking happy right now."

She moves to stand in front of me. "Is that because you escaped suspended confinement this time, or you get to deal with me for the rest of your life?"

She presses into me, and I link my hands behind her back. "Both."

"You were very brave to do that in there. At least it didn't really get stuck this time."

"I was starting to panic just thinking about it, but you made it better."

She looks at the ring on her finger. "How soon do you think we can make this legit?"

I cock an eyebrow. "In a hurry?"

"Damn straight I am. Don't think I haven't noticed how those Kings hussies have been floating around you thinking you're some cheater they can sink their fangs into."

I let my head fall back against the wall. "Andie, you're absurd."

"Oh, am I, Pretty Boy? Well, sucks to be you then because you're stuck with me."

"I think I'm good with that."

She pushes up on her tiptoes, grinning. "You feeling better?"

I pull her to me and wrap my arms around her. "I say we make this legit as soon as possible."

Six Months Later

ANDIE

A year. It's been a year, and here I am again. Different stadium. Different crowd. Same, but different man.

"You going to be ok singing for thousands of raging fans?"

I stand in the tunnel with the Kingsnakes, a cup of hot tea in my hand, leaning up against the metal barricade that separates me from my husband. My black knit dress fits snugly, showing off my curves under a new fitted leather jacket with some additional ruffled flare and my favorite sparkly silver heels.

I lean over the barricade to get just a little closer. "I guess we'll find out. Are you ready for the first game of your last season?"

Sean's contract is up after this season, and he's decided it's time to give his body a rest and see where else he can lend his efforts.

"I'm ready to spend all my days and nights with you and Ax and our little girl." His hand slides over my little growing bump, leaving it there, hoping to feel movement.

"We're ready for you," I hear the PR assistant say behind me.

I push up to my toes. "Be safe, ok?" I press my lips to Sean's and then step back, knowing it's time for me to do what I came to do.

"I'll do my best. I love you."

I grin. "You still suck, but you're growing on me."

The corners of his light blue eyes crinkle as he smiles, that beautiful smile I will never ever tire of making come to life.

I lean over for one more quick kiss and leave him with his team as I make my way to my spot in the middle of the field. I reminisce as I take the mic, waiting for the players to be announced and gather on the sideline before me.

A year ago, I stood in a spot just like this, but it was completely different. I stood before a crowd, needing to let go of one life and have the courage to take up another. I was terrified of the unknown, of the possibility that letting go meant never being whole or loved again.

Ladies and gentlemen, please rise for the singing of the national anthem by Grammy Nominated Best New Artist, Andie Greyson. Please remove your hats and place your hand over your heart.

But there was a pair of blue eyes, wearing number twenty-four that stood just as he does right now, who pushed me to do it. I didn't know it then, but sometimes that's all we need. Someone to dare us, but we have to take the leap, to jump to the other side to find out what might be waiting for us there.

At the time, I could've never imagined I'd be here. I've found unconditional love and partnership I've not known. A family of my own and another in Sean's that Ax and I've been welcomed into with open, loving arms. A career that fits me perfectly in a way I could only dream of. A life so full, I can't possibly ever do enough right to deserve it.

The tapping of the drums fills the stadium as the flag is marched forward and held high. Tears threaten to escape as I take it all in.

I breathe, finding Sean again, his eyes fixed on me, and everything that stirs within me calms. It's all just as it should be. I smile, watching the corners of his mouth turn up ever so slightly. My love for him overflows.

Josh was my first love, and a piece of my heart will always reside with him. I can't help but think of him tonight as the flag rises before me, and I know up in one of those boxes way up high, our son is listening, expectantly waiting for me to sing.

Josh sacrificed his life doing what he was born to do, and he loved me until the end. I had to take the leap, but he helped lead me to a new life, all by entering me into a silly little competition that's somehow led me to exactly where I belong.

Keep reading for a sneak peek of book 3 of

Abandoned Brothers Series

Available at: **authorstacywilliams.com**

Chapter 1

LEX

The thick liquid swirls around the rim of my wide-mouth glass. I watch the translucent streaks recede into the blood-red pool. The sour smell is pungent and isn't helping the waves of nausea rising in my stomach as I try to keep my miserable heel-clad feet from running out the doors.

This is what I want. This is what I want. This…is what I want.

You know that feeling you get in the very depths of your gut when something isn't quite right? The one that sets off warning bells or sirens that are supposed to kick you into high gear and generate action.

Some people call it instincts, others the gift of fear. I'm not exactly sure what it is or where it comes from, but over the past few months, I've gotten really good at ignoring it. Tonight, every form of internal alarm system is going off, and it's so loud I can't hear anything else.

I tip my glass to the side, wondering what would happen if my unsteady hand slipped and this detestable, fermented sludge ran down the front of my stiff ivory-colored dress.

"Alexandra."

The startle of a familiar mousey voice prevents the first drop, and I turn to see Gail Chambers making a beeline for me with a group in tow.

"Alex, these ladies are my best friends. They've known Seth since he was a toddler and have been dying to meet you."

The tiny, prim, and proper woman loops her arm through mine like we're best buds. It's not that Gail isn't friendly. She's just never been that fond of me, or really, I'm not the princess she imagined for her son.

The women gather around, and I squeeze back, unsure I want to be included in their little plastic circle. I realize there's a frightening similarity between the dress I have on, which I hate, and the style and appearance of my future mother-in-law and her posse. My stomach rolls again, and I clench my teeth, forcing a polite smile as she introduces me to each of her friends.

I offer my hand, receiving each meticulously pampered and manicured one in return. The last desperate housewife offers one of those prissy handshakes that involves only a few awkward fingers, clearly appalled by my rough, grease-stained hands despite my light pink polish.

A nervous laugh escapes Gail as her friend studies her hand, ensuring I didn't leave any residue behind. "Oh, yes, I told you all how Alex volunteers to help her grandfather out in his garage from time to time." *Volunteers?* "Young women these days and their need to master the skills meant for the opposite sex."

This is what I want. This is what I want. This is...

I inhale, scanning the overly decorated room for Seth, needing rescue. When I don't spot him, my alarm system activates the panic mode. My one cracker and cheese rises in my throat, a cold sweat creeps up the back of my neck, and my feet tingle with the urge to sprint to the nearest exit.

While the former county fair beauty queen and her band of BFFs babble on about necessary skill sets and changing times, I stare into the glass in my shaky hand, contemplating a spill as my escape plan.

"So, you work on automobiles, then?" One of the women, whose name I can't remember now, asks with just a little too much condescension in her tone for me to really care to answer her. But because I'm mostly polite, I respond kindly.

"Cars, trucks, SUVs, things with engines." I force my lips upward just a little as they all half laugh.

The laughter halts as they study me like I'm some kind of rare foreign species, which is my cue to find somewhere else to be in this twinkle-light-flower-infested room.

"Alex is taking some classes and assists Seth at the firm, but once they're married, you know how it is. Wifely duties take over."

Her ability to make excuses for my line of work never ceases to amaze me. Helping Seth move his office furniture doesn't even remotely qualify as working for his firm, and as far as schooling, I'm enrolled in a single program working toward an ASE certification, as in Automotive Service Excellence.

School was never my deal, but working with my hands, specifically on cars, is where I belong. I grew up in my grandpa's garage, filled with foul-mouthed men and the scent of oil and brake fluid. Those men are my family, and that garage is my life.

I want to get married, have a family, and work on cars. That's my dream. It's simple. It's not flashy or grand, but it's mine. But here I stand in a room full of people who will never understand me or the thrill of diagnosing a broken vehicle, repairing it, and returning it to its grateful owner.

The pool of women I've encountered in my life that seem to understand my career choice could be counted on one hand. There are even fewer men who appreciate it for more than assuming I'm some chick who tinkers under a hood. Women in the garage are rarely accepted, but someday, Grandpa's garage will be mine, so I'm doing what I can to give myself the best leg up when that day comes.

Wanting no part of the load of crap being shoveled out here, I excuse myself. "It was nice meeting you all, but I need to find Seth."

They all nod in unison.

"I'll catch up with you later about riding together tomorrow for your final dress fitting." Gail chimes in an overly eager tone that causes my feet to move even faster.

I weave my way through people, most of whom I've only briefly met over the past two years, searching for the man who's supposed to be helping me through this. The one who's supposed to be standing by my side yet seems to disappear when I need him most.

These are his people, his family, and his friends. If I had it my way, I'd meet him at the courthouse, foregoing all this pomp and circumstance. Unfortunately, my ideas were vetoed immediately once Gail got involved. But maybe this extravagance is giving me the time and observance I need to put things in perspective.

I stop at the bar to set down the glass of wine that I didn't order and would never drink, although chugging it is an appealing idea if I didn't think it would come right back up. Then again, maybe that's not such a bad plan.

"Hey, pal."

I turn to the man who's taught me everything I know, his slightly wrinkled gray button-down shirt only mildly fitting over his short, broad frame. He leans an elbow on the bar, surveying the room.

"Hey, Grandpa."

"Your mom messaged me. She got caught up at work."

I nod, wishing I could get back to working on the truck that came in this afternoon with a valve cover leak.

"This is quite the set-up. You doing alright?"

My eyes roam over the room filled with people and things representing nothing of the world I belong to or my preferences. The white linen covered high-top tables with elaborate pale pastel floral centerpieces and hundreds of twinkle lights strung from one end of the room to the other. It's all elegantly stifling and stiff, just like my dress.

I tug at the scratchy material around my neck. "Yeah, it's all a little…bright." I spend my days in coveralls or jeans covered in grease and grime, T-shirts, and flannels. All this flowery vibrance is nauseating.

Grandpa chuckles next to me. "That it is. How are your nerves? It's only a couple of days."

I can't meet his gray-blue eyes because this man will see right through my shaky conviction. "They're holding on." I try to joke, but it comes out flat.

In my peripheral, I see one of his bushy gray brows arch as he studies me. I pretend to search the room again, attempting to ignore his prying eyes.

"No one is forcing you to do this."

My head snaps in his direction. I'm used to my grandpa being blunt, but this comment came out of nowhere.

"What?"

He rests his back against the bar, turning his attention to the room full of men and women who appear to be dressed for the Kentucky Derby rather than what was supposed to be an informal pre-wedding gathering for friends and family, AKA Gail's friends and family.

"All this," he gestures around the room with his head. "I just want to be sure that this is what you envisioned when you think about the rest of your life. Seth is a good guy, but he's not…"

Don't say it. Don't even say it.

My entire body tenses, and I stop him before he says it, turning to face him. "Grandpa, this is happening. This is what I want." A sour taste fills my mouth just saying it, my stomach in full revolt.

He doesn't look at me, likely knowing I'm full of crap. I hear him release a long breath through his nose, and there's that slight whistle that's always there.

"Sometimes the comfort and reliability of a Buick seem like a safe bet, but a Mustang…it's where real fun and living happens."

I stare at him as he pushes away from the bar, the man who's raised me, at least where it's counted most–the one who knows me better than anyone. He just had to do it. But this is what I can't handle right now. I can't have him putting thoughts in my head that don't belong there. Thoughts that haven't belonged there for a very, very long time but never cease to go away no matter how hard I try. Thoughts I don't have space in my head for, especially tonight.

The rotten old fart drops a bomb of wisdom and leaves me standing here as he heads back to the fresh trays of cream puffs and crab cakes.

He just had to say it. He just had to put it out there.

I glare at his back as my dress suddenly shrinks around my chest, and my need to flee escalates. *Where in the hell is Seth?!* I move towards the doors leading to a small deck needing fresh air.

I push out into the brisk night air filled with the overwhelming stench of cigar smoke.

"Alex." Seth's voice catches me off guard. He stands off to the side, surrounded by all of his college buddies and their ladies. "Come here and hang out with us."

My feet stay put as I glance back over my shoulder at the party inside that's for us, and yet we've spent the whole evening apart. *What's new?*

My positive attitude hits rock bottom, and my desire to be here evaporates like the billowing smoke around me. Evidently tired of me not listening, that little voice of my innermost being screams. *This is NOT what I want!*

Seth takes another puff of his cigar and closes the distance between us. He leans down to kiss my cheek, and the smell is repulsive. I wrap my arms around myself as my skin breaks out with goosebumps from both the chill and the recognition of what's happening, of what's been happening that I've chosen to ignore.

"We've been catching up." He shrugs off his jacket and places it around my shoulders. One of his long arms comes around me and pulls me toward his friends.

I join their little smoke-filled group, trying not to breathe while an unspoken war rages within me. *Buick. Mustang. Buick. Mustang. Buick. Mustang.*

As the Buick starts talking next to me, all I can think is that the Mustang is long gone. My heart sinks yet again to the toes of my overly-priced and horrendously uncomfortable shoes.

"So, Alex, does this mean we all get free oil changes when we're in town?" One of the guys asks, pulling me from battle. When I realize who said it, it's accompanied by a smug smirk, like it's some kind of joke. *Pompous dick.*

"It's buy ten, get one free." My voice is quiet as my mind spins with sudden awareness.

The women in the group giggle like I said something funny, and I feel Seth's arm slide around me. "Alex runs the shop. She's got guys to handle the oil changes."

I've got guys to handle the dirty work? Gag me. I'd change oil every day for the rest of my life as long as I don't have to sit behind some computer or work in an office.

This is not new–these comments, the cute little jokes, and this weird type of protectiveness, like I need help explaining the work I do because it can't possibly be serious. I guess for the first time, I'm hearing them loud and clear. It's not my problem these people are too close-minded to think a woman might actually like fixing things…like cars.

It's time for me to go before I melt down and make a fool of myself in front of people who really don't care to know me other than I'm becoming Seth's wife. *Seth's wife. Seeeettttthhhh's wife.* I'm not even sure who that's supposed to be because I'm afraid it's not me.

I've been a flight risk for the past two hours. *If I'd been listening to that bossy internal voice, it's actually been much longer.* But now, my timer just went off.

"Actually, I have a valve cover leak waiting on me," I announce to no one in particular, pushing Seth's jacket off of my shoulders and handing it back to him.

He frowns. "What? You're leaving?"

"Yes." My heart starts to race with the need to run…*Mustang.*

"Are you alright?" He follows me to the doors.

I stop, looking up at his freshly shaven face and golden brown eyes while my heart hammers away at the thought of what I'm about to do.

"What do you think of this dress?"

"What?" His brows tip in so far they almost meet.

"This dress?" I whisper, looking down at the stiff, ugly, plain material covering my body. "What do you think of it?"

He studies me like he's noticing I'm wearing a dress for the first time. "I think you look beautiful. It's stunning."

My heart sinks into a pit of disappointed despair. *Buick. Mustang. Buick. Mustang. Mustang. It's always been a Mustang.*

"I have to go."

I swing open the doors, and all the bright whiteness of the room shocks my senses into flight mode. I make a run for it, not taking even a second to think about anything or anyone that might get in my way.

Acknowledgments

I have so many to thank. I'm not even sure where to begin and how to say it all, so here we go.

To my husband, your love, support, and encouragement never end. Thank you for helping me with all of the behind-the-scenes stuff that I am no good at, for picking me up when I want to stay lying on the floor feeling defeated, but most of all, for loving me so much more than I will ever deserve. Your love makes me able to write these stories and know that this kind of love actually exists. I love you forever and always.

To my kids, there are no words. You guys are my biggest dream come true. Thank you for sharing this journey with me, cheering me on from the sidelines, pumping your fists every time another book is sold, and being patient with me when my head is in another world. You guys make this all so much better. These books are for you. I hope someday they show you the kind of love story I wish for you with all my heart.

Mama, my number one fan and reader of all first drafts. Thank you for reading this story many times, for your complete and honest feedback, and for helping me get this story just right. I love you so much.

Roger, thank you for reading another romance, making sure all my football content is accurate, and for your love and support as I wind my way through this endeavor.

Lauren, girl, thanks for reading my stories, for your unending love and support, for being my best friend, and for the endless crazy text threads no one on earth would ever understand. I love you forever.

Abby, thank you for reading and finding all of the things no one else does. Your comments are seriously my favorite and bring so much joy to my editing process. I love you and miss you.

Natalie, thank you for reading this story, helping me make it the best it can be, for your love and friendship, and for helping me remember why I'm doing this when my insecurities get the best of me.

Lizzie, thank you for reading another one of my stories, giving me all of your thoughts, and helping me make this story as realistic as possible.

Allison Buehner, my editor, thank you for polishing this story and helping make it shine. I'm so grateful for your help and support.

Last but certainly not least, to the lost and those searching for a place in this world–a place to belong. I pray that you keep searching and don't give up even when it feels like you'll never get there. Sometimes, we just don't fit in the world we were born into, the ones we get lost in, or the ones we had no say in at all. We find ourselves sitting dark, afraid to step back into the light. Who knows what we'll find or what others will see when we do? It's terrifying and hard, and can feel a whole lot safer to just stay where we are. What you should know is it's never too late to choose a different path, take a step in a different direction, or decide it's time to take a leap into the unknown. One step at a time is all it takes. Be brave. You're worth it. You'll find your place. And sometimes, it finds us.

About the Author

Stacy Williams lives with her husband and children in Illinois. She writes in five-minute increments between homeschooling and extracurricular activities. She's spent years dreaming about writing love stories that, in a worn and broken world, remind us of what we're truly made for.

authorstacywilliams.com

 @stacywilliams.writes

stacywilliams.writes

Made in the USA
Monee, IL
14 March 2025